THE
HOMECOMING

THE
HOMECOMING

CARSTEN STROUD

CENTURY

Published by Century 2013

2 4 6 8 10 9 7 5 3 1

First published in Great Britain in 2013 by
Century
Random House, 20 Vauxhall Bridge Road,
London SW1V 2SA

www.randomhouse.co.uk

Addresses for companies within The Random House Group Limited can be
found at: www.randomhouse.co.uk/offices.htm

The Random House Group Limited Reg. No. 954009

A CIP catalogue record for this book
is available from the British Library

ISBN 9781780891064

The Random House Group Limited supports the Forest Stewardship
Council® (FSC®), the leading international forest-certification organisation.
Our books carrying the FSC label are printed on FSC®-certified paper.
FSC is the only forest-certification scheme supported by the leading
environmental organisations, including Greenpeace. Our paper procurement
policy can be found at www.randomhouse.co.uk/environment

Printed and bound by CPI Group (UK) Ltd, Croydon, CR0 4YY

For Linda

Among the dead there are those
who still have to be killed.

—FERNAND DESNOYERS, 1858

Perhaps the universe is suspended on
the tooth of some monster.

—CHEKHOV, 1892

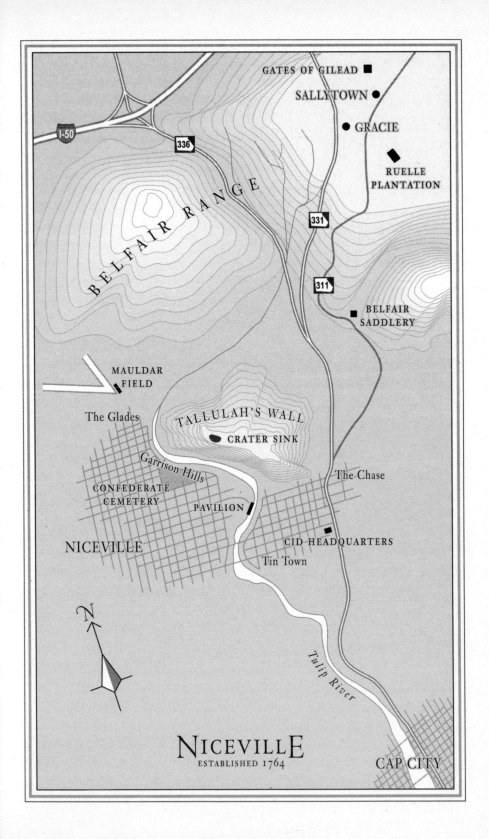

GATES OF GILEAD ■
SALLYTOWN ●
● GRACIE
◆
RUELLE
PLANTATION

I-50

336

331

311

BELFAIR
SADDLERY

BELFAIR RANGE

MAULDAR
FIELD ◢

The Glades

TALLULAH'S WALL

● CRATER SINK

Garrison Hills

The Chase

CONFEDERATE
CEMETERY

PAVILION

NICEVILLE

CID HEADQUARTERS

Tin Town

N

Tulip River

NICEVILLE
ESTABLISHED 1764

CAP CITY

After the Fall

What the Military Term "Vertically Deployed into the Terrain" Actually Means

There was this Chinese Lear, first in line at Mauldar Field, locked and loaded, an arrow in a full-drawn bow, jets spooled up, brakes smoking, flaps flapping—the tower phone starts to shrill—a loud metallic howl—John Parkhurst, the tower boss, snatches it up, and what he gets—he told the cops later—is this shrieking raging rant from this loud-mouthed—

Okay, to help this make sense, Parkhurst is a part-time Pentecostal minister, so when he's talking to the cops he uses the word *individual* instead of something stronger—anyway, the guy on the horn is claiming to be an FBI agent, and what he wants—at the top of his lungs—is for that *curse word curse word* Chinese Lear to be *stopped right where it is*, held on the runway, locked down, and when Parkhurst—who's kind of a fussy older guy who should probably have been a dentist instead of an air traffic controller—asks for a badge number, well, the guy completely *loses* it—starts to curse again—*uses the F word*—and is halfway through a phrase that starts with *you dumb c-word* and ends *you-know-where*—so Parkhurst slams the phone down.

Two minutes later the Lear, a 60 XR Luxury Edition—ten mil easy—powers up into the sky, climbing steep, riding the thunderbolt—the twin jets so loud they rattle windows for a mile around, and Parkhurst sits back, stares at the phone, his ears still on fire, and he says *dear me* and *oh my* and lets out a sigh and starts shaking his head, thinking, *and on the Lord's Day too.*

But . . . other than that nasty bit of business . . . he got himself calmed down and looked around at the other guys—most of them staring back at him wondering what *that* was all about—and then he looked out the windows and by God's Good Grace it was still a lovely Sunday morning in the spring and when he glanced up at the shining blue sky there wasn't a cloud to be seen . . . okay, maybe, except for something kind of odd away there in the southeast. It looked like a smudge of black smoke. Or perhaps blowing leaves.

Parkhurst, having taken spiritual refuge in the Old Testament, pondered the smudge for a time, idly speculating on its nature.

Meanwhile, a thousand feet up and a half mile downrange, the Chinese Learjet dipped a wing and banked gracefully to the south.

As Parkhurst drifted through Psalms, a flicker of unease twitched at the back of his mind. He turned to check the Doppler radar. The smudge came back as a diffuse return, essentially undecipherable. So he used his binoculars to get a closer look.

It took him a second or two to get the target in focus, and another second to make sense of what he was seeing, but once he figured it out, his throat clamped up and his chest went cold.

It wasn't a cloud of smoke, or leaves. It was a flock of crows. A very *big* flock of crows.

Parkhurst jumped onto the radio—*Flight zero six five emergency China Lear alter your course immediately to bearing*—but by then, given the speed of the jet, it was just too damn little too damn late. Parkhurst got a brief return transmission from the copilot—*tower we are*—followed by a shrill Chinese curse.

The scarlet and gold jet, glittering in the morning sunlight, punched straight into that flock of crows and burst out the other side, its fuselage streaked with blood and matted black feathers, the starboard engine trailing a thin plume of blue smoke. The jet was already losing altitude.

The pilot was on the radio again—*tower this is Flight zero six five we have multiple bird strikes repeat multiple bird strikes—visibility zero*—then there was only crackle and static.

In the tower they all stood in stunned shock as the Learjet skewed to port—its nose dipped—the leftward bank quickly turned into a roll and then a rapidly narrowing spiral—the nose dipped—dipped farther—the plane went into a nosedive—the radio came back to life—the pilot had reverted to Hakka and was screaming into his mike—in the background they could hear voices and shouts and metallic racket of the airframe juddering—the pilot came back in English—*tower we are going in we are going in.*

They all heard one last transmission—*tell my son*—then a hoarse cry—the Lear slammed into the ground two miles away, right in the middle of the fourteenth green of the Anora Mercer Golf and Country Club.

It exploded into a yellow and red and black fireball that flared outwards and rose up into the sky. A few moments later the guys in the tower felt the shock wave hit the windows, a dull percussive thud, followed by a rolling boom.

There goes my career, Parkhurst was thinking. And then, as an afterthought, *poor souls.*

A thousand feet above the crash site the flock of crows re-formed, drew into a tight cloud that took on the shape of a scythe as it flew low across the town, wheeling and soaring, filling the cool clear air with their brassy cries, and then it rose up in one coherent mass and disappeared into the east in the direction of Tallulah's Wall.

There was a graveyard silence in the tower except for somebody at the back of the room, who said, in a small voice full of awe, "Holy shit."

Parkhurst swallowed with pain and got onto Fire and Ambulance. While he was calling it in, one of the other controllers, a new kid named Matt Lamarr, studied the flight roster for a moment.

He looked up at the other guys, all of whom were still staring out at the mushroom-shaped cloud rising up from the golf course, except now they were barking and yapping and snapping at each other like a pack of deranged Labradoodles.

"Hey, dudes," he said over the din, and then he said it again, louder. "Dudes!"

Everybody but John Parkhurst turned around to stare at him.

"What?"

"Morgan Littlebasket took his Cessna up at 10:22 hours? Right?"

"Yeah," said one of the guys. "So what?"

"So, like, where is *he*?"

The Niceville black-and-whites got to the scene of the Learjet crash in four minutes, followed closely by the fire crews. The fireball was raging and pools of jet fuel were burning off all around the splash zone. It was just too hot to work the blaze. There wasn't much for anybody to do other than to wait for it to die down and check for collateral injuries around the perimeter.

All they found was one lone vic wandering around in a daze, a crumpled little man with a heavily damaged nose and a badly singed face who identified himself as Thad Llewellyn.

From what they could decipher of his hysterical ramblings it sounded as if his wife had been in the center of the impact zone when the Lear came screaming down into the fourteenth green.

Her name was Inge and apparently she'd been holding the pin for him while he was trying to chip his way out of a sand trap.

The patrol guys refrained from making the obvious hole-in-one jokes—at least in the guy's hearing—and gently helped him into a cruiser and sent him off to Lady Grace Hospital, lights and siren if you please.

Then they set up a ribbon barrier to keep the bystanders at a safe distance—mostly groundskeepers and a few folks who'd been having Sunday brunch in the Hy Brasail Room—and settled in to wait for the flames to subside to a workable level and the duty supervisors to show up.

In the meantime they watched the wreck of the Lear burn down into a debris field of shattered metal and glass and body bits out of which rose a billowing black cloud with bright orange fire at the center. The wind was carrying the smoke eastward, away from the caravan of cop cars, but they could feel the heat coming off it even from a hundred feet away. The fairway grass was blackened all around the site.

Basically the entire fourteenth green was a smoldering crater fifty feet deep and a hundred feet across. Which is what happens when an aircraft vertically deploys into the terrain.

Nick Kavanaugh and his partner, Beau Norlett, got to the scene a few minutes later. The fire trucks were stacked up along the cart lane and people in HazMat suits were out there spraying foam all over the place. The EMT vans were parked out of the way, the paramedic crews leaning against the front bumpers or standing around talking in clusters. Nothing for them to do. There were no survivors. Whatever was left of the passengers and of Thad Llewellyn's wife, Inge, would eventually get tagged and bagged by the Forensics guys or the Transportation Safety Accident Investigation crew.

Nick rolled their navy blue Crown Vic up behind a big black Suburban with SUPERVISOR printed across the tailgate in bright gold letters. It was Mavis Crossfire's ride. Nick looked across at Beau as he opened the driver's door.

"Let the LT know we're here. Tell Tig that Staff Sergeant Crossfire is on the scene too. Then go see what the First Responders have to say."

Beau Norlett was a young black guy shaped like an artillery round. Raw, but eager and tough, and getting more useful every day. He and Nick had only been partners for a week now, but it had been one hell of a tour. A bank robbery with six killed, including four cops. A wealthy older woman named Delia Cotton gone without a trace, and her elderly gardener, a man named Gray Haggard, gone with her. A hostage-taking at a church which required the services of a police sniper. And just yesterday, his wife's father, Dillon, vanished from his office up at Virginia Military Institute, not seen since.

And now this.

A hell of a week.

"Will do, boss," said Beau, who was still running on the adrenaline high of the last few days. Since the Belfair and Cullen County Criminal Investigation Division unit had high sartorial standards—at least Nick did—he'd bought two new suits, a Kors and a Zegna, and three pairs of Allen Edmonds shoes. At his salary, with a wife and two kids, this was a major investment.

"They got a coffee truck over there, Nick. Want a coffee? Honey bun?"

"Coffee would be great, but don't call me honey bun in front of the harness guys."

Beau laughed, picked up the handset, flicked the SEND tab. Nick closed the door and took a moment to wring out the kinks before he put on his suit jacket. He was in charcoal gray today, with a black shirt. No tie. It was too damn hot. He slipped his gold detective shield onto his belt, tugged at the Colt Python he carried in a holster on his right side, and surveyed the scene, getting his head into the game again.

At thirty-two, Nick was young to be a CID detective, but he had served eight years with the Fifth Special Forces, so his thirty-two wasn't like the thirty-two-year-old hairball who is still living in your basement trying to finish his doctoral dissertation on Gender and Race Bias in Neo-Kantian Hermeneutics.

Nick was just over six feet, gray-blue eyes, blue-black hair graying at the temples, still taut and fit, married to Kate Walker, a family practice lawyer, whom he adored and who, he hoped, adored him back, which, most of the time, she did.

He walked up to the driver's side of the Niceville PD Suburban and tapped on the window. Mavis Crossfire grinned back at him as she powered the glass down. A big-boned pink-faced woman with short-cropped red hair and smile lines around her pale blue eyes, she was in harness this morning—a crisp dark blue uniform with a big gold badge on her Kevlar vest and staff sergeant stripes on her sleeves.

"Nick. Top of the morning."

Nick shook his head. "Top of the morning?"

"You're Irish, aren't you?"

"I was born in California."

Mavis smiled, took a sip of coffee from a thermos with an Ole Miss logo on the side, nodded her head in the direction of the crash site.

"There's a hell of a thing."

"Yeah. Any survivors?"

"Not a chance. And another vic killed when it came down on top of her."

"Do we know who she was?"

"Inge Llewellyn."

"Jeez. Thad Llewellyn's wife? Plus-sized Nordic lady with a voice that could cut glass?"

"That's her."

"Tough week for Thad Llewellyn. First his bank gets robbed, and now his wife gets hers on the fourteenth green. Does he know yet?"

"He was over there in a sand trap when the jet came down. First Responders found him wandering around the fairway with no eyebrows. Saw it all."

"Where's he now?"

"Black-and-white took him to Lady Grace. They've sedated him."

"I sure hope so. Poor bastard. I heard it was a crow strike?"

Mavis nodded.

"Tower saw it happen. Lear smacked straight into the flock. Thousands of birds. Never had a chance. Now get this. There's *another* fire crew over at the base of Tallulah's Wall, picking through a wrecked Cessna. Tail numbers come back as Cherokee Nation Trust. Inside is a crispy critter named Morgan Littlebasket."

"I know that name."

Mavis nodded, looking at her notepad.

"Yes, you would. That would be *the* Morgan Littlebasket, head of the Cherokee Trust and all-around Very Inflated Person up in Gracie. Tower guys say he showed up for a joyride at oh-nine-hundred this morning. Seemed a bit distracted. Fooled around with a pre-flight check and then took off around ten twenty. Went south. Witnesses say he buzzed those old trees along the crest of Tallulah's Wall. Then he came down, skimmed along the Tulip River for a half mile, powered up again and banked left, rose up to maybe five, six hundred feet, altered course to the northwest, leveled out, and flew himself right smack into the middle of Tallulah's Wall."

"Straight and steady flight?"

"Not a weeble or a wobble. In like a bullet."

"Man," Nick said, smiling at her. "What do you figure was going through his mind?"

"The windshield, and thanks for the setup."

"Maybe a suicide? Any note? Any last words?"

"Nothing so far. We've got people going through his house right now. Could have been a stroke or a heart attack. We'll have to wait and see."

"He's got daughters, doesn't he?"

"Two. Twyla and Bluebell. Lost the mother to cancer a while back. Her name was Lucy. Twyla's sort of Coker's main girl, by the way."

"Perky black-haired thing? Big brown eyes and candy-red lipstick? Curves like a French staircase? She's a killer. I've seen her at the Bar Belle with Coker."

"Apparently you have."

"Young for him, isn't she?"

"No comment. But Coker has that Clint Eastwood thing going for him, you gotta admit. And you'd be amazed how many gullible young girls think police snipers are sexy."

"Do you?"

"No. I'm more inclined toward your ex–Special Forces steel-jacket CID detectives with flinty eyes and a gigantic weapon named after a snake."

"Mavis, I never suspected."

"I wasn't talking about you. Anyway, I've got cars on the way to their homes, break it to them both as easy as they can."

"We got a time frame for when Littlebasket hit the wall?"

"Various witnesses pinned it at 10:41."

"And twenty-odd minutes later that Lear over there flies into a cloud of crows?"

Mavis nodded.

"That's what I was thinking. Littlebasket hits Tallulah's Wall, the explosion spooks all those crows that live in those trees around Crater Sink. Flock takes off and heads northwest. Enters Mauldar Field airspace just in time to get into the Lear's flight path."

"So just wrong time, wrong place."

"Yeah. A thing like this, everything's gotta go wrong in exactly the right way, but when it does, when all the dominoes fall, Bob's your uncle."

"I never know what that means."

"Neither do I. Guess it's like, there you go."

"We know anything about the passengers on the Lear?"

Mavis looked down at her notepad.

"Plane was owned by a Chinese trading company based in Shanghai. Daopian Canton Incorporated. Two thousand Fortunate City Road. Pilot and copilot were employees of the company. Three other passengers, also employees. Top dog was a man named Zachary Dak. Title was Director of Logistics."

"Where were they going from here?"

"Filed a flight plan for LAX to refuel and then on to Honolulu and then Macao."

Nick worked through that.

"Macao? What were they doing in Niceville? Something to do with Quantum Park?"

"Says on their entry visa that they were looking at real estate for a possible branch office."

"Who'd they meet with? A local agent? Somebody out of Cap City?"

Mavis gave him a tilted look. "What are you thinking?"

"Don't know. I'd just like to know who they met with. And why. Five Chinese nationals, a private Lear, and now they're garden mulch. We should be ready for a whack of questions from the State Department. Where were they staying? The Marriott?"

"Yes. Checked in Friday, flight crew and the three civilians. Separate rooms all around. Rented a Lincoln Town Car from Airport Limos. It's still parked in the lot at the Marriott."

"I don't know. Something's . . . not right."

Mavis had known Nick long enough to take his instincts seriously.

"The manager on duty is Mark Hopewell. I've already called him and he's pulling together whatever he has. Also, there's a retired deputy sheriff at the Marriott, Edgar Luckinbaugh. Works as the senior bellman.

Edgar pays attention. I could go have a talk with him, see what he knows about these guys."

"Or I could," said Nick. "I know Luckinbaugh. He strings part-time for Coker, one of his CIs."

Nick was quiet for a moment.

"Mavis, somebody should give Boonie Hackendorff a heads-up about this. The Cap City FBI will sure as hell get queried by State. I don't want Boonie to get caught flat-footed."

"I'll see he gets the report. Right now he's got his hands full."

Nick heard something in her tone.

"Yeah? Why? What's up with Boonie?"

Mavis had been sitting on this for a while.

She gave Nick an anticipatory grin.

"Well, it looks like, maybe an hour ago, on Highway three six six, just past the Arrow Creek on-ramp, State Patrol clocked Byron Deitz at one-forty, pulled him over, a hostile stop, guns out, the whole deal. He was in that fat yellow Hummer. They found a pill bottle full of ecstasy in the cup holder beside the driver's seat, plain sight, so they cuffed Deitz and did a routine search of the Hummer. Guess what they found in the tailgate?"

"Please don't make me."

"Cash from the First Third robbery in Gracie."

That rocked Nick.

Rocked him right back.

Byron Deitz was his brother-in-law, a thug and a wife beater. Kate's sister was married to the guy. Just last night Beth had finally gotten one too many smacks in the mouth.

She'd packed her kids into the SUV, told Byron she was going to a hotel, and called Kate on her cell. When he'd left for work this morning, Kate and Beth were still in the sunroom talking it through. Nick was planning on dropping in to see Deitz later in the day, straighten him out, a righteous meet that had been too long coming.

But this?

The First Third robbery had happened last Friday afternoon. Take was at least two million five, maybe more. Four cops had been executed during the pursuit.

As much as Nick loathed the guy, he found it hard to believe that Deitz, who was retired FBI himself, could have had anything to do with something as ugly as the cold-blooded slaughter of four cops.

"How'd they know it was from the First Third?"

"Still had the bank bands on it. A big fat sheaf of brand-new hundreds. They also found a Rolex that was part of the stuff stolen from the safety-deposit boxes."

"I don't—I just don't believe it."

"Believe it," said Mavis. "It gets better. Deitz connects to this Learjet crash too."

"How?"

"Parkhurst said somebody called the tower about a quarter to eleven, ID'd himself as Byron Deitz, says he wants the Chinese Lear on the runway to be held until he gets there."

"*Deitz* did this?"

"Parkhurst can't confirm the voice, but the caller ID was BD SECURICOM, which is Deitz's company. I called the number back when I got here, and got Deitz's voice mail."

"So it really was Deitz."

"I'd say so. The caller claimed to be FBI, but when Parkhurst asked for a badge number, the guy lost it, started screaming, swearing—"

"That's Byron."

"All over. Parkhurst hung up on him, cleared the jet for takeoff. After that, things went all rat-shit and he never thought about the caller again until the First Responders started asking him questions. I was about to go up and talk it over with Parkhurst right now. You wanna—"

"Let me get this straight. Deitz was on his way *here*."

"Looks like he was on the cell phone screaming at Parkhurst when the State Patrol guys clocked and locked him. Anyway, you wanna come along? Maybe we'll find out something."

Nick stared at her, trying to take all this in.

"If Deitz did the First Third, he killed four cops. Why is he still alive?"

"Early in the day, Nick. He could still be dead by sundown. Patrol is taking him to their HQ up in Gracie. Boonie Hackendorff is on the way up to see that the FBI gets a piece of him. First Third is a multistate bank, so it's a federal beef."

"Jesus. Mavis, does Reed Walker know?"

Reed Walker was Kate's brother. A blade-thin guy with the air of a raptor about him, intense, aggressive, crazy-brave, he drove a Police Interceptor pursuit car for the Highway Division of the State Patrol and was, in Nick's opinion, certifiably nuts. Two of the cops who had been killed in the First Third robbery were his personal friends, one of them a guy he had trained with at the Police Interceptor Training School. Reed was up in Virginia, looking for Kate's father, who had not been seen since Saturday afternoon.

Mavis was ahead of him.

"It's covered, Nick. Marty Coors called him up at VMI and told him to stay there. He said if Reed came flying back and showed up anywhere around Deitz he'd shove him into the back of a dog car and let one of those werewolves chew on him. Reed's handled. For now, anyway."

A silence.

"Anything on that, Nick? On Kate's dad?"

Nick looked at his hands, shook his head.

"Not so far. There's a state cop up at VMI, name of Linus Calder. He's doing everything he can. I was supposed to chopper up there and help, but now we have . . . this."

He made a gesture, taking in the crash, all the cops, and the media trucks that were finally arriving on the scene.

"So he's just . . . gone?"

"There's more to it, Mavis. When I can, I'll fill you in."

"But not now?"

"Can't. Sorry."

"Why?"

"Because you'd think I was a fucking fruitcake if I told you the whole story. I don't believe it myself."

"I already think you're a fucking fruitcake."

"I know. So do I."

Mavis studied his face for a moment, saw what was there, and set the thing aside.

For now, anyway.

"So what do you want to do about this rat-fuck right here, Nick? CID has jurisdiction. So far."

"Man. What a cluster . . . can you stay with it?"

"I'd love to."

"Talk to Parkhurst, Mavis, if you don't mind. Follow up on the Deitz connection from this end. And give Boonie a wake-up on this Chinese national thing, will you? Before State and the FBI director land on him?"

"I will. What are you gonna do?"

Nick looked back to see where Beau was. He was in the middle of a group of Niceville uniforms and, from the grin on his face, talking trash, having a good time.

"I'm going to have to call Beth and tell her."

"Maybe not right away? Wait and see how it shakes out."

"Deitz won't be able to talk his way out from under a sheaf of stolen cash."

"No. But if you give it a bit you'll have more to tell Beth than what we have now. And there's her kids to consider. The more you know, the better."

"You think?"

"I do. Give it an hour. By then Marty Coors and Boonie Hackendorff will have talked it over. The picture will be clearer."

Nick took the advice.

It was a call he didn't want to make at all.

"Okay. Good advice. Well, I'm gone."

"What are you gonna do?"

"Go see Edgar Luckinbaugh at the Marriott."

"Take him a box of Krispy Kremes. The honey-glazed ones. He loves them."

Love May Be Blind, but a Few Years of Marriage Will Fix That

While Beau Norlett and Nick Kavanaugh were cruising over to the Marriott, Nick's wife, Kate, and her sister, Beth, were sitting in the glassed-in conservatory at the back of Kate's town house in Garrison Hills, a neighborhood of antebellum Spanish Colonial town homes with wrought-iron galleries and cloistered gardens. It was a pretty spring morning and they were alone. Beth's two kids, Axel and Hannah, eight and four, were sound asleep in one of the guest bedrooms.

Through the leaded glass of the sunroom Kate's garden, a grassy slope which led down to a stand of pines and willows, was bright with marigolds and hydrangeas and roses. A soft dappled light played on the windows and the lawn, and on Beth's drawn and weary face.

Although Beth was only four years older than Kate, and had the same kind of pale skin and fine-boned Black Irish features, her expression had hardened in the last few years and her eyes were wary and guarded. Kate was having an iced tea, but Beth was well into her fourth scotch and rocks. Her long red hair hung limply down her pale cheeks as she stared into the heavy crystal glass, gripping it so hard her fingers were white.

"It started with the air-conditioning—"

"The fight?"

Beth gave Kate a wry smile.

"Not much of a fight. He's got a hundred and fifty pounds on me. The house was hot, the kids were whining, and Byron was all in a lather about something that happened at work. Something connected to that awful bank robbery on Friday."

"Did he say what?"

"Only that the robbers got away with all of the payroll draw for everybody at Quantum Park, that it was all Thad Llewellyn's fault, and since BD Securicom was responsible for security at Quantum Park he was going to get a lot of heat for it. I tried to tell him that wasn't true, but he wasn't going to hear it. He said I didn't know what the bleep I was talking about and I never bleeping did, so how about I just shut the bleep up."

"In front of Axel and Hannah?"

"No. They were in their rooms. But I'm sure they heard. When Byron goes off, I think they can hear him in Cap City. It wasn't anything the kids hadn't heard before."

"But last night was different?"

Beth sighed, took a sip of scotch.

"Not different. It was just, suddenly, *enough*. Maybe it was the heat. I just didn't feel like trying to calm him down anymore."

"He hit you."

Not a question.

Beth nodded.

"Not the first time. But I think perhaps the last."

"Beth, do you have money of your own?"

Beth nodded, not looking up.

"Where is it, Beth? Because if Byron really believes you're not going back, he's the type of man who would drain the accounts and hide the assets."

Beth looked up at Kate.

Her eyes were greener than Kate's, and with the tears, they shone like emeralds. She had a fresh bruise along her left cheekbone, a raw purple and green stain with a deep bloody scratch in the middle. From his FBI ring, Beth had explained, while Kate was dressing it.

"Do you think he would? Really? What about the kids?"

"Beth, I'm a lawyer in family practice. It happens all the time. I just wrapped up a case on Friday, a horrid creep named Tony Bock. He spent a year tormenting his ex-wife and—"

"Tony Bock?"

"Yes. Why? Do you know him?"

Beth was looking a little shocked.

"Well, in a way. The reason Byron was so cranky last night was because the air-conditioning had gone on the blink. NUC sent out a guy to fix it, his name was Tony Bock—"

"Short, squat guy with a face like a frog? Black hair and bad skin?"

"Well, he wasn't pretty to look at. But his name was definitely Tony Bock. How odd, isn't it?"

"Bock works for Niceville Utility, I know that. He's a bad person, Beth. Just so you know."

"Okay. If I ever see him again, which I won't."

"Anyway, my point is, guys like Tony Bock and your husband, if those guys are willing to punch you with a closed fist—Tony Bock used to beat his wife too—why would they draw the line at taking all your money?"

Beth reached up and touched the bruise, wincing slightly as her fingertip met the skin. Last night, while Nick had gotten Axel and Hannah safely tucked into bed, Kate had used her digital camera to take several shots of Beth's face. She had also walked Beth into the master bedroom and demanded to see the rest of her body. When she did, she felt a bolt of pure anger flash through her chest. It was clear from the bruises beaten into Beth's blue-white skin that Byron had done this sort of thing before. Often. Kate took shots of these old injuries as well. While she did, she tried to think of a way to kill Byron that wouldn't get her life in prison.

Nick could find a way, she had thought at the time, *and he'd be happy to.*

Here in the conservatory, looking at Beth's face in the soft sunlight this morning, Kate was still thinking it. It must have been on her face, because Beth managed a smile.

"No, honey, we can't kill him," she said.

"Was it that obvious?"

Beth even laughed.

"Kate, Reed and I always thought you could kill people if you wanted to."

"Byron's lucky Reed *didn't* kill him. I know Nick wanted to. But you always held them off."

Beth looked away, and then came back.

"Reed wouldn't have just beaten Byron up. He'd have hurt him badly. Badly enough to lose his job. Maybe even killed him. He has a terrible temper, you know that. And Nick is just as crazy, only with him it's under better control, maybe because of the war. And isn't it true that wife beaters who get that sort of punishment, sooner or later, they find a way to take it out on the wife or the kids—"

"Not if they're dead."

"But this is real life, Kate, and you can't kill them, because you'll go to jail. Besides, I thought . . . I thought he'd stop. I did love him, once. He was always so . . . sorry. So crushed."

Kate shook her head.

"Oh, he's sorry all right. Sorry for himself, sorry that he has to be sorry. And after a while he'll be mad at you again for making him feel sorry. Beth, he's never going to stop until somebody stops him. They never do. You cannot ever go back to him. Never."

Beth was crying again, in silence, deep, wracking sobs. She fought for control.

"I know that. But we can't stay here."

"Yes you can. The house is too big for us as it is. It's just the two of us."

"What about Rainey Teague? Isn't he coming to live with you soon?"

"Yes. So that makes three."

"Well, that's what I mean. You've already got Rainey Teague coming. Poor little kid. Abducted, traumatized, an orphan. Now you're going to clutter the place up with three more fugitives from life? Why don't you just open a shelter for abused kids and be done with it?"

"Family's enough, Beth."

"Rainey's not family."

"He will be. Look, Beth, we have five bedrooms and four baths. Plus the carriage house at the back. There's even a second kitchen in the carriage house. Dad rebuilt this house for a large family. You could even have your old room back."

Beth's face altered.

"Dad . . . I can't believe he's gone."

Kate took a breath, a shaky one.

"He's *not* gone, Beth. He's . . . missing. And only for a few hours. I talked to him yesterday. He was supposed to come down and see us—"

"And he never showed up."

"No. That's right. He didn't. But maybe he needed to do some research—"

"Oh sure. Research about what?"

Kate's answer was careful.

"I had asked him to look into a few . . . family things. Maybe that's what he's doing right now. When he's working he loses all track of time. It's only been a few hours, Beth."

Kate wasn't going to say anything to Beth about what the Virginia state cops had found in Dillon Walker's office up at VMI. Beth had enough to think about. The time would come, but not yet. Beth started to cry again, choked it back.

"But where is he, then? And why is he missing? You've tried his cell. No answer. Why doesn't he call? It's not like him, Kate. It just isn't. I don't understand any of this . . . What does Nick say? What does Reed say? Are they doing *anything*?"

"There's a Detective Calder up at VMI. He's working on it right now. He'll call us as soon as he finds Dad. Or Reed will. In the meantime, you're staying."

Beth straightened up, stiffened her back.

"No. I'm a grown woman. With two kids. I can deal with this. We can go to a hotel."

"And if Byron shows up at the hotel door? Which he will. What then?"

"Kate, Nick can't stay at home and be my bodyguard. He has a job. So does Reed. And so do you."

"We'll work that out. Nick's not the only one with a gun around this house."

"You have a gun?"

"I have a Glock pistol, and I know how to use it."

"Is it loaded?"

"Nick says if a gun isn't loaded it's a paperweight. Anyway, Nick is going over to see Byron later today. So Byron may not be as big a problem for you as he likes to think he is."

"Byron won't like that. He'll get right in Nick's face."

"I hope he does. Then he can get a piece of what he's been giving you. If he actually assaults Nick, Nick will put him in a hospital, and then he'll arrest him for assaulting a police officer, he'll go to jail for that, and for domestic assault on you. I have digital proof of that. Maybe he'll even do county time. I'd love to see him deal with the people in Twin Counties Correctional. Ex-FBI? A wife beater? They'd corner him in a storage shed and have a party. He'd be lucky if they didn't geld him."

This was said in a flat voice, without inflection or a trace of melodrama.

Beth stared at her.

"It's happened," said Kate. "Just ask Nick."

"God. You really are angry, aren't you?"

"Yes, I am. And you should be too."

Beth sighed and leaned back into the sofa, sipping at her scotch.

There was a silence.

Kate drank a bit of her iced tea and studied Beth's face, seeing the hardness go out of it and traces of her old life come flowing back in.

"He was trying to kill you, Beth. I hope you understand that. Maybe not your body. But you. They want to suck the soul out of you. That's what guys like Byron do."

Beth let out another shaky sigh, put her head back, closed her eyes. After a moment she said, "I always thought Byron had an empty place inside him and he was desperately trying to fill it and no matter how much I tried I just couldn't help him."

Kate leaned over, put her hand on Beth's arm, gently, moved in to give her a soft kiss on her bruised cheek. Then she pulled back, smiled sweetly, and said, "What utter crap."

The phone rang.

"Hey, Kate, it's Reed. You hear about Byron?"

If a Bear Falls in the Forest

At around the same time that Kate was getting the latest on Byron Deitz from Reed Walker, Staff Sergeant Coker of the Belfair and Cullen County Sheriff's Department was rolling northbound on Highway 311 about ten miles south of Gracie, smoking a cigarette and enjoying the way the sunlight was making the sweetgrass glow on the slopes of the hills rising up all around him.

He was in his main ride, a black-and-tan Crown Victoria Police Interceptor with large gold six-pointed stars on the doors and an LED light bar on the roof that was visible from Mars when it was turned on. Staff Sergeant Coker was in a very good mood, all things considered, because it was a lovely morning and he was all gunned up and armored to the teeth and he was cruising along in his favorite vehicle and, to cap it off, he and his good friend Charlie Danziger had just gotten away with a bank robbery in Gracie a couple of days back that had netted them around two million dollars in cash and valuables.

He and Charlie Danziger went all the way back to the Marine Corps, and Charlie, up until a few years ago, had been a sergeant in the State Highway patrol. More recently, Charlie had been the Route Manager for Wells Fargo Armored Trucks, a position that had given him a lot of insider knowledge about large cash deliveries to local banks.

Such as a delivery last Friday of over two million to The First Third Bank in Gracie.

Danziger and the wheelman, a burn-scarred hardcase named Merle Zane, had done the actual robbery, and Coker, the best police sniper in the state, had taken care of the inevitable police pursuit with a Barrett Fifty.

Results: four wrecked squad cars, four dead cops, two dead media types who were in a Live Eye chopper following The Chase, and, sadly, a little later, the regrettable necessity of shooting Merle Zane in the back, just to keep things tidy. Merle Zane had last been seen stumbling into a pine forest with one of Charlie Danziger's nine-mill rounds buried in his right kidney.

All in all, it had been a hectic afternoon, but in the end very profitable for Coker and Charlie Danziger.

Coker was idly turning over in his mind the various ways in which these newfound assets could be deployed for maximum sensory stimulation when his radio came to life and his cell phone rang.

He checked the call display—C DANZIGER—flicked it to voice mail, and picked up the police radio handset.

"Coker."

"You're supposed to say your car number, Staff Sergeant Coker."

"I forgot it, Bea. What's up?"

"I'm not Bea. I'm *Central*."

Coker grinned, which seamed up his wolfish face and made him look even meaner than he already looked.

"Okay, Central. What's happening?"

"Citizen is calling in a 10-38 at 2990 Old Orchard, wants immediate assistance."

"That's Ernie Pullman's ranch, isn't it? He can handle a damn dog call himself. He's got more guns than the Bass Pro Shop."

"It's not a mad dog call. It's a mad bear call. I only said it was a 10-38 because we don't have a radio code for a mad bear. Can you take this, Coker? We got nobody else in the sector."

"Where is everybody?"

"Most of our units are assisting State. Looks like the State guys have made some huge bust on Arrow Creek and everybody's rolling on it."

"Who got busted?"

"State's not saying. Some guy in a big yellow Hummer. Shots fired."

Coker worked that through and decided not to ask any more questions about a big yellow Hummer.

"Okay. Who was the caller?"

"Ernie himself. He sounds pretty upset."

"Ernie can shoot a bear as well as I can."

"He says there's a problem with that."

Coker sighed.

"Okay, I'm rolling. Is he still on the line?"

"Yes."

"Tell him to gimme five minutes. Out."

Coker sighed, flicked on the light bar, and hit the accelerator. He also scooped up the cell and flicked the voice mail button.

"Coker, this is Charlie. Where you at. Call me. It's important."

So Coker did.

"Charlie?"

"Coker. Where are you?"

"I got a 10-38 at Ernie Pullman's ranch—"

"Ernie can't handle a mad dog?"

"It's not a—look, Charlie, what's up?"

"I'll meet you at Ernie's."

"You sound a little spooked, Charlie."

"I am."

Ernie Pullman's Rocking Bar Ranch was more of a county dump than a ranch, with a big fenced-in yard littered with old tractor parts and rusted-out car bodies and assorted useless junk. Ernie's double-wide slumped down in the middle of this, looking like it had been dropped there from a great height. As Coker pulled into the drive he heard a horn beep, and a large white Ford F150 pickup filled up his rearview mirror.

Coker got out of the cruiser, stretched out his legs, waited while Charlie Danziger extracted his six-foot-something frame from behind the wheel.

Charlie had long white hair and a big white handlebar mustache. He was from Montana and looked it. Coker was from Montana, too, but he looked more like a Marine Corps DI, which made sense, since he used to be one.

"What's up, Charlie?"

"Where's Ernie?"

"Bea says he's out back, dealing with a mad bear."

"Pissed-off mad or crazy mad?"

"We'll have to go see."

"We gotta talk."

"I hate it when you say that."

"First off, let's see where Ernie is. It's not something I want to go gabbing about in front of the worst damn drunk south of Sallytown."

They made their way around to the back of the double-wide. There was another yard back there that ran down a muddy slope to a large stand of mixed timber—oaks and pines and alders in the main, with a few soaring poplars sticking up above the rest. There was a very large black clump about three-quarters of the way up the tallest poplar, and a smaller blue and white clump a few yards higher. The smaller blue and white clump was yelling at them and waving a hand.

The bigger black clump didn't seem to be doing much of anything. Coker and Danziger stood there for a minute, taking it in.

"That you, Ernie?" Coker shouted.

"Who the fuck else?" yelled Ernie Pullman. "Shoot the fucking bear, will ya."

Coker looked at the bear. It wasn't moving at all. He looked at Danziger.

"You bring your Winchester?"

"It's in the truck."

"The carbine or the long gun with the scope?"

"The carbine."

"Think you can hit that bear with a carbine? All I got is my shotgun and this sidearm."

"I can hit the bear with a thrown stone, Coker."

And then, in a lowered voice, "You want to hear what I got to say?"

Ernie was still yelling at them.

"How long you been up there?" Danziger called.

"Almost an hour."

"How'd you call 911?"

"My cell, you asshole. I had it with me when the bear showed up. Charlie, shoot the fucking bear, will you?"

"Bear looks dead to me," said Coker.

Ernie did not find this amusing.

"Well, he was pretty fucking lively when he chased me up this poplar."

"Maybe he's just napping," said Danziger, in a soft aside to Coker. "Is it legal to shoot a napping bear?"

"Have to look it up," said Coker.

He looked up at Ernie Pullman, who was a good fifty yards away, and then looked at Danziger.

"Okay. He's far enough away. What's on your mind, Charlie?" he said, in a quiet voice.

"You haven't heard yet?"

"Well, I heard the State guys made a hostile stop on a big yellow Hummer near Arrow Creek. Only one big yellow Hummer in this part of the state."

"You're right about that."

"They popped Deitz?"

"Yep."

"He dead?"

"Not yet."

"They find the cash you stuck in the back of his ride?"

"They did. Plus that Rolex."

"So they're thinking what we want them to—"

Ernie, who had been watching them talk quietly together about God knew what, felt the need to draw their attention back to the matter at hand.

"For Chrissakes, shoot the fucking bear!" Ernie screamed. "My hands are slipping."

"They are too," said Danziger, quietly, to Coker. "You can see him sliding down a bit there."

"Shoot the bear!" screamed Ernie, now verging on the repetitive.

Coker lit up a cigarette, smiled at Danziger.

"So they've got Deitz," he said, still in hoarse whisper. Danziger nodded.

"I guess we'll haveta see how it plays out."

"We will."

Ernie was now sliding faster. He had stopped saying anything coherent and was just sort of shrieking and crying.

The bear still wasn't moving.

"Stop screaming, Ernie," Danziger yelled. "You'll wake him up. Maybe you can just sorta slip around him."

Ernie said several unkind things in a very loud and excited tone. He was about ten feet from the bear, sliding down toward it by inches, and it looked as if the bear was now wide awake.

It let out a low moaning growl and shifted its position and growled again, this time with much more authority. Ernie stopped screaming, but he was still slipping down the tree trunk.

"Pretty sure that bear's not dead," said Coker, in an aside to Danziger. "Looks real active now."

"He does, doesn't he?" said Danziger. "Maybe I should go get the Winchester?"

"Probably should," said Coker.

The Book of Edgar

The Quantum Park Marriott Hotel and Convention Center occupied ten acres of rolling grasslands about halfway between the Belfair County Regional Airport—known locally as Mauldar Field—and Quantum Park itself, an enclosed, razor-wired, and well-guarded research and development center set out on the northwestern edge of Niceville.

Quantum Park was the base for a selection of anonymous feeder firms that did peripheral R and D for prominent outfits with names such as Lawrence Livermore, Motorola, General Dynamics, Northrop Grumman, Lockheed Martin, KBR, and Raytheon.

Through no coincidence at all the security firm handling the complex needs of Quantum Park was an outfit called BD Securicom, the *BD* standing for *Byron Deitz*, who, until his recent transfer to a new position as the lead suspect in a bank robbery, had been its CEO and sole proprietor.

With a facility such as Quantum Park nearby, and an airport right at hand, the Niceville Marriott was doing a brisk trade in business travel, its success reflected in the elegant Frank Lloyd Wright–style complex of residential suites, the wave pools, the workout areas, the huge convention hall next door, and particularly the low-ceilinged central foyer clad in yellow limestone and floored in highly polished slabs of oak stained a rich, glassy auburn the color of a horse's eye.

Along one side a huge gas fire flickered behind a forty-foot glass wall, and on the opposite side an equally giant aquarium glimmered in tones of tourmaline and teal set off by schools of scarlet fish that drifted and flashed under the downglow of tiny halogen lamps.

Behind the fire wall was a Starck-style restaurant known as SkyLark— surprisingly good French fusion and a major draw from as far north as Gracie and Sallytown. Behind the aquarium was a brass-and-hardwood long bar known as the Old Dominion, where, on any weekday evening, you'd have to work damn hard to avoid all the local players who gathered under a huge panoramic oil painting of the Battle of Chickamauga.

Holding court there were men such as Bucky Cullen Junior, whose family owned most of Fountain Square, in the heart of Cap City's financial district, or Billy Dials, who ran Niceville's largest hardware and lumber supply store, or Niceville's Mayor-for-Life, Dwayne "Little Rock" Mauldar, the only son of Daryl "Big Rock" Mauldar, who had graduated as a Four-Letter Man from Regiopolis Prep, survived two combat tours in Vietnam, and gone on to play six years as a starting linebacker with the St. Louis Cardinals.

They were Great White Sharks, all three of them, with dead-fish eyes and jolly airs and graces, with rolls of fat at their collars and diamond pinky rings and loud voices, and they heartily approved of anyone who heartily approved of them.

These creatures were usually surrounded by a school of human moray eels and mud cats and lampreys. Maybe it was the aquarium.

All in all, the Marriott was a pretty snazzy place and not in any way tarnished by the arrival at the main entrance of a gleaming navy blue Crown Vic that, although referred to as "unmarked," could not have screamed *cop* any louder if the word had been spray-painted in red all over the hood. Beau Norlett was at the wheel with Nick riding shotgun as he pulled to a stop under the stone canopy.

An older man in a civilian version of Army dress blues stepped up and opened the door for Nick, saluting smartly as he did so. Tall and lanky, with a body that may at one time have been well muscled but now looked dried out and spidery, he had oversized ears and a marine crew cut and a sardonic expression on his sallow face.

A shining brass plate on his crisp blue uniform was engraved with the letters EDGAR.

"Detective Kavanaugh," said Edgar Luckinbaugh, as Nick stepped out of the car. "We've been expecting you."

"Thanks, Edgar. This very large guy on the far side is my partner, Detective Norlett."

"Sir," said Edgar, offering Beau a far less precise salute, displeased with what he was seeing.

"Welcome to the Marriott."

Beau, well aware that Edgar was displeased, and why, returned it with precisely the same level of insolence. He also decided to "forget" the big box of honey-glazed Krispy Kreme donuts they'd brought along for him. Edgar led them through the glass doors and into the cool shadows of the lobby.

Faint music came from everywhere, a lilting piano sonata. A slender Asian man with porcelain skin and stony black eyes watched them as they crossed the gleaming floors. Small and neat, in a well-cut black suit and lavender shirt, he was sitting behind a French escritoire with his tiny hands resting on a large green leather notebook. He smiled at Nick as Nick glanced over at him.

His name was Mr. Quan and he was the concierge, which explained the black suit and the lavender shirt but not the oversized bow tie in chrome-yellow silk. Perhaps nothing could.

Nick was halfway across the lobby when his cell phone rang. It was Kate.

"Hold on a second, okay? I gotta take this."

He stepped away a few feet, leaving Beau Norlett and Edgar Luckinbaugh alone to consider, in a stiff and stony silence, each other's salient deficiencies in character and tint.

"Kate, how's Beth?"

"Well, Reed called. What's this about Byron being arrested?"

Nick sketched out the basics.

Kate was a quick study.

"Do you really think he had anything to do with that awful robbery?"

"I'd find it damn strange if even Byron was dumb enough to keep cash from a robbery-murder beef lying around in his truck. But the Chinese angle, that's another story. How's Beth taking it?"

"She's shocked. But not sad. I don't think anything Byron did would surprise her. She's downstairs right now, talking to Axel and Hannah."

"Did Reed have any news about your dad?"

"Not yet. He's driving back down today. I told him to come here. Can you get back for dinner?"

Nick looked at his watch.

"I think so. I guess a family meeting is in order?"

"Yes, it is. Please try to make it. There's a lot going on. I've asked Beth and the kids to stay with us for a while. We could fix up the carriage house for them. Is that okay?"

"You're still feeling the same way about bringing Rainey Teague home too?"

"I am. He'll be out of physio soon. He has to go somewhere. I'm his guardian."

"Full house, Kate."

"Yes. For a while. Maybe it would be good for Rainey to have other kids around."

"It might."

Would it be good for Axel and Hannah to have Rainey around? he was thinking. *That's the question.*

"Nick . . . are you okay with all this?"

A pause.

"I will be, Kate. I will be."

"Thank you, Nick. You know how much this means to me. Can you really make it home for dinner? Reed will be here by then. We can talk about everything. Okay? The whole family?"

"I'll be there. Look for me by moonlight, though Hell should bar the way."

"The Highwayman got shot, didn't he?"

"I won't. Love you, babe."

"Me too. Bye."

Nick could see that Edgar and Beau had been together long enough to perfect their dislike. He tried to ignore the tension between them as Mark Hopewell, the duty manager for the day, young and keen and looking like a gun-locker in a three-piece suit, came around from behind the registration desk with a troubled expression on his face.

"Detective Kavanaugh. I'm so sorry to hear what happened at Mauldar Field."

"Thanks, Mark. This is Detective Norlett. Edgar, don't go," he said, as the bellman turned to leave. "We'd like to talk to you as well."

"We can use my office," said Hopewell, leading them back around the registration desk to a small, cluttered room, harshly lit by a brutal blue fluorescent buzzing overhead. Hopewell poured them coffee—it smelled marvelous—and handed it around. Nick sat, Beau loomed, Edgar hovered, and Hopewell perched himself on the side of his desk, holding a sheaf of papers in his large pink hands.

"Can I ask, Detective—"

"Mark, we know each other. I'm Nick, okay?"

Mark nodded, but couldn't manage a smile.

"Thanks, Nick . . . were there any survivors?"

Nick shook his head.

"You're Air National Guard, aren't you?"

Hopewell nodded.

"Then you know the phrase 'vertically deployed into the terrain.'"

Hopewell winced.

"Jeez. Where did it come down?"

"Middle of the fourteenth green at Anora Mercer. Killed a woman on the green, injured her husband."

"What caused it?"

"Bird strike. Flew into a flock of crows."

"Man. I did that once in an Apache. One of those damn Canada geese. I mean, only one. We had to auto-rotate from six hundred feet."

"Better you than me. Are those the papers on these guys?"

Hopewell handed them over.

"Yes. Everything we have on them, including calls received and made. Flew in from Shanghai, checked in on Friday, five rooms booked a month in advance. Charges went on an Amex Centurion card presented by Mr. Zachary Dak. Not an ounce of trouble, kept to themselves. Stayed well clear of the boys in the Old Dominion. Dinner at SkyLark—the pilots at a separate table—and according to Mr. Quan, they spoke a kind of Chinese he called Hakka—Quan didn't like to hear it and said they were 'peasants'—Quan's a Mandarin. Guess it's a class thing. Other than that, they didn't stand out in any way at all. That is, until this morning."

Nick looked up from the papers.

"This morning? You mean the crash?"

Hopewell shook his head.

"Nope. Before that. Edgar here can tell you the story. I was interviewing an applicant in one of the meeting rooms. Edgar . . . ?"

Luckinbaugh straightened up, showed a mouthful of tombstone teeth, and tugged an old Sheriff's Department notebook out of a side pocket.

"Yes sir," he barked out, and began to read from his notebook in the strangled syntax of a cop testifying in court. Nick stopped him after the second repetition of "the subject was observed."

"Jeez, Edgar. You're not up in front of Judge Teddy. Just lay it out straight, okay?"

Edgar looked disappointed, and he folded the notebook away with a disapproving frown.

"Well, okay . . . Like Mr. Hopewell says, I was on the portcullis—"

"The what?"

"Edgar calls it that," said Hopewell. "It's an old word for the entrance to a fort."

"Edgar," said Nick. "Please."

"Sorry. I was on the main doors. Time marker was nine-forty-two hours this ay emm. Black Benz Six Hundred pulls up out front, marker was alpha delta nine seven six nevada bravo—"

Nick looked at Beau, who gave him back a wide grin and shook his head, moves which Luckinbaugh picked up but chose to ignore. There was a right way to do things even if these young pups didn't appreciate it.

"—driver was a big ole cullud fella name of Phillip Holliman—"

The word *cullud* landed on the floor with a dull clank. Everybody but Beau tried to ignore it.

"Deitz's guy," said Nick.

Luckinbaugh nodded.

"Yes. I take the keys and as he's walking inside he asks me what room Mr. Zachary Dak is in and I say well Mr. Dak and his party they all checked out earlier this morning and Holliman he says what the—he utters an obscenity or two—and then he asks me how long and I say maybe thirty, thirty-five minutes—well, I figure Holliman was like to explode—his face goes all purple and his eyes get big and he grabs me by the arm and says I gotta take him to Dak's room right this—obscenity— moment do I get it and I start to say well I can't without Mr. Hopewell—"

"Did you take Holliman to Dak's room?" Nick asked, thinking that maybe letting Edgar read from his notebook might have been a better idea.

"Yes sir, pardon me, Mr. Hopewell, but he was making a scene and there were guests coming and going and he was snarling and yapping at me and people were staring at us so I says okay and I took him to Mr. Dak's suite—the Glades—and no sooner do I slide my pass card in the slot than Holliman he just crashes right by me—the maid hasn't been there yet so the rooms are all in a hooey and Holliman he goes charging from the living room to the master and the bath like a crazy man and all the time he's swearing and growling—I thought he was gonna pitch a fit—and then he comes back and grabs me and he wants to know are they all gone and I say yes sir they all took a shuttle up to Mauldar Field—all gone every fucking one he says, right in my face, gettin' his cullud spit on my cheek and all—and I say yes and then he's on the cell phone—has it at his ear—"

Luckinbaugh stopped, took a breath.

"Now Detective Kavanaugh, at this point I will have to refer to my notes, because what he said on the phone is I think revelant to the case—"

" 'Relevant,' you mean?" put in Beau, which got him a stern look from Luckinbaugh.

"Yes sir, that's what I said. Revelant. So I gotta read the transcript if it's okay?"

This was addressed to Nick. For Luckinbaugh, Beau was now invisible.

"Yes it is, Edgar. You go ahead."

Luckinbaugh, suppressing a triumphant sneer at Beau, tugged out his notebook, flipped through the pages, and then began to read aloud.

"Exchange went as follows, Detective Kavanaugh. Holliman says 'they're gone Deitz' from which I implied that he meant his boss Byron Dee—"

" 'Inferred,' " said Beau, who just couldn't help himself. "*Inferred.*"

"That what I said."

"No," said Beau. "You said 'implied.' That means to assign a quality or state to something by indirect reference. 'Inferred' means to draw an inductive meaning—"

"Beau," said Nick.

"What if I did? Same damn thing," said Luckinbaugh, arriving at a verdict on the kid and filing him away under *uppity.*

Nick gave Beau a head shake and Beau managed a blank expression. Edgar shrugged his shoulders, settled his feathers, and resumed . . .

"And I was close enough to hear the response from Mr. Deitz, which

was 'Gone? Who's gone?' to which Mr. Holliman replies 'Zachary Dak
and his whole crew. They checked out thirty minutes ago. They're in the
wind' and Mr. Deitz says 'Jesus and what about the item—' "

"Deitz said 'the item'?" Nick asked. "His exact word?"

Luckinbaugh nodded gravely.

"His word exactly. He said 'what about the item?' "

"Did you have any idea what he meant?"

"No sir. But from his tone I figured whatever it was, it was real important. I'm a go on, then?"

"Please."

"So Holliman says 'I'm standing in their room. There's nothing here.
Nothing. They're taking the item with them. They were always going to
take it with them' and Mr. Deitz says 'Jesus H. Christ on a fucking crutch'
and Mr. Holliman says 'yeah well I'll give him a call then if you think
he'll help' outta which I *implied* was Holliman being sarcastic and then
Mr. Deitz he says 'no wait—the Lear. It's at Mauldar Field. That's a half
hour from the Marriott. Call the field boss, tell him not to give that Lear
clearance to take off until I get there' and Mr. Holliman cuts in saying
'I'm just a security guard Deitz' and Mr. Deitz starts screaming at him so
loud that Mr. Holliman pulls the phone away from his ear and Deitz is
saying 'tell him whatever—make sure that plane never gets spooled up.
Go. Now.' And then Deitz hangs up and Holliman is staring at me."

"Did he say anything to you?"

"Yes sir. He walked up to me and stuck a finger in my chest and he
says 'you heard nothing you follow Edgar not a fucking thing are we
clear' and I said 'yes sir we are clear' and Holliman shoves me out of the
way so stern I bounced off the door and he's gone."

There was a silence as everyone took this in.

"The item?" said Nick, more to himself than to the others. "Mark,
did they put anything in your safe?"

Hopewell shook his head.

"Not a thing. And the in-room safe was never touched."

"So you and Edgar, you never saw this Dak guy with anything that
looked unusual."

Both men shook their heads.

"Did they ever meet with anyone on the premises?"

"Not that we saw," said Hopewell. "I asked Mr. Quan if he had performed any services for them. He said he had ordered up a black Lincoln
Town Car from Airport Limos and he had provided a detailed map of the

town. Other than that, he found a source for a kind of green tea they liked."

Hopewell paused, seemed to be working out how to say something.

"There was something Quan said, I thought was funny at the time. Funny odd, I mean. He's Mandarin—or at least he speaks it—but he used a word that I always thought was Cantonese, and the way he used it, after what I'm hearing, I was wondering—"

"Uh, Mark . . . is there a point?"

Hopewell grinned.

"My wife says I wander, Nick. The word was '*gway-lo*,' which, when Quan uses it, he means it as an insult for white folks. It means ghosts, and I guess the idea is we're all so pale we look like ghosts. But this time he used it to describe Mr. Dak and his people. So what I was thinking is, did he mean it literally?"

"You mean ghosts as in *spooks*?" said Beau.

"Yeah. Yes. So I asked him just a while ago and he got all antsy and weird but finally he said that to him they all 'had the stink of *guangbo*' on them. I asked him what '*guangbo*' meant and he said they were like the Chinese secret police and that everybody in China hated them."

"Nice work, Mark. We'll need a statement from Quan too. Has the maid done their rooms yet?"

"No. Once we realized that there had been a crash and that you'd be coming over, I had all of their rooms locked and sealed."

"When was the last time their rooms were cleaned?"

"They'd have had a turn-down service at ten last night. But the rooms are all cleaned before noon, depending on when the guests are out."

"So almost twenty-four hours, then?"

"Yes."

Nick looked at Beau.

"Call the LT, will you? Tell him we'll need Forensics out here to go over the rooms. Mark, we'll try to be subtle, but this crash, these guys are Chinese nationals, so the State Department and maybe the FBI will be getting involved. And this connection with Byron Deitz . . . something's not right here."

"I been turning it over," said Luckinbaugh. "I got a notion, you want to hear it."

"We do," said Nick.

"Well, Mr. Deitz's company was security for Quantum Park," said Luckinbaugh. "Lot of high-tech stuff there. Secret stuff. Maybe that's why they were here. The Chinese guys. Maybe 'the item' was something they took from Quantum Park?"

Everybody stared at Luckinbaugh. It was as if a stuffed and mounted bluefin had begun to recite Catullus. He was a bigot but apparently he was also a pretty good cop.

"Oh Jesus," said Nick. "That's damn good, Edgar. Makes sense. And I sincerely hope you're wrong."

Luckinbaugh shrugged, but looked pleased.

Another silence.

"Edgar, did any of these guys send anything off by FedEx or drop anything in the mail?"

Luckinbaugh shook his head.

"No sir. Mr. Hopewell took the liberty of checking the mail drop box. Nothing there. And no FedEx or UPS pickups on a Sunday. Their drop boxes are empty too. And the shuttle took these guys right to Mauldar Field, no stops to drop anything off. If they had it when they left here, then they had it with them on the plane when they took off."

They all contemplated that.

"Well, I guess we know where it is now," said Beau after a moment. "Whatever it was."

"In a crater on the fourteenth green," said Nick.

"Yes sir."

Nick stood up.

"Okay, Mark, Edgar, thanks a lot."

"What's going to happen now?" Hopewell wanted to know.

"Beau and I are going to go on up to Gracie, get a sit-down with Byron, see what he has to say about all of this. We'll get our CID people in here, get your statements, bag the rooms, check out their contacts. In the meantime, we'd be grateful if you said absolutely nothing about this to anybody. There were media trucks at the crash site. Sooner or later they'll figure out where the victims were staying. They'll be all over you."

"They won't get a thing from us," said Hopewell.

"Damn right," said Luckinbaugh, with a final defiant glare at Beau. Nick and Beau headed for the car, with Luckinbaugh following behind. He opened Nick's door for him, and he was still frowning at the back of Beau's head as they pulled away.

"Made a friend there," said Nick.

"Probably not," said Beau, grinning. "His type just gets on my nerves."

"I inferred that," said Nick.

A pause, while Beau accelerated onto the main road and turned north. Gracie was about seventy miles away, on the east slope of the Belfair Range.

After a while, Nick said, "Cullud spit?"

"Yeah," said Beau, looking grim.

"Shit's still out there, isn't it?"

"Yeah. But not as much as you'd think. Times have changed. You run into it, this part of the state, it's mainly with the older guys, especially the county deps."

"Well, it's not in here, Beau."

Beau shot him a sideways smile.

"No?"

"No."

"Then why you making me drive?"

The Term "a Criminal Lawyer"
Is the Opposite of an Oxymoron

Marty Coors was standing in the cement-block basement of the State Police HQ holding cells a few miles out of Gracie. The holding cells were twenty feet underground, protected by walls a foot thick, with closed-circuit cameras everywhere you looked and every kind of sensor and trip-wire device and mantrap you could order up from *The Great Big Book of Totally Sneaky Stuff.*

Coors was staring at a sheet of bulletproof mirrored glass. The glass made up one whole wall of a SuperMax containment cell. Inside the cell, sitting on a steel chair bolted to the concrete floor of a barren blank box, shackled in just about every way it is possible to shackle a guy without entirely covering him in chains, was the Man of the Hour himself, the one and only Byron Deitz.

But since the lights inside the SuperMax cell were not turned on, all that Marty Coors could see was his own reflection, a six-foot-three-inch muscled-out ex-marine in his early fifties with a face made for radio and steel gray hair cut so short his scalp glowed pink in the sun. His eyes were in shadow as he stood in a pool of light from an overhead fixture.

Marty Coors was the CO of this sector of the State Police and right now it was his personal duty to see that the piece of human waste currently being held inside the SuperMax containment cell lived to see the next morning.

This he was doing by being the only living human being on level four of the cellblock. Level four had only one cell, known to the troopers based here as the Bull Pit, and Marty Coors was looking at it right now.

Coors was convinced to a moral certainty that every one of the twenty or thirty state troopers and county cops and even the three FBI types crowding the main floor concourse of the HQ center would cheerfully pop six rounds of hollow-point into Byron Deitz's skull if he gave them a sliver of an angle on him. Or, if pushed, beat him to death with their bare hands.

This was because Byron Deitz had just been caught with pretty clear and convincing evidence that he had been involved in an armed robbery during which four police officers had been literally executed, two state, one county, and one of their own pursuit drivers, a fine young man named Darcy Beaumont, which had left Coors with only one pursuit driver for his entire sector, Darcy's best friend, Reed Walker.

Two media mutts had also been killed when their news chopper had been shot down, but, to be honest, nobody gave a flying fruitcup about them, because, really, did *anyone* give a flying fruitcup when a couple of vultures circling a fresh kill got themselves all shot to shit?

No, they did not.

The memorial service for these four young men was scheduled for the following week, at Holy Name Cathedral down in Cap City. So far, law enforcement people from all over America, from Canada and the UK and Europe, were slated to walk behind the hearses. Three police pipe bands were due to attend, including the NYPD Emerald Society Pipes and Drums, the U.S. Corps of Cadets Pipes and Drums from West Point, and the Virginia Military Institute Pipes and Drums.

It was shaping up to be the largest memorial service for fallen police officers ever held in the South, with expected attendance being estimated at somewhere around ten thousand people.

And this was all happening because of two hundred and twenty-odd pounds of meat and gristle chained to a chair on the other side of this sheet of glass. The main reason Coors was unarmed was because he really didn't trust himself all that much either.

He reached out and hit a wall switch beside the glass and a bank of fluorescent lights flared up inside the SuperMax cell. Deitz was slumped over in the chair, asleep, so when the lights went on his head came up with a jerk.

Appearance-wise, Byron Deitz had never been a figure one could contemplate with a joyful heart. He did not walk in beauty like the night. In fact, he slouched in warthog ugly like a Hangover Monday in Barstow, with a big bald head stuck like a cannonball on a neckless torso that might have been a shaved grizzly carcass. The fact that he had been well and truly tuned up by the arresting officers was written—let's say tattooed—all over his face. He straightened up, glared through the glass, knowing somebody was out there. His grating snarl came through the loudspeaker in the wall over the window.

"Where's Warren Smoles? I want my lawyer. I'm not saying a fucking thing without Warren Smoles in the room."

Coors pushed the TALK button.

"This is Captain Coors—"

"Marty, you prick."

"We've called Smoles. He was down in Cap City. He's flying up right now. In a police air unit. He'll be here in an hour. Anything you need right now?"

"You could take these fucking chains off me, Marty. I'm in your SuperMax cell. My company designed and built it. My contractors put it in. Whaddya figure, I built in a secret door in case I ever ended up here? Besides, I gotta hit the can."

"I'll see what I can do," said Coors, killing the speaker. He left the lights on. From what he could see, Deitz was still talking. From how red his face was getting, it was probably something unpleasant. His radio beeped. He picked it up.

"Coors."

"Captain, Nick Kavanaugh's here. He's asking to see Deitz. What do you want me to say?"

"Tell him I'll be right up. And send a team down here to get Deitz to the can. It's okay to take the girdle off him. Just ankle chains and the belt shackles. He's not going anywhere."

"Will do, Captain."

"No sidearms, remember. Just the muscle and the Taser if you need it. Reliable guys only, got it?"

"Hey, Cap, they're all reliable."

"You know what I mean, Luke."

"Roger that. They're on their way."

When Coors got out of the elevator in the main lobby, the entire space was jammed full of uniforms, big blocky men and solid, capable-looking women, young and old and right in the middle, the black and tan of the Sheriff's Department, the charcoal gray of the State Police, even a few navy blue uniforms from the Niceville PD.

He saw Mickey Hancock and Jimmy Candles, the shift supervisors for the Belfair and Cullen County units, standing talking to Coker and his buddy Charlie Danziger. Danziger was a tall, cowboy-looking older man with a white handlebar mustache, and Coker was a top kick with the county. Coker was the unofficial go-to police sniper for pretty much every agency in this part of the state. He was wiry, silver-haired, and had something of a gunfighter air about him, with pale eyes and a tanned leathery look. He and Charlie Danziger were in civilian clothes, Coker in a charcoal suit and Danziger in a white shirt, jeans, and cowboy boots. Danziger's connection to the case was that one of his Wells Fargo trucks had delivered the cash only an hour before the robbery.

When the elevator doors binged open, everybody in the lobby, including Coker and Hancock and Candles and Charlie Danziger, turned to look at Coors. It was like being gunned by a room full of wolves, all set faces and ferocious attention. The talk, whatever it had been, fell silent. Coors moved through the crowd, making eye contact, letting everybody know who was running this room. They all gave way as he passed. There was no muttering, but there were a few unfriendly looks.

He reached his office, a glassed-in square with a view of the rest of the operating area and the front doors. Nick Kavanaugh was there, along with his new sidekick, the kid named Norlett.

Boonie Hackendorff, the Special Agent in Charge of the Cap City FBI office, was leaning on the wall opposite Coors' desk, a large big-bellied man with a round red face and a neatly trimmed beard. He had his suit jacket open and Coors could see he was carrying today, a gray Sig in a Bianchi holster.

Everybody looked up as Coors came in.

"Gentlemen."

"Jeez, Marty," said Boonie Hackendorff, "can you feel what's going on out there?"

Coors came around, sat in the chair behind his desk, laid his hands on the table.

"Hell, yes," he said. "Reminds me of Tombstone just before the Earps took their walk. Nick, how are you? Any word on Kate's dad?"

Nick shook his head.

"Got a DT named Linus Calder up at VMI, he's on it. So far, no sign of him."

"He's what, in his eighties? Could he have just wandered off?"

"That's what we're hoping," said Nick.

Coors nodded.

"I hear Mrs. Deitz is with Kate?"

"Yes. She walked out on Byron last night. Took the kids. I think she'll be with us for a while. Boonie, you're gonna want to talk to her, I guess."

"Yes. But not today. She's been through enough. Okay, we're all hanging here, Nick. What the hell went down at Mauldar Field?"

Nick laid it out for them, from takeoff to wipeout, and what they had learned from Hopewell and Luckinbaugh.

Boonie Hackendorff was not pleased.

"Are we saying that those five guys who augured in were Chinese fricking spies? And that Deitz was working with them?"

Nick shook his head.

"Only solid thing we can say is that Deitz is connected to them. He might even have been trying to stop them from doing something."

Boonie was clearly thinking Homeland Security, a Bigfoot agency that nobody ever wanted to deal with.

"And Deitz used the word 'item'?"

Nick nodded.

"No idea what he meant?"

"Not yet. Like I said, might have been something Deitz was trying to recover, something the Chinese guys had taken—stolen—somehow."

Boonie shook his head.

"That doesn't square with Holliman saying 'they were always going to take it with them.' "

"No. It doesn't," said Nick. "That sounds more like Deitz was expecting to get the item back."

"Which sure sounds like he gave it to them in the first place," said Marty Coors.

"We can't assume it. All we can do is follow up. Boonie, you might want to get on to the people at Quantum Park, get them to start an inventory check, see if anything's missing."

"We're going to have to bypass all the Securicom people, go direct to the companies themselves. Jeez. I gotta make a few calls."

Boonie went toward the door, saw all the uniforms out there, all staring back at him through the glass, and hesitated.

"Use my gun room," said Coors. "Nobody there. Close the door."

When Boonie was gone, Coors leaned back in his chair.

"What do you make of Deitz having a wad of bills from the bank thing in his own truck?"

Nick leaned forward.

"I think it stinks of a plant. Not even Byron Deitz is dumb enough to leave a hundred thousand in stolen money lying around in his truck."

"Deitz is a greedy guy, Nick. And he's been dirty before, back when he was with the FBI, how he got 'resigned.' "

"I knew he was forced out. I've never heard what he did. Records were sealed."

Coors reached for a pack of cigarettes, remembered he had quit, found a stick of gum and popped it into his mouth.

"Sealed as part of a plea bargain. Whatever he did, four mob guys ended up in Leavenworth. Still there. Very pissed off, from what I hear."

"Who are they?"

"Guy named Mario La Motta, zipperhead named Desi Munoz, another guy named Julie Spahn. Fourth guy, De Soto something, he died a few years back. What I heard, Deitz was into something with them, figured out they were all about to get busted, flipped the whole thing into a 'case' he was working—lying shit—but rather than deal with another corrupt FBI story line in the media, the Feds gave him credit for a mob bust and Deitz took early retirement. That's how he was able to get licensed to run security for a place like Quantum Park."

"Quantum Park people never knew?" asked Beau. Coors popped his gum, shook his head.

"File was sealed. FBI does the background check on all those applications, and they sat on it. So it was like it never happened."

"Unbelievable," said Beau, looking at the closed gun room door. They could hear Boonie's voice through the metal. He sounded unhappy.

"Did Boonie know about this?"

Coors shook his head.

"Couldn't say, Beau. I doubt it. Agency was protecting itself. They'd have no trouble keeping their field guys in the dark, not if it meant keeping the lid on a 'rogue agent' scandal. I guess we should fill him in when he comes out of the gun room. Only fair. I only heard this story maybe a year back. By then Deitz was in solid. Nothing to be done without him screaming about his rights."

"How'd *you* find out, Captain Coors?" asked Beau.

Coors smiled, popped his gum again, and tapped the side of his nose. Beau nodded.

"So how do you think we should play this?" asked Nick. "The jurisdictional issues are a mess. We have a whole bunch of things cooking off right in our faces and if the national security sector lands in the middle of this, Deitz is liable to get jerked right out of our hands."

Coors sat forward, thumped the table.

"Main thing I care about, who killed our guys? I mean, fuck these dead Chinese mooks, fuck whatever got stolen from Quantum Park. For that matter, fuck national security. All I want is for whoever slaughtered our boys to take a spike at Gun Hill."

"Then we have to figure a way to keep Deitz here, in Gracie, where we can work him," said Nick. "And you're right, Deitz is our only hook. Either he had a hand in this robbery, in which case he knows who else was involved—because there's no way Deitz could manage a Barrett .50 the way that shooter did—"

"Deitz is no kind of shooter at all," said Coors. "I've seen him at the range. He can hardly manage a pistol, let alone a Barrett .50."

"And if he didn't have anything to do with it, the guys who planted the stolen money in his Hummer sure as hell did, and even if he doesn't know it, somewhere, somehow Deitz connects to them. They *chose* him. They had to have had a good reason. So, either way, Deitz is our only link to them."

The phone on Coors' desk bleeped at him. He picked it up, listened, and then said, "Okay. Keep him in the car. And stay down the road. Don't let any of our people see him. And don't let him get near the media crews. He starts one of his All Cops Are the Spawn of Satan speeches to any of the television crews outside, our guys will beat him to death. So stay clear, you got it? Good."

He hung up, looked at Nick and Beau.

"Warren Smoles is here."

There was a general groan.

"Here in the HQ?" asked Beau.

"No. I got two of our guys keeping him in a plain brown wrapper a mile down the line."

"They won't be able to do that for long," said Nick.

Coors grinned.

"Yeah. He's already calling it unlawful confinement. They took his cell phone too. He went postal."

"What'd they tell him?"

"Security precautions for his own safety."

"He buy that?"

"Hell no. And I don't give a fuck. That showboating air bag is staying right there until we figure out what to do about—"

Boonie came out of the gun room. His face was wet and red and he had taken his tie off.

"Well, here we go. I just got off the line to D.C. State Department is sending an investigator to monitor the crash investigation. And get this. They may be bringing somebody from the Chinese Embassy with them. I'm gonna have to lee-aze with them. What the fuck does 'lee-aze' mean?"

"It means it's your turn in the barrel," said Coors.

"That's what I thought. Fuck them all. Okay. So, to cut to the chase, whaddya wanna do with Deitz?"

They all tried to look blank.

"Don't even start with me," said Boonie, shaking his head. "I know none of you give a rat's kidney about a buncha dead Chinamen, or if any spy shit was stolen from Quantum Park. All you want is who killed your boys, and Deitz is all you got. He had the money. We have him. You want to keep him close."

"That's right," said Nick. "And you'd let us?"

Boonie blew out air, patted his shirt for the cigarettes he had given up around the same time Marty Coors did, rolled his eyes, and sat down on the edge of Coors' desk.

"I'd take him away from you guys for the bank thing in a heartbeat, if that's all it was. But this Chinese deal changes everything. It's only a matter of time before the DNI lands on us, maybe even the CIA, and then nobody will see Byron Deitz again this side of Jordan. They'll use him in some poodle-faking espionage stunt with the Chinese that'll fall flat on its ass like always and none of us will ever be able to find a trace of him in a hundred years. Tell you the truth, that's all I give a fuck about too. These were *our* people. But to pull it off, we're gonna need a stunt. Any ideas?"

There was a silence.

"How's his blood pressure?" Nick asked.

"Deitz?" asked Coors.

"Yeah. His heart, liver, that kind of thing."

They all looked at each other.

Nobody said anything for a while.

"We'll need a tame doctor," said Coors.

"We'll need him right away," said Nick.

More silence.

Boonie reached over, took one of Marty Coors' gum sticks, started chewing on it as if it were a toothpick. The effect was not pretty, but then neither was Boonie Hackendorff.

After a time, Boonie smiled around the gum.

"I think I got just the guy," he said.

Warren Smoles had long, luxurious white hair that he combed straight back in a leonine flow that perfectly framed his deep-set brown eyes, his strong jaw, his lofty forehead. He may have been tanned a buttery brown, but it was hard to tell under the pancake makeup that he had put on before he arrived. Right now he was standing out in the parking lot of the State Police HQ, surrounded by media people, a bright flood lighting him up like a roadside Jesus, if Jesus had been wearing a double-breasted navy blue pin-striped suit over a pale pink shirt with a white English-style collar and a pale blue silk tie held in place with a gold collar bar.

Warren Smoles was where he liked to be, where he was born to be, right in the middle of a media scrum, doing what he did best, which was to lie his ass off with style, wit, and ferocious conviction.

Nick, watching him on the television set in the Lady Grace Hospital cafeteria, surrounded by a squad of Niceville cops, was thinking that you had to hand it to the guy.

He had arrived on the scene only four hours ago; he had spent less than thirty minutes consulting with his client, and another half hour playing hardball with Boonie and Nick and Captain Coors while they arranged Deitz's helicopter transfer to the intensive care unit here in Niceville.

And now Smoles was out there on the hardpan, claiming complete mastery over every detail of the case, and the media mutts were hanging on every word. The fact that Smoles knew damn well that the tame doctor—a Lady Grace heart surgeon who was Boonie's brother-in-law—was using a preexisting blood pressure issue that Deitz had as a pretext for admitting Deitz as a critical care case, didn't seem to be slowing him down at all.

Smoles had completely signed on to the stunt, since he knew as well as they did that if they didn't find a powerful excuse for secure medical custody right here in Niceville, Deitz would be swallowed up on a national security finding, never to be seen again by mortal men.

And then where would Warren Smoles be?

So he was in top form this afternoon.

"As clear a case of evidence planting as I have ever encountered," he was saying, in his rolling baritone, his eyes alight with righteous fury, his expression one of outrage and indignation. "We have the savage killing of law enforcement officers at the hands of unknown felons—an abominable act that I decry with every fiber of my soul, as does my client—but instead of launching a serious professional investigation, the FBI and local agencies, having utterly failed to crack this heinous case, have conspired together to lay the guilt at the feet of an innocent man—by the way, a very sick, no, a critically ill innocent man—he has only now been diagnosed by a doctor as suffering from atherosclerotic ischemic heart disease and severe hypertension—he has been medevacked only two hours ago—as you all witnessed—to the intensive care unit of Lady Grace Hospital in Niceville, where I will make sure that he receives the critical care that will be needed to save this poor man's life, a man who, I might add, is a pillar of the community and a highly decorated member, now retired with honor, of the very same agency, the FBI, that is now deliberately scapegoating—"

Nick clicked the set off, stood up, and faced the Niceville police officers.

"Okay. You all have your assignments. Nobody gets near the custody wing, let alone the lockdown where Deitz is. And that includes any and all state and county guys. And I'm going to have to ask you guys to stay out of his room. I don't want Smoles to have any pretext for a beef against any of us. His room is as good as a cell, he's shackled down, and the male nurses up there are used to prisoners. I know you all feel like seeing this guy dead, but there's more to it than that. A lot more. You got any questions, any doubts about your ability to carry out your duties, you go explain it to Staff Sergeant Crossfire and she'll reassign you."

"What about Smoles?" a cop asked from the back of the room.

"By law Warren Smoles must have free access to his client, within reason, especially if we're going to ask Deitz any questions about the case. But I want to know when he arrives. As you can see, Smoles is still up in Gracie shooting his face off. But he'll be down here tomorrow morning, just in time for the morning news feed. Until then, other than his docs and the nurses, nobody gets to see Byron Deitz."

Everybody nodded, everybody seemed to get it, and Nick broke up the meeting. Beau was leaning against the back wall, and they both watched in silence as the cops filed out of the room.

Beau pushed off the wall.

"What about us?"

"We're going to go talk to Deitz right now."

"You just told everybody that nobody but the medics could get in to see him. How are we going to get around that?"

"They're guarding the lockdown wing."

"Yeah?"

"Deitz isn't in the lockdown wing."

"Where is he?"

"He's in the underground parking lot, sitting in Mavis Crossfire's Suburban."

"Jesus. Who's watching him?"

"Mavis is watching him."

"All by herself?"

"Yes."

Beau nodded.

"I hope he doesn't pull something on her."

"I hope he does. He could use another beating."

They found Mavis Crossfire's Suburban parked in an out-of-the-way corner of the subbasement parking level, backed into a narrow slot with concrete walls on both sides. Mavis was at the wheel, eating one of the Krispy Kremes that had originally been intended for Edgar Luckin- baugh. She looked up, a wary flicker, as Nick and Beau came out of the gloom, her hand going down to her sidearm. But then her face bright- ened into a cheerful smile and she opened the driver's-side door.

"Hello, boys. Busy day?"

"Yeah. How's Deitz?"

"See for yourself."

She stepped around to the passenger-side door, popped it. Deitz was stretched out on the rear bench seat, still in his prison jumpsuit, shackled at the waist and ankles, the chains run through a ringbolt in the floor of the backseat.

He was sound asleep.

"Man," said Nick. "Did you slip him something?"

"He wanted a smoothie. I popped an Ativan into it. He hasn't had any sleep in twenty-four hours."

"How long's he been out?"

"He went out as soon as I parked. How's it going upstairs? I can't get any radio down here."

"Smoles is all over the news. According to him, local law enforcement is the Antichrist."

"Is Smoles coming in tonight?"

"No. He'll want a fresh news cycle in the morning. Change into a better suit. Get his makeup redone. It'll take CNN and Fox a while to get their trucks down here and set up. Smoles wants us to do a perp walk for the cameras around two. He asked us to get a couple of Deputy U.S. Marshals lined up for that."

"Why U.S. Marshals?"

"They make better TV, he says. I guess we better wake Byron. We're going to have to get him tucked away in lockdown."

Mavis took out her ASP baton, poked Deitz in the side. He moaned, twitched, opened his eyes.

"Shit," he said. "Where am I?"

"In the basement at Lady Grace. Nick here wants a word with you."

Deitz sat up, his chains clanking, leaned into the rear seat, closed his eyes, and put his head back on the neck rest.

"I got nothing to say to Nick, Mavis."

"Maybe," said Nick. "But I have something to say to you. You're going to want to hear it."

Deitz opened his eyes and looked at Nick. There had been a tone in Nick's voice. It sounded like an opening. An angle he could work.

"How's Beth and the kids? I figure they're with you."

"They are. Beth is leaving you."

"Jeez. There's a bulletin. Alert the media."

"You stepped in it pretty good here."

Deitz closed his eyes.

"Fuck you, Nick. I'm tired. Go away."

"In a minute. I said I had something to say."

"I'm not telling you one fucking thing. Where's that asshole Smoles?"

"He'll be back here tomorrow morning."

"What's all this shit about me having a heart condition? All I got is high blood pressure, and who the fuck wouldn't, they were in my shoes?"

"We're just trying to keep you local, keep you out of the hands of the federal government. Saying you're too sick to be transported is how we're doing it. Smoles signed off on it. He knows that national security will be all over you for the Chinese thing—"

Deitz grinned.

"Those fucking Chinks. They really all dead?"

"Yes. We're still looking for the item."

Deitz was just a bit too still and his face just a bit too blank.

"What item?"

"The one you and Holliman were so worked up about this morning at the Marriott."

Deitz thought this over.

"I hear that Lear went straight in at five hundred miles an hour."

"Nowhere near. Maybe two."

Deitz laughed, opened one eye.

"Good luck trying to find jack shit in a smoking crater like that. Even if there *was* jack shit to find."

"We don't need to find the item, Byron. We just have to figure out what's missing from Quantum Park. All *that* takes is a thorough inventory check."

"Still doesn't prove I had dick to do with it."

"The government isn't going to want to *prosecute* you, Byron. They just want to *use* you. You go down that rat hole on a national security finding, you'll never see blue sky again. You might even end up in a Chinese prison."

"Why the hell would that happen?"

"Five Chinese nationals died this morning, died while trying to leave the country with a top-secret device—"

"You don't know that."

"Okay. I only *suspect* it. I'll bet my 401(k) that you damn well *know* it. So the State Department can claim it was an accident until their lips fall off. Chinese government won't believe that, not for a minute. And if you think Zachary Dak didn't use your name to his bosses, you're kidding yourself. Five of their guys are down, in a ten-million-dollar plane. We have information that says they were *guangbo*—spies. Secret police. Their bosses lost face and they'll need your ass to get it back. Washington will give you up in a flash. They'd rather hang it on you than run the risk that the Chinese would think *they* had something to do with it. The country needs Chinese money a lot more than it needs you. So you need to think about it."

From the expression on his face, Deitz was.

"Well, that's all I wanted to say," said Nick, straightening up. "This is the last time we'll get a chance to talk like this. Once you get into that lockdown ward upstairs, it all runs on auto. Eventually the spooks will arrive, and you'll be gone. You have a nice night, Byron. I'll kiss the kids for—"

"Fuck the kids. Are you offering me something or not?"

"I think somebody planted that money on you—"

"No shit? You should be a detective."

"And I think there's a *reason* they picked on you. It's pretty obvious that whoever planted it has a connection to the robbery. So if you help us with that, maybe we can do something about the Chinese angle."

Deitz opened both eyes.

"You don't really give a fuck about the Chinese thing, do you?"

"Not really. Not my jurisdiction. I just want the people who killed those cops. I think you might even know who they are."

Nick could see the cartoon *thinks* bubble floating above Deitz's head.

"If I had information about who they were and didn't report it, I'd be an Accessory After. Draws the same penalty as if I actually did the bank."

"Hard thing to prove *when* you figured it out. Could have been a minute ago, and here you are reporting it right away, like a good citizen. So. Do you know who they are?"

Deitz said nothing for a while.

"I don't *know* who they are. I got a few theories."

"Now's the time to talk, Byron."

Deitz looked at Mavis, then came back to Nick.

"Can you really keep the government off me?"

"I think so."

"How?"

"If you're assisting the police in a multiple-cop-killing case, even Jon

Stewart would go nuts if a pack of nameless spooks stepped in and shut that down just so the president could keep the Chinese friendly."

"How would the media find out?"

"Smoles would be happy to take care of that."

Deitz put his head back, closed his eyes.

They waited him out.

"I'm gonna want to talk to Smoles."

"You do that."

"I will."

"I'd do it soon."

What Dreams May Come

Nick made it home long before moonlight. Beau dropped him off outside Kate's town house in Garrison Hills just as the sun was going down. A golden light was slanting through the live oaks that framed the cream-colored facade of the house. Lights were on inside, a soft glow filling the tall French windows. He could hear voices, and music. The scent of steaks cooking on the barbecue grill in the back garden drifted on the air.

Beat down, depressed, sleepless for almost twenty-four hours, Nick slowly climbed the curving steps that led up to the main floor landing.

As he reached the doorstep he could hear children's voices coming through the ornate black doors. Axel and Hannah, Beth's kids. They sounded happy.

He stopped for a moment, leaned his back against the wrought-iron railing, listening to the murmurs of life inside the house. The double doors had two arch-shaped stained-glass panels set into their rising curves. He could see silhouetted figures moving through the light.

At that moment it came to him that his old life with Kate had ended yesterday, and that from now on everything would be different.

They had been alone, quietly and happily alone. Now there would be Beth, and Axel, and Hannah.

And in a while, when he got out of physio, they'd have Rainey Teague, and all of that poor kid's troubles along with him—kidnapped—missing for ten days—discovered buried alive in a sealed crypt—both parents committing suicide—in a coma for a year. The prospect of having Rainey in the house was a stone in his heart. In Nick's mind, Rainey was tied to the essential *strangeness* of Niceville.

Even the disappearances of Delia Cotton, of Gray Haggard, and the unexplained absence of Kate's father, Dillon, had barely registered with the people of the town. But they sure had with Nick.

And only last night, right here where he was standing, right on these steps, Kate had opened these same black doors onto a *thing* that had no explanation, no framework, no reason to exist that fit into any of the outer world's reality. It was utterly strange, and it was *hostile*—hate-filled, hungry, mindless—something out of a nightmare world, something alien and terrifying and inexplicable.

They both saw it, Nick and Kate.

And they both saw the woman—the *image* of the woman—who had stepped out of that old mirror in a haze of green light and confronted the *thing* in the doorway. They had recognized her from an old picture. It was a woman named Glynis Ruelle, who had died in 1939. This had actually happened last night.

Or had it?

Maybe none of it had been real.

Neither he nor Kate had spoken about it since. Beth's emergency call, her arrival in the middle of the night, the kids crying, all of this had driven the memory of the woman in the mirror, and the thing at the door, into the background.

And in the morning, the call about the plane crash at Mauldar Field had taken his mind off everything but his work. Now he was back home, and it was all in front of him again.

Hesitating on the landing, his hand on the latch, listening to the kids playing and the talk of the adults inside, Nick felt that he was an *outsider* in Niceville, that he didn't belong, that whatever was going on in Crater Sink, in Niceville, whatever was going on with Rainey Teague and all the missing people, whatever had created that swirling black nightmare at their door, it had nothing to do with him, and it never had, and it was nothing he'd ever be able to understand, or ever hope to change.

It was in his mind to turn away, to go back down the steps, to walk away up the hill, walk away from Beth and Axel and Hannah and Reed and even from Kate, walk away from Rainey Teague and all the inexplicable forces he represented.

Just go quietly away under the branches of the live oaks, under the Spanish moss, vanish into the evening darkness, just keep walking until Niceville and all of its mysteries were miles behind him.

Go home to California, find a way to get back into the Army, or even try for the Marine Corps. Find an *ordinary* life, a *comprehensible* life.

Save himself.

As if.

He opened the door and Kate was there with a drink in her hand and a kiss for his cheek. Married men live longer than single men, and there's a reason for it. He kissed her back, and held it long enough to get a whistle from Reed.

They ate in the formal dining room, the walls covered in family photographs, all of them sitting around the long gleaming table, under the Gallé glass chandelier that their mother, Lenore, had brought back from Paris thirty years ago. Kate was at her usual place at the end of the table nearest the kitchen. Nick was at the other end, his back up against the fireplace screen, Reed at his left hand and Axel at his right, Beth and Hannah down the middle. Sterling-silver platters of roast potatoes and cobs of corn and sliced tomatoes and garden salad and barbecued steaks covered the center of the table.

There were decanters of lemonade for Axel and Hannah, and three bottles of Veuve Clicquot were chilling in an ice bucket on the oak sideboard.

A fourth, popped and fizzing, was in Reed's right hand, and he was filling a quartet of crystal flutes lined up in front of him. When the flutes were full they were handed along and everyone looked to Kate for the toast, even Axel and Hannah, both kids looking solemn and a bit shell-shocked.

"To Beth and Axel and Hannah. Welcome to a happy home."

"I second that," said Reed, leaning in to give her a kiss on the cheek and then putting a hand out to Beth. Everybody pinged their glasses, Axel and Hannah clanked their tumblers, and the food got handed around.

Axel, eight, a slender, solemn boy with large brown eyes and a full head of curly brown hair that hung down into his eyes, looked around the table with a puzzled expression. Nick saw the question forming in his eyes and he leaned over to listen to him. As he did so it cut him to the quick to see the boy flinch in a reflexive move. He had been doing that for a couple of years now, pulling back if any male adult came too close.

"I heard Uncle Reed say that Dad was arrested. Was it because he hit Mom?"

Looking at the boy, Nick settled on the simplest answer. Axel had all the time in the world to learn the whole story.

"No, it wasn't. He was arrested for driving too fast. And for fighting with some police officers. But your dad should never have hit your mom. Not ever. Men *never* hit women. Or little kids. Never."

Axel looked a little hunted.

"Axel, did your dad ever hit you?"

Axel looked at his plate and shook his head.

"Not really," he said, still looking down. "But he yelled a real lot. And he'd lean down and get real close. And he shook me sometimes. Hard. It hurt my neck and made my head ache. I didn't like it when he did that."

"I guess not. It was wrong for him to do that."

Axel leaned in closer, spoke in a conspiratorial whisper.

"He hit Hannah once. Mom doesn't want anyone to know. He hit her because she made a mess in her diaper and Mom let it get on the new rug in the movie room. Dad was pretty mad about that because it was his special room and nobody was supposed to go there but Mom wanted Hannah to see a movie and her player was broken so we went in Dad's special movie room and that's where it happened and Dad came home and saw it. Mom was holding Hannah and Dad was hitting Mom like he does when he gets all mad and Hannah was crying so he hit her too. That's why she can't hear out of that ear anymore."

Nick couldn't help glancing down the table to where Beth and Hannah and Reed were busy talking about getting the carriage house ready for Beth and the kids to live in it.

Hannah was a round, plump, angelic little girl who had just turned four, still quite babyish, with large blue eyes and hair so blond it was almost white. She had pale skin and a slightly loopy smile and a wonderful sense of humor.

She had a habit of tilting her head to one side if people were speaking to her, and she always focused on their lips while they were talking. She also had trouble getting some words out right.

He knew this was because she was deaf in her left ear. It hadn't occurred to him that she was deaf because her father had slapped her so viciously on that ear that he had damaged her hearing. The realization left him with nothing to say.

Like all kids who have to live with unpredictable parents, Axel had developed an acute ability to sense what was going on in the minds of adults in his world. Axel read Nick pretty well.

"It's okay, Uncle Nick. Don't you worry about her. Mom took her to a doctor. She's going to get a hearing aid. She'll be okay."

She will now, he thought.

And so will you.

Nick knew then that no matter what happened here in Niceville—and he had a feeling it was going to be very bad before it got better, if it ever did—he was going to do whatever it took to keep these people safe.

There was a full moon that night. It shone in through the master bedroom window, a streaming blue light that pooled on their bed. It was so intense that it woke Kate up.

Through the gauzy drapes she could see it hanging there, a huge blue-white sphere surrounded by a misty aura, now gliding majestically into a bank of clouds. The room grew dark.

Nick was asleep, at rest, the worry lines fading, making him look years younger. The house was silent. Beth was down the hall in the guest room. Axel and Hannah were sleeping downstairs, on a pull-out sofa in the rec room, where they had fallen asleep while watching a DVD of one of Kate's favorite movies, *The Kid*, with Bruce Willis.

She looked at her bedside clock. It was almost three thirty. She lay back on her pillow and tried to make some sense of the disorder that had come into their lives. She tried not to think of where her father might be. She would have to think of it sometime, but not right now. Tomorrow was a Monday, and Mondays were expressly created for dealing with things like that.

She closed her eyes and was drifting off to sleep when she *felt* rather than heard a sound, a soft, thudding impact, and then a jingle of metal on metal. It was coming from outside. It sounded like it was in the backyard just below her window. She looked over at Nick.

Still asleep.

She slipped out of bed, careful not to disturb him. He was a light sleeper, and tended to snap fully awake if he heard anything out of the ordinary, a habit he had picked up in the wars. She was surprised that the sound hadn't wakened him.

Kate went to the window and looked down into the yard. She heard the thump and jingle again. There may have been a shape, a shadow there, in the middle of the backyard. A big dark shape.

The yard lights shut off automatically at midnight, but she had a remote on the windowsill that would turn them back on. She was reaching for it when the moon came out from behind the clouds again. The yard filled with moonlight.

A huge horse stood there in the backyard, pale golden in color, although it was difficult to distinguish color in moonlight. It had a long white mane and four white hooves with feathery white hairs all around them. It was enormous, one of those farm horses—what did they call them?

A Percheron or a Clydesdale or a Belgian.

It was cropping the lawn, now and then stamping a hoof and shaking its massive head, making its harness jingle faintly. She stood and stared down at it for a long minute, thinking that it was a magnificent animal, wondering how it had gotten into their yard, where it had come from, and what she was going to do about it.

She looked back at Nick.

Out cold, on his back, his mouth slack. Kate knew how exhausted he was because she was in the same state. Kate, a girl of the South, wasn't afraid of horses, even gigantic horses. Deep down they were all the same, prey animals, and if you kept that in mind and moved quietly and slowly when you were around them, you could handle them. Nick could stay sleeping. He needed it more than she did.

She got into her dressing gown and ghosted down the back stairs and through the sunroom. She could see the animal through the glass, big as a house, the moonlight glistening on his hide like silver on gold. His head was down and he was still working on the lawn. Kate pushed the glass door back, slowly.

The horse jerked its head up, snuffled at her, thumped a hoof the size of an anvil into the ground with enough force to send a tremor through Kate's body, and then went back to ruining her lawn.

Kate walked slowly up to him, feeling the cool moisture of the grass under her bare feet, seeing her shadow on the lawn in the moonlight.

She reached the horse's head, bent down, and touched his forehead. He lifted his head, snorted, and huffed at her. His breath was as hot as an oven and he smelled of horse and hide and grass. He moved his head slightly to the left, staring down at her with one huge brown eye.

She saw herself reflected in it, oddly distorted, a silvery figure bathed in light. The animal snorted again, and stepped back and away. He turned—massively, ponderously, like a great wall of hide and muscle—and he walked away from her, his hooves thumping into the grass, his long tail twitching, his heavy flanks moving.

In spite of her fear, as if hypnotized, Kate followed him into the forest at the bottom of her garden, to a shadowed place lit with shafts of moonlight. He disappeared into the dark. She stood there, hearing him moving away over the stones, hearing his hooves clip-clop through the little river there. She stood still, holding her breath, feeling a kind of humming presence all around her, an electrical charge filling the night.

Everything changed.

Kate was standing on the banks of a broad mud-brown river. It surged and hissed behind her, slow and powerful and immense. The air smelled of river mud and wood smoke and growing things. She was at the end of a long avenue that ran under an arch of live oaks so large and ancient that their branches met in the air above the lane. At the far end of this green-shaded avenue was a great mansion with a gallery that ran all across the front. Grecian pillars supported the gallery.

It was a fine old house, a plantation house, and Kate recognized it from a large oil painting that hung in the dining room at the golf club.

It had once belonged to relatives of hers. Lenore, her mother, had an old closet door in their house, made with painted panels taken from this plantation house after the Civil War. The panels were faded and dried, but you could still see the pattern on them, jasmine flowers on a pale background, hand-painted, according to Lenore, by an artist brought in from Baton Rouge.

"This is Hy Brasail Plantation," Kate said to herself. "Why am I here?"

She realized she was asking a ghost horse a question. A horse that was nowhere to be seen. The lunacy of this struck her, but the strangeness remained. So did the plantation.

Hy Brasail Plantation
Southern Louisiana, 1840

It was the afternoon of the ninth of July in the year 1840. Today was London Teague's sixty-third birthday and his third wife was dying. Her name was Anora Mercer. Anora Mercer had been a famous beauty, one of the celebrated Mercers of Niceville and Savannah. There was a time when London Teague had persuaded himself that he adored her. But that was when Cathleen, his second wife, was still alive. While Cathleen lived, Anora was forbidden fruit. Cathleen died by her own hand the following year and was refused consecrated ground. Her grave now lay beneath the jupiter willow at the center of the box maze. It had been London Teague's experience that the fruit untasted was usually the sweetest. So it had been with Anora.

Now Anora was leaving too.

Her illness had come on her three days before, during the night. In the morning she would not wake, and when she finally opened her eyes and tried to speak, her voice was lazy, as if she were disguised in drink, and her eyelids drooped. She complained of languor and pain throughout her body. The fever grew upon her and her lips became cracked and dry. She felt the weakness spread from her body into her hands, and in a while could not raise a cup to her lips. Her breathing became harsh and rapid. Soon she fought for every breath.

The medical men had arrived and contemplated her through their pince-nez, stroking their sideburns. The ague, they intoned with heavy sighs. And perhaps a touch of the miasmic fever. They told the women to exhibit tincture of laudanum at need, to have her bled, and to put her in the salt baths. They then presented an outrageous fee, took themselves down to the river landing, and flagged a packet back to Vacherie.

Anora's state grew dire.

The sickness spread. Her face began to swell and bruises bloomed along her thighs and across her belly. Her throat closed in upon her so that no food could be taken, only lemon water and chamomile and sheep marrow mixed with brandy. Nothing seemed to stay the advance of this sickness and now, two days later, it had stolen away all of her beauty.

Yet she fought on, and the women tended to her. At three o'clock this day a parson from South Vacherie had drawn up in a hired dog cart, a Mr. Horace Aukinlek, S.J., a jaundiced cadaver with a gotch eye and a stammer. He now loitered in the music room, his moldy black frock hanging on a chair and his hobnails defiling the second-best ottoman as he thumbed through Psalms with a cold collation and a flagon of cider at his elbow.

By late afternoon it was clear to all that Anora could not hope to recover. Already the mask of death, the skull face, was rising up from beneath her skin, stretching it as tight as a painter's canvas, and her color was a waxen yellow.

Riders had been dispatched to Niceville to inform Anora's people there, her godfather, John Gwinnett Mercer, and his family, but this was a distance of six hundred miles and had been done more as a sign of respect than with any hope of a return before her struggle had ended.

John Gwinnett Mercer was a volatile man and he had not looked with favor on Anora's betrothal to a man forty years her senior, a man already twice widowed and rumored to be a rake.

London Teague would not risk a serious rift with Mercer, a wealthy man with great influence in New Orleans and Memphis, so the riders had been sent, at punishing expense.

And still Anora lingered.

Go, Teague thought, but did not say, when he came in to stare down at her, the women bustling about the sickbed. But it was in his mind.

This unwillingness to die in a timely manner was simply selfish malingering. It was womanish and weak. Anora was like an actor whose part in the play had ended, yet she would not leave the stage.

Her selfishness had put the pressing business of Hy Brasail in irons. A sad cold supper had been laid out in the summer kitchen, stale corn bread and hard-boiled eggs, a slab of mutton and a balthazar of Sillery in a silver ice boat. Their girls, Cora and Eleanor, were whining and moping in the deer park and the two boys, Cathleen's sons, Jubal and Tyree, unwilling to watch Anora die, for they loved her dearly, had taken themselves off to Plaquemine to offer a novena.

The house slaves were all caught up with caring for Anora and, because she was beloved by the people, the work of the plantation had effectively come to a halt. And his money was slipping away.

In heaven's name, woman.

Just go.

At sunset the women put Anora's wasted body into a ladder-back chair and carried her up the servant stairs to the Jasmine Room, softly singing "Annie Laurie," Anora's favorite song. The Jasmine Room had a view of Hy Brasail's great avenue of live oaks, considered one of the jewels of southern Louisiana. Riverboats passing by along the Mississippi often lingered in the bend, backing water so the passengers lining the rails could admire it.

The avenue was made of twenty-eight massive spreading oaks, fourteen to a side, planted long ago by a Creole merchant who had gone back to Spain to fight Napoleon and gotten himself bisected by chain shot on the ramparts of Valladolid.

The oaks of Hy Brasail marched in a stately progression down to the riverbank, their branches interlaced above the deer park to make a kind of leafy green cathedral. At the far end of the avenue the river glimmered in the dying light.

This was Anora's favorite view, and she had often expressed the wish that she might, on a far distant day, die with this view before her.

As they carried her up the stairs Anora had called weakly for Teague to sit by her, but he could not abide sickness of any kind.

It repelled him.

He gave word and Second Samuel brought Tecumseh around to the front of the house. Teague mounted up on his big hammer-headed roan and cantered down the shaded avenue without looking back at the French doors of the Jasmine Room, where he knew she would be watching. At the gates he wheeled left and went for a long gallop upriver, all the way past Telesphore Roman's place, fifteen furlongs or more, all the time thinking she'd surely be gone by twilight.

But when he came cantering back up between the live oaks early that evening, Second Samuel was there, a standing rebuke on the porch steps, and in his thick West Indies accent, with a touch of his old defiance, he told London Teague that the lady of the house was still struggling brave against it, yes she was.

As Second Samuel took the reins from Teague and stroked Tecumseh's heaving barrel, Teague could plainly see in the old man's yellow-rimmed eyes and the set of his leathery jawline that there were loose talk and murmuring in the slave quarters.

Teague watched Second Samuel lead Tecumseh away to the stables, thinking that his head boy, though not yet fifty, was now a bent old wreck. Second Samuel had been with London Teague ever since Teague's people got run out of Hispaniola.

Teague, who consulted the cat whenever dumb insolence or persistent sloth made it necessary, had never taken it out of its bag to flay Second Samuel's back. But the sheer impudence of the man—

Teague felt a ribbon of hot bile in his throat and his vision went dim. He put his right hand on the grip of the pistol in his belt.

After a while he took it away.

No man who mistreated his livestock could have good standing down in New Orleans, good standing with the men who counted, and London Teague was in great need of good standing with the men who counted.

Second Samuel was a hundred feet away, leaning in to talk softly to Tecumseh, who had known him since he was a colt, when Teague called out to him.

"Samuel, has Talitha been found?"

Second Samuel turned to look back, tugging on Tecumseh's halter. The horse could smell the mares and did not want to stop. He whinnied and capered, but Second Samuel held him tightly, thinking about the question and what it might mean for Talitha, who was his oldest daughter, and a sore trial to him.

Talitha had gone missing from the big house on the night that the lady had been taken poorly and she had not been seen since. She had been absent before—she was a willful girl and liked to go on walkabouts. One time she had wandered overland and through the marshes as far as the outskirts of South Vacherie—but she had never been gone this long. It was now the afternoon of the third day and this was a breach that could no longer be overlooked. Teague saw the hesitation in the man's face but let it pass.

"Not rightly yet, Mister London."

"Who's looking?"

"Mister Coglin's men, I believe."

"With the dogs?"

"Not yet, Mister London. Those dogs is unruly in the chase and tend to do damage. Don't want no damage done to the stock, you always says."

Teague nodded, dismissed him with a wave, and went slowly up the steps and across the creaking boards to the open doors. The front hall was empty, but the house stank of sickness and death. In keeping with the ancient custom, the great gilded mirror in the front hall had been draped with black cloth, as had all the other mirrors in the house.

The Irish believed that the spirit of the newly dead would enter an uncovered mirror, and live there, in between the two worlds, trapped forever.

So the mirrors were all draped.

Teague drew in a breath and held it.

Death.

The house reeked of death and dying. It flowed like a miasma down the main staircase and pooled around his boots. He glanced into the music room and saw that it was still infested by Mr. Aukinlek. He exhaled, smacked the dust off his jodhpurs, scraped his boots on the brush bars by the doors, and went looking for his tobacco pouch.

A few minutes after midnight Teague was sitting in a cane rocker on the gallery outside the Jasmine Room, still in his riding clothes, his blue jacket hanging off the chair rail behind him. He was smoking a bent briar full of latakia, his boots propped up against the railing.

Through the open glass doors behind him he could hear the soft voices of the women tending to Anora, and the singsong monotony of Aukinlek's voice as he administered the Last Rites, and under that Anora's fretful murmuring as they wiped her body down with vinegar sponges and dabbed at her swollen lips with ice.

He pulled in a wheezing breath, shook his big shaggy head. Even the smoke from his pipe couldn't quite cover the smell of a sickroom.

He pushed himself up out of the cane rocker and walked a short way down the gallery, his spurs clanking, the old boards groaning under his weight, passing by very close to Kate, who was standing in the shadows by the French doors. Kate smelled the tobacco on him as he passed, and the rank sweat in his clothes.

Teague was a big, thick man, well over six feet and two hundred pounds, and most of it was still muscle. But he was feeling his years tonight. Their weight lay heavy on him, the necessary things that had been done, and the troubles that had come of them.

And there was something about the gallery tonight that troubled him. He felt a *presence* in it, felt that he was being watched, appraised, and not by a loving eye. He was being *judged*.

His conscience, perhaps? Not likely. It never had before, and he had given it a great deal of cause. He shrugged this feeling off, dismissed it.

At the corner of the gallery he put his shoulder against the pillar and looked out into the night, feeling the life of Hy Brasail Plantation in the dark all around, the steamy heat lying over it like a woolen blanket.

It was too hot for sleep, so most of the people were gathered under the cottonwood trees by the horse paddock, the red glow of their cheroots flaring up in the dark. There were girls down by the Mississippi singing "Shall We Gather at the River" as they washed themselves. Somewhere belowstairs a brat was grizzling. The whining turned into sobbing and then rose up into a grating howl that was abruptly cut off by a meaty smack.

Under the live oak branches fireflies flickered through the hanging shreds of moss. A faint breeze was rolling in off the river, bringing the fertile aroma of saw grass and river mud. The shack windows glimmered with lantern light. Wood smoke drifted in the dark and he could hear the faint tinkling of a mandolin coming from the overseer's house on the far side of the peach orchard. Out by the stables came a deep, trumpeting whinny, followed by a booming crack as Tecumseh kicked out at the timbers of his box stall.

He heard the gallery boards creaking behind him and turned to see a black shape standing in the shadows, a sliver of yellow light lying on her cheek, her eyes hidden in the dark.

Talitha.

He stepped away from the gallery railing, moving into the shadows with her.

"What the hell are you doing up here?"

Talitha spoke, a throaty whisper.

"She still lives?"

"She does," said Teague, in a hoarse, angry whisper, keeping his distance from the girl. "How can this be?"

Talitha moved closer to Teague, stepping into the shaft of light from the window. Teague looked into her almond-shaped eyes, her half-open lips, the way the simple cotton shift lay on her rounded body, her high breasts, her taut nipples under the thin fabric. He could smell her and his blood began to rise up. Talitha was like a sickness to him. Even in a slave cot she was the devil to pay.

"I don't know. No one ever lasted this long."

"Where have you been?"

A silence, and then a flash of white as she smiled up at him.

"Why? Did Mister London miss me?"

More bloody insolence.

"Answer the question."

"I been over by Thibodaux," she said, with a sly tone. "In our secret place. I been waiting. I thought you'd come looking."

"While Anora's dying and the house is in a shambles?"

"You come before, Mister London. You come lots of times."

"You have drawn attention, girl. And now you come sneaking up the staircase at night. What if you had been seen?"

"I know how to not get seen, Mister London. All good slave childs know how to do that."

"It was stupid to come here. It was stupid to run off that same night. It looks poorly to the people. Already there is talk. You drew attention. Do you still have the animal?"

She lifted her hands into the light. She was holding a wicker sewing basket, the lid held down with scarlet ribbons.

"Yes. But now your lady is surrounded by the house women. There is no way to bring it close to her again. In this heat, in the dark, it's danger-ous to handle. It will strike at anything on a night like this."

Teague was silent for a time, listening to the voices from the sick-room, someone singing "Annie Laurie" in a childish voice. They sang it to her when she was asleep. He came back to Talitha.

"She is dying. There is no need to take the risk. You should not be up here. Go down through the summer kitchen. Wait in the box maze by the jupiter willow. I'll come down to you."

"Soon? I'll make you forget the lady again."

"Don't chide me," said Teague, his temper rising up. Talitha held out the wicker basket, shook it teasingly. Teague stepped back. The animal inside the basket made a sound like a kettle and the wicker sides bulged as it coiled.

Talitha showed her teeth.

"You *better* come soon," she said with fire, "or maybe I'll take me another. Mister Telesphore, he been looking at me that way."

Teague raised a hand, but she slipped away from the blow, making no sound at all. Teague watched the darker shadows where she had disappeared for a long minute, thinking about her. Kate stood nearby, listening to him wheeze, smelling his scent, tobacco and leather and sweat, thinking about him.

Teague felt a chilly hand on the back of his neck and shook his head like a heavy horse. Then he turned and walked back up to the open French doors, passing close by Kate and, it seemed to her, avoiding the space in which she stood.

He stopped at the threshold, took a deep breath, and stepped into the sickroom.

It was lit by candles set on chairs all around Anora's bed, and one of the houseboys—Cutnose, or one of his brothers—was sitting in a corner, tugging on a cord connected to a fan of embroidered cloth suspended from the beams. The fan moved ponderously back and forth, making the candle flames flicker and sending crazy shadows dancing around the walls.

In the bed Anora was a small doll-like figure, shrunken and emaciated. Her eyes were closed and her rich black hair—all that was left of her beauty—lay fanned out in a shining arc on the satin pillow. Her yellow hands were folded on top of the coverlet and a rosary made of peridot lay tangled through her fingers.

The house women—Flora, Jezrael, and Constant—looked up from their rosaries as Teague came into the room. Mr. Aukinlek had his back to the windows and did not hear Teague step in. He was reading a Psalm—"Oh Lord let them be ashamed and confounded that seek after my soul—"

"Enough," said Teague, cutting through the prayers. "Leave us. All of you."

The women rose without a word, Cutnose too, and all seemed to shimmer out of the room. Aukinlek turned to say something portentous, but a look at Teague's face reduced him to a stammer and he too was gone. Teague came over and looked down at Anora—who had not opened her eyes or stirred in any way—and then he glanced around the room.

The Jasmine Room was named so because Anora had commissioned an artist from Baton Rouge to come and hand-paint a bower of jasmine onto the ceiling and halfway down the walls. It was a light and airy room, with tall sash windows that opened onto the gallery. The carpet and most of the furniture had been cleared away to make room for the daybed and the salt bath and a long trestle table littered with washbasins and fresh cloths.

All that was left of the original furnishings was an ancient mirror in a gilt baroque frame—not a large mirror, no more than thirty inches on a side, but it was precious to Anora because it had come down to her through the Mercer line and had once been in her grandmother's bedroom in their town house in Dublin.

It was said to have come originally from Paris, where the Mercers had once been the Du Mêrcièrs. This was before the Terror, and few of that branch had escaped the guillotine. The mirror was all that was left of those times, and so it was a treasure to Anora, a fragment of all that had been lost by the Mercers and the Gwinnetts over the centuries.

In keeping with the custom, the mirror was draped tonight, a stark black rectangle floating in the middle of a field of painted jasmine.

Teague pulled up a rickety wooden chair and sat down on it. The frame creaked under his weight as he leaned back and crossed his legs. Anora's breathing quickened and in a moment she opened her eyes, glancing around the room with a frightened expression until she settled on his face.

The frightened look changed into a calm, direct regard, although the light in her hazel eyes was dimmed and her face was nearly unrecognizable.

She moved her lips but no sound came out, only a series of dry clicks. Teague poured water into a silver cup and held it to her lips, using his left hand to lift her up so that she could sip at the rim. Her body was as hot as a cookstove and her linen tunic was soaked.

She managed to swallow the water and Teague laid her back down. She closed her eyes for a time and then looked at him again.

"I've been asking for you, Lon . . . Where have you been?"

"I had to go up to see Telesphore. Business."

"I saw . . . I saw you ride away. You never looked back . . . but then you never do."

A pause.

"Why were you asking for me, Anora?"

Another long wait while Anora seemed to go deep inside herself and then struggle back to the surface.

"The . . . girls, Lon. Will you see to them? Especially Cora. She won't . . . understand."

Teague sighed and held his temper.

"If you mean will I see to their interests, your godfather has taken great care to do that himself. Their money is as safe as yours has been. Little good it has done for us, for our affairs, but that was John Gwinnett Mercer's wish."

Anora closed her eyes and was silent for a time. Teague watched her chest rising and falling under the sheet. It looked like a bird was caught in the fabric, a febrile flutter only.

"You . . . will have the tontine, Lon, when I am gone. That will see your . . . affairs set aright. What I wish . . . what I . . . *require* . . . of you . . . is that you *care* for them, Lon, as you care for Jubal and Tyree. Cora is only six, and Eleanor not yet eight. They will need you. You have a great capacity to love, Lon . . . as you once loved me . . . let them see your love for them. You are their father. They are your blood as well as mine."

Teague had already decided to send Cora and Eleanor to Niceville, to live with the Mercers or the Gwinnetts. He had no use and no patience for wet-nursing a pair of useless infants, especially since their resources were so well sequestered. As that was also John Gwinnett Mercer's work, let him bear the burden of raising them up.

As for Jubal and Tyree, at thirteen and fifteen they were finally at a useful age and after they had gone to Trinity in Dublin and then away for their Grand Tour of Europe, they could come back as ripened men and see to the affairs of Hy Brasail. But there was no need to speak of this to Anora.

"I will do right by the girls, Anora."

"*Our* girls, Lon. Yours and mine. I have your word?"

"My word, Anora. They will not want for care or good company. That I pledge."

This appeared to satisfy her.

She was quiet for a time, and the sound of nightjars and cicadas seemed to fill the room. Her skeletal fingers twitched at the peridot rosary in a fretful way, but her face was still. The chair creaked as he got to his feet. She opened her eyes as he stood by the bed, looking down at her.

"Will you kiss me, Lon?"

He hesitated, and then leaned down to kiss her on the cheek. Her skin was hot and damp. She lifted a bony hand and clutched at his cravat, pulling him close. She lifted her head, kissed him on the lips, and fell back, her eyes fixed on his.

She did not release him.

Her lips moved. She was saying something. He leaned closer. She swallowed and tried again.

"You have killed me, Lon."

He pulled back but she held him.

"No. Do not lie to my face. This is my last hour and there is no time for any more lies. When it bit me, I saw it, slipping away across the comforter. It was a harlequin coral. I know who put it there. I know why she put it there. So do you."

She released him and reached for the rosary again, her eyes closing.

Teague's face was hot but his chest was icy cold. He looked at the pillow under her head. She was on the threshold. It would only take a moment of pressure to help her cross it. Kate saw his huge hands twitch, his long fingers spreading, and knew his mind. Teague forced himself to be calm.

"If this is true, about the snake, and I do not give it any countenance, why have you not spoken?"

"I was . . . weary . . . weary of . . . you. Weary of your ways. I loved you once. Now I am ready to go."

"Who . . . who have you told?"

"No one. I won't have the children know."

"Anora . . . this is simply not—"

Her hand came off the sheet, fingers spread.

"No, Lon. I won't have your lies be the last words I hear. Send for Constant. I must sleep."

"Anora . . ."

"No, Lon. Go. For heaven's sake . . . just go."

Teague stood and stared down at her for a time, but it was as if he was the dead thing in the room. She was still alive, barely, but she was as gone from him now as if she were already in her family's crypt in the Niceville churchyard. His head was reeling with the urgency of only one thought . . .

Who else knows?

And the answer came back.

Talitha knows.

Anora slept, a sleep so peaceful after such pain and struggle that at first Constant and Flora and Jezrael thought she might have passed. Constant laid a fearful hand on her breast, lightly, and they all smiled when she felt the flutter of Anora's heart. It was shortly before three in the morning and the life of Hy Brasail was at its lowest ebb. A wind was sighing in the branches of the live oaks and a lantern set on the river landing burned in the dark, a single yellow glimmer in a moonless night. Constant rose, leaned over to kiss Anora's forehead, and then they all slipped silently from the room.

A candle by Anora's bed burned low.

Kate stood by her bed, looking down at the dying woman. She heard a dry rustle, the sound of wings. A swarm, a cloud of dragonflies came to the windows and ticked against the glass, a vibrating green shimmer in the candle's light.

The mosquito netting that tented Anora's bed rippled gently in the night wind. Anora fell into a deeper sleep, and now her life began to flicker and fail. Kate could feel her going.

She drew away into the shadows.

Anora awoke abruptly from a sensation of falling and saw within the candle's glow a figure sitting on the rickety wooden chair beside her bed.

It was a young girl. Talitha.

She was sitting up straight, her knees tight together and her ankles primly crossed. Her strong brown hands were folded on top of a wicker sewing basket. She was looking into the middle distance with a somber expression and a faraway air, but when Anora stirred, Talitha looked down and smiled at her.

"What are you doing here?" Anora asked, a tremor in her voice.

"I am here to make amends, Missus, if I can."

Anora looked for the cord that rang the night bell, but it had slipped to the floor. Talitha bent over and lifted it up and laid it down on Anora's breast. She held her hand there, gently, and then patted Anora's fingers.

"You don't need to be afraid now, Missus. I can't hurt you no more."

"No. You've already killed me, have you not?"

"I have, Missus. And now I have come to . . ."

"Atone?"

Talitha looked puzzled.

"Missus Teague, I do not know what that word means."

"It means to make up for the wrong you have done. Is that the creature, in that basket?"

Talitha looked down at the wicker basket on her lap. She lifted the
cover and reached inside. Anora's throat tightened and it was in her mind
to pull on the cord, but something held her.

Talitha lifted her hand out. Coiled around it was a snake, not small,
perhaps thirty inches or so. It had a small tapered head with a yellow
band around it, and its body was banded in bright red and dark green, the
bands separated by a smaller ring of vivid yellow. It twisted and writhed
in Talitha's grip, its tongue flicking like the antennae of a moth.

Talitha lifted it up and turned it in the candle glow. Two tiny shards of
yellow light glittered in its jewellike eyes.

"The harlequin coral," said Talitha, seeming to be transfixed by the
snake as it lifted its head and stared back at her.

"Be careful," said Anora, in a whisper.

But Talitha only smiled and draped the snake around her shoulders,
where it coiled and tightened and settled, a brightly colored enameled
necklace.

"It can't hurt either of us now," said Talitha.

"Then why have you brought it here?"

"I will be buried with it, I believe."

They were each silent for a time. Anora was looking at Talitha, trying
to see her clearly, but her image kept fading and then coming back again.
Talitha seemed to feel her flickering attention.

"Missus, will you do what I ask you to do?"

"What do you want?"

Talitha turned and lifted a hand, pointing at the ancient gilt mirror
hanging on the wall. The black cover was gone and the glass reflected the
room, the pale white woman in her bed and the young black woman in
the chair. The candle flickering low.

"Will you get up and look in the mirror?"

"I can't."

"I believe you can, Missus. You must try."

Anora tried but was unable to rise. Talitha bent over her and lifted her
in her strong young arms, carried her across the floor, and set her down
carefully on her bare feet, the two of them framed in the mirror, two
silhouettes with a corona of candle glow around them. Anora was trem-
bling. Talitha stepped in and held her in both her arms, kissed her gently
on the cheek.

"Don't be afraid, Missus. There's family on the other side of the glass. Daddy says this mirror was opened by your own people, when they was living in Paris, France, a long time back. He says a lot of your family got put to death in what they called the Terror. Many of them was put under a machine. When the thing was done, the executioner took their heads from the basket and held them up to this mirror, the very one that been took from their own home where they all once lived, so they could see themselves in it one last time. They meant it to be cruel, because life was still in them, and they could see what been done to them, but it was the last thing they looked at, and they sent their spirits into it, and that is how this mirror got opened. That is the story my daddy told me."

Anora stared into the mirror, seeing only herself and Talitha, embracing each other, and the sickroom a dim image behind them. And something else. In the farthest corner of the room she thought she could see a shape, standing in the shadows, a pretty young woman in a pale night shift.

The woman looked familiar to her. Perhaps she was the ghost of a woman she had known, or would someday know. Or perhaps she was simply having visions. Her head filled with green light. If Talitha had not been holding her she would have fallen. Talitha's body was as cold as hers was warm.

Talitha kissed her on the temple.

"Good-bye, Missus. I am sorry for what I done."

Anora tried to touch her, but there was a window of rippled glass between her and Talitha. She held up her hand against the mirror and Talitha lifted hers on the other side until their palms touched. Talitha spread her fingers out, covering Anora's hand with her own. Anora could feel the chill in Talitha's hand even through the mirror.

"Are you coming with me?" Anora asked.

Talitha shook her head.

"No, Missus. I wish I might. I can't."

"Yes you can. I forgive you. It's not too late for you. You can go to the pastor at Plaquemine and confess. To a judge. You can . . . atone."

"Missus, I believe I done that already. For what I done to you, Mister London has killed me."

"Killed you?"

"Yessum. Mister London has killed me with a rope down in the box maze and now I am hung in the jupiter willow with a note I never wrote pinned to my dress. Mister London, he don't collect I never got my letters, but Second Samuel knows."

She paused for a moment, as if listening.

"They calling for me now, Missus. My run is done. I am bound for unconsecrated ground, because I am a whore and a murderess. I only come to take you to the mirror. Remember me to Second Samuel, if you can. He was a fine daddy to me, and I am sorry I was such a bad daughter. If you see him one day, on your side, I beg you tell him so, for me."

Talitha took her hand away and stepped back from the mirror. She felt something lying at her feet. Anora's body lay on the ground, a small dead thing. In the mirror there was only one reflection. Her own. Talitha lifted Anora's body and carried it back to the daybed, laying it down softly. She lifted up the sheet and placed it over her, leaving her face uncovered. She arranged the body into a peaceful pose, twined the peridot rosary around Anora's fingers.

Then she picked up the candle, looked around the room one last time, saw Kate standing there, watching her. She touched her finger to her lips, and then blew the candle out.

Down in the jupiter willow Talitha's corpse turned slowly in the river wind, a crushed snake twisted around her neck, a note pinned to her dress.

> I kilt the missus
> With this snake
> and now I am dead
> Jesus heal me

In the mirror hanging on the wall of the Jasmine Room, Anora Mercer stood looking at her own body lying on the daybed. Then she looked up at the young woman in the white slip and smiled at her.

Anora turned away and walked down a winding lane between oaks and willows until she came to a sunlit clearing full of emerald green dragonflies. They fluttered and hummed around her, a vibrating cloud of shimmering green. She could feel the thrumming power of their wings.

Through the cloud of dragonflies, as if through a mist of green light, she saw a tall house on a sun-dappled street lined with live oaks draped in

Spanish moss. The house was pale cream stone and it had high sash windows and the interior was filled with a golden afternoon light that put a warm glow on the rooms and the furniture.

A blond-haired boy in a navy coat and gray trousers was standing at the foot of the curved staircase that led up to the entrance. He had a rucksack in his hands, and he was standing with his head down, his long blond hair covering his face, as if he had not yet seen the woman waiting on the landing. Another boy, smaller, with curly brown hair, was standing beside him, their heads together, as if conspiring at something. The woman on the landing had shining black hair held back by a silver pin. She was smiling down at the boys. The woman looked like her, so much alike they could almost be sisters. The woman on the landing glanced up, saw Anora there, and raised her hand.

Anora recognized her. She was the young woman in the white slip, standing in the shadows of the Jasmine Room. Anora tried to wave back, but the vision turned into a dazzle of green light and the dragonflies took her away.

In his empty bed London Teague lay awake and stared at the ceiling, thinking of the girl in the jupiter willow, sick with dread of the morning. The lantern on the river landing glimmered in the dark. Beyond it the Mississippi rolled down to the Gulf of Mexico, down to the Civil War, down to the future, leaving Hy Brasail Plantation and all her people far behind in the moonless southern night.

Sunlight streaming in through the gauze curtain of her bedroom woke Kate up. She glanced at the bedside clock. It was almost seven. Nick was already out of bed. She could hear him in the shower. The smell of bacon and eggs came up the stairwell, and children's voices came with it, Axel and Hannah. It sounded as if they were talking to Eufaula, the ethereal young girl who came each weekday to cook and care for the house.

Kate pulled the covers back and slipped out of bed. She went to the window and looked down into the yard, seeing the sunlight on the flowers and the green shadows at the bottom of the yard, where the pines and oaks crowded up against the hill. She could see the water bubbling and frothing along in the creek that ran through the little forest there.

She realized that she was looking for hoofprints on the lawn, and it came to her that she had dreamed a strange dream the night before, about Hy Brasail Plantation and the people who had lived and died there. She could feel the details slipping away and she fought to keep them in her mind. She felt it was very important to remember.

When Nick came out of the shower Kate was sitting at her desk, still in her nightgown, writing in a notebook, head down, fixed and concentrated. She didn't look up when he kissed her on the back of her neck. She sighed with pleasure, but she kept on writing. He didn't ask her what she was writing, and she didn't tell him. She didn't want to tell him that she was writing about a dream and the dream was about the Teague family, and it wasn't a good dream at all.

Nick left her there and went in to dress.

It was Monday morning, and Niceville was waiting for them all.

Six Months Later

Three Men in a Federal Prison Come Up with a Simple Plan

Leavenworth Prison, a gray stone temple under a match-head sun far off on the Great Plains of the American Heartland: the General Population Common Room was steamy and hot and packed with heavyweight cons. The low-ceilinged windowless space stank of sweat and testosterone and the ammonia reek of potato-peel screech.

Although these guys were all seasoned cons, every man in the room was staying away from the three men on the battered green vinyl couch in the middle of the common room.

The men, two of them thick as old buffalos, slab-sided and weathered, and one a thin, graying, wispy man who looked impossibly ancient, were paying close attention to a CNN newsreel playing on the big flat-screen bolted to the wall.

The screen was covered with chicken wire but the men—Mario La Motta, Desi Munoz, and Julie Spahn—could clearly see the heavy-muscled bald-headed guy with the biker goatee being perp-walked from an EMT vehicle by a couple of paramedics. Two Deputy U.S. Marshals were flanking the medics, and a guy who was obviously a plainclothes cop was walking along behind them.

They're walking this guy up the marble steps of the county courthouse in this small southern U.S. town that the CNN banner was calling Niceville.

The perp was wearing a bright red jumpsuit and flip-flop sandals. His ankles were chained and he's got his cuffed hands linked to a steel ring on a wide leather belt at his waist. The belt, for obvious reasons, buckles in the back.

The Deputy U.S. Marshals—a heavy-bodied black woman with flat gray eyes and this gigantic white guy with a red face and long blond hair down to his shoulders—are looking tight and worried. So does the cop, a sharp-planed guy with salt-and-pepper hair, wearing a navy blue suit, a white shirt open at the collar. He has a large stainless-steel revolver in a belt holster, from what they could see probably a Colt Python. He had a gold oval badge clipped to his belt. He looked straight ahead at the backs of the two marshals. The expression on his face was flat and he had shark eyes for the media crowd.

The Deputy U.S. Marshals were bulling through the press crowd like a couple of NFL linemen, the detective in the blue suit following in their wake.

The press were pressing in all around—why they're called the Press—shoving mikes into faces, shouting inane questions, clutching at sleeves and shoulders. One big guy in a Banana Republic safari jacket stuck a fat furry mike with a LIVE EYE 7 logo on it into the face of the detective in the blue suit, striking him a glancing blow on the cheekbone. There was a quick flurry of movement—the camera jerked and the scene goes chaotic—it steadied and the man in the safari jacket was lying on his back at the bottom of the stairs, arms and legs waving like an overturned beetle.

The CNN camera zoomed in on him, and then panned back up to the blue-suited cop, who has already turned away. The rest of the media crowd pulled back a few feet.

The U.S. Marshals, who saw nothing of this, and if they had would have enjoyed it immensely, got the perp to the top of the stairs, where the prisoner somehow managed to break away and look back down at the crowd on the steps, his face red and his mouth bent into a nasty snarl, and now he's yelling something which La Motta and Munoz and Spahn can't hear because of all the noise in the common room.

"That's him," said La Motta, pointing a fat pink finger at the screen. "That's The Fuckhead," giving it the capital letters.

La Motta's voice sounds like it's coming from the bottom of a drainage ditch. He's got thick black hair which he combs straight back and waxes down with Bed Head. Since he's carrying three hundred pounds of muscle and fat on a frame built for maybe one-eighty, this makes him look like a walrus but nobody has ever told him this.

"Yah think?" asked Munoz, being sarcastic, because there's no fucking way any of them is ever gonna forget The Fuckhead. Desi Munoz is as bald as a trailer hitch and has bushy black eyebrows that he combs straight up like he's hoping one day they'll be long enough to start looking like hair.

"Byron Deitz. In the freaking flesh."

"What's going on this time?" asked Julie Spahn.

They'd been following the Byron Deitz saga ever since the spring, when the media story about the First Third robbery and his connection to it had first broken.

"They're taking him to another one a those fucking jurisdiction hearings. The Feds want him remanded to D.C. to face that espionage beef. Local guys want him to stay. They're saying he's got a heart condition— that's why the EMT guys are there—Feds think it's bullshit and they want his ass in D.C. Deitz is saying he knows who really did the bank, but he's not gonna tell until the Feds drop the spy thing. It's what you call a stalemate."

"They ever get the money back?"

"Not so far," said Munoz. "Still out there somewhere. Fucking millions, floating around. Not a sign of it in six fucking months."

"Who's the cop in the blue suit?" asked La Motta. "Looks like a nasty piece of work."

"Onna crawl there," said Munoz. "At the bottom."

La Motta peered at the words streaming along the banner at the bottom of the screen.

FOX NEWS REPORTER ASSAULTED BY LOCAL CID DETECTIVE AT REMAND HEARING FOR COP KILLER SPY

"What the fuck is 'local cee eye dee'?"

"Criminal Investigation Division. Bigger than the local cops but smaller than the state investigation guys. Cover maybe a buncha counties and shit."

La Motta didn't get it.

"What's a local CID guy doing on the perp walk?"

"Cop's name is Nick Kavanaugh. Kavanaugh is Deitz's brother-in-law," said Munoz. "Deitz married a chick named Beth Walker, she's older sister to Kavanaugh's wife. I guess they figure Kavanaugh can get Deitz to talk—you know, family and all that shit. Ain't working so far."

"How do you know this shit?"

"I asked the block boss. Swanson. He owes us."

"No shit. Where'd he get it?"

"He gargled it onna web."

La Motta thought this over.

"Maybe this cop's a way in to Deitz?"

"Maybe," said Munoz, looking doubtful. "Looks like a tough nut. You could crack a tooth on guys like that. Swanson says the guy used to be a war hero, got a shitload of medals. Was inna Special Forces, over there in Raghead-istan. I dunno. Maybe the wife or the sister would be easier."

La Motta nodded, went quiet.

Spahn pointed at the screen.

"This jerkwater town—what is it again?"

"Niceville," said Munoz, smiling. "It's down inna southeast, few miles outta Cap City."

"We got any people in this shithole?" asked La Motta.

"In Niceville?"

"Yeah."

"Not yet. But we gotta do something about Deitz, that's for sure. Soon as we get out."

"Nobody's forgetting that," said Spahn, smoothing him down.

"We're just sitting here, our thumbs up our asses. Be good if we had a guy down there now, do some advance work for us. Get the lay of the land."

Spahn grinned.

"The lay of the land? Wasn't that your wife?"

"Fucking funny, Julie."

La Motta went inside for a bit, remembering what Deitz had done to them, came back, shaking his head. They all remembered it just fine. They had been remembering it every day for eighteen hundred and forty-seven days. They'd be out soon. Fucking Byron Deitz wasn't going to have that long to wish he had never fucked with them. Maybe eighteen hours. Maybe less.

"So they still didn't find the money yet?" Spahn wanted to know. "The shit Deitz stole?"

La Motta and Munoz shook their heads.

"Not yet," said La Motta. "Swanson says it's still out there. Six fucking months. That means it's hidden pretty good. I figure Deitz is gonna sit on it until he gets out. Then he cashes in."

"Three million bucks, rotting inna storage locker somewhere," said Munoz, shaking his head. "Money rots, you know, less you keep it in a dry place. Remember what it was like, trying to keep all that money in fucking New Orleans?"

"Or it's inna basement somewhere, fucking rats making nests outta it," said La Motta.

A pause, while they all thought about the money.

Julie Spahn had the last word on it.

"That fucking money is *ours*."

A House by the Side of the Road

A sunlit fall afternoon in the Garrison Hills section of Niceville. Kate was waiting for Rainey Teague and Axel Deitz to come home from Regiopolis Prep. She did this whenever she could, waited on the stairway like this, so Rainey and Axel would see her standing there when they turned the corner. Both boys needed to see someone waiting for them.

Axel's mother was working from Mondays to Fridays down in Cap City, as a civilian employee of the FBI, a job engineered for her by Boonie Hackendorff, the Special Agent in Charge and a family friend. Beth's daughter, Hannah, just turned five, spent the week in Cap City with her mother, at a day care facility maintained for FBI staff. Beth and Hannah made it home on weekends.

Their father was still in Twin Counties Correctional, awaiting the outcome of a long and complicated federal appeal demanding that he be remanded to Washington, D.C., to face a charge that he had conspired to sell national defense information to a foreign nation, specifically China. Apparently the Chinese government had taken the view that the death of their people was an act of aggression on the part of the U.S. intelligence agencies.

The matter was being fought out in various jurisdictions, from the State Department and Justice all the way down to the screamers on talk radio. Kate had followed the ins and outs of the case. She felt it could go either way. Byron might get sent to Cap City for a trial, or he could end up on a plane to Beijing, wrapped in heavy chains.

As for Rainey, his father, Miles, was lying stiff, cold, and dead in the white Greek Revival temple that was the Teague family crypt in the New Hill section of Niceville's Confederate Cemetery. Miles was on the second shelf from the top, just below an ancestor named Jubal Teague, and across the way from Jubal's brother, Tyree Teague. Miles had a small mahogany box tucked under his right hand that contained what little they could find of his head.

Jubal and Tyree were the sons of the infamous London Teague. He wasn't there. No one knew where London Teague's body was. No one cared. He was rumored to have died of syphilis in a brothel in Baton Rouge, or possibly it was Biloxi, a bitter old man given to gin and violence.

London's son Jubal seemed to have lived an honorable life, serving with distinction as a Confederate cavalry officer during the Civil War, the same war that saw his brother, Tyree, cut down by Union grapeshot at Front Royal.

Jubal Teague went on to become the father of a deeply unpleasant man named Abel Teague. Deeply unpleasant men seemed to reappear in the Teague line fairly often. Like his grandfather London's, Abel Teague's body was not in the family crypt either, for roughly the same reasons.

Kate had undertaken an informal study of the Teague line, keeping her interest a secret from Nick, whose instinctive unease around Rainey had, over time, receded, or had appeared to recede. She had no desire to have that unease flare up again. So here she was, standing on the landing, waiting for the last of the Teagues to come down Beauregard Lane. And there they were.

Her heartbeat jumped a groove, like a needle in an old vinyl record, but she calmed herself. Lately she had been doing a lot of that. Two weeks ago, she'd gotten a heads-up call from Alice Bayer, Delia Cotton's ex-housekeeper. Nick had gotten Alice a job as attendance secretary at Regiopolis.

Alice had called to say that Rainey and Axel had been skipping a lot of classes lately, and she wanted to know if there was anything she could do to help, because "she really felt for those young men, for what they'd both been through."

This was very much on Kate's mind as she watched the boys coming up the sidewalk. They were wearing baggy gray slacks and white shirts, each with a sky-blue-and-gold-striped tie and a navy blue blazer with a gold pocket crest, a crucifix bound up in roses and thorns, the insignia of Regiopolis Prep. This was the Regiopolis school uniform, a uniform Rainey had worn since he was four, but Axel had only recently acquired.

About Rainey, the Jesuits at Regiopolis Prep and the therapists from the Belfair and Cullen County Child Protection Agency and the doctors and the various law enforcement agencies involved in the Rainey Teague Case—it was one of those cases that seemed to demand capitals—had all agreed that, after the emotional trauma he had been through, what Rainey Teague needed most was continuity and predictability.

Rainey had grown two inches in the last months, and his physiotherapy had ended weeks ago. Now he was a strong, fit young boy. Axel adored him, as younger brothers sometimes worship older brothers. Axel felt that Rainey could do no wrong. Kate hoped he was right.

Rainey and Axel reached the foot of the steps, heads down, immersed in a low and, from the sound of it, intense conversation, neither of them seeing Kate standing there.

Kate was about to speak when she caught a flash of green over in the square, in a patch of slanting sunlight, by the sparkling fountain.

A woman was standing there, in a white dress, or perhaps a nightgown, looking back at her.

By some trick of the afternoon light through the trees, the air around her had a greenish glow, as if she were standing inside a swirling cloud of emerald sparks. The woman was thin, and looked as if she had been ill for a long time, but she had glossy black hair. Her face looked familiar, as if Kate had seen her once, in a dream, or perhaps an old movie. The woman was very still and seemed to be staring intently at the house.

Kate was overcome with a strong sense of déjà vu. A name floated up into her consciousness.

Anora Mercer

A tremor ran through her body. Not fear. Painful regret? Vertigo? Was she losing her mind?

Kate lifted a hand to her, and the woman—if she was there at all—raised her hand in response.

Kate almost called out to her.

A wind stirred the trees around her and the sunlight shimmered into a translucent green shadow and when it steadied again the image was gone.

Kate heard Axel call her name, and when she looked back down at him, he was staring up at her.

Her smile faltered and died away.

"Axel, you look terrible. What happened?"

Axel tilted his head and looked at her through his long brown hair, his eyes dark with anger. His shirttail was hanging out and the knees of his slacks were stained with mud.

Kate came down the stairs and took him by the shoulders. He was vibrating like a plucked string. When he opened his mouth to speak, Kate saw blood on his teeth. She looked over at Rainey, who was standing over Axel with a protective arm laid across the smaller boy's shoulders.

"He had a fight with Coleman Mauldar," said Rainey. Kate felt her heart sink.

Coleman Mauldar was the only child of the mayor of Niceville, a jovial and ruthless man whom everybody called Little Rock.

Coleman was barely fourteen, but thanks to the roulette wheel of genetics, sixty pounds heavier and a foot taller than either Rainey or Axel, strong and quick, a gifted athlete, full of charm and mischief. He and his followers, Jay Dials and Owen Coors, had been making Rainey's school days a misery ever since he had been abducted a year and a half ago. Now that Axel was living with him, Axel was getting his share of the abuse.

"What happened, Rainey?"

Axel wiped his face, straightened his back, cut in before Rainey could speak.

"They were calling him Crypt Boy again. So this time I smacked him one."

"We got into a fight with them," said Rainey. "But it didn't last long."

"What happened?"

"Father Casey broke it up. He said it wasn't fair, because they were bigger than us."

Axel wiped his nose on his sleeve.

"They're never gonna stop," Rainey said. "I'm Crypt Boy and Axel is Cop Killer's Kid. They followed us home today, calling us names, until we got to the corner there. I wish my dad were here. He would have taken care of them."

This of course cracked her heart, but she kept it hidden from the boys.

Kate had resolved to talk to the boys about Alice Bayer's call, about skipping classes—this was her main reason for being here today to greet them—though what they had just said made it difficult to bring it up right now.

But her sense of injustice was on fire.

Working as a family practice lawyer had brought her in contact with a lot of childish stupidity and meanness, not all of it committed by children.

But when it was . . . Rousseau thought that all children were innocent until corrupted by the adult world. Rousseau was dead wrong.

There was a bit of grave evil in every child, but in a few children, grave evil was all there was and all there ever would be.

People didn't like to think this, but in family law, and in Nick's world, it was a fact of life. On his own, Jay Dials was a decent kid, from a good family—his father owned Billy Dials Town and Country, a building supply store on South Gwinnett—and Owen Coors was the son of a state police captain, Marty Coors, a close friend of Nick's.

Jay and Owen knew right from wrong well enough. But in Kate's opinion, when they got with Coleman, things changed.

Behind his good looks and his cheerful manner, Kate believed, Coleman Mauldar was a sadistic monster, and right at this moment she felt she could do almost anything to him, hurt him badly, just to make him stop.

Axel and Rainey were looking at her and what she was feeling must have been written on her face.

"So if Coleman is bad," Axel asked, "is it okay to hurt him back?"

I'd love to, Kate was thinking.

"We're going to have to do something about this. Axel, your mom and I will go have a talk with Father Casey about all of this. In the meantime, both of you come in. We'll get you cleaned up."

Axel nodded, seemed to shake off his bad mood. Axel was a resilient kid, in some ways tougher than Rainey. He came up the stairs in a lighter mood.

Rainey stayed down on the street, looking across at the park with the fountain.

Kate, coming up behind him, caught the hunted look in his large brown eyes.

She turned to follow his look, thinking about Coleman Mauldar and his . . . his *minions*. If they had the nerve to follow him here, if they were loitering in the park over there, they were going to bitterly regret it. They were going to bitterly regret a lot from now on. Kate was going to make a project out of Coleman Mauldar.

"Are you looking for Coleman?"

Rainey looked up at her, his expression blank, and then back out at the square.

"No. I was looking for somebody else."

"Somebody else? Who?"

"Nobody," he said, turning away. "Just a person I saw once."

"In the park over there? Just now? Because I thought I saw a lady in white standing in—"

"No," said Rainey, slipping away. "It was nobody. Nobody at all."

Zero to Sixty in Four Point Three Is Good but Sixty to Zero in One Is Not

At around the same time that Kate Kavanaugh was tending to Rainey and Axel and considering various ways to murder a fourteen-year-old boy, her brother, Reed Walker, was roughly ninety miles northwest of Niceville, rolling southbound on Side Road 336 with the golden brown hills of the Belfair Range filling up his windshield.

His radio beeped at him.

"Charlie Six, what's your twenty?"

Reed's gun belt creaked as he leaned forward to pick up the handset. His ride was brand new and he'd racked the driver seat back as far as it would go to make room for his six-foot-two frame. This made it a reach for the handset, but it was a lot easier on the knees.

"Charlie Six, I'm southbound at mile marker thirty-one on Side Road 366. That you, Marty?"

"It is. You going for the barn?"

"Roger that, boss. I've been on since oh-four-hundred. Shift ends at sixteen hundred hours."

"Not for you, my friend. Kentucky's telling us they had a car go jackrabbit at the state line with us. Lost him in a turnout. Last they saw he was heading our way, maybe forty miles east of your twenty, westbound on the interstate."

Reed Walker was getting this call because he was at the wheel of a Ford Police Interceptor with a 365-horsepower mill that could get him from zero to sixty in under five seconds, and the northeastern part of the state was his operational zone.

The car was navy blue with State Police markings that were visible only when the light hit the car at a certain angle. It was a blunt blue bullet with big fat tires, a NASCAR-certified steel roll cage all around him. It had a muscled-up hunchbacked look, as if it were bulked out on steroids. It was squat and mean and tight and had a rack of steel bumper bars up front, run-flat tires, an LED light rack so bright that when he lit it up you could see it from two miles away. Its top speed was classified but during the shakedown trials at the training ring over in Pinchbeck, Reed had run it out to one-ninety and he could feel the car aching to do better than that. And he would have let it, if the pit boss hadn't stopped him.

He figured it was fast enough and steady enough to blow the doors off anything with wheels and a lot of things with wings. Reed loved this ride more than a K-9 cop loved his dog.

Reed was pulling a one-eighty turn and punching the pedal back up to speed while Marty Coors got the descriptors and read them out—

"Georgia says it's a Dodge Viper—"

Be still my beating heart.

"Matte black. Kansas plates a vanity plate—hotel alpha romeo lima echo quebec utah india november—*harlequin?*—registered to a Robert Lawrence Quinn—born June 13, 1965. No wants no warrants. VIN comes back as a Chipa Edition Viper . . . Christ . . . stats say this brute tops out at two hundred— You think you can take this car?"

"Any given Sunday, boss. I'm at the on-ramp now. Have we got a visual yet?"

"None of our guys, but minutes ago several citizens called in a black sports car—couldn't make the type and moving much too fast for plates—at mile marker three four five westbound—"

"Coming right at me, then. I'm gonna lay back here by the embankment—"

"Citizen says the car was a blur—"

"Can we get air?"

"Negative, Reed. Air's doing cover flight on a prisoner transfer convoy—"

"Byron Deitz? Nick still babysitting him?"

"Yeah. He's in the transfer van with him right now. They're bringing him back from another one of those extradition hearings."

"So no chopper for me?"

"You're on your own, Charlie Six—wait one—"

Marty Coors cut away.

In the following silence, Reed sat at the wheel, taking in the world around him, seeing it as if this might be his last hour. The afternoon light was sliding sideways across the interstate—long blue shadows from the pine forest crawling out onto the blacktop. Through a break in the pines he could see a small herd of whitetail deer, grazing the kudzu and wildflowers. They always came down from the Belfair Range in the fall.

Traffic on the interstate was sparse, just a few minivans and SUVs, now and then a transport or a tanker. Light traffic was a good thing. If this Viper showed up—and it was due at any moment—the chase would be right into the setting sun, and a wandering civilian hidden by the glare could kill him. Reed was thinking, *Can I catch a Viper?*

The U.S. Marshals prisoner transport van—a rectangular tin box on squishy tires—swayed and lurched along the Cap City Thruway like a big blue rhino on a skateboard. The sound of the tires on the road and the rhythmic *knock-knock-knock* of the diesel engine filled the interior of the van with white noise. And there was a leak somewhere, because they were getting blowback from the tailpipe, so the air inside the prisoner compartment was stale and hot.

Sitting on a steel bench across from a silent and sullen Byron Deitz, Nick Kavanaugh was mainly concentrating on not throwing up. Deitz, shackled by the ankle to a ringbolt in the floor, had his big meaty fists bunched into his belt and his small black eyes fixed on Nick's face, his fat lips tight. Nick stared back at him without blinking.

Their close association over the last few months had given each man a new perspective on the other. Where there had previously been intense dislike and contempt, now there was open hatred.

Their route, the last run for Deitz, this month anyway, was a direct trip northwest from Cap City to Niceville, a distance of about fifty miles.

The convoy was doing a careful fifty-five, going through the flatlands below Niceville, the four-lane blacktop lined with lodgepole pine and pampas grass. Through gaps in the pines you could see the sunlight glinting on the rippled surface of the Tulip River as it curled through the farmland to the west of the highway.

The light was hazy and golden, classic late fall in the South, long shadows sliding across the road as the sun slipped down into the west.

Through the pitted windshield of the transfer van, past the hulking shapes of the two Deputy U.S. Marshals up front on the other side of the steel mesh, Nick could see a big black Suburban, no markings, maybe fifty yards ahead. There were two Cap City FBI guys inside the Suburban, both wrapped in Kevlar, wired up and loaded for bear.

If Nick looked to his right through the rear window slits, he could see a steel gray State Police car coming up behind, flashers on, a couple of up-armored state cops staring back at him through the windshield.

Keeping company two hundred feet overhead was the state chopper that Reed Walker really could have used right now. The two marshals—Bradley Heath, the big blond guy with the shoulder-length hair, and Shaniqua Griffin, the beefy black chick—were the same two cops that La Motta and Munoz and Spahn had been watching on the CNN feed up at Leavenworth. These two, partners for only a month, disliked each other intensely and therefore were not much given to witty banter, so the mood inside the van was not the teensiest bit sparkly. Nick went back to staring at Byron Deitz and Byron Deitz went right on staring at him.

Reed stiffened and sat up in his harness. In the distance, over the wind in the pampas grass, came the sound of sirens . . . his radio popped back . . . "Charlie Six switch to tactical."

Reed did.

The burst of adrenalized chatter and choppy cross talk came as no surprise. It wasn't every day that you got to chase a runaway Viper down the interstate. The whole depot was pumped. Days like this, you'd pay to do the job.

"Echo Five, I just got my doors blown off by a black Viper tinted windows no ID on the driver he's westbound at mile marker three five four—"

"Roger that," another voice cut in—female—sounded like Kris Lucas—the dog unit trooper—"I'm about a quarter mile back—"

"Went by me so fast I thought I was stopped—"

"So you got out to pee—"

In the background of the call Reed could hear the sound of her engine winding out, and the dog—his name was Conan—in the back going totally nuts.

"No way I'm staying with him—I'm maxed out at one-fifty, my ride's shaking like a paint mixer and he's a black dot getting smaller every second—is Charlie Six out there?"

Reed was rolling slowly along the on-ramp, the heavy car rocking slightly from the race cam, keeping the crest of the curve high enough to shield him from that Viper—he wanted the element of *holy shit where'd this guy come from* when he appeared out of nowhere and started to climb up his ass—and mile marker 354 meant this Viper was about five miles away.

If he was doing what it would take to leave Kris Lucas' dog unit in the ditch he'd cover that five miles in less than three minutes. Now Reed could hear the high-pitched whine of a race-tuned engine, a wailing scream coming faintly on the wind—sirens trailing far behind.

He keyed the handset.

"Dog Car, this is Charlie Six—I can hear him. I'm gonna take him at the three-six-six on-ramp—I'm gonna climb right up his butt—you fall back, Kris—I don't want you to blow a tire—those units aren't set up for this—let me have this—"

The engine whine got louder and now he could just make out a tiny patch of matte black streaking down a long decline a mile out. The black dot was carving a risky path through light traffic—shifting from lane to lane—weaving through the crowded sections.

Amazingly, all the civilian traffic was holding pretty steady, getting off the road as the chase swept by, staying in their lane if they couldn't—using their mirrors *and* their brains, he figured. Maybe they'd seen enough episodes of *World's Wildest Police Chases* to learn how to drive when they were in the middle of one.

And it had been his experience that American interstate drivers were, on the whole, a pretty competent lot. It was only around the cities that things got crazy.

He could see the faint flicker of police flashers a long way behind the Viper, their sirens barely audible. Reed felt his heart rate start to climb as he tightened his harness. He put the handset into the cradle and punched SPEAKER just as the Viper disappeared into the hollow of a road dip at a half mile away.

"Jimmy, I got him—he'll be on me in seconds—I'm rolling—"

"Echo Five says he's doing one-seventy easy—how much blacktop will this take?"

Reed visualized the next twenty to thirty miles of interstate that ran west from here—rolling hills, big slow curves, the sun going down, shining right in his eyes—three interchanges—the Holland Creek overpass at four miles—then a long, empty stretch of about fifteen miles—the Side Road 440 ramp—two miles later the Super Gee Truck Stop and Gas Bar—four acres wide and lit up with arc lamps, semitrailers coming and going—had to get *that* blocked—and, thirty-eight miles from exactly here, a huge toll plaza that crossed all four lanes at the Pinchbeck Cut. And the toll plaza had spike rails that could be raised to shred the tires of any vehicle that tried to run it. What would happen right after that to any car moving at a hundred and eighty miles an hour was going to be deeply memorable.

Reed did the math—at one-eighty the car would cover three miles in sixty seconds—thirty-eight miles in—*Jesus*, he thought, *the next thirteen minutes are going to be really interesting*—

"I'm gonna need all the snow gates dropped on every ramp between here and the Pinchbeck Cut—"

"Already done—"

"And get on to Rowdy at the Super Gee—get on the CB band, warn the truckers still in the chute, and tell Rowdy nobody leaves that lot until we have this guy in cuffs—"

And then a shattering engine blast as the Viper cleared the dip, low and fast, a panther-like bulge to its flanks, eating up the road, front end inches from the ground.

He got a brief glimpse of two white faces through the windshield—two white males, one with a beard—the car flashed past with a Doppler wail—and the Viper was *gone baby gone*.

"Jimmy, I'm moving—"

"Roger that—"

Reed flicked the sound down to a low rumble—from now on this was between the black Viper and his Ford Interceptor—he heard Marty Coors saying something about County Sheriff units getting into blocking positions—the chatter seemed to fade away and he was accelerating down the on-ramp, tires smoking, the engine winding up with a throaty roar, a weight driving him back into the seat, his body getting heavier and heavier, his arms rigid on the wheel, his right foot jamming the pedal down.

This must be what it's like to ride the rocket down in Cape Kennedy. What a rush.

The car skittered a bit as it thumped over the rumble strip, straightened up, and shot down the highway like a shoulder-fired missile—he glimpsed a red minivan in his side mirror—a pretty blond woman with an open mouth and big eyes as he flew out in front of her—up ahead the Viper was a black dot—he fixed his eyes on that black dot as he felt his car come on the cam.

Christ, this thing could *fly*.

The HUD—the heads-up display—was projecting his speed onto the lower edge of his windshield—bright red numbers—65—71—78—now the Viper wasn't getting smaller quite as fast—Reed had his light bar on and the siren wailing—the road curved and the sun moved right into his face, a blinding glare. He flipped the visor down.

The HUD numbers were rippling up—95—120—140—148—157—169—172—that crushing weight as the thrusters kicked in—the car felt like a cruise missile under his hands, hugging the terrain, slicing through the curves—he could feel the blacktop thrumming up through the wheel.

Up ahead the Viper was weaving a narrow black ribbon through the traffic. Christ, one dumb move by a civilian and there'd be car parts and body bits for a quarter mile. Reed felt his anger building as he watched the Viper thread a closing gap between two converging cars—red brake lights flared as the drivers slammed on the binders—blue smoke boiling up from their tires.

Son of a bitch, he said to himself, as the red numbers flickered on his windshield—170—173—179—he jigged around an SUV that had come to a full stop right in the middle of the highway—heard a cry and saw a man waving at him as he flashed past.

The Viper was close now, maybe a hundred feet, and getting closer every second. The guy at the wheel had to be looking at what was filling up his rearview and thinking *holy shit who is this guy?*

Reed picked out the sweet spot on the Viper's lower left side where he was going to ram it with the bumper bars. One tap at this speed, and a two-hundred-thousand-dollar car turns into a spinning top. Yards . . . feet . . . inches . . . he saw the Viper's tail squat down suddenly and the tires blur as the driver punched it harder, trying to get whatever the car had left. The Viper leapt ahead, like a spurred horse, and began to pull away again, fifty feet, sixty—shrinking.

Man, thought Reed, putting the pedal to the floor and holding it there, *you had to love American engineering.*

That Viper is a thing of beauty.

Reed was in the *zone* now, and everything around him became a seamless river of color and sound flowing past, the radio chatter fading away, the howl of the engines growing faint, nothing in his head but the sound of his own breathing and the steady hammering of his heart.

There were only two points in this universe: the bulging hood of his car and the fat black ass of the Viper—he fixed his eye on the Kansas plate—HARLEQUIN—in navy blue letters on a pale blue background, the Kansas State Wildcats logo—a license frame made of chrome chain links—LITTLE APPLE FINE CARS—the details burned into him as he came closer and closer.

The world darkened for half a second and the sound of his own engine boomed back at him as he flashed under an overpass.

Reed saw the black letters of the sign on the side of the bridge—SIDE ROAD 440—and he realized they had covered twenty miles. Two miles to the Super Gee Truck Stop. Eighteen more miles until they reached the Pinchbeck Cut toll plaza.

At these speeds he had less than six minutes to take this car out. His eyes cut to the HUD numbers—183—187—192—195—the car felt light under him and there was a minor but worrying vibration in the steering wheel. He knew that at speeds like this a tiny twitch of the wheel, or something tumbling into the road, and he'd be airborne in a death spin that—

"Charlie Six, got a bulletin for you—"

Reed flipped the speaker volume up again.

Marty Coors was on the line, his voice tight.

"Go, boss—"

"Kentucky boys say they've got a white male shot dead in the washroom of a Shell station in Sapphire Springs—they ID'd him as Robert Lawrence Quinn—Kentucky has closed-circuit video of two white males leaving the Shell station in Quinn's black Viper—face recog made them as Dwayne Bobby Shagreen and Douglas Loyal Shagreen—used to be strikers for the Nightriders—White Power mutts—both wanted by multiple agencies for rape, felony assault, armed robbery—consider armed and dangerous—Reed no matter what don't you close with these guys until we can get backup—"

"I'm inches from his ass, boss!"

"Back off a bit, Reed. I mean it."

"We got a window of five minutes before we hit the Pinchbeck toll—we gonna take them there?"

"Word is we let them through—"

"What? No goddam way."

"Yes, goddam way. Plaza is full of civilian staff, full of civilian traffic, propane tanks for the shed heaters. If that Viper goes airborne, hits people, hits propane, there'll be hell to pay—"

"Word from who, boss? That asshole governor?"

"This transmission is being taped, trooper."

Reed got his temper reined in.

"Okay. Okay. I'll back off a few feet. If I'm gonna stay on him, you gotta get me that chopper—you gotta clear the highway for fifty miles out—I'm gonna need eyes in the air—"

A short wait, voices off.

"Roger that—"

Reed was now less than fifteen inches off the tail end of the Viper—it looked like the Viper had nothing left—topped out at 201 miles an hour—he could see the tower sign for the Super Gee coming up on his right side—lit up like a beacon—there was something spread out along the side of the road—a long low mass of ragged color—he was going too fast to make out what it was—if Reed struck the Viper with his bumper bars at this speed it would be nothing less than an execution.

Maybe these two assholes were looking for it. Suicide By Cop after one last wild—there was something coming out of the passenger-side window—a hand, gloved, something in the glove—a heavy black pistol—the muzzle tracking around towards his windshield—muzzle flare and blue smoke and a big heavy bullet struck his windshield, starring it, a bull's-eye of cratered shards—

"Gun! He's got a gun—I'm taking fire—"

Nick looked up as the female marshal picked up her radio. She spoke once, a staccato bark, a silence, another bark, and then she hooked the handset back, turning around as she did so. At the same time they could all hear the chopper winding up and pulling ahead fast—Nick could see the machine banking to the northwest, rotors spinning—

"State needs the chopper, Nick—they've got a trooper in a pursuit car taking fire—"

"Call sign?"

Shaniqua looked puzzled.

"Didn't get it."

A burst of engine noise and the sudden wail of a siren—the State car passed them on the left, a slate gray blur accelerating away, and disappeared into the distance, strobe lights flaring red and blue, followed closely by the big black Suburban with the two FBI guys. In a moment, they were all alone on the thruway. Deitz was sitting up and taking an interest in his surroundings.

"We lost the Feds too?" Nick asked. Shaniqua nodded, her flat gray eyes wide.

"Yeah. Two guys in the car being chased, they're wanted by the FBI."

"Please get the call sign of the State car taking fire."

Shaniqua blinked. She didn't know that Nick had a brother-in-law running a chase car for State. She turned around, spoke into the handset, turned back.

"Call sign is Charlie Six. A Sergeant Reed Walker. You know him?"

"Yes. Is he hit?"

Another blink, and another brief exchange on the handset. Nick listened, wishing he was there instead of here, wishing he had his own radio with him. He didn't even have a gun right now. Against the rules to sit inside the prisoner box while wearing an issue sidearm. His Colt Python was up front with the marshals, in a lockbox on the floor.

Shaniqua twisted around again—"Can't make it out—sounds like he's being shot at—the cross talk is—"

"Put it on the fucking speaker, lady," said Bradley Heath, a low Tennessee drawl in a voice as deep and smooth as a cello.

Shaniqua huffed at his tone but she hit the SPEAKER tab and the van filled up with the electric crackle of police cross talk on the State channel. Nick recognized Reed's voice, flat and steady, but tight as a plucked wire.

"—not backing off Jimmy he'll just keep—"

"Repeat disengage Charlie Six disengage—"

"Negative Jimmy he'll just keep shooting—"

A sharp cracking report, and under that a boom like thunder, and then another crack, all of it in the background of Reed's transmission.

"I'm slowing but so's he—I just got two more rounds in the windshield—he's leaning out the passenger window—this is nuts—I'm not just gonna lay back here and let him light me up—I'm gonna move in and take him out—"

"Negative Charlie Six—"

Reed again, calm, steady, but adrenalized.

"I'm right by the Super Gee—the truckers are all standing there—they're right on the side of the road—he could turn that piece on them any sec—oh jeez—brake lights brake lights—the guy's jamming back on me—I'm on the binders—oh man here he comes—"

Reed kept his mike on but stopped talking.

They heard a rising siren wail and then a huge metallic *clank*, and then another—Reed swearing, teeth gritted, his voice a guttural snarl—and then the clatter and clanging of something tumbling along the highway—something big and made of iron—the earsplitting shriek of metal on road—Reed's transmission cut off abruptly and the interior of the marshals' van was suddenly jammed full with an intense and painful silence.

After a long pause, Deitz decided now was a good time to make a helpful comment.

"Hey, Nick," he said, his tone jovial, "sounds like your boy just got his ticket punched—"

Nick stepped up and crossed the space between them—Deitz was getting to his feet, his shackles rattling, his heavy fists coming up, moving into a boxing stance, a fighting guard, chin low—Nick bypassed all that Queensberry crap and drove his fist over Deitz's guard and straight into the tiny furrowed space between Byron Deitz's right and left eyebrows, feeling the nose cracking like a walnut, feeling the impact of his punch all the way up his arm and into his pectorals and deltoids and then down into his hips.

Deitz crossed his eyes under Nick's fist and his thick legs got all wobbly and his head slammed backwards into the wall of the marshals' van, striking it with a clear bell-like bong. Deitz bounced back, his nose bubbling blood, but he was sliding now.

Nick stepped back and let him fall.

A high-pitched female voice was blaring at him and he turned to see Shaniqua twisted around and banging a fat fist on the prisoner mesh, Bradley Heath shouting at her, trying to catch her arm—

"Hey, you can't be pounding on my goddam prisoner—" But her voice was cut off and ridden down by the cello note of Bradley Heath's awestruck, almost reverential *Holy shit* and everybody but Byron Deitz turned around to look back out at the road, where a sleek amber shape with brown eyes ringed in white was rising up in the air to meet the windshield.

"Deer—a deer!" Nick heard Bradley Heath's hoarse growl, as the van shuddered and dipped—Nick, reeling, clutched the stanchion at his left—Heath was stiff-legged on the brakes and the squishy tires were starting to fold . . . everything seemed to stop moving . . . Nick saw the way the muscles rippled under the deer's pelt, saw the terror in its wide brown eye . . . a heartbeat . . . another—the buck hit the windshield square, two hundred and sixty pounds of tightly packed meat and muscle and bone slamming into a big flat wall of glass moving forward at sixty miles an hour. The effect was nothing less than spectacular.

The windshield exploded in a shower of glass beads as the deer smashed through it. The carcass smacked Bradley Heath and Shaniqua Griffin square in the face and upper body, crushing them from the chest up, cracking their skulls like raw eggs and then—still moving at about fifty miles an hour—the entire mass of disintegrating gore and bone and viscera struck the steel prisoner mesh immediately behind them, bending it into a concave bowl and shearing off nearly every one of the rivets that held it in place.

Most of the meatier bits got stuck in the mesh, but Nick, still on his feet, transfixed, caught the full force of the semi-liquid wall of brains and bodily fluids and bone splinters that hurtled through the screen, coating the entire inside of the prisoner box with blood and ruin.

Nick felt the wave hit him full on—it was as hot as black coffee and stank of copper—blinded, he went backwards and down, banging his head on the floor, and lay there next to Byron Deitz's unconscious body as the van, driverless, veered sharply to the right, left the road, went air-borne as it hit the verge rail, descended ponderously again, and landed on the right front wheel, which blew up on impact.

The van, making a grinding metallic groan like a freighter striking a reef, rolled majestically onto its right side, struck hard and bounced once, dropped back to earth, and then gouged a furrow through the pampas grass and red earth about fifteen feet wide and forty yards long, mainly with the upper right edge of the roof.

At forty-one yards and a couple of inches the leading edge of what used to be a federal marshals' van and was now a loose confederation of auto parts and assorted biological material struck a stand of lodgepole pine and slammed to a sudden halt—sixty to zero in one—rapidly eject-ing an undifferentiated mass of deer and dead deputy parts that flew out the shattered windshield and spread itself all over the pines and painted the pale gold pampas grass with a fan of scarlet and pink and purple chunks for a radius of fifty feet.

———

Nick Kavanaugh lived through this, although he didn't come around until the medevac chopper got him onto the roof of Lady Grace Hospital in downtown Niceville seventy-nine minutes later, and even then he was only awake enough to recognize the round pink and badly bearded face of Boonie Hackendorff, whose worried expression got more worried as he replied, in response to Nick's faint whispered question, that no, Byron Deitz had not been killed in the crash and was, as of this point in time, nowhere to be found.

"In the wind" were Boonie's exact words.

"And Reed? Is he okay?"

Boonie Hackendorff's face went pale around the edges. His eyes were wide and full of regret.

"Reed's alive. A lot of other folks, not so much."

These were cryptic words and the effort involved in trying to decode them carried Nick off into the following darkness.

Thursday

Mr. Harvill Endicott Comes to Niceville

Business at the Quantum Park Marriott Hotel and Convention Center was brisk on this lovely Thursday morning, but the central foyer happened to be nearly empty. A few stragglers from a convention of mechanical engineers were holding up the long bar in the Old Dominion off to the left.

When the tinted glass doors of the front entrance swished open and Edgar Luckinbaugh escorted a tall and bookish-looking older man in an English-cut blue suit across the polished oak slabs to the registration desk, Mark Hopewell had a lot of time to speculate upon the precise nature and character of the man before him, holding out an American Express card, his thin-lipped smile revealing a set of smoke-stained teeth.

His accent, when he spoke, was neutral, neither southern nor northern, neither European nor North American. A mid-Atlantic man, thought Hopewell, who felt that the man's presentation was neutral, neither imperious nor overly friendly, as is often the case with business travelers.

"Good morning. The name is Harvill Endicott. I believe I have a reservation."

Hopewell tapped a few keys, looked up with a cheerful smile, and agreed that this was so, welcoming Mr. Harvill Endicott to the Marriott. He slid a form across the granite surface of the desk and watched as Mr. Endicott filled it out and signed his name in an elegant flourish, setting the pen down gently beside the form.

When he looked up again, Hopewell was slightly disconcerted by the impression that Mr. Endicott's eyes were almost completely colorless. This, combined with his blue-white skin and his thin purple lips, gave him a cadaverous air that sent a vague tremor of unease through Mark Hopewell's young and impressionable mind. If Mr. Endicott was aware of this effect, he gave no sign.

Hopewell glanced down at the registration card, noting that under "BUSINESS" Mr. Endicott had written "Private Collector and Facilitator."

"Is it business or pleasure, sir?"

Endicott smiled again, a much more open and friendly smile.

"I suppose it's a bit of both, Mr. Hopewell. I requested a suite with a view of the town, one not on the ground floor, if possible. With windows that open to the air? And a terrace? I'm a smoker, as you may have been warned. And high-speed Ethernet in the room?"

"Yes sir. All taken care of. We have you in the Temple Hill Suite, one of our finest. It is a smoking suite, as you requested, and it has a large terrace, one of only three in the hotel. It's on the top floor, quite secure. It's named after the estate of Alastair Cotton—"

"The Sulfur King," finished Endicott.

"You've heard of him?" Hopewell said, obviously surprised. Endicott inclined his head.

"I have made something of a study of the area," he said, gathering up his card and the papers and slipping them into an inside pocket.

"I requested cars as well?"

Hopewell nodded, pleased to be pleasing.

"Yes sir. You asked for a black Cadillac DeVille and a beige Toyota Corolla. We have them in valet parking. The Cadillac has a GPS screen, as you requested. Just ring for the valet and whichever vehicle you request will be brought around whenever you wish."

"Thank you, but if you would just send the keys to my room, and let me know where to find the cars, I'd greatly prefer that. I come and go at irregular hours and I don't wish to be a burden to the staff."

"Not at all, Mr. Endicott. I'll have the keys and the garage map sent up right away. Is there anything else I can do, sir?"

"Not that I can think of right now."

"Then enjoy your stay. We have a concierge desk, as you can see," he said, inclining his head in the direction of a French escritoire behind which sat, primly erect, a tiny Oriental man in a black suit.

Hopewell watched him cross the oak floor, thinking that Mr. Harvill Endicott did not seem the sort of man who would do anything at all for pleasure, or, more accurately, what Mr. Endicott would consider pleasurable might be something quite unpleasant to know about.

———

"Yes, thank you, the suite is perfectly fine," said Endicott, tipping the bellman, whose name tag identified him as EDGAR. This Edgar creature was fidgeting about the suite, poking at this and fussing with that, seemingly unwilling to leave, although Endicott had tipped him twice, once at the lobby door and again four minutes ago, for a total of nine dollars, which ought to be enough for any damn bellhop.

"May I help you?" Endicott said, with an edge. Edgar Luckinbaugh stopped twitching at the curtains and stiffened, and, mumbling something about the thermostat, shuffled across an acre of beige carpet to the door.

Endicott closed it with emphasis, turned away with a sigh, and considered the suite.

It was large and full of light, and, as promised, it offered a splendid view down a long grassy incline to the town of Niceville, about five miles to the south and east.

He opened the French doors and walked onto a large stone-tiled terrace with a gallery railing. The air was sweet and scented with harvest smells, with cut grass and turned earth, and the sun was warm on his cheek.

Niceville was a snug-looking town situated in the looming shadow of a long limestone barrier wall that, according to his researches, was a thousand feet high.

He smiled, patting his suit pocket and pulling out a heavy gold cigarette case and a battered Zippo lighter, in gleaming brass, with the crest of the First Air Cavalry on the side, a black-rimmed yellow oval bisected with a black bar, a black horse head in the upper angle.

He flicked it and put a light to a Camel, drew the smoke in with real pleasure, considering the view before him.

Niceville was shrouded in live oaks and pine with, here and there, a brighter green swath of willows. A number of church steeples pierced the canopy of trees, and a golden, hazy light lay upon it, even at this early hour. Sunlight rippled on the broad brown back of the large river that carved a meandering course through the middle of the town.

The Tulip, he recalled, noting the way it swept in a big, aggressive bend past a large stand of willows that lined the western bank. That would be Patton's Hard, if his memory served.

The way the water eddied and swirled there probably meant a whirlpool, he thought, and given the force of that big river, a dangerous one to get caught up in.

The ascending sun was lighting up the roofs of houses, glinting off window glass and storefronts, and sending a shimmer along the tracery of overhead wires that stitched together the older portions of the downtown area.

A pretty sight, taken as a whole, and full of gentle light, except for that portion of Niceville still in the shadow of that wall. The way Niceville lay spread out beneath it made the cliff face look like a gigantic tidal wave looming over the town.

He sighed, finished the cigarette, stubbed it out against the railing until it was dead and cold, and dropped the broken stub into a separate compartment inside his cigarette case, snapping it shut with a metallic click. He would flush the butts down the toilet later. Endicott considered it prudent not to leave his DNA scattered about.

He turned away to the suite itself, which was nicely done in creams and beiges and oak panels, a thick Berber carpet under his feet. The requisite flat-screen television, an expensive and overly complicated coffee-maker, a minibar and a refrigerator, a bar sink, glasses and cups.

Along the way was a marble-walled bath, verging on the sybaritic, and down another short hallway lined in mirrors he found a large master bedroom with a king-sized bed and far too many pillows.

Edgar had set Endicott's luggage down on a padded bench at the foot of the bed, a matched pair of saddle-leather cases. Endicott picked up the heavier one—easily, although it weighed eighty pounds. Endicott was stronger than he looked.

He set the case on the bed, thumbed the pressure locks hidden along the sides, and lifted the lid. Inside, laid out neatly, were a Toshiba laptop and various peripheral computer devices, a pair of Zeiss binoculars equipped with a laser range finder, a module that looked like a window-mounted GPS that was actually a laser surveillance mike with a video camera. He also had an electronic key-code analyzer, a compact set of Dremel battery-powered machine tools, a silver box containing a stainless-steel syringe and a large glass vial filled with hydrofluoric acid, a shiny blue device that looked exactly like a Motorola cell phone but was actually a Taser stun gun, a Streamlight high-intensity flashlight, and a shiny gray Sig Sauer pistol, a P226 9-mm Parabellum, along with a cleaning kit, a reasonably efficient sound suppressor—never used—four boxes of Black Talon rounds, fifty to a box, and three spare fifteen-round magazines.

Unloaded, of course, since keeping the magazines loaded all the time ruined their springs, which would, sooner or later, cause a round to jam in the pistol slide, which would get you killed.

Although Endicott really had taken a cab in from the airport, he hadn't flown in. Not with this sort of gear. He had driven up from Miami in a nondescript GMC Suburban. It was now stowed away in long-term parking at the airfield—under another name—full of gas and spare gear and a steel valise chained to a ringbolt in the cab floor. The valise contained lots of cash and several different IDs and another Sig.

He lifted the Toshiba out of its slot and carried it over to the desk set up behind the long sofa that faced the television. This meant he could work with his back to the side wall, with a clear view on the left to the wall of windows and the terrace, and on the right to the only other way into the suite, which was through the heavy black-stained doors that led out into the hotel hallway.

He walked over to the coffee machine, sorted out how to get a cup of espresso, punched the ON button, and walked back to his Toshiba, carrying the extendable Ethernet cord that provided the hotel's high-speed connection.

He plugged it in, turned on the machine, and was connected in thirty seconds. He went immediately to the news section, found a tab for LOCAL BREAKING in the Cap City region.

In a few minutes of clicking around, he had established a number of interesting facts, the most spectacular of which—amateur video was included—showed the dramatic end of a high-speed chase that had happened the previous afternoon. A black sports car—possibly a Viper—was being pursued by a state trooper driving one of those new Ford Interceptors. The pursuit was taking place along a stretch of interstate to the north and west of Belfair County.

The video—shaky but serviceable enough—showed the two cars, less than a yard apart, streaking through a section of highway walled in with tall pines.

As the cars came abreast of a large truck stop called the Super Gee, it looked as if someone in the passenger seat of the Viper was shooting at the following pursuit car with a pistol—Endicott could not make out what sort of weapon.

The cars were flying past a number of people who were standing along the side of the highway near the truck stop perimeter—*as if they were at a NASCAR track, the idiots*—and then, in a blurry and confusing sequence, the black Viper jammed its brakes on, forcing the pursuit car to rear-end it.

The Viper, rebounding, went into a long, slow spin that took it—like a scythe—straight through the crowd lining the roadside.

Bodies flew everywhere—not all of them in one piece—and smoke and dust obscured the scene.

The pursuit car, still on its wheels, emerged from the dust cloud, the driver clearly fighting for control. He managed to steer the car away from the crowd now being mauled by the Viper. You could see the brake lights on the pursuit car flashing, see the blue and red flare of its light bar, brilliant against the smoke and wreckage behind it.

The car weaved and rocked and finally came to stop in the gully-like median that separated the east- and westbound lanes of the interstate.

The camera did a crazy erratic zoom to the face of the young cop behind the wheel as he popped the door and stepped out onto the grass, his face flushed and angry.

At the bottom of the screen ran a crawl—

EIGHT KILLED AND THIRTEEN INJURED AS POLICE CHASE GOES WRONG ON I 50

The driver of the pursuit car was named, a Sergeant Reed Walker, of the State Patrol.

The men in the Viper, described only as Wanted Felons, had both been declared DOA at Lady Grace Hospital a few hours later.

According to the summary, Sergeant Walker, who was uninjured but described as "shaken up," had been assigned to desk duty pending an independent inquiry. Under a subheading titled OTHER REGIONAL NEWS, there was a short piece describing a rollover on the Cap City Thruway fifty miles to the south of Niceville that had killed two federal officers and injured a local detective. A prisoner had escaped after the crash.

The prisoner was described as "Byron Deitz, 44, white male six three two hundred and fourteen pounds brown eyes black goatee shaved head. An overnight search of the area failed to discover him. He is now considered at large. Last seen wearing a red prison jumpsuit and lime green sandals—"

"Dear God," said Endicott, half aloud. "Shouldn't be too tough to spot him."

"—prisoner may have taken the sidearms of the two dead deputy marshals as well as a police radio and a cell phone belonging to the injured detective. If seen alert the police but do not approach as Deitz is considered Armed and Dangerous."

"I would be too if I were being dragged around the county in an outfit like that."

Endicott leaned back in the chair, staring at the computer screen with half-closed eyes, sipping at his espresso—it was nearly scalding. Maybe he could sue, like that old bat at McDonald's.

So Deitz is out.

That complicates things.

Or maybe it simplifies them.

He leaned forward, tapped a few keys, and brought up a Google Earth image of the countryside that lay between Niceville and the northern limits of Cap City.

It was mostly tilled earth and farmland, with the occasional horse ranch scattered here and there, and what looked like a large sandpit or stone quarry about a mile off the main road, connected to it by a narrow track. The Cap City Thruway was a four-lane affair that meandered in a lazy, looping way north and west from Cap City to Niceville, with a few country roads branching off. It looked like ugly country for a fugitive, and Endicott had a healthy respect for the men and women of the Deep South when it came to the question of firearms and a certain freewheeling vigilante streak in the culture down here.

If I were Byron Deitz, and I was tricked out like a circus clown, would I wander about the hinterland, an open invitation to getting my torso ventilated by any passing farmhand with a Remington 700 right there to hand?

I would not.

I would get myself into one of these ranch houses or farm buildings I see here on Google Earth and I would use my boyish charm—and one of those borrowed pistols—to improve my wardrobe and, if possible, to call upon a friend—if I had any—to come to my assistance.

Endicott knew enough about the wiles of local law enforcement to realize that the people hunting for Byron Deitz would have reasoned along the same lines, and would no doubt have spent the last several hours making damn sure that Deitz wasn't hiding out in any local residence or in any of the outbuildings attached. Yet, hours later, Deitz was still being described as "at large."

Ergo . . . someone was *helping* Byron Deitz.

Based on what Endicott knew of Byron Deitz's character, and he had made a rather exhausting study of the man, it seemed unlikely that anyone would come to his aid out of brotherly love. Take that away and what remained was either fear or self-interest.

Or both.

Probably both.

So who might the leading candidates be? Endicott had a file full of the most salient details surrounding the Gracie robbery, but one fact that had formerly not been known had just been conveyed to him by a local source. The fact was in an e-mail. Endicott opened it. It concerned an internal stock transfer at Deitz's security company.

> Local sources also confirm that a transfer of voting shares controlled by Enterprise Syndicate, Byron Deitz's personal corporate shell, had been prepared and was ready to go into effect as soon as Byron Deitz signed it, which had not yet happened.
>
> This transfer would give an entity known as Golden Ocean Ltd. a 50 percent share of the voting stock. The sole proprietor of Golden Ocean Ltd. was Andy Chu, formerly Deitz's in-house IT expert.

"Fascinating," said Endicott, leaning back and almost but not quite lighting up a cigarette. "The inscrutable Chinaman is still with us. What handle did Andy Chu have on Byron Deitz that would make him hand over half his company to a pencil-neck rice burner? And how did Andy Chu find it in the first place? And where does this leave Phil Holliman? In the rear with the gear?"

About the blackmail?

Simple.

Andy Chu was an IT geek.

They know how to find out stuff.

And finding something rotten in Byron Deitz's background wouldn't be much of a challenge for a computer geek with a serious grudge. From his own readings in the Book of Byron, Endicott was persuaded that Deitz hadn't so much moved through life as slithered, leaving a slimy residue.

The most probable scenario right here was that Chu had found out about Deitz's deal with the Chinese and had threatened to go to the cops unless there was something in it for Andy Chu.

Endicott had more espresso, sipping it carefully—it was still too hot—while he gave the state of affairs some consideration.

He had information that a compromise was about to be reached between the U.S. State Department and the Chinese government regarding the disposition of the Byron Deitz affair. Although the information was oblique, it seemed to Endicott to be distinctly possible that Byron Deitz was about to be handed over to the rough justice of the Chinese in exchange for a loosening of some troublesome Chinese trade barriers.

In terms of Mr. Endicott's assignment, this would have been an unacceptable outcome.

The original idea had been to pry Byron Deitz loose from the authorities while he was still being held in what was probably an amateurish local lockdown here in Niceville, take him to a private and soundproof location, and, with the help of the Dremel tools and a syringe of hydrofluoric acid—that stuff was nasty enough to make a ceramic cat howl—allow Deitz to unburden himself of the crushing moral weight of two and a half million dollars of stolen cash.

This part was to be videotaped, full HDMI with surround sound and, when they finally got sprung from Leavenworth, provided to La Motta, Spahn, and Munoz for their viewing enjoyment. Deitz was not expected to be around for his film debut.

But if Deitz was shipped off to the Chinese before Endicott could reach him, Endicott's mission would be deemed a failure by his bosses in Leavenworth, who did not look lightly upon failure. Life, however, as Muhammar Qadaffi had once observed, was what happened to you while you were picking out a new feather boa.

Deitz was not on the way to China.

Deitz was out and on the run.

So, assuming that Deitz had gone safely to ground, the trick was to get a tail on Deitz before the good guys did. He was going to need that cash to disappear, and when he pulled it out of whatever hole he had hidden it in, Endicott was going to be right there to help.

But who was helping Deitz?

There were only two viable candidates.

Phil Holliman, his Second in Command.

For why?

Loyalty, long association, abiding friendship?

Unlikely.

With Deitz out of the picture, as far as he knew, there was nobody around to pin his name on the Raytheon stunt—Holliman sure as hell *knew* about it even if he was just Deitz's errand boy. And now he was the top guy in BD Securicom, although he might not know that Deitz was about to hand over half the company to that geeky Chinese dork down in IT. And it was a moot question how long the Feds were going to let a private security firm with a felon for a CEO handle the perimeter control for something as vital to the national interest as Quantum Park.

Endicott felt it was reasonable to rule out Phil Holliman, at least provisionally.

Which left Andy Chu.

For why Andy Chu?

Because if he didn't help, Deitz might not be alive to sign that stock transfer, and, on a more basic level, if he didn't help, Byron Deitz would find a way to reach out and kill him.

Down in the lobby the curious bellman named Edgar found something plausible to do in the cloakroom until Mark Hopewell took his coffee break in the Old Dominion bar. Mr. Quan, the concierge, was off doing something diligent for a visiting potentate of the Shriners.

Seizing his moment, Luckinbaugh stepped around to the registration desk and, with a few practiced keystrokes, tapped into the system.

Edgar Luckinbaugh had been a deputy sheriff for Belfair County until he had suffered the misfortune of getting caught while dipping into the Belfair and Cullen County Law Enforcement Benevolent Fund.

His misfortune in this matter had more to do with exactly who had caught him doing it.

In the normal course of these things, he'd have been detected by a simple audit and handed over to Internal Affairs to be dealt with according to the rules. But he had not been caught by a simple audit. He'd been caught—through a fluke—by a Staff Sergeant Coker.

In Coker's Court of No Appeal—he sat as both judge and jury—assorted petty criminals and other flawed characters who had come to his attention were offered a choice between becoming contributors to Coker's wide-ranging informal intelligence file on who was doing what to whom in and around Niceville and the counties, or, if they so chose, being handed over to the proper authorities forthwith, to reap what they had sown.

Not surprisingly, everyone who had appeared before the bench in Coker's Court of No Appeal, Justice Coker presiding, had taken Door Number One.

This made Coker a better source of sensitive information about the darker side of Niceville than anything contained in Boonie Hackendorff's database in the FBI office down in Cap City, which, unknown to Boonie, had already been hacked into by Charlie Danziger, who was no slouch at this sort of thing himself.

So it came to pass that when Edgar Luckinbaugh stood in the dock before Justice Coker, he had also chosen Door Number One.

After his honorable retirement from the Belfair and Cullen County Sheriff's Department a year later, Coker had gotten him a job at the Marriott, Niceville's largest and most luxurious hotel, where all the best people came to stay.

There his bellman duties allowed him to develop a great deal of information about the people who checked in and what business had brought them to town. Most of this information was as deadly dull and boring as the contents of a United Nations press release on anthropogenic climate change.

Some, however, was more intriguing, and Coker had been able to profit from Edgar's researches in various subtle ways, not all of them evil.

A few of them, such as the detection of a brutal pedophile, the exposure of several con men and fraudulent stock promoters, and the arrest of two men wanted for a contract killing in Texas, resulted in real benefit to the people of the town.

In the matter of Harvill Endicott's arrival at the Marriott, Luckinbaugh, an observant fellow, had noted that the airline tags attached to Mr. Endicott's luggage were from an airline that had never offered flights into Mauldar Field, yet Mr. Endicott had arrived in an airport limousine.

This piqued his ex-cop's curiosity.

Then, while shifting Mr. Endicott's extremely weighty luggage about during the man's arrival, Edgar had managed to pass it through the metal detector that he kept in the bellman's locker and found that the larger case was fairly bulging with heavy metal objects.

A moment's work with a pick had revealed to Edgar the contents of Mr. Endicott's case, and an inventory was duly recorded. Particular attention was paid to the Sig Sauer pistol.

Now Edgar was at the registration desk, completing, as quickly as possible, a dossier on a Mr. Harvill Endicott that would, when finalized, be forwarded to Coker for his reading pleasure.

The last element that Edgar managed to extract during his investigation was that Mr. Endicott, a single business traveler, had ordered up two cars, one of them a highly visible black Cadillac and the other a horrid Toyota Corolla, tan in color, that was so utterly invisible as to be a perfect surveillance vehicle.

During his time as an investigator with the county, Edgar and his partners had frequently deployed exactly that sort of anonymous Japanese vehicle to great effect. Interesting.

Very interesting.

Deitz Was in the Wind

Endicott, thinking about the Deitz thing in his hotel room the morning after the accident, got it almost exactly right. Spectacular though it had certainly been, Byron Deitz missed the part where the deer hit the windshield because he was lying in a heap on the floor of the prisoner compartment with blood bubbling out of a dented nose and his mind in a far-off world where bright blue butterflies sang arias from *Rigoletto* in tiny voices that sounded like wind chimes. This fleeting diversion came to an abrupt end as the leading edge of the marshals' van hit the wall of pines and came to a sudden stop, unlike everything inside it that wasn't strapped down, including Nick Kavanaugh and Byron Deitz.

However, Deitz had not traveled quite as far as Nick, who didn't come to a halt until he hit what was left of the—fortunately springy—mesh cage behind the driver's seat. Deitz slid only thirty-nine and a half inches, since that was the length of the chain that ran from his ankle to a ringbolt welded to the floor of the van.

The chain stopped Deitz from breaking his neck on a stanchion behind the passenger seat, but it also wrenched his ankle as it snapped taut at the end of its length. The pain in his ankle overrode the pain in his nose—it was of a far higher order—and jerked Deitz out of singing-blue-butterfly world and back into full consciousness.

He lay there, blinking up at the side of the van, wondering for a time how the side of the van came to be the *ceiling* of the van. Further, how did everything get all red and sticky and why did the van smell like a butcher shop? While he was on the subject, how did he get all covered in gore and bits of squishy stuff?

He closed his eyes, regrouped, shook his head, regretted that immediately, and opened his eyes again. He saw Nick Kavanaugh lying in a crumpled heap, jammed up against what looked like part of the prisoner cage. His chest was going up and down pretty regularly, but there was a gash over his left eye and he was covered in blood and tiny pink bits of something that could have been bone.

Still alive, Deitz thought.

Hopefully not for long.

After wiggling his toes and fingers, Deitz managed to get it together enough to sit up and brace his back against the wall—no, the roof—of the van. He looked around and tried to piece it all together.

Up front, two dead deputies.

Wrapped around said deputies, something large and furry and shapeless, with hooves.

Blood and chunky bits and glass all over everywhere.

Van lying on its side.

Conclusion: they'd hit a deer.

Deitz figured the driver had gotten distracted by the fact that his brother-in-law over there had just pounded him into La-La Land. With one punch.

For a mid-sized switchblade of a guy, Nick could hit damn hard. If they ever had a rematch, Deitz was going to bring a baseball bat.

He leaned back, touched his nose—that hurt—moved his right leg—that hurt too—and considered the current state of affairs.

No sirens yet.

So this just happened.

The deputies are dead.

Nick isn't.

Yet.

I'm alive, but chained to the floor.

Or the wall.

Whatever.

First thing on the To-Do List.

Get free.

How?

Get the key.

It wasn't a pleasant task, dealing with the key, which was in the female marshal's coat pocket, under a pile of deer bits and gore.

But Deitz was motivated.

He got the key.

Andy Chu was one of those Asian guys who don't actually have an actual age. If he wore a ball cap backwards and rode a skateboard you'd figure he was maybe twelve, a skinny butter-colored kid with big black eyes pulled up at the corners and ears that stuck out in a wonderfully presidential way.

Put him in a pair of baggy flannel pants and a checkered shirt that flopped around his skinny ass and you'd . . . well, you'd have Andy Chu, sitting at his desk in the IT offices of BD Securicom playing World of Warcraft online—his avatar was a seven-foot-tall Viking named Ragnarok who had a magical battle-axe and a hauberk of solid gold and all the Valkyrie chicks were totally crazy with cyber-desire for him and Chu was about to manifest a gigantic—of course his cell phone rings.

He picked it up with a weary sigh and looked at the call display.

CHESTER MERKLE

Who the hell was Chester Merkle?

Only one way to find out.

He hit ANSWER and complicated his already complicated life beyond all recognition.

Chu got to the construction yard trailer that Deitz was hiding in about forty minutes later. He'd passed the scene of the crash a mile back. The big blue van was lying on its side, surrounded by cop cars and ambulances and fire trucks. Men and women in various uniforms were milling about in brisk and purposeful ways and a medevac chopper was just settling onto the northbound lane as a wide, fleshy woman tightly constricted by the black and tan uniform of the County Sheriff's Department waved him through.

According to the directions Deitz had given him, the trailer was being used as an office for a large quarry operation, recently shut down, probably because of the recession. The owner of the quarry was a guy named Chester Merkle.

The actual Chester Merkle was off seeing Bruges with Mrs. Merkle and her younger sister, Lillian, for whom Chester Merkle had a secret longing that he would once again fail to consummate in Bruges, even though he was paying for the whole damn trip.

Chu pulled up in his navy blue Lexus and stopped at the chain-link fence with the faded sign on it that read:

MERKLE'S QUARRY
IF YOU WANT TO POUND SAND
YOU'VE COME TO THE RIGHT PLACE

Chu shut the engine off. The trailer, a double-wide, had a sagging roof and the windblown sand had blasted off most of what may have been its pale gray paint. There was chicken wire over the windows and the door, which was shut, had a large steel padlock on it. There was no sign of Byron Deitz and Chu was giving serious thought to just starting the car up and driving away when he heard Deitz's voice, from a distance, echoing around the huge sandy pit beyond the gate.

"Get out of the car."

This is where he shoots me, Chu was thinking, but he got out anyway because what the hell else was he going to do? He stood beside the vehicle, waiting for a bullet with an air of dignified resignation that was a credit to his line.

"Open all the doors."

Chu did just that, all four of them.

"Now the hatch."

Chu did, although it seemed unlikely that if he *had* called the cops, there would actually exist anywhere on the planet a cop stupid enough to let himself get picked as the guy who has to get into the trunk.

"Step away from the car."

Chu did this too.

There was a shuffle of gravel and Byron Deitz slid clumsily down a rock pile off to Chu's left, where he had been waiting all along.

Since Andy Chu hadn't been fully filled in on all the details of Deitz's escape, this barefoot apparition in a blood-soaked jumpsuit limping towards him with blood running from his bashed-in nose and a large pistol in his hand, the muzzle pointing directly at Chu's crotch, gave him a bit of a shock.

"Jesus," he said, in spite of himself. "What happened?"

"We hit a deer," said Deitz, as he came up, bringing with him the reek of blood and sweat.

Up close he looked worse.

"You bring what I asked?"

"It's in the trunk."

"Move back here."

Chu did, and watched as Deitz stripped out of his jumpsuit—naked he was all muscle and beef and bone—and cleaned himself off with the Wet Wipes as much as he could—brisk, efficient work—Byron Deitz was fully alive to the situation he was now in.

Then he pulled on the Securicom uniform that Chu had taken from the change room locker, a crisp white shirt with black shoulder flashes and black slacks with a thin red stripe down the sides. The uniform belonged to Ray Cioffi, who was off duty and, conveniently, about Deitz's size and weight. It took Deitz a few minutes to get squared away, during which Andy Chu looked into the sky expecting to see a chopper and then down the lane expecting to see red and blue flashing lights.

But nothing came.

It would.

Within an hour the state chopper had overflown this site and shortly after that a cruiser came down the lane to check the trailer and the grounds, but Deitz was ex-FBI and he knew how to clean a scene. The troopers walked around the site, rattled the lock on the gate, climbed the fence to check the door of the trailer, but there was nothing to see. Since they didn't think that anyone had gotten into the trailer they didn't look inside it, and it followed that they didn't find Chester Merkle's phone inside, and therefore they didn't check whether any calls had been made from the phone, because if they had, they would have seen a number that, shortly afterwards, they might have discovered belonged to a man named Andy Chu, who worked at BD Securicom. And that would have been that. But they didn't, so it wasn't.

Back at the scene of the rollover they had brought in the dogs, who got one snootful of all the guts and gore scattered all over the place and, after a whispered conference, expressed their regrets and respectfully declined to participate.

So, all in all, a bit of a failure on the part of local law enforcement.

By the time they were fully into the challenging work of failing to detect anything remotely useful, Byron Deitz and Andy Chu, taking the side roads, were well on their way to Andy Chu's neat wood-frame rancher at 237 Bougainville Terrace in the Saddle Hill neighborhood of southwestern Niceville.

Chu had a garage with an automatic door, so Deitz stayed low until Chu got the Lexus parked inside and shut the engine down, his heart going like one of those miniature gas engines they put in model planes. Much to his surprise, Deitz didn't shoot him as soon as the garage door powered down.

"Got anything to eat?" was what he said.

Well, not quite exactly.

Because of his nose, it actually came out as, "God addy ding doo ead?"

Either way, it eased Chu's mind.

For now.

The Shocking Price of Arugula

Around noon on the same Thursday that Mr. Endicott was reviewing his options in his suite at the Marriott, pain brought Nick back out of the dark. He was dimly aware of previous periods of consciousness occurring randomly through a long and difficult night, fragmented images of doctors frowning at him under cold blue lights, and two large nurses standing over him, talking across his naked body, in Italian, about the shocking price of arugula.

This more recent awakening, into a milky light pouring through a window, seemed nearly normal, as if he were coming out of a sound sleep.

He opened an eye and Kate was looking back at him, her face drawn and pale.

She smiled at him, leaned forward, and kissed him on the cheek. She smelled wonderful. He hoped he did too, but he doubted it. Kate leaned back in the chair, still holding his hand.

"You're supposed to say 'Where am I?' "

Nick tried a smile.

It hurt, but he did it anyway.

"Where am I?"

"Lady Grace. It's about noon Thursday. The day after you were in the accident. Basically, they say you're fine. I have no idea how, but they say you are. Your eye is okay, they just put a bandage on it to protect the bone around the socket. You cracked something called the supraorbital process. You're only groggy because they sedated you. They had to. You were thrashing around a lot and they couldn't get any X-ray images. You also have an injury to the knuckles of your right hand that the doctors—and I—believe may have been acquired just prior to the rollover."

Nick lifted his right hand.

The knuckles were swollen and there was a spreading bruise along the back of his hand.

"I may have punched Byron in the nose."

"That's what I thought. Good for you."

"How do I look?"

"Like a public service announcement."

"That bad?"

"No. Not really. As I said, you're basically okay. The doctors think you're made out of hickory. The X-rays showed nothing. They say anybody else would have cracked a rib or broken his neck. But not you."

This was said with a tremor, but she rode on over it.

"You have a lot of Niceville friends, Nick, for a boy from Away who's only been in town for three years. Your partner, that nice lad Beau Norlett, he was here earlier, but he had to go on a call. Tig Sutter looked in. Jimmy Candles and Marty Coors and Mickey Hancock. Lemon Featherlight was here, out in the hall, talking to Rainey. Mavis Crossfire phoned to ask about you. And I saw Charlie Danziger in the lobby and he was asking after you."

"Where Charlie Danziger is, there's usually a Coker."

"No. Coker and every other county cop are all out looking for Byron. Along with most of the CID and a lot of the state guys too."

"Maybe I should have punched him harder."

"Maybe you should have. Just out of curiosity, why did you punch him at all? Other than because he's a mean stupid bully who richly deserves a beating. I loathe all bullies. I surely do."

Nick told her, the short version.

"And that's when the deer showed up? While everybody in the van was yelling at you?"

"Basically."

Kate smiled, her eyes bright, tears welling up behind them.

"You could have been killed, Nick. You toad. Then where would my life be?"

Nick put his hand back on top of hers, said nothing, but held it there until she cried it out a bit. She took a tissue from a box on the table beside the bed, held it to her eyes, rubbed her nose, crumpled it into a ball inside her fist.

"There are people in the hall, waiting to see you."

"Rainey?"

"And Axel. And Hannah. And Beth. And Boonie Hackendorff. Also Reed—"

"Reed. How is he?"

"He's fine. I mean, physically. Emotionally, he's pretty banged up. Marty Coors put him on suspension until the inquiry is over."

"Still has a badge and a gun?"

"Yes. But no regular duty. For now."

"What the hell happened?"

"You don't know?"

"No. I checked out right after Boonie told me that people got killed."

Kate told him the story, including the final butcher's bill. Eight dead—one more hanging on in the OR but expected to go soon—thirteen injured, four seriously. The traumas were down at Sorrows in Cap City. The rest were here in Lady Grace, including the dead ones down in the morgue.

Nick listened carefully, seeing it play out on the movie screen at the back of his skull.

"What'd those truckers think it was, the Indy 500? Lined up along the road like it was a claiming race? Jesus. Stupid as hell."

"Yes. It was stupid. It wasn't Reed's fault at all. The men in the Viper were shooting at him. Reed thought they'd be just as happy shooting at the people lined up at the Super Gee. Marty Coors was telling him to back off, and then the men in the Viper jammed on the brakes. Reed tried to swerve, but not soon enough—"

"There's not a lot of leeway at two hundred miles an hour."

"No, there isn't. But you know how it is. Civilians get killed during a police chase, even if it's their own damn fault, somebody in a uniform has to pay."

"What about the guys Reed was chasing?"

Kate made a face.

"The Brothers Shagreen? What do you always say? Best thing you could say about them is they're dead. One of them, I think his name was Dwayne Bobby, was still alive at midnight, but I don't think anybody was going to heroic lengths to save him. He died by two in the morning. It's possible one of the OR nurses was standing on his oxygen tube at the time. They're not down in the morgue with the good people, by the way. State is holding them in a refrigerated meat truck at their HQ."

"In that line of truckers, was there anyone we know?"

"Yes. Billy Dials' brother."

"Jeez. Mikey?"

"Yes. He was killed. Not instantly. It was bad. Billy's taking it pretty bad. They were close."

"Anybody else?"

"No one we know. Thank God. Will you see Rainey? He's pretty upset. About you. And he's been having a tough time lately. At school. Now Axel is catching it too."

"Catching what?"

Kate filled him in on the bullying that was going on, Coleman and what Kate was calling his "minions."

"Marty's kid is in on this?"

"According to Rainey and Axel."

"Of course. Send him in. If Axel's there, send him in too."

"They'll only let one person in at a time."

"Okay. Start with Rainey, then."

Kate got up and went to the door, while Nick managed to get himself into a more upright position. Rainey came in wearing his school uniform and an anxious expression, Kate following behind with a worried look.

Nick gave him a smile and Rainey put out a hand for a formal shake. They hadn't reached the hugging stage yet. Perhaps they never would, although Nick was ready to try. Rainey studied Nick's face while they shook, as if searching for something.

"God, Nick," he said, after a moment. "You look awful."

"Thanks, kid," Nick said, smiling—his smile wasn't reassuring, but he hadn't seen his face in a mirror yet. "You look pretty good yourself."

"What was it like?"

"The rollover?"

"Yeah. Was it scary?"

"No. It was sort of . . . busy. A lot going on."

"Kate says it was a deer?"

"Yes. A buck, actually."

"And those two marshals got killed by it?"

"Yes," said Nick, pushing the image down.

"The deer—the buck—was it standing in the road?"

"I wasn't looking at the time. But probably not. Probably running along the shoulder, or trying to cross the lane. When a deer thinks it's being chased, it will run straight for a while, and then it will cut sharp, right or left. They're quick and nimble. Whatever's chasing it—a coyote or a cougar—it usually gets deked out of its shorts and the deer's gone. Only when what's chasing the deer is a car, if the deer cuts to the left, he's going to cut right out in front of the car."

Rainey thought this over, filing the data.

"You were with Axel's dad, in the truck. Everybody says he got away."

Nick nodded, feeling suddenly tired.

"Yes. He did."

"Axel's scared of his dad, you know."

"I know, Rainey. I'll talk to him about it."

Rainey saw Nick fading.

He shot a look at Kate, who nodded.

"You coming home soon?"

"I hope so."

"Good."

Something in his expression caught Nick's eye.

"Kate says you and Axel are having trouble at school? With Coleman and those guys? Jay and Owen? When I get out of here, I'll go talk to Little Rock. And Captain Coors. He's a friend of mine. He'll talk to Owen. Okay?"

Rainey shook his head.

"It'll only make it worse. Father Casey already talked to them. It just makes them mad. And then they tell everybody at school that Axel and me are snitches. And wimps."

Rainey paused.

"What I'd like . . ."

"Yes?" said Nick.

"Can't we do something about it ourselves? Me and Axel. We've been talking about it."

Nick glanced at Kate, and then came back to Rainey.

"Like what, Rainey? Axel got into a fight with Coleman. So did you, last week. Do you want to fight him again?"

"We already tried that. You saw what happened. I got my clock cleaned. So did Axel. He's too strong."

"He shouldn't have let it happen at all, Rainey," Kate put in. "He's supposed to be a sportsman, isn't he? Isn't fair play what Regiopolis is all about?"

"Not for us," said Rainey, but softly.

Nick was curious.

"Okay. Fighting didn't work. What would you do, then?"

"Axel says we should tell Coleman that Axel's father escaped so he could come and kill Coleman."

Nick and Kate rolled with that, but it shook them both to hear the venom in Rainey's voice.

"Rainey, I don't think threatening a schoolkid with murder is the way to go here."

Rainey considered it for a while.

"Maybe he could get kidnapped like I did. Only they wouldn't bring *him* back."

Silence followed while Nick and Kate worked out a way to deal with this.

Kate spoke first.

"Rainey, I know Coleman's a bad person, but we don't want something like that to happen to anybody."

"It happened to me."

"Yes, it did," said Nick. "And that sucks. And one day I'll find the people who did it, and we'll make them sorry, won't we?"

"Nick," said Kate, a warning tone, but Rainey cut in.

"We could make Coleman look in the mirror."

"The mirror?" said Kate, her heart in her throat. Rainey turned around and faced her.

"I remembered. The mirror in Moochie's window. I was looking at it the day when it happened—"

"The day what happened?" asked Nick carefully.

"The day I got kidnapped. I was standing on the sidewalk in front of Moochie's. I was looking at the mirror in the window. The gold one with all the curly stuff in the frame. It's really old. We could find out where it is and make him look at it. Maybe he'd disappear too."

They both stared at the kid. And they were both thinking exactly the same thing, because that mirror—the same antique mirror that had been in Moochie's window—was sitting at the back of the linen closet in the hallway outside their bedroom right now, wrapped in a blue blanket. It was still where they had put it six months ago. He knew because he checked it regularly, the way you check a loaded weapon. Had Rainey found it?

Kate was about to ask Rainey exactly that, and Nick was about to stop her, when there was a knock at the door. Kate opened it and Reed Walker was there, in his State uniform, cool and crisp and looking grim, his Stetson in his hand and his thick black hair cropped short.

"Sorry to cut in, Kate—I know, I know—one at a time—but I just got a call and I have to go—I wanted to see Himself—"

Nick admired Reed although he felt that if he stayed at the wheel of a Police Interceptor he was not likely to see the far side of fifty. He sat up and grinned at him as Reed came over and stood by the bed, setting his hand on Rainey's shoulder.

"Christ, Nick, you look—"

"Like a public service announcement?"

Reed showed his teeth, a sardonic smile which furrowed his lean face. Rainey, who seemed to have a case of hero worship when it came to Reed, broke in to ask Reed about the chase, what was it like, who were those two guys in the black Viper, why was the license plate HARLEQUIN, was that a clue?

Reed slowed him down enough to tell him the highlights without dwelling too much on how utterly miserable he was feeling at this moment.

Rainey took it all in, then went back to the bad guys in the Viper.

"But those guys, who were they?"

"A couple of White Power guys. Outlaw bikers. Dwayne Bobby Shagreen and Douglas Loyal Shagreen. Both of them were wanted on multiple felony warrants from all over the South—"

"Where are they now?"

Reed hesitated.

"Well, they're dead, Rainey."

"Yeah. But dead where?"

"In a refrigerated truck parked next to the State Police headquarters in Gracie. Why, you wanna go see 'em?"

Rainey lit up.

"Could I? Could Axel come too?"

Kate, who felt Reed wasn't beyond it, stepped in. "No, you can't. And Axel can't either."

Reed smiled down at Rainey.

"Kid, I saw them. Two huge ugly dead guys. The way they look would give you nightmares. Gonna give me nightmares."

Reed looked back at Nick.

"The heck with the Shagreens. How are you?"

Reed stood for a moment, getting a rundown on Nick's status, his smile fading.

"We haven't got Deitz yet," he said, after Nick had given him a brief sketch of what happened in the van. "No sign of him."

"Somebody's helping him," said Nick.

"Has to be, considering what he was wearing. I understand he might also be wearing a broken nose?"

Nick looked at Kate, who shrugged and smiled.

"Well, I may have adjusted it a bit."

"Was he in shackles?"

"Yep."

"Risky. Was there a camera in the van?"

"Yep."

"Hit him anyway?"

"Yep."

"Why?"

"Seemed like the right thing to do."

"Why are you talking like that Spenser guy in the Robert Parker novels?"

"Am I?"

"Yep."

"You two," said Kate, "should take this act to Vegas."

"Kate tells me Marty has you on a desk?"

Reed's expression shifted into gloom again.

"No. Not on a desk. I'm suspended. Full pay, but don't come into the office until he calls me."

Silence in the room.

Everyone who knew Reed Walker knew that the job—driving an Interceptor—was the central axis of his life. Everything else turned around it. Without that pivot, that center of gravity, what would Reed Walker do? Fly off into space?

Reed shook that off, grinned down at Nick.

"So. Are you gonna lie around here all week nursing your boo-boos or you gonna get up and go looking for Deitz? I figure, since he spent a lot of time smacking Beth around, you and me have a special interest."

Kate was on her feet, the Irish in her rising.

"Reed! Nick's not going anywhere—"

"Is this a bad time?" said a laconic Texas-tinted voice from the door. Everybody turned to look, and there was Boonie Hackendorff filling up the doorway and blocking the light from the hall.

"Yes, it is," said Kate, still winding up.

"Good," said Boonie, stepping lightly through the door, grinning broadly, bringing with him the scent of lime, of cinnamon breath mints and a strong afternote of cigar.

"I hate sneaking sideways into a room. I prefer to make an entrance."

"Fine," said Kate. "Now let's see you make an exit. Nick's only sup-posed to have one visitor at a time. This is turning into a parade."

Reed stepped in.

"Actually, Kate, Boonie's got business with Nick. Beth's here, with the kids. Maybe we can all go get a bite of lunch? Let these two talk."

He looked at Rainey, who was oddly absent. Rainey shook himself, refocused, said, "Sure. Can I have a mimosa?"

Reed looked down at him.

"That troubles me on so many levels, kid."

"Yes, you can have a mimosa," said Kate, taking his hand and pulling Rainey to his feet. "So long as your uncle has a Shirley Temple."

She came over, gave Nick a kiss that he could feel in his knees, gath-ered up her things, shot a glare at Boonie.

"Don't you be dragging my husband off anywhere, Boonie. You follow?"

And they were gone.

There was a silence, while Boonie and Nick considered Kate and all her ways.

"Hell of a girl," said Boonie after a pause. "You ever notice she says 'You follow?' just the way that guy said it in *The Sting*?"

"The big guy, played the Irish hood everybody was so afraid of? Doyle Lonnegan?"

"Robert Shaw."

"Yeah. Now you mention it, she does."

"Consider yourself warned. How you doing, anyway? Can you move around at all?"

"What do you have in mind?"

"Think you can make it to the morgue downstairs?"

"I look that bad?"

Boonie's jovial mood darkened.

"No. I mean, it's . . . Look, I got a problem here, and I don't want to take it back to D.C., or even to the rest of my people at Cap City."

"Why me?"

"Nick, when you were in the war, I guess you saw a lot of dead bodies, right? Maybe saw a lot of weird shit?"

Nick gave him a sideways look.

"You could say. That's what war is all about. Stacking up those dead guys. Plus there were cookies."

Boonie looked pained, embarrassed.

"Jeez, Nick. I meant no disrespect. I'm asking a serious question. I know it's maybe stuff you don't wanna talk about, but I can't think of anybody else to ask."

"This all about a particular dead body?"

Boonie looked down at his hands.

"Yeah. It is. Thing is, nobody—right now anyway—nobody can know I'm asking you in on this. I mean, the jurisdictional thing and all. There'd be blowback out of D.C., maybe even with the State guys. Not Marty Coors, no. Nor Mickey Hancock . . . plus, there are . . . other things, about this body, details I don't want to see go anywhere else. I know I can trust you to shut up. I'm not sure about the rest of my guys downtown. This is career death for me, I handle it wrong. Like I said, can you move?"

"I can sure as hell get my ass downstairs."

Boonie looked uneasy, but committed.

"You not gonna faint on me, or pitch a fit? 'Cause if you do, Kate will surely tear me a new—"

"I'm fine. I promise I won't die on you."

Boonie took it in, nodded.

"Can we do it now? I got a guy with a wheelchair outside. You can ride down—"

Nick was already standing, in his slippers, reaching for a thick blue robe. He lashed it tight around his waist, looked white around the edges, got his color back, and said, "Let's go."

Boonie was going for the door.

"I'll go get the wheelchair guy—"

"Boonie, you bring a wheelchair into this room, and you'll need a flashlight and a crowbar to get yourself free of it again. You follow?"

"I follow."

Coker and Charlie Danziger Have Another Frank Exchange of Views

Charlie Danziger was aware that he reminded people of Sam Elliott—he was tall and lean and craggy and he had a big white mustache, and now that he wasn't with the State Patrol anymore he wore his faded blond hair on the longish side. So Charlie Danziger, who liked to think of himself as an original, did what was possible within the narrow scope of choice that nature had given him to counteract that effect.

This afternoon he was counteracting the Sam Elliott effect by sitting on the front porch of his ranch house in the foothills of the Belfair Range, watching his horses run on the downslope of his front forty while drinking Italian Pinot Grigio, a flowery white wine from Valdadige that Danziger was convinced the real Sam Elliott wouldn't tolerate as a barbecue starter.

The anti–Sam Elliott effect of this was diminished a bit by the fact that he was wearing a clean white shirt and a pair of boot-cut jeans faded by the actual sun and he had on the battered bloodstained old navy blue Lucchese cowboy boots that he was, in his own eccentric circle, notorious for.

The noon hour of this lazy Thursday was passing, sliding into the west—and the sun was putting a hazy autumn glow on the Belfair Range behind him and on the black hides of the six Tennessee Walker–Morgan crosses that he was letting run wild down the hill. A lovely sight, marred only by the tan-colored County Sheriff's Department car that was rolling along the Cullen County side road about a mile away.

Danziger eased himself forward in the old wooden chair he was sitting on, groaning as he did so since the bullet hole in the right side of his chest still smarted a bit, even after all these months. Perhaps if he'd had the slug taken out by an ER doctor instead of an Italian dentist named Donny Falcone it wouldn't be smarting quite so much.

However, since he'd acquired the chest wound by getting himself shot by a guy who had, just two hours before, helped him rob the First Third Bank in Gracie, Danziger took the view that going to a real ER doctor instead of Donnie Falcone would have been a bad decision.

Danziger bore the guy who shot him no grudge since the guy, a decent enough fellow named Merle Zane, had only shot him because Danziger had shot Merle Zane first, and in the back at that.

Danziger leaned forward in the chair, poured himself a fresh glass of wine, watching the distant dust trail of that County car as it got closer and closer. It was slowing now, getting ready to make the turn into the long gravel drive that curled and wandered its way up the quarter-mile-long grassy slope to Danziger's place.

It was too far away to make out the markings. Could just be a social call. Danziger, ex–State Patrol, was on good terms with local law enforcement, good enough to go fishing down in Canticle Key with Marty Coors and Jimmy Candles and Boonie Hackendorff, all of them members of the same National Guard unit.

Still . . .

He reached down beside him and picked up the Winchester carbine that was leaning on the wall. He didn't have to rack it to put a round in the chamber. That was movie stuff, done mainly for the sound effect.

If a gun isn't loaded, it's a paperweight, his sainted mother used to say, usually when she was getting loaded herself.

He cocked the hammer back, sighed heavily, got to his feet with a groan, and walked to the edge of the porch, setting his glass down on the railing and holding the Winchester muzzle down along the seam of his pants.

He squinted a bit against the glare of the sun on the patrol car windshield as it made the final turn and rolled up the grade, coming to a stop in the middle of the turning circle.

At this range, Danziger ID'd the car by its numbers. It was Coker's official ride. He was a staff sergeant in the County Sheriff's Department.

Coker was from Billings. Danziger was born in Bozeman. They were a year apart in age, Coker fifty-two, Danziger fifty-three. They'd met in the Corps a long time back and were about as tight as two cranky twice-divorced cops could manage. Danziger kept the Winchester in close and waited.

Coker shut the engine down, popped the door, and got out slowly, six feet of ropy muscle with skin tanned copper brown. He leaned his left hand on the roof of the cruiser and smiled across it at Danziger. Danziger figured his right hand was resting on the butt of his service Beretta.

"You gonna shoot me with that carbine, Charlie?"

"Depends on why you're here, Coker."

"Guess you've heard the news?"

"Deitz is out."

"Yes."

Coker ran his left hand through his bristles, set it back on the roof.

"Sorta complicates things a bit, I guess."

Danziger nodded, cracked a big smile.

"Got that right, my friend."

A silence.

"Well, you gonna offer me a beer, or what?"

"Outta beer. How about a glass of wine?"

"Jeez," said Coker, wincing. "That Dago cat piss all you got?"

"Might have a lime cordial back there."

Coker laughed, a short sharp bark, pushed himself off the roof of the cruiser, and came around the front. He was in his patrol uniform, tan with brown flashes, his six-pointed gold sheriff star glittering in the afternoon light. He came to the foot of the stairs, looked up at Danziger.

"I guess we need to talk."

"I always hated that phrase. Whenever Barbara used it, I knew I was in deep shit."

"Well," said Coker, grinning up at him, "I believe that about covers the situation."

Danziger went inside and brought out the bottle, frosty from the cooler, and a heavy glass tumbler for Coker. Coker was sitting in the other ancient wooden chair, tilted back against the boards, his boots up on the railing. Danziger, looking at him, got that classic image of Henry Fonda as Wyatt Earp in *My Darling Clementine*.

He handed him the tumbler, sat down in the other chair, tilted it back against the wall. Boots on the railing. His bloodstained blue cowboy boots. Coker sipped his wine, cradled the tumbler in his hands, and nodded at Danziger's boots.

"Them's what did us in, my friend. Those damn blue boots."

"*Them's?*"

"Okay. *Those.* If you hadn't worn them to the fucking robbery, then that Thad Llewellyn banker guy wouldn't have told Deitz that one of the gunmen was wearing blue cowboy boots and Deitz wouldn't have put you and them—*those*—boots together."

"I wore them because they're my lucky boots."

"So you keep telling me. Only reason Deitz hasn't told the cops yet is they haven't let him off the Raytheon beef. If they had cut that deal when they still had him, we'd be playing out the last part of your favorite movie right now."

"*The Wild Bunch?*"

"Yeah. At the end, where they fight the whole Mexican army and they all get killed."

Coker was right.

Coker was the best police sniper in this part of the state. They called him in for all the really bad ones. Coker was also the guy waiting in the Belfair Range when those four cops came barreling up the defile, right on their asses, he and Merle Zane with the black Magnum.

Coker had taken out the two media types in the news chopper first and then all four of the pursuit cars. Five rounds from the Barrett .50 he had borrowed from Armories.

Six dead.

The take had added up to two million one hundred and sixty-three thousand dollars, plus random jewelry from the safety-deposit boxes.

And one stainless-steel box with a Raytheon logo on it. Inside that, the disk-shaped guidance module that Coker had named the cosmic Frisbee.

If you had asked either of these men why they did that, robbed the bank, took the cash, killed four cops—being cops *themselves*—well, both of them would have looked at you for a long while and then one or the other of them would have said something along the lines of *who is this asshole and how did he get in here?*

Coker sipped at his drink again, and they sat there for a bit, watching the stud horses gallop on the hillside.

"So," said Coker, after a while. "Got any suggestions?"

"I been thinking about it, ever since I heard. Coupla things come to mind."

"And . . ."

"You could shoot me out of hand, right now, tell everybody you just dropped in and found me counting the cash, and then we slapped leather."

"Slapped leather?"

"You know. Had a gunfight."

"*Slapped leather?*"

"It's from the movies, dammit."

"What was the movie? *Cabaret?*"

"Okay. Forget that," said Danziger. "Where's the cash now?"

"It's not cash anymore. Got it into the Mondex system."

"How'd you do that?"

"Boxed it up and FedEx'd it to our guy at that limey bank in the Channel Islands."

"Boxed it up? *Boxed it up?* Are you fucking nuts, Coker? What did you say it was?"

"Tax records. Nothing bores the shit out of people more than tax records."

"Did it get there?"

Coker reached into his shirt pocket, pulled out two navy blue cards, each with a large gold chip embedded in it. Embossed on the front side, in holograms, were the letters PNG BANK. He held the cards out to Danziger.

"Pick a card. Any card."

Danziger took the one on the left, flipped it over. There was no signature line. Just a small square of dots made for a scanner.

"What's the PNG Bank?"

"Papua New Guinea. Based in Port Moresby. Our guy says Qadaffi was one of their clients."

"Well, if they're good enough for Muhammar . . . this one of those, what you call 'em . . . ?"

"Used to be called Mondex cards. These are sorta like those, but all the data is triple encrypted. They can be traced, but it's not easy, especially if they get churned by the holding bank."

"What's *churned* . . . no, never mind. I could give a shit. What's on them? I mean, how much?"

"Little over a million on each. That includes the money we took from Deitz for giving him back his cosmic Frisbee."

"That was five hundred thousand. Plus two million one hundred and sixty three thousand from Gracie—"

"Minus the one hundred thousand you stuck in the back of Deitz's Hummer when you were putting the Frisbee in the glove box."

Danziger was quiet for a time, doing the math.

"We're short maybe four hundred thousand."

"Cost of doing business."

"With the limey?"

"Yeah. He had to clean a lot of currency. Sixty pounds of it. I say four large for a service like that is dirt cheap. Anybody we could have taken it to in Atlanta or Vegas would have asked for fifty percent."

Danziger studied the card for a while.

"Is this safe to use?"

"It's not like a credit card or an ATM card. It's more like a computer and a cell phone. You can send cash over the phone, you can use any kind of currency, and if the guy you're dealing with has a Mondex card too, then you can just transfer cash back and forth right there on the street. No bills no coins no receipts. No stores, no banks with security cameras—"

"So it's just like cash?"

"Yeah. Only it's all on that computer chip there."

"What if I lose it?"

"Like I said. It's cash. You'd be fucked."

Danziger nodded, slipped the card into his shirt pocket.

"You okay with this?" Coker asked.

"Hell, I'm fine with it. But it kills Plan B."

"Which was?"

"Plant the cash somewhere where Deitz controls the facility, and then rat him out. Not even Deitz could talk his way out of actually having all the stolen cash in his possession."

"Wouldn't have worked."

"Why not?"

"The Feds went all over everything Deitz owned, home and office and his beach house. Deitz cooperated, because he knew damn well he didn't have the cash. It turns up later, someplace they already looked, not even the Feds would buy it."

Danziger had nothing to say to that.

"Besides," said Coker, pouring himself more wine, "there's Twyla."

Twyla Littlebasket was Coker's girlfriend. She was a Cherokee dental hygienist, formerly employed by Donnie Falcone. She wore tight-fitting powder blue dental hygienist smocks that buttoned all the way down the front, and white stockings. Her father had been Morgan Littlebasket right up until six months ago, when he flew his plane into the side of Tallulah's Wall. Twyla had brown eyes and long black hair as shiny as a crow's wing. A figure that could cause heart palpitations in a yak.

Due to an oversight, Twyla had stumbled on the cash one day shortly after the robbery, mainly because Danziger had left it lying out on the counter at Coker's place.

They had talked about shooting her but neither of them could bring himself to shoot a sexy dental hygienist in a baby blue dress that buttoned all the way down the front.

So they'd cut her in for a share instead, which she took, smiling sweetly even though it made her part of the conspiracy and therefore as guilty as they were, which didn't really bother her because, deep down, she had larceny in her the way crocodiles have teeth.

"What about her? She worried about Deitz?"

"She's fretting. I told her we'd come up with something. She said it was too late for stratagems and schemes. She said there was only one sensible thing to do."

"What was it?"

"We go find Deitz and kill him."

"Did she? My, my. Our Twyla continues to amaze. Well, I'm game. The field is going to be a bit crowded. Every law enforcement guy in the state is thinking exactly the same thing. Plus remember that guy, the guy who found out Twyla's dad was taking pictures of her in the shower, got ahold of them and e-mailed them to Twyla?"

"Tony Bock."

"Yeah. Him. Remember what he said, when you and Twyla paid him a call?"

"After he pissed himself and fainted, or before?"

"Didn't he say that Deitz's IT guy, Andy Chu, was blackmailing Deitz? That he had film of Deitz meeting with the Chinese?"

"Yeah. I put that fact in my back pocket, figured we could use Chu for something, down the line."

"What was he blackmailing Deitz with?"

Coker turned it around in his mind.

"Chu probably knew about the deal with the Chinese."

"Wasn't there something about four guys in Leavenworth?"

"Yeah. You're right. Mafia guys, if I recall. Heavy hitters. Bock said that Chu found out Deitz had fucked them on an inside job back when he was with the FBI. When it went south and the Feds were closing in, Deitz cut a deal in exchange for testimony. They let him resign, and the four Mafia guys went to Leavenworth."

"Where they still are?"

"Far as I know," said Coker, patting his tunic for a cigarette, pulling out a pack of Camels, offering one to Danziger.

"You figure they got a TV in Leavenworth?"

"Sure."

"You figure they saw Deitz on it, getting busted for taking down a bank and walking away with a couple of million?"

Coker inhaled on the cigarette, blew it out, grinned through the smoke at Danziger.

"Charlie, I do believe you're not just a pretty face after all."

"Thank you."

"Mafia guys have long memories. If they think Deitz has money—"

"They'll send somebody."

"Maybe already have."

"Could be."

A silence, while they worked out the angles.

"Okay. Crowded field," said Coker, "but we gotta do it. Law is one thing, but if a mob enforcer gets to Deitz and puts real voltage through his nuptials—"

"We'll be next. Guy won't give a shit about due process or evidence. He'll come right at us. Come to think of it, that's probably what Deitz is planning to do right now, wherever he is."

"Be nice to know who this mob enforcer guy is."

Another silence. Danziger broke it.

"Who was this guy Edgar Luckinbaugh was going on about?"

Coker took a sip of his Pinot Grigio, silently wished for bourbon, set the glass down.

"The guy who checked into the Marriott?"

"Yeah. Orville Hender-something."

"Harvill Endicott."

"Edgar said he had a shitload of heavy metal in his case. A Sig, couple of boxes of ammo. Some gear looks like an interrogation kit. Rented two cars. Caddy and a shit-box rice burner. Think he's the guy from Leavenworth?"

Coker thought it over.

"Edgar said he looked more like a dying minister on the run with the poor box. Tall skinny guy, old as dirt, sort of a pale blue-looking guy, according to Edgar. Bloodless. Sound like a Mafia shooter to you?"

"Yes," said Danziger, with feeling. "He does."

Coker glanced over at Danziger, nodded.

"Duly noted. We get a moment, let's go look him over. From a distance. Sound good?"

"No. We get a look at him and maybe he gets a look at us looking at him. If he's a smart guy, he'll know why we're tailing him. I say we put Edgar on him. He used to be an investigator with the county. A pretty good one. He's got the street smarts, and he's done surveillance before."

Coker wasn't sold.

"Single-man surveillance is a bitch. And what if he gets burned and the guy turns around on him?"

"Better Edgar than us. Besides, he could use the money. Being a bell-hop pays poorly."

Coker thought it over.

"Okay. Works for me. Will you put him on it? Tell him we'll pay five hundred a day."

"He'll have to call in sick at the hotel."

"Five hundred a day ought to cover that."

"Okay. I'll call him today."

"Tell him to be careful, will you?"

"I will. So Twyla says we gotta kill Deitz?"

Coker nodded absently, watching the horses wander, thinking about Harvill Endicott.

"Twyla have any suggestions on how we were supposed to find Deitz? I mean, everybody in the state is looking for him, but they haven't got him yet. That means somebody's helping him."

They both sat and watched the horses. Danziger was thinking that if there was such a thing as reincarnation, it wouldn't be so bad to come back as a stud horse.

"I got a theory about how we find Deitz," said Coker, after a pause. "We wait a while, he'll come barreling right up that road, guns a-blazing."

"I thought about that, and we can't let that happen."

"Why not? You think we'd lose?"

"Think about it. Deitz gets free, any normal guy in his situation is gonna try for Mexico or Canada. But instead he comes straight at you and me? Even if we kill him, a lot of people are going to wonder why he did a crazy thing like that."

Coker mulled that over.

"Good point. So what do we do?"

"Somebody's helping him, right? I mean, hiding him and backing him up. Maybe whoever it is, he's already dead in his own basement and Deitz is using his car and his money. Otherwise Deitz would already be back in jail. So think about it, Coker. If it's not Phil Holliman, who basically hates Deitz's guts, who's the next logical choice?"

Coker thought about it for a while. Danziger went to dig out another bottle of Santa Margherita. When he came back, Coker was just shutting down his cell phone. He grinned at Danziger, a berserk light in his yellow-flecked eyes that always made Danziger feel like smiling.

"Guess who's not at work today?"

Dead Man Talking

Like most morgues, the morgue in Lady Grace Hospital was in the sub-subbasement. When the elevator doors slid back, both Boonie and Nick got that smell right away. Bad meat and Lysol and Dustbane and clammy air. Death itself. A long, narrow corridor, badly lit, filled with voices and bustle but nobody visible. As they walked down the hall they passed a couple of autopsy rooms, figures in dark green scrubs bending over something laid out on a steel table, bare feet sticking out, as blue as Indian corn, the figures talking low, heads together, hands working. Blood on their sleeves. That god-awful fluorescent bar hanging low overhead as if these guys were playing poker instead of turning a human body into a meat canoe.

They passed on down without looking in and saying hello and nobody came out to ask them what their business was, if any.

At the far end of the long dark hallway was a set of stainless-steel doors. No windows. When they got close, a short, blocky Hispanic attendant pushing a gurney emerged from a side hall and banged the big steel button that opened the double doors. While they hissed open he noticed Boonie and Nick coming down the hall, and his face opened up in a cheerful grin.

"Special Agent Hackendorff," he said, in a thick Spanish accent. "You in here again?"

"I am," said Boonie, as the Hispanic guy looked Nick over, Nick in his hospital gown and paper slippers and big blue bathrobe.

"You brought one that can walk?" said the attendant. "Usually we have to roll them in. Like this one," he said, tapping the sheet covering the corpse. The dead man's feet were sticking out. They were still pink.

"Looks new," said Boonie.

The guy nodded.

"He's number nine. They just lost him. We're putting him in cadaver storage with the other eight. Hell of a thing, that Super Gee thing. Niceville gets weirder every year."

He looked over at Nick, smiled.

"I'm Hector. You look familiar."

"I'm Nick Kavanaugh."

"Thought so. Seen you around. You're with the CID, right?"

Boonie was shaking his head.

"Hector, Nick's not with the CID. Nick's not even here. Nick never was here. You follow?"

Hector looked puzzled, and then he brightened.

"Oh yeah. I get it. The Traveling Dude in Drawer Nineteen."

"That's right," said Boonie.

Hector tapped his nose, turned away, and pushed the gurney through the doors and on into a large, harshly lit, and chilly room lined in steel doors, three high and covering both walls.

Waving over his shoulder, he disappeared into what looked like a large meat locker at the far end of the room. Boonie led Nick over to a stack of drawers, the last one on the left. Each drawer had a stainless-steel door on it, marked only by a number. Number 19 was the middle door in the stack.

Boonie stopped in front of it, sighed, and seemed to slump into himself.

"Not sure I'm up to this," he said, smiling at Nick. "Ever since I ran into this case I haven't been myself. Now I'm about to do it to you."

Nick considered Boonie's face, all the humor gone from it, and the new age lines around his eyes.

"If you can handle it, so can I."

Boonie nodded, tugged at the latch, and opened the door. There was a body inside, naked under a sheet of plastic, lying on a steel shelf. Frigid air flowed out from the compartment and pooled around their feet. The air smelled of stale meat and frost. Boonie rolled the shelf out and stood on the far side, facing Nick across the corpse.

"Do it," said Nick.

Boonie pulled the plastic sheet back, revealing the pale blue body of a middle-aged man, lean and well muscled, with an ugly purple burn scar running from his left pectoral up the left side of his neck. He might have been a good-looking man in life, but now he was a horror. His eyes were two ragged black pits filled with dried blood. Pieces were missing from his cheeks. His nose was gone, nothing left of it but torn cartilage. His left ear had been bitten off and his right earlobe was just a bloody nub. His lips were gone, revealing a set of strong white teeth in a ghastly parody of a smile.

The autopsy docs had sliced him open from his throat down to his crotch, the classic Y-shaped incision used to open up a body. He had been stitched back together, not carefully, with thick black nylon thread. There was what looked like an entrance wound in his throat, right under the jaw, made by a small-caliber weapon.

Nick looked up at Boonie.

"This is Merle Zane, right?"

Boonie nodded.

"In the flesh. Mostly. I've been keeping him on ice for six months now. Let me lay it out for you, you'll see why. Fingerprints match a Merle Zane, born in Harrisburg, Pennsylvania, November 17, 1968, raced stock cars—made it to NASCAR—no priors until he was booked into Angola on an aggravated assault beef after he took a tire iron to a couple of pit guys. Did five years. Out for good behavior. Was working for a couple of classic car dealers called the Bardashi Brothers. No idea how he got recruited into the Gracie thing. But this is him. They found him lying up against a tree, in that big old pine forest that runs up into the Belfair Range. Maybe two miles from the Belfair Saddlery. As you can see, he's been chewed on a bit, coons and coyotes and such, and he's got that hole in his throat there. It's a through-and-through. Left a much bigger hole on its way out the back of his neck. Docs found fragments of a .38-caliber slug buried near the top of his spine. More about this slug in a minute. I'm not gonna turn him over because, tell you the truth, I just don't want to, but he's got another bullet wound in his back, lower right side, maybe from a nine-millimeter, and you can see here he's got a grazing wound on his left shoulder."

"All from the same weapon?"

Boonie shook his head.

"Can't tell."

Nick looked down the man's torso.

"You say he's been shot in the back, but I'm not seeing an exit wound. Slug should still be in there. Too fragmented? Hit the hip bone maybe?"

"No. Here's where things go bat-shit. Somebody took it out, whatever it was, and then stitched him back up."

Nick took that in, or tried to, and failed.

"No. Got it wrong. That makes no sense. I remember you guys put it together. They take the First Third on Friday afternoon, they run, pursuit guys get shot to shit by a third guy at the north end of the Belfair Range, and these guys lay up in the Belfair Saddlery while the whole state is looking for them. They had a dispute—you guys found brass all over the place. A lot of rounds. Zane takes one in the throat, another in the lower back, maybe as he's turning to run, he makes it to the woods, goes maybe a couple of miles, sits down by the tree—"

"Goes into shock and dies," said Boonie. "State of decay and stomach contents put the time of death as somewhere between five and midnight—on the Friday. The day of the robbery."

"And then somebody—maybe the guy who shot him back at the Saddlery—comes along and takes the slug out of his back?" Nick said, following it through. "But not the one in his throat? That's just . . ."

"Crazy. But that's how it looks, Nick. Also, all the brass we found lying around at the Saddlery was nine-mill. The slug that went into his throat was a .38. Not a Special. An old Smith and Wesson slug. They stopped making those rounds back in the twenties. Not powerful enough. From the lans and milling marks on one of the larger fragments, D.C. said there was a better than even chance that the slug came from a Forehand and Wadsworth revolver. Forehand and Wadsworth was a Worcester, Mass., company that went out of business in 1890."

"I don't get it. We're saying the guy who shot him came back later, dug out his own round, sewed the wound up—"

Boonie was nodding.

"And then he puts a bullet into this guy's throat using a revolver that has to be a hundred and twenty years old? Is this what we're saying?"

"This is what this corpse is saying. And there's more. The thread used to sew up this guy's back after the bullet came out? It stopped being made in 1912. It's an old-fashioned kind of cotton twine they used to make on plantations and such. Can't be found anywhere these days."

"Maybe it was from the Saddlery?"

"Maybe. Since these guys burned the Saddlery down, we won't ever know. Now, Nick, I got a few other things to say and you're gonna have to stand here and let your mind take it all in. Okay?"

"I'm still here."

"Setting aside the whole scenario we've just been talking about—which in my opinion is utter horseshit and makes no fucking sense at all—the autopsy guys established that the wound in the throat was postmortem—"

Nick started to speak, but Boonie held up a palm.

"The wound was postmortem by as long as forty-eight hours. State of decay proves it."

"What?"

"Yes. What. As in *what the fuck*?"

"So whoever did the throat wound . . . was probably not the same guy who did the back wound?"

"That's how I see it. This guy was shot twice. Once when he was alive. And two days later, when he was dead. Want to hear the rest?"

"Not really."

"Me neither. Sometime during those forty-eight hours, the guy had been bathed. Soaped down. Rinsed off."

"How do you know that?"

"There was soap residue in his hair. Would you like to hear what we found out about the soap?"

"No."

"Denial. It's not just a river in Egypt. It's a brand called Grandpa's Wonder Soap—"

"Let me guess. It's real old."

"Yes. Grandpa's Soap is still in business, but the materials in this soap residue—the oils and stuff—they stopped using them back in the twenties. Then there's the clothes this guy was wearing. Hobnailed farm boots, lots of rough wear, from a maker in Baton Rouge who went out of business in 1911. Initials inside the boot, *JR*, burned in with a hot—"

"The initials, again?"

"*J* and *R*. In both boots. Size ten. Faded jeans in a style Levi hasn't made since—"

"Let me guess. The twenties."

"And the shirt he had on was one of those old-timey types where the collar is separate, gets pinned on with those coppery rivet things? It was starched white and bleached a lot. The material was worn so thin it was almost like paper."

Nick had nothing left to say, but Boonie did.

"There was gunpowder residue on his right hand."

"Even after somebody washed him?"

"Yeah. Must have been. Residue was from a kind of cordite mixture they used to make .45-caliber ammunition. First World War stuff. And now we come to the dirt."

"Okay. The dirt."

"On the back of his shirt—which by the way had no hole in it where the bullet in his back would have gone through—"

"Somebody changed his *shirt*?"

"Let me finish. The shirt had these stains on the back. Like he'd gone down hard onto his back. Forensics found pollen there, and plant mate-rial, and soil particles. Long story short, based on the combination of plant types and soil composition and pollen and a bunch of other shit I can't understand, they figure the shirt—if not the dead guy wearing it—had hit the ground—flat on the back—somewhere up north, on the far side of the Belfair Range, probably up around Sallytown."

Boonie fell into a silence, going inside, his expression a mix of puzzled anger and depression. Nick wasn't feeling anger or depression. He was feeling dizzy and, if he wanted to be honest, scared. Something was wrong in Niceville, and this traveling corpse was part of that wrong.

"Boonie . . ."

Boonie looked up at Nick, hoping there was an explanation that he had missed, and that Nick could explain to him, and then all this would go away.

Nick hesitated.

If he started down this road, there was no telling where it was going to end.

"You know Lemon Featherlight."

"Yeah. He's a drug squad CI. Seminole. Was in the Corps for a while. Did well in combat but not so good in peacetime. Lacy Steinert over at the probation and parole office got his Dishonorable changed to a Gen-eral Discharge. Long black hair, sharp face like a hatchet, dresses like a fashion guy. Hangs out at the Pavilion, getting paid to bang the Ladies Who Lunch."

"Yeah. Well, I don't think he's still doing the escort thing—based on what he was doing with the Corps, Lacy got him into a helicopter pilot course—and he was a help to me in the Rainey Teague investigation. About a year after it happened—Rainey was still in a coma right here at Lady Grace—Lemon was in a beef with the DEA—a flake case but he was going away on it—"

"Fucking DEA. They've flaked more of my CIs than I can count. Agency's got no reason to live."

"Anyway, Lacy Steinert asks me to meet him, says he has background on the case . . . I won't get into it . . . but he made a few good points."

"Like what?"

"Like how fucking weird the whole thing was. Think about it, Boonie. The kid disappears into a mirror—"

"Not really—"

"No. But that's how it looked. And ten days later we find him inside a sealed barrow in the Confederate graveyard. Inside the barrow was a guy who was killed in a duel on Christmas Eve in 1921. The guy's name was Ethan Ruelle. Remember that. We get Rainey out, he goes into a coma for a year. And then one day he wakes up."

"I follow. But where we going?"

"On the day Rainey woke up, Lemon Featherlight was going to visit him. Right upstairs in this building."

"Why Lemon?"

"He was tight with the kid. He knew the parents, used to . . . visit the house . . ."

Boonie's face changed.

"Jeez. Not Sylvia?"

Nick lied his face off and said, "No, not Sylvia." Boonie let him. He knew what Featherlight's rep was like. But he said nothing more on that topic. Niceville had its seamier side, even on Quality Street, just like everywhere else.

"So every now and then he'd come to see Rainey, talk to him, figured maybe the kid wasn't that far down, maybe he could hear voices . . . anyway, on the day Rainey wakes up, Lemon is coming up on the elevator, and the door opens, and there's this guy standing in the hall, waiting. Later on, when things calmed down, Lemon described him . . .

Tall, tall as me, shaved head. He had that yard boss look, or like a DI, no looking away. Straight at me, eye to eye . . . he was wearing farm

clothes. Rough jeans, heavy boots—looked old—the boots—marked
up and dirty—jeans with the cuffs rolled up. His belt was old and worn
and cinched in tight, way past the last hole, as if he had lost a lot of
weight, or it was borrowed from a bigger guy. Wide across the shoulders, looked real strong, thick neck with what looked like a burn scar
on one side, had on an old plaid work shirt, shirt looked paper thin,
like it had been washed too much. He was carrying a canvas bag, on a
strap over his shoulder. It looked heavy. It had markings on the side.
Black Army stencil. First Infantry Division, and the letters *AEF.* He
moved . . . funny . . . as if he had a stiff back . . .

Boonie didn't like this at all.
"Lemon speak to the guy?"
"Yeah. The guy said his name was Merle and he said something about
being sent there by a Glynis Ruelle. I checked the records. Glynis Ruelle
was married to a guy who was killed in the First World War. He was in
the First Infantry Division, American Expeditionary Force. His name
was John Ruelle—"
"Fuck. As in *J* and *R*? The initials in those old farm boots?"
"Probably. John Ruelle's brother lived through the war, but he was
pretty maimed. His name was—"
"Ethan Ruelle. Who was in the grave where you found Rainey."
"That's right."
Boonie walked away again, stood with his back to Nick, his big round
head shaking back and forth.
"Boonie, I don't like this either. But we have to deal with it. On the
back of the mirror that Rainey was looking at the day he disappeared,
there was a card, with writing on it. Flowery sort of script. It said '*With
long regard, Glynis Ruelle.*' "
Boonie came back again, shaking his head.
"Nick, Rainey Teague came out of the coma—"
"On the Saturday. Right before Lemon got to him. The docs were
already working on him. Later on he said that a guy named Merle had
talked to him, and that's why he woke up."
"Merle. Rainey said *Merle*?"
"He did. He also talked about dreaming that he was on a farm with a
lady named Glynis."
"Fuck. Fuck me sideways."

"That about covers it."

"And this is the *same* Merle we got here, the asshole who got his ticket punched on Friday afternoon. The day before."

"That's what we're looking at."

Boonie looked down at Merle Zane's ruined face, as if maybe the guy would start talking, come up with a few answers.

"You got Lemon's phone number?"

"Yeah. Somewhere on my phone."

"Call him. Get him down here. I think he's yanking our chains. I think he's behind all of this shit. He's pulling a stunt."

Nick was shaking his head.

"No. He's not. Boonie, there's a lot of this I haven't talked to anybody about. Other than Kate. And Lemon Featherlight."

"Why not?"

"To be straight, I just didn't want to. Even now, I wish I could just forget about it."

"And Lemon knows part of this stuff?"

"Yes."

"Then I mean it, Nick. Call him. Get him down here. Please. Send a cruiser if you have to."

"Now?" said Nick.

"Now," said Boonie, and then he rammed the tray back into the freezer and slammed the door.

A Hard Kid to Like

After lunch with the family—neither Rainey nor Axel got a mimosa—Reed went back to his apartment to wait for a verdict on his career that might take weeks to come down.

Although Beth had intended to go with Kate and the boys to Regiopolis, there had been a cancellation at Hannah's audiologist—the wait times for appointments were very long—so Beth was taking Hannah for a hearing-aid fitting, apparently a long and complicated business. So Kate drove Axel and Rainey to Regiopolis Prep in time for the boys to catch the rest of their Thursday afternoon classes.

Kate stopped the Envoy a short distance past the iron gates and shut the engine off. On the far side of the black spear-tipped wrought-iron fence that enclosed the grounds, the school loomed through the willows and oaks that dominated the lawns and gardens, a sprawling red sandstone castle built in the Romanesque style. Boys were lying around on the lawns and under the trees, and a game of flag football was under way on the playing field.

Rainey and Axel sat in the rear seat and looked out at the school grounds, their faces pale and worried. They made no move to get out.

"Look, boys, maybe now is the time for us to go in and talk to Father Casey?"

Rainey, his head down, his long hair hiding his face, shook his head emphatically.

"No, Kate. Please."

Axel was silent.

Both of them seemed oppressed and frightened.

Axel was staring out the window at some boys playing in the park. She saw a tall red-haired kid running with the ball, chased by a pack of boys. The sound of their shouts and laughter came across the lawn.

"That's Coleman playing football, isn't it?"

Both boys jumped at the name.

"Yes," said Axel. "They don't have Latin until two forty-five."

"Wait here," said Kate, and she popped the door. Rainey was objecting—shouting at her—and Axel looked worried, almost guilty.

She closed the door anyway, and stalked through the gates, headed for the football field, weaving through the kids lying around on the lawn, her eye fixed on that tall redheaded kid. Somewhere behind her she could hear Rainey and Axel calling her name, faint and far off.

But she went straight on.

When she was within ten yards, she called out, in what Nick had described as her Addressing the Jury voice.

"Coleman. Coleman Mauldar."

The game came to a ragged halt as the boys turned to look at her. She saw that Jay Dials and Owen Coors were there as well, both boys lean and strong, clear-eyed and long-haired, as most of the Regiopolis kids were.

The secret to happiness?

Old Money, Good Genes, and Dumb Luck.

Coleman tossed the football to Jay Dials, said something in a low voice, and then came across the field to the towering willow where Kate was waiting.

The rest of the boys went back to their game, running on the wide-open space, shirttails flying, their voices shrill and wild on the wind.

In the afternoon light Coleman's astonishing good looks were impossible to miss, his light green eyes and that cascade of rich red hair, his white shirt open to reveal a taut, tanned chest that rippled with muscle, his easy smile, only slightly wary.

"Miz Kavanaugh. Hello. How are you?"

"Coleman, can you answer a question for me?"

"I can try," he said, his smile faltering.

"How much bigger are you than me?"

He didn't like the question at all.

"Than you? I don't know, exactly."

"I'm five four and I weigh a hundred and fourteen pounds. How much credit would you get from those kids over there if you were to knock me down?"

"Knock you down?" he said, stepping back, his smile gone. "Ma'am, I would never hit a gir—a woman."

"Never?"

His face was hardening up.

"No. Never."

"Why?"

"Why?"

"Yes. Why wouldn't you ever hit a woman?"

They were both speaking softly, and the wind in the trees was loud enough that their conversation wasn't carrying beyond the arc of the willow they were standing under. Overhead the branches were hissing and sighing as the wind moved through them. The air smelled of green leaves and cut grass.

"It's not . . . right. It wouldn't be fair."

"Why not?"

"Because . . . you just never do it. There's never a good reason to hit a woman. And because I'm bigger and stronger than you. Besides, all the guys would . . . they'd think I was a . . ."

"Jerk?"

Coleman was quiet for a bit.

"Look, Miz Kavanaugh, I think I know what this is about. It's about Rainey and Axel, right?"

"You know what they've been through, don't you? Rainey lost both his parents, he was abducted by strangers, he was in the hospital for a year. As for Axel, I'm sure you know the news—his father is a bad man, and now he's out there somewhere, doing God knows what. Axel's terrified of him, has been all his life. The last thing Axel needs is another big strong male beating the crap out of him. But you got into a fistfight with Rainey last week and another one with Axel yesterday—beat him up, right over there by the chapel doors."

Coleman rose up at that.

"Miz Kavanaugh . . . Axel came at me. He was going all ape on me . . . all I did was stop him—"

Kate was holding up a hand, palm out, her face white with anger.

"Coleman, we both know what's going on with you and those boys. You can't seem to find it in your heart to give them a break. You and Owen and Jay have names for them—"

"Names?"

"Don't play dumb with me, Coleman. Rainey is Crypt Boy and Axel is Cop Killer's Kid, or something like that—"

Coleman's face was going through a number of alterations, and getting redder.

"Ma'am, I truly have no idea what you're talking about. Owen and Jay and I—we never called those kids anything like that—"

"Where were you yesterday afternoon?"

Coleman's expression cleared.

"Yesterday afternoon . . . around when, ma'am?"

"Wednesday. Yesterday. After school."

"Ma'am, after school yesterday we had football practice. The Blue Knights are playing Sacred Heart Falcons on Sunday. They killed us last week. So Father Robert is making us run their playbook—"

"You never followed them home from school, calling them names?"

"No ma'am. We didn't."

"You deny it?"

"Look, Miz Kavanaugh . . . this is crazy. None of this is right. I mean, you've got it all crazy."

"You're saying you didn't follow them home yesterday? You and Owen and Jay?"

"That's right."

"Can you prove it?"

Coleman started to bristle.

"Yes, I can prove it. Every practice they do roll call. Like in the Army. We were all there. Owen and Jay. And me. It'll be on Father Robert's attendance sheet. We can go get him right now. He's in his office."

He turned and started across the lawn, stiff and angry. Kate called to him.

"No . . . wait."

Coleman stopped, looked back at her, visibly angry but controlling it. She walked up to him.

"You're telling me the truth, aren't you?"

"Blood of the Holy Virgin. Honest."

Kate didn't want to start deconstructing Axel and Rainey's allegations in front of this boy.

But the lawyer in her was persuaded that this witness was telling the truth.

"Then I apologize. I'm truly sorry I accused you."

Coleman cooled down as she spoke.

"Rainey says he and Axel were followed home yesterday? By Regiopolis kids?"

"Axel said so."

"Then I'll ask around. Because if they did that to them, that's not right. No. It's not right."

"You don't deny teasing them? Getting into fights with them? Making fun of them?"

Coleman shook his head.

"No. I guess I don't. You get together with the guys, it starts out sorta fun. But then it . . . it gets nasty. Mainly Rainey. Axel, he just sorta goes along, and he'll stick up for Rainey. Most of the guys kinda admire Axel for that. He's a fighter. But Rainey . . . he knows how to get under your skin. He's good at that. He knows right where to stick you. He told me that this was the best I was ever going to be, a dumb jock in a jerkwater school in Crackerville, and that I'd grow up to be a loser car salesman who drinks too—"

Coleman cut that off, and hardened up.

"Like I said. Rainey knows where to stick it."

"I know he's difficult. He has lots of reasons to be difficult. So does Axel. And you're a school leader. You should be . . . helping them both . . . and Owen and Jay. They need good role models, boys their age. Loyalty to each other, that's what this school is all about. Instead you're letting yourself down, and them, and the school."

She was losing force and conviction with every word. Doubt was flooding through her.

"Look, Coleman, now that we've talked I think I may have been wrong about you."

"Thank you. I'm sorry I got hot. My dad is always asking me to prove I'm not . . . Look, are you taking this to my dad? Because these days he's got a real bad temper. He won't say why, but I don't like to cross him when he's like that."

"No. If I can't get to you right now, right here, then no one ever will. I'm not going to talk about this to anyone."

Coleman was looking at her, a number of emotions playing on his face, and Kate began to think there might be hope for him after all. It was Rainey and Axel she was worried about now.

"Is Nick angry? Is he going to come after me?"

That stopped her.

"Of course not. God no. He doesn't even know I'm here, and he won't ever know. Anyway, he wouldn't come after you even if he did. He thinks this is between you and the boys. It's for you all to settle it fairly."

Coleman stared back at her, his face solemn.

"Okay," he said, after a long time.

"Okay what?"

"Okay. I'll try to help them. Both of them."

"You'll try?"

She looked into his eyes and her heart went out to him. Having Little Rock Mauldar as a father . . . She knew the man pretty well and most of what she knew she didn't like.

"You'll really try to be kinder?"

"Yes. I will. I mean, I have tried, and Axel's okay—especially when he's not around Rainey—Rainey, he's a hard kid to like, Miz Kavanaugh. Like I said, he's got a mean mouth—he can be pretty harsh, the kind of things he says, and he's not all that nice to the Green Jackets—the juniors and the newbies—he picks on them—and sometimes he says really weird things. But you're right. Those two have been through a lot. Father Casey says we should cut them some slack. So I'll try harder, Miz Kavanaugh, I promise you that. And if I change, about Rainey, then Owen and Jay and the rest of guys will go along. They already like Axel a lot."

She looked at him for a while longer, and was suddenly afraid she was going to cry.

"You know, I believe you. And I thank you."

He smiled at her, and put out his hand, and she shook it, smiling back, feeling her heart lighten as she did so.

Coleman waved and ran off to his game. She stood and watched the boys play for a while, wishing that this was Rainey's life.

He's not all that nice to the Green Jackets.

He's got a mean mouth.

He's a hard kid to like.

Liking Rainey hadn't come easily to Kate either.

Maybe there was more to this than she thought. Maybe she and the boys could have a talk about this. Go somewhere right now where they could all have a heart-to-heart. But when she got back to the SUV, the boys were gone.

After a long and increasingly frustrating search of the Regiopolis grounds, Kate went inside to the clerical office to see if Alice Bayer was around, but the woman behind the glass wasn't Alice.

The woman said no, she hadn't seen Rainey or Axel come in at all today. She added that both boys had taken to leaving early a couple of days a week. But that was okay because they had brought in a note.

A note?

Kate asked to see the note.

After sniffing at Kate for a moment, and pursing her mouth, the woman opened a file and riffled through it, retrieving a piece of paper and handing it through the slot in the glass partition.

It was a handwritten note, done in green ink, with a fountain pen, on linen card stock, a soft cream color.

Please let my son Rainey have Early Leave for the next little while. He's helping me with a project.

Thanks so very much.

Sincerely,
Sylvia Teague

Kate stared at the note. She knew this writing well. It was Sylvia Teague's hand, as clear and crisp as always, and she wrote in green ink, with a Montblanc that had been willed to her by Johnny Mercer, a distant relative.

She pulled herself together.

"Has Father Casey seen this note?"

The secretary shook her head.

"I don't think so. I mean, I didn't see the need. It's routine attendance stuff. That's our job here. Attendance and Records. And after all, the note *is* from his mother."

"It's not from Axel's mother. Axel's mother is Beth Walker, my sister. Why are you letting Axel miss classes as well?"

The woman got distinctly chillier.

Kate was surprised that ice didn't form on the glass panel between them.

"Axel told us his mother works in Cap City, with the FBI down there. I asked for some kind of confirmation from her by phone or e-mail. The next day I got an e-mail directly from her, giving us permission to release Axel as long as he was going to be with Rainey. I have it . . . wait a bit . . . here it is."

She had riffled through a file folder marked PERMISSIONS LIST. She held the paper up for Kate to read through the glass.

Beth_walker12@gmail.com

To

attendance@regiopolispreparatory.org

 Yes, Axel has my permission to leave school early as long as he is accompanied by Rainey Teague. Please call me at 918-347-6021 if you need clarification. Elizabeth Deitz

"Did you call that number?"

"Yes. Of course. I got her voice mail and left a message."

"Was it returned?"

"I'm sure it was. Otherwise we wouldn't be letting the boys have Early Leave, would we? And the note here is signed by Rainey's mother. It's her signature, that much I do know."

"And how would you know that?"

The woman's mouth got tighter.

"Why, we have her signature on record. Alice is particular about permissions. She insists that every parent has to come in and sign this signature form personally. Otherwise, if we just send the form home, the boys will sign it themselves, the rascals, and then where would we be?"

"Do you have my sister's signature on file?"

"Not yet. Axel is a new student this term. Your sister—I suppose—has been too busy to come in and sign the card. I imagine all the trouble her husband is in has something to do with that."

This was said with an unmistakable air of smug malice. Kate took a closer look at the woman behind the glass. She was one of those Front Office Virgins, a plump whipped-cream sundae of a woman with swirly hair and cherry red lips and small black eyes hidden behind round rimless glasses. She was looking decidedly wary and defensive.

"I'm sorry," said the woman, with an edge. "I don't believe we've met. May I ask what your interest is in this matter?"

Kate didn't smack her, but of course there was the glass wall between them.

"I'm Kate Walker—Kate Kavanaugh, I mean. I'm Rainey's guardian. And Axel and his mother and sister live with us. It's all in the registry book behind you there, if you cared to look. Are you aware that no one really knows where Rainey's mother is?"

The woman shook her head, making the twin disks of her glasses glitter in the light from the desk lamp beside her.

"Well, she must be around somewhere, *dear*, because when we asked for a note from his mother so Rainey could have Early Leave, Rainey came right back on the very next day with that note you have in your hands. I checked it with her signature form, just like I said—"

"Forgive me, but I don't know your name."

"Oh no," said the woman, simpering, "how could you? My name is Gert Bloomsberry. I'm only here on a temporary transfer from Sacred Heart."

"I see. Miss Bloomsberry, is Alice around?"

Gert hesitated, and then leaned forward, speaking in a conspiratorial whisper.

"Well, keep this to yourself, but that's why I'm here. Alice hasn't been in to school in over two weeks. She sent us an e-mail saying she was going to be away for a while and not to worry. She had some sick days coming."

"Do you have that e-mail?"

The woman frowned at Kate.

"Of course. But that's a personal correspondence and I am not at liberty to—"

"Alice lives up in The Glades. Has anyone gone up there to see if she's okay?"

"Yes. Of course. She has a small house on Virtue Place—isn't that just so cute? Alice, I mean, living on Virtue? Anyway, Father Bernard dropped in on his way to the airport. The lights were on and everything looked fine. He knocked but nobody came to the door. Her car was gone. There was a note on the front door. GONE TO SALLYTOWN. BACK SOON."

"Was it signed?"

"Father didn't say."

"Has anyone called the police?"

Gert recoiled at the idea.

"*Goodness* no. The *police*? We all figure she's gone to see a friend."

"Let me understand this. Alice has been missing for two weeks on the strength of a single e-mail and all you've done is send somebody over to read a note on her door? What if she's lying dead on the other side of that door? Why are you all taking this so calmly?"

"Dear me, Miz Kavanaugh, you *are* an excitable girl, aren't you?"

Kate managed not to pound on the glass.

The woman rolled on, oblivious, admiring her hands on the desk in front of her.

"No, Alice Bayer is much loved. We all feel she's entitled to a little fun in life. She works so hard, you know? Everybody around her admires the way she runs Attendance, the interest she takes in the boys. She knows them all by name, and where they like to hang out, places like Patton's Hard—God knows *that's* a bad place, what with the river there and the whirlpool and all, but they all go there, the school skippers, Rainey and Axel too, and if they start in to skipping classes, well, Alice has been known to go down there, drive down to Patton's Hard, and bring them back to school by their ears, and that's certainly what I call taking the mickey out of those—"

"How do you know that Rainey and Axel go down to Patton's Hard?"

Patton's Hard was a mile-long stretch of parkland that ran along the Tulip. The willows there were the oldest trees in Niceville. It was a dank, dark, and dangerous place. Kate and Beth had hated Patton's Hard since they were children.

"Why, they told the other kids, didn't they? Bragged about it. Told the Green Jackets. The little kids in Junior School. Said they have a fort down there. They've been telling those little boys all about the ghosts that live there, on Patton's Hard, under the willows, daring the kids to go there with them. Father Casey had to—"

There may have been more, but Kate was already on her way to the Envoy.

She kept the note.

Deitz Guns Up

Deitz came out of Andy Chu's shower wrapped in one of Andy Chu's bath towels. One of his best bath towels, but if he was still alive after this was over, Chu was going to burn it in his backyard barbecue.

He was waiting for Deitz in the kitchen, picking away at what was left of lunch—kung pao chicken, which he hated, because he hated all Chinese food. He was staring out the window at a tan Toyota that was parked up the street. It had been there for a while now. No one was in the car, but now that he was *harboring a fugitive* he had developed a level of situational awareness that bordered on painful.

Speaking of painful, he was aware of Deitz looming at his shoulder, smelling lemony fresh.

"You get the stuff?" said Deitz, speaking in a more normal voice now that the swelling in his nose had gone down. His black biker goatee was gone.

"Yes, I did. It's all in my—in your—room—in the master bedroom."

"What about the wig?"

"That too. I got a large, since all they had was women's stuff."

"They have what I was looking for?"

"They did. Exactly what you ordered."

Deitz grunted, turned, and lumbered out of the kitchen. Chu considered just making a run for it, opening the kitchen door and bolting down the street. There were drawbacks.

The main one was the Blackmailer's Dilemma.

It had been implicit, although unspoken, in Chu's deal with Deitz about the shares in Securicom that Chu knew about the scam with the Chinese to copy the Raytheon module. He had followed Deitz around during those two days and he had videotape of Deitz meeting with that Dak guy down in Tin Town. Therefore, the corollary was, Chu Knew Too.

And failed to report it.

As a matter of fact, quite the opposite. He attempted to benefit from the knowledge by blackmailing his boss.

As a person here on an E-1 visa, Chu knew that if any of this came to light, he'd be lucky to get away with ten years in a federal lockup, after which he'd be put on a plane back to Shanghai. What might be waiting for him in China did not bear thinking about, especially since he was involved—however peripherally—in the death of Mr. Dak and his associates, all of whom were sure as hell *guangbo*, which was the Chinese secret police.

Hence, the Blackmailer's Dilemma, and therefore no headlong dash down the sidewalk crying out for succor.

There was a lot of banging of drawers and slamming of closets—as a roommate Deitz was pretty loud—and a few minutes later Deitz came back into the kitchen. Chu was waiting for him, feeling that whatever the hell Deitz looked like, Chu had to approve. This turned out to be a challenge.

Deitz didn't walk into the room so much as manifest into it. He was carrying a black leather valise and wearing an off-the-rack Hugo Boss suit in charcoal over a pale gray shirt, no tie. On his feet he had a pair of glossy black Allen Edmonds wing tips over dove gray socks. He had even requested a scarlet pocket square.

In short, from the ground up, he looked pretty damn good, like a designer refrigerator or like one of those retired NFL linebackers who get jobs as halftime commentators on Fox and CBS—hyper-snazzy in a vaguely alarming way.

But all this ended at the neck, or that slightly narrower part of his body where most men would usually have a neck.

Deitz's connection between his shoulders and his skull was a thick cone of sinew and muscle and bone that tapered upwards just enough to blend into his skull, which narrowed a bit from there on in, although not enough to come to an actual point.

Deitz had addressed the goatee issue by hacking it off with Chu's Braun waterproof electric razor, a process that the razor did not survive. He dealt with the bruising around his eyes and the disorderly state of his nose by putting on a bit of cosmetic cover-up that Chu had bought at Walgreens.

It was thick and chalky and while it did hide the bruises, it made Deitz look like a French mime. The problem of his blackened eyes—now more of a yellowish green—was neatly solved by a pair of those bug-eye wrap-around sunglasses that all the highway cops were wearing.

So far, so good.

Where this all fell apart was the wig.

Deitz had been specific.

He wanted a long shiny blond wig, long enough for the hair to come down to his shoulders.

"Like one of those guys on the WWF, okay?"

Chu, asking no questions—every man's sexuality is his own business—had paid two thousand dollars for the thing that was resting uneasily on the summit of Deitz's skull right now, a luxurious sweep of golden hair—guaranteed human, all the way from Denmark, he had been assured—cut into an artfully ragged fall across the forehead, the rest hanging down in a long blunt wave that pooled on his shoulders.

There was no way to get around it.

Deitz looked like Anna Wintour.

Or at least like Anna Wintour's head stuck on the body of a gigantic troll in a Hugo Boss suit.

Please don't ask me what I think.

"What do you think?"

Chu was silent for a time.

If he let Deitz go out in that wig they wouldn't get half a mile before kids on the side of the road would be throwing stones at the car as they drove by. Dogs would chase the car down the street, yapping and snapping. This would attract the attention of the cops, who would not pass up the chance to have a chat with a large ugly guy wearing an Anna Wintour wig, if only just to have something to tell everybody back at the station.

At that point, the jig, as these Americans like to say, would be up, and not just for Byron Deitz.

"Have you looked in a mirror?"

Deitz said nothing for a bit.

"Yeah. I did. I thought I looked pretty good."

"Do you know who Anna Wintour is?"

"No fucking idea."

"Well, you look just like her."

Deitz got much redder than normal.

"Make your fucking point."

"She's a famous fashion broad. Gay guys dress like her on Halloween.

If you had a tiny black dress on, and stiletto heels, the look would be complete."

Deitz calmed down a bit, breathed out.

"Shit. You're sure?"

"I am."

"Fuck. I thought I looked sort of like Arnold back when he was playing Conan the Barbarian. Or maybe a football player. They're all wearing their hair long these days."

Chu shook his head.

"Not Conan. Not football. Anna."

Deitz thought about it.

"Lose the wig?"

"Lose the wig."

Deitz took it off, flipped the lid of Chu's garbage can, and dropped it in on top of the kung pao chicken.

Two thousand dollars.

Gone.

"Fuck it then. We'll go with what we got."

"Where are we going to go?"

Deitz opened his suit jacket. He had a large gray steel pistol shoved into his belt.

"We're gonna go see a guy about my money."

Endicott was parked a quarter of a mile away, in the black Cadillac, listening to Chu and Deitz talk in Chu's kitchen. He had his Toshiba open on the passenger seat, the screen showing the sound and video feed from the surveillance gear in the Toyota Corolla he had parked down the street from Chu's house at 237 Bougainville Terrace.

About the size of a GPS module, and stuck to the Toyota's windshield as they always are, the device had an attached laser sound detector mounted on the left side mirror that focused on the glass windows of Chu's living room. By detecting nano-sized variations in the glass, the laser could translate the vibrations into sound. In this case, the sound of Chu and Deitz talking about Anna Wintour. The device also had a camera, so Endicott could track, from a safe distance, who was coming and going at Chu's house.

Earlier he had watched as Chu drove away, alone, according to the device's infrared camera, which read body heat signatures inside houses and vehicles. Since Deitz and not Chu was the focus of Endicott's attention, he stayed put.

Chu had come back about two hours ago, and now—judging by the conversation—they were about to go see a guy about his money.

Excellent.

"*We're* going?"

Deitz took off his glasses, giving Chu the full Deitz glower. In his head he could hear a sound like somebody cracking walnuts. It was coming from somewhere very close. Deitz had not yet figured out that the walnut-cracking sound was Deitz grinding his teeth. He ground his teeth when he was angry or frustrated or tense. Since he was hardly ever anything else, the walnut-cracking sound was in his head quite a bit.

"We are. I got a spare piece. You ever fire a gun?"

"Byron," said Chu, summoning all his persuasive powers, "I cannot go off and get into a gunfight. I'll just freeze up, like that translator dweeb in *Saving Private Ryan*."

"What the fuck are you talking about?"

"What about Phil Holliman? He's your muscle guy."

"I'm not sure I can count on Phil. He's sitting pretty right now, running Securicom. If they let Securicom keep the Quantum deal when the contract runs out this month—and they might—he'll be in clover. I show up on his radar, the best way he clears himself with the Feds is to rat me out. There's no percentage in this for Phil."

"Can't you use one of the guys? There are mean guys in the outfit. Ray Cioffi, for instance?"

"I don't need a bunch of mean guys, Chu. I just need a driver, a guy to get me there and cover my back while I go in."

He leaned down and fumbled in the valise at his feet, brought out another huge steel pistol, dropped the mag, racked the slide back, held it so Chu could watch as he shoved the mag back in, smacked it home, and released the slide. He thumbed the de-cocking lever and held it out to Chu.

"There you go. It's ready to rock, so don't blow your foot off. I got this from Shaniqua. It's a Sig. Point and shoot. Fifteen rounds. Use both hands."

Chu took it from Deitz. It was as heavy as a bowling ball and as far as Chu was concerned about as useful.

"Byron—"

"No. Fuck that. You're going. I've given the thing a lotta thought. I'm not leaving you sitting around back here, going all pale and shaky on me. You're in a spot here, Andy. You fucking did it to yourself. You put yourself right here in the fucking ten ring. For a while there, sitting in the slam, I thought about all the ways I'd like to fuck with you. But then I realized you weren't the problem. The assholes who set me up, those guys are the problem. You *know* I didn't steal that fucking money. Nick and Boonie and all the local guys know I didn't steal that money. They're just squeezing me with the Chink thing because they think I know who *did* steal that fucking money. And I do. I know *exactly* who did that fucking bank and I'm gonna go take the money away from them. Then I'm gonna kill them. Both of them. Then I'm gonna call Warren Smoles and he's gonna set up a deal with the Feds and if I handle it right—recover the money—kill the cop killers—I'll be a fucking hero and the Raytheon beef will disappear."

"Who are they? The guys who really did it?"

"Haven't figured that out, hah? I'll give you a hint. Go find out who I paid five large to so I could get my Raytheon thing back."

Chu knew that Deitz had ransomed back his module, and that the only people who could have had it to ransom *from* were the people who robbed the bank. But the payment went to a Mondex card, and although he had tried, he had never been able to track the card all the way to an end user. He had gotten as far as the Channel Islands and hit a wall. He wasn't going to tell Deitz this anytime soon.

Anyway, Deitz had moved on.

"So I figure, bottom line, you and I are in the shit together. So man up, put the fucking gun in your pants—no, not down the front, you dumb-ass—on the side there—good—now put your coat on, get the fucking car keys, and saddle up."

Chu made one last effort.

"Look, Byron, the guys who robbed that bank killed four cops and two civilians doing it. Whoever they are, they're serious people and they're not going to be easy to get to. And they have to know you're out. Won't they be expecting you to come after them? You'll be walking into a trap. They'll probably kill us both."

Deitz said nothing for a moment, and Andy Chu's heart began to beat again.

Not for long.

"Doesn't matter. I can't stay out that long. Every cop in the state is looking for me right now. Pretty soon the FBI will start thinking about who might be helping me. You're not at work today. You just spent five thousand on clothes that are four times too big for you. Plus that fucking wig. Soon as they look at that, we'll have the SWAT guys landing on your roof. I got a limited amount of time to take care of these pukes, and I'm not going to dick around with being fucking *tactical*. Okay?"

Chu sagged into himself, found a trace of courage in there somewhere. What the hell. He was hip-deep in self-inflicted shit. Maybe he was about to get what he deserved.

"Yeah," he said. "What the fuck. Let's go."

Deitz grinned at him.

"Know what, kid? You got potential. Now let's go kill something."

Endicott watched the computer screen as Chu's garage door slid up and Chu's blue Lexus rolled down the cobbles. The brake lights lit up, and then the car headed off up Bougainville.

Endicott started the Cadillac, put it in gear, and glided silently down the road, now and then glancing at the Toshiba screen. He had attached a GPS transponder to the Lexus during the night—Chu's alarm system wasn't much better than a bunch of tin cans tied to a string—and now he could follow that Lexus wherever it went.

Where it seemed to be going was north on River Road. Endicott sat back into the satiny leather seats—Cadillac. No better car in the world—you can keep your BMWs and Audis—and thought about what he had just heard:

You know I didn't steal that fucking money. Nick and Boonie and all the local guys know I didn't steal that money. They're just squeezing me with the Chink thing because they think I know who did steal that fucking money. And I do. I know exactly who did that fucking bank and I'm gonna go take the money away from them. Then I'm gonna kill them. Both of them. Then I'm gonna call Warren Smoles and he's gonna set up a deal with the Feds and if I handle it right—recover the money—kill the cop killers—I'll be a fucking hero and the Raytheon beef will disappear.

It had never occurred to La Motta or Munoz or Spahn—or for that matter to Endicott—that Deitz hadn't stolen that money. In the world they all inhabited, *innocence* was not a word that tripped lightly off the tongue.

Endicott looked at his cell phone, considered asking for advice from his source down here—Deitz's own lawyer, Warren Smoles, as crooked a man as ever choked down a scruple with a double shot of Tanqueray. Another thought?

Was it possible that Deitz *knew* he was being listened to? That this was all showbiz?

No.

It wasn't.

He'd only been on Deitz for two days and he had already decided that Deitz had the situational awareness of a mollusk.

Shortly thereafter, Endicott reached a conclusion. No calling Warren Smoles, or Mario La Motta, or anyone else.

All of this was just too damn interesting for that. He watched the red dot as it accelerated north on River Road, now just crossing Peachtree.

He reached for a Camel, lit it up, rolled down the windows, and opened up the moon roof. If you smoked in a rental car, they charged you five hundred dollars to clean it. Endicott could afford it, but five hundred was outrageous.

"You know I didn't steal that fucking money."

The Chinese guy was probably right—and for a pencil-neck geek he had serious stones—but he and Byron Deitz were probably going to die this afternoon. It would be interesting to see who was going to do the killing.

He pulled on his cigarette, blew smoke out through the moon roof, smiling.

Excellent.

The Outside Wants In

Lemon Featherlight got to the Lady Grace morgue about fifteen minutes after Nick called him. Nick didn't send a cruiser because Lemon would have told the cop where and how to insert his cruiser and that wouldn't have gone well.

They watched him coming down the long, dark hallway, a tall, lean silhouette in a black tee and jeans, passing into and out of the pools of light from the overheads, his boots hitting solid on the terrazzo.

He walked up to the steel doors where Boonie and Nick were waiting and stood there under the light, a handsome but angular, even cruel, face, his deep-set eyes in shadow, long black hair pulled behind his ears, his mouth a thin line and his hands at his sides.

"Nick. How are you?"

Nick smiled.

"Banged around a bit. My own damn fault."

"I heard the van hit a deer."

"A buck."

"Big one?"

"Full-grown. Killed the driver and the shotgun guard. The van went down and I woke up with Boonie here crying salt tears over me."

Boonie snorted but said nothing.

"I saw Reed in the hall. How's he doing?"

"Not well. Marty Coors grounded him until a hearing."

"I saw the video. He's lucky he walked away."

"Lot of people didn't," said Boonie. "You ready to do this?"

"I'm here," he said, still looking at Nick, ignoring Boonie, whose expression was equally stony.

"Where is this guy?"

"In here," said Nick, hitting the steel button. The doors hissed open and Nick led them back into the storage sector, Boonie following as if Lemon were already in custody. They gathered in front of Drawer 19.

Nick looked at Boonie, who opened the door and tugged the tray out. He pulled the sheet off the way a matador swirls his cape. If he was expecting Lemon to pass out from the shock, he was disappointed.

Lemon stood there, hands folded at his buckle, his face impassive, as Nick, with Boonie's occasional assistance, laid out the details of the autopsy report and the related forensics.

When he was finished, Lemon looked across the tray at Nick.

"It's him. That's the guy."

Boonie sighed, put his hands on his hips.

"You can see this guy is dead, right?"

Lemon looked at him without expression.

"Yes. I can."

"And you believe us when we tell you that this guy right here died maybe twenty hours before you say you saw him in the hallway outside Rainey's hospital room."

Lemon nodded, waiting for the rest.

"So. Did anybody else see him?"

"Maybe," said Lemon. "Have you asked?"

Boonie's face got darker.

"It was six months ago. I only just heard about this."

"Now you have. You're right here in the hospital. Go ask the people on that floor. And in the lobby. I'll wait."

"On your say-so?"

Lemon shrugged.

"Agent Hackendorff, I really don't care."

Boonie bristled.

"Look, Featherlight, I can make your—"

Nick broke in.

"Boonie, stop being such a hard-ass. Lemon's a stand-up. I know you don't like what he is telling you. I didn't like telling you my part either—"

Lemon looked at Nick.

"What part did you tell him?"

Nick went through it, Rainey using Merle's name when he woke up, talking about Glynis Ruelle. The writing on the back of the mirror. When he was finished, Lemon kept on looking, the question clear in his pale green eyes.

Nick shook his head.

"No. Not the rest of it."

Boonie groaned, stepped back, and looked at them both.

"The *rest* of it? There's more?"

Nick and Lemon exchanged a glance, and then they both turned to Boonie.

"Yes," said Nick. "There's more. You want to hear about it?"

Boonie said nothing for a time, glaring down at the corpse on the steel tray.

"Sure," he said, with a sudden smile. "I mean, after all this crazy shit, how weird can it be?"

Nick signed himself out in spite of the howls from the docs and the nurses—possible concussion—danger of a clot—internal bleeding—and they took Boonie's black Crown Vic across the river to the Pavilion, a riverside restaurant and shopping complex built out on a cedar plank boardwalk that ran in a broad curve along the river.

The day was warm and clear, with just a bite of fall in the wind. The

Tulip was racing past the railings, a deep, rumbling vibration as it swept around the pylons. Beyond the railings the sunlight glimmered on the water as it roiled and churned. Along the riverbanks bougainvillea vines grew thick, and dense colonies of pampas grass nodded in the breeze. Upriver, the old willows on Patton's Hard glowed with an inner light.

They got a round table under the awning at the Bar Belle and a pretty waitress with a retro forties look and a figure to match took their orders—beer, beer, nachos, and a carafe of Chianti—smiling over her shoulder at Lemon as she left them. Boonie held up his hand, palm out.

"Nope. No more weird shit until I get myself outside a Beck's."

So they sat there, waiting, in an uneasy silence, broken a minute later by a cell phone ringing. There was the usual reflexive scramble through pockets until Nick came up with his.

KATE

"Well, I'm a dead man," said Nick.

The phone rang on, shrill and insistent. He had a brutal headache and the crack in his . . . his what? His supraorbital process? Well, that hurt too. Maybe signing himself out without calling Kate wasn't such a good idea. And what Kate would have to say about it when she heard would probably render him sterile. He was about to find out.

"Hey, Kate—"

"Where are you?"

"I'm at the Bar Belle, with—"

"I'll be there in twenty minutes."

"Okay, babe, listen, I was just going to call—"

The line was dead.

He put the phone down on the table. The other two men looked at each other and then at Nick.

"Kate?" asked Lemon.

Nick nodded. A commiserative silence followed. Their drinks arrived and he picked up his wine, took a long drink.

"We should have given her a heads-up," said Boonie.

"She's on her way over."

Boonie winced.

"Shit. Right now?"

"Twenty minutes away."

"She'll kill me. She told me not to take you anywhere. I'm a dead man."

Lemon smiled at him, a sardonic grin.

"Still time to make a run for it. You might even make it to the Canadian border."

Ignoring him, Boonie lifted his Beck's, took a long swig, set it down with a dismal sigh.

"Hey. What's the worst that could happen?"

"It could be me instead of you," said Lemon.

Boonie took another drink, leaned back.

"Okay. We got twenty minutes. Can you tell me what you gotta tell me in twenty minutes?"

They managed it. In the end they had to ask Boonie to stop interrupting. He finally did, and they got to the end of it, at least the end so far.

Boonie had another Beck's in front of him. But now all he was doing was staring down into it. When he started to talk it was a curveball.

"Nick, did I ever tell you what Charlie Danziger told me a while back?"

"No. What'd he say?"

Boonie looked around the boardwalk. The place was filling up with the happy hour crowd, bright, sparkly people in all things Hilfiger and Armani. In the forested hills that led up to the base of Tallulah's Wall the warm lights of The Chase neighborhood showed through the trees. Across the river on the eastern banks traffic was booming up and down Long Reach Boulevard. On the Armory Bridge one of those navy blue and gold streetcars of the Peachtree Line was rumbling over the river, shiny and glittering in the sun.

In spite of the disordered state of his own mind, it seemed to Boonie that on this sunlit afternoon Niceville was doing quite nicely, thank you. Boonie came back to them, speaking in a low voice, a voice for the table.

"Charlie. You know he was still a staff sergeant with State when Kate's mother died in that rollover on the interstate. What, maybe six, seven years ago?"

"Seven."

"So Charlie was one of the First Responders to the scene. Kate's mother . . . what was her name?"

"Lenore."

"Yeah. Charlie said Lenore was still alive. He could see he wasn't going to be able to get her out without killing her, so he just sort of got inside the wreck with her and held on to her while he was waiting for Fire and Rain to get there. Lot of blood. Lady was in pain. Nothing Charlie could do but hold on and . . . you know . . . try to be soothing. Comforting."

"Charlie's a good man," said Nick. "The State IAD guys screwed him. I mean, *really* screwed him."

A silence, while the two cops at the table thought about how Internal Affairs cops lived with themselves. Lemon, who had been a marine, knew something about getting screwed by vindictive MPs, but he didn't say so.

After a moment, Boonie went on.

"Anyway, so Kate's mom was going into shock, in and out of consciousness. Charlie's just holding on to her, trying to get her to stay with him, not slip away. But she's going. He could tell. She opens her eyes and looks at Charlie and she says, 'She uses the mirrors.' "

Nick had heard this from Kate, the night of the . . . the night of the mirror. But he let Boonie tell it. It seemed to be helping him.

" 'She uses the mirrors.' She said it a couple of times, like she knew she wasn't going to make it and she wanted Charlie to remember it. A couple of minutes later, just as Fire and Rain gets there, she slips away, Charlie still holding on to her. Charlie said he'd never forget it, that look in her eyes. Like you said, Nick, a good man."

There was a long silence.

Boonie seemed to shake himself, like a dog coming out of the water.

"So let's review," he said. "And this time, you two don't interrupt me."

He sat forward, spreading his hands out on the tablecloth. Inhaled, and then exhaled.

"Okay. This Glynis Ruelle lives in the mirror you've got in your upstairs closet. I know, I know, it's a gate or a portal or whatever, but that's what it comes down to. This mirror has been around a really long time. Far back as Ireland in the 1790s. We think Glynis died in the thirties, but since the archives got burned in 1935 we can't be sure. Somehow or other, inside the mirror world, Glynis can make things happen in the outside world. *She uses the mirrors.* She has a way of knowing what was making people disappear—Delia Cotton, Kate's dad, this Gray Haggard guy whose shrapnel bits you found on the dining room floor of Delia Cotton's house—and so she recruits Merle Zane to help her somehow. She keeps him in a midway state between life and death so he can do . . . something . . . up in Sallytown. Something that involves a guy named Abel Teague, Rainey's distant relative, who had done a girl wrong, a girl named Clara Mercer, Glynis Ruelle's younger sister. How'm I doing?"

"Very well," said Lemon. "Except there's also the fact that Abel Teague used extremely slimy methods to get Glynis Ruelle's husband and his brother sent off to the war, and when Ethan came back—maimed—Abel Teague arranged for a gun-hand—a Haggard, by the way—to call him out and kill him on Christmas Eve in 1921."

Nick said nothing. He was looking down into his glass and remembering.

Boonie took a drink, went on.

"Thank you. That too. So she has every reason to hate this Teague guy. And Merle Zane pulls it off—whatever it was we don't know—based on what you tell me, probably a gunfight—and during it he gets himself shot dead for the *second* time—hence the dirt on the back of his shirt—yes I said *hence*—and he suddenly zaps back to being the dead guy with his back up against a pine tree two miles into the Belfair Range."

He paused, took a drink. They all did.

"The next thing that happens is that something like a black swirly thing shows up at your door—you and Kate—Kate thinks it's her missing dad—she opens the door—there's this black cloud there—and then the mirror lights up, Glynis Ruelle steps out of the mirror and onto your living room rug and she says something like 'Clara, stop, Abel Teague is dead'—I guess because Merle managed to kill him in that gunfight—maybe we oughta send somebody up to Sallytown to see if Abel Teague's corpse is lying around in a ditch somewhere—anyway Clara stops—the black thing goes away—you and Kate get blinded by this green light—it ends—Clara and Glynis are gone—the lights are back on—Kate turns the mirror facedown on the rug. Have I got that about right?"

"You do," said Lemon, aware of Nick's silence.

"And you saw this yourself?" he asked Lemon.

"No. But we were in phone contact during part of it. I was over at Sylvia Teague's house, going through her computer—"

"Going through Ancestry files. So only Nick and Kate saw this part, the swirly thing at the door?"

"That's right," said Nick, coming back.

Boonie was quiet for a while.

"Okay, no offense, Nick, but . . . have you thought about this being a stress thing? From the war?"

Nick tried not to rise up at that, because he had considered the possibility.

"It occurred to me. But what about Kate? And none of that would change the thing that happened to Rainey Teague. Everybody saw that. No, believe me, I've tried. We're stuck with this damn thing."

"Strange things do happen in the world," said Lemon. Boonie—who was warming to him—smiled and said, "Tell me one thing compares to this."

"The entire world. What it's really made of. I read a book, about particle physics. Quantum mechanics, that kind of thing? What we're looking at, right here—you, me, Nick, the river going by—it's all just an energy field. I know, I know—but it's true—"

"There was a guy in my unit," said Nick, "had this saying written on his helmet: *God made the universe out of nothing, and if you look real close, you can tell.*"

Lemon nodded.

"That's exactly what I mean. So if all this is just a field of energy, maybe there are places where that energy field can get . . . bent. Warped."

"You mean like with magnets and iron filings?" Boonie asked.

"Yeah. Like that. Or gravity. Things are only heavy because the earth is actually pulling on . . . everything. Including you and me. But we can't see it, can we? Maybe there's something like that in Niceville."

Boonie snorted.

"What? Like Crater Sink?"

Lemon was going to say *Yes, exactly like Crater Sink*, but they saw a big black SUV come rolling into the parking lot, Kate at the wheel.

"She's here," said Boonie.

"She is," said Lemon. "So, what do you think?"

Boonie watched as Kate climbed down out of the truck and stopped for a moment beside it to search the crowds in the Pavilion.

"I think," said Boonie, as Kate made eye contact with him and started walking towards them, "I think I believe you. God help me. And I have no fucking idea what to do about it."

"I don't think there's anything anybody can do about this. Except avoid it. Maybe there's a rational explanation for all of it. Maybe not. Maybe Lemon is right and there's a force that's . . . twisting things . . . bending reality . . . in Niceville. I'll tell you where I come down. You know what the patrol guys say. FIDO."

"Fuck it. Drive on," said Boonie.

"That's it exactly. I say fuck it. Whatever it is, we can't touch it or do a damn thing about it. So fuck it. Drive on."

"What about Merle Zane?"

They all rose as Kate walked up the stairs onto the terrace. Nick smiled at her, but he was speaking to them.

"Put him in the ground, Boonie. Put him in the ground under a heavy stone and walk away."

Kate wasn't smiling.

She stood and looked slowly around at the three of them, finally coming back to Nick. She coldly assessed his state of health for a few seconds.

Nick waited for it.

Boonie and Lemon braced themselves.

Kate let out a long sigh.

"Nick, you're an asshole."

"He is," said Boonie. "I tried to stop him."

She fixed him with a glare.

"And you, Boonie, are a lying hound."

"That he is," said Nick.

Lemon said, "Hey, I'm an innocent bystander."

She shook her head, sighed heavily.

"I could really use a drink."

A general ripple of relief and the resumption of normal breathing. Since her drink was Chianti and there was a carafe of it on the table, all that was needed was another glass, which Lemon got up to fetch. Kate took a chair across from Nick, at Boonie's right hand. Boonie opened his mouth to start up an apology, but she lifted her hand.

"No apologies needed, Boonie. I never expected him to stay in the hospital anyway. He hates hospitals. He says people die in them."

"They do. You look beat, babe," said Nick.

"I am beat. I am beat up and beat down. I've been getting schooled in real-world parenting. Apparently I'm a gullible fool."

Nick glanced at Boonie, and then back to her.

"Rainey?"

"Yes. Rainey. And Axel. They've been skipping classes. Leaving early. As far as I can tell, since the first week of the term. I think they've gotten into Beth's e-mail service too, because they're probably sending phony e-mails to cover themselves—"

"They're faking e-mails?" said Nick. "They're too young to hack into—"

"Don't kid yourself," said Boonie.

"He's right," said Kate. "Those boys are on Axel's iPad all the time. They know more about the Internet than Mark Zuckerberg. And they're both lying to us about Coleman and Owen and Jay. It turns out they haven't been following them home, or picking on them. No Crypt Boy and Cop Killer's Kid. I mean, there's the usual conflict, but that's what boys are like. Rainey and Axel have been handing us—Beth and you and me—a line of pure bullshit."

"Like most kids," Boonie said.

He had raised two girls all by himself, one now happily married and the other happily in the Navy, and getting them there had nearly killed him.

Kate sighed again, smiled up at Lemon as he came back with a glass, filled it, and handed it to her.

"Thank you, Lemon. I've been telling these guys about Rainey and Axel. They've been skipping classes. Faking notes and e-mails. Playing hooky."

"And going where?" Lemon asked.

She looked up the river toward Patton's Hard.

"I think they're spending a lot of time up there," she said, nodding toward the place. "Under the willows."

"If they've been playing hooky," said Nick, "then we'd have gotten a call from Alice."

Kate took a sip, held the glass in front of her, and frowned at her reflection.

"That's another thing that's bothering me. Alice Bayer doesn't seem to be anywhere around. I talked to her temp, a horrible person named Gert Bloomsberry, who was thrilled to tell me that Alice hasn't been at the school in over two weeks. According to Gert, Alice probably went off to see a friend—"

That got Nick's attention.

"Alice wouldn't bail on her job for *any* reason. Not that woman. She put up with Delia Cotton for ten years. Never missed a day."

Kate agreed, and said so with real heat.

"One of the teachers went up to her house. The car was gone and there was a note on her door. It said she'd gone to Sallytown and she'd be back soon. The priest knocked, but there was no one home. They've been calling, but all they get is her answering machine."

"I don't like that," said Boonie.

"Neither do I," said Nick.

"Then you won't like this either," said Kate, reaching into her briefcase and bringing out the note she had taken from Gert Bloomsberry. She laid it on the table so everyone could see it.

Nick picked it up, read it, set it down.

"You see my problem," said Kate, a comment for the table. "Since most of us believe that Sylvia is dead—where did this note come from?"

Lemon leaned forward, picked up the note.

"I think I know," he said, which got the full attention of everyone else.

"When we were still trying to figure out what was going on, Nick and Kate asked me to run through Sylvia's computer to see if there was anything on it that would help. I went over—"

"How'd you get in?" Boonie asked. "There's a security lock on the door."

Nick and Kate looked at him.

Boonie shrugged.

"I had a drink with Mavis Crossfire. The Teague house on Cemetery Hill is on her beat. Now that nobody lives there, she makes it a point to see it's okay."

"And the house is fine," said Lemon, with an edge. "I have the code. I go there from time to time, just to take care of the yard. If she sees my truck in the driveway, Mavis will come in for a beer. The thing is, this note—Sylvia has a file box of them, on the shelf in her office. At least she did last time I was there."

Boonie didn't get it.

"But why would she keep old notes?"

Kate knew why.

"That paper is expensive. Sylvia had money, but she was frugal about things like this. And she was meticulous about her handwriting, as you can see. If she made a mistake, she'd start over, but she'd keep the old note in case she wanted to use the other side for something."

Lemon was holding the note.

"There's nothing wrong with this one."

"Yes, there is," said Kate. "I was thinking about it on the way over. There's no date. Sylvia always put the date under her signature. If you look close, you can see that the note has been shortened. You can see the scissor marks. Somebody cut the date line off. She must have made a mistake on the date line, so she put it aside and took out another piece of paper. You know what this means, don't you? Nick? Lemon?"

"Yes," said Lemon. "Rainey's been in that house. His old house. Probably with Axel. They've figured out the code—"

"I have it written in my planner," said Kate. "I guess they're going into my purse as well."

Nick stood up, angry, his face set and pale.

"Where are the boys now?"

Kate sat back, her expression one of sorrow and worry. "I don't know. Rainey's not answering his cell. Axel has his iPad turned off. I called Beth at the audiologist's office, and she hasn't heard from them either. I tried Rainey's cell phone GPS locator online and it's not working. His phone's a Motorola, so the only way to kill the GPS is to take the battery out. They're not at home. I have no idea where they are. They left the truck while I was confronting Coleman. Maybe they're at Sylvia's house right now."

"Did you fill Beth in on the whole story?"

"No. I just said they were playing hooky. She can't leave the doctor's office until the fitting is over. She says she'll meet us as soon as she's free."

"Well, let's you and me go—"

Several things happened at once.

Nick's beeper went off.

And so did Boonie's.

Then Nick's cell.

Nick looked at his beeper first.

911TIG

The 911 code meant CALL IN NOW. TIG was Tig Sutter, Nick's boss at the Belfair and Cullen County CID. Boonie was already talking into his own cell. Nick had Tig on the line a moment later. Some intense and terse exchanges followed. Kate and Lemon traded looks, and Lemon shook his head.

"It's not the boys, Kate. Relax."

Nick had a short, sharp exchange on the cell. He closed the call just as Boonie finished his.

"It's Deitz," said Boonie, looking at Nick. "He's rolling in a dark blue

Lexus. Niceville PD is tracking him right now. Up in the north end. You coming?"

Nick looked at Kate.

"You just got out of the hospital, Nick," she said. "Are you really in good enough shape to go?"

Nick took her question seriously.

"Yes. I am. I wouldn't go if I weren't. It wouldn't be fair to the rest of the cops."

"Then go," she said. "Lemon and Beth and I will find the boys."

Well, No Matter What Happens, There's Always Death

Chu and Deitz were heading northeast, toward the intersection of North Gwinnett and Bluebottle—Endicott following along about a mile back—Endicott was listening to complicated New Orleans jazz by Irvin Mayfield—when Deitz looked up through the moon roof and saw a small olive-drab dot floating just above the canopy of transplanted palm trees that shaded The Glades. For a while he paid it no attention, flying dots being a dime a dozen near an airport.

The Glades neighborhood was a parklike development of fifties-style housing done in a Coral Gables style. It had once been Niceville's most prestigious suburban development. But Niceville had overrun it and swept on by and now it was run-down and the palm trees were weary and tattered. Coker had a bungalow in The Glades.

After they got through with Danziger, Deitz intended to go pay Coker a visit.

They were well into Niceville's northern suburbs now and the afternoon rush hour was building up. The Galleria Mall was coming up on their left, a collection of box stores and theme restaurants like the Rainforest Café and Landry's and T.G.I. Friday's, all of it surgically attached to one of those gigantic Bass Pro Shops. The parking lot was already jammed.

Jesus, look at those saps, Deitz was thinking, looking at the cars and

SUVs packed into ten acres of parking, the lights of the stores flashing and blinking, the people milling around. *Spare me the fucking burbs.*

Chu had the radio on and he was listening to something sappy with a lot of strings and horns. Chu seemed to be doing okay. He was quiet, but that was only natural.

The cars and trucks and buses flowed around them and Deitz had the comfortable feeling of being just one anonymous vehicle in a glittering river of steel and glass. He was starting to feel like he was a street player again, like he was *operating*.

The gun on his belt helped the feeling. It was a bit like being back in the FBI, before he'd totally fucked his career.

He'd seen a couple of Niceville PD cruisers, but they weren't paying any special attention to him. He was staring at the dark green dot—a chopper obviously—but not really focusing on it.

He was having happy thoughts about what he was going to do to Charlie Danziger when he finally had him down on the ground.

First thing, those blue boots were—okay, now wait a fucking minute.

What the hell is that chopper doing?

It was a quarter mile away, gliding along real slow, on a perfectly parallel path with their Lexus, and at about the same speed.

It wasn't a traffic chopper.

Deitz squinted at it, trying to see the marking on the tail boom. It wasn't a Eurocopter . . . From the color and the silhouette, it looked more like a Huey. Who the hell still flew Hueys these days?

He got the answer a second later.

The Air National Guard.

"Chu, get into that mall. Turn now. Go slow, but get us into—"

Chu was jerked out of his reverie by the steel in Deitz's voice. It rattled him, but he braked to make the next left turn at a large neon sign with shooting stars all over it:

The Galleria Mall
The Best Deserve The Best

"What is it?" Chu was asking, his voice going up a couple of octaves, but Deitz was watching a black SUV about eight cars back, in the right-hand lane, big and bulky, with tinted windows. He had seen it before, but trucks like that were everywhere.

"Just make the turn. Go slow. Use your signals."

"Is it the police?"

"Yes. I think so."

"What are we going to do?"

"Get us into the covered parking area. That's gonna take out the air unit. We can deal with the guys on the ground. Just don't make any crazy moves. Drive as if this was where we were going."

"How long have they been following us?"

Deitz thought about it while he watched as the black SUV braked, hesitated, and then moved on down the street. Which meant they were passing the Eye onto another surveillance unit.

Deitz got the implication. They wanted to know where Deitz was going. Otherwise they'd have just scooped him up as soon as they had their team squared away.

They thought he was going for the money.

Greedy bastards.

"Don't know. They just handed us off."

"Handed us off?"

"Never mind," he said, as Chu rolled the Lexus into a huge covered parking area. Chu stopped at the bar, pressed the button for a ticket. The bar lifted. There were about ten cars lined up behind the Lexus, and none of them looked official. Which didn't mean a thing.

The trick was to get on foot and get lost in the crowd. Deitz wished he had brought the wig, if only to change his outline in a mass of people. He wasn't nervous, or scared. He checked his mood and realized he was wired up and engaged. He'd run this sort of game hundreds of times himself. He knew how it was played. And he played it pretty well.

"Go up three levels. There's a walkway across to the upper level of the mall. Park near it."

"Am I coming with you?"

Deitz gave him a carnivorous grin.

"Oh yeah. You're coming. You're not gonna want to miss this."

Chu found a slot six spaces away from the Promenade Walk.

"Back it in," said Deitz, looking for anybody on foot. As soon as the Lexus had taken that turn into the parking lot, they'd have gotten people out on the ground. But unless they were a dedicated surveillance unit, and not a bunch of feckless locals, the people on the ground would be easy to spot. And they'd be jumpy, because now there were civilians all over the place, and dead civilians killed careers. Chu got the Lexus parked, shut it down, started to pull the key.

"Leave it," said Deitz.

Chu didn't ask why.

Because one of us might not be coming back.

They were out on the deck.

"Take your jacket off, put it over your arm," Dietz said, while he grabbed the black valise out of the rear of the Lexus. "When I tell you, put it on again. Keep the gun in your pants. You okay?"

Chu's mouth was too dry to get any words out, so he just nodded. Deitz smacked him on the shoulder, a ferocious grin creasing his beefy face. Chu realized that Deitz was having *fun* and he wanted Chu along to share it with.

At that point he knew that if the opportunity presented itself, he was going to have to shoot Deitz in the back. Often.

He hoped he could do it.

Deitz waved him on ahead, and they were moving, slow and steady, across the walkway, the glitter and glare of the big covered mall opening up before them, various and beautiful and new, and full of the dull roar and canned music and the shuffle and scuffle and chatter of a couple thousand people that make malls a pretty good facsimile of hell.

"Where are we going?" Chu asked, as they turned left and headed along the upper balcony, keeping close to the storefronts. Deitz inclined his head in the direction of a large gatelike structure, apparently made out of huge wooden logs.

A family of stuffed bears stood outside the gates, all of them on their hind legs, in that charging-grizzly pose that they were probably NOT doing when they got themselves drilled in the skull. A sign in cartoon log letters above the gate read BASS PRO SHOP, and a large crowd was milling about the entrance.

"Why there?" Chu asked, trotting to keep up with Deitz, who was picking up speed.

"They sell guns," he answered, just as someone shouted at them from off to their left—Deitz and Chu turned as a large guard in a Securicom uniform popped out of nowhere and took a brace with his handgun pointed straight at them, barking at them:

"Freeze—freeze or I'll—"

Deitz shot the guard in the knee.

The guard shrieked, a whistling howl, and went down, his weapon clattering across the tiles.

"We're not killing anybody," said Deitz, over his shoulder, as he trotted toward the guard through a crowd of terrified shoppers, most of whom were now running in every direction but the one that had a Deitz in it.

Chu noticed that the order of fleeing did the shoppers no credit—it was the dads leading by fifty feet, trailed closely by the older sons, with the women and toddlers bringing up the rear.

Deitz was bending down over the sweaty face of the guard, whose cheeks were pulled back in a rictus of pain.

"Jermichael Foley, you dumb fuck," said Deitz, taking a knee beside the guard. "Don't we always say *Leave the takedown shit to the cops?* Don't we *always* say *that?*"

Jermichael Foley was nodding vigorously, trying to stop the bleeding in his knee. Deitz prodded the entrance wound with his index finger, which drew another steam-whistle shriek from Jermichael.

"Jeez, Mr. Deitz, you *shot* me!"

"Yeah, but only in the knee, so I hope we can still be friends. I'm afraid that knee's fucked for good, though. Your own damn fault."

He patted the guard on the shoulder, plucking his radio out of his belt. He walked over and picked up the guard's weapon, the inevitable Glock 17. All around him the citizens had utterly fled and he and Chu were alone in a kind of courtyard in front of the Bass Pro Shop entrance. Two employees wearing plaid shirts and bib overalls were busy trying to close the rolling glass doors that sealed the store off.

Deitz lifted the Sig and fired two rounds at the employees. The two employees promptly gave up their efforts and disappeared at a dead run into the dimly lit recesses of the store.

Which was mammoth, two gigantic floors stuffed with every kind of sporting gear the American Male would ever want: boats, fishing rods, more boats, canoes, tents, binoculars, all things camo in every woodland color. Here and there an array of stuffed animals lurking on top of display cases.

And all along the upper balcony, row upon row of guns—rifles and shotguns and handguns—all of them visible to Chu as he stood there. He was trying to figure out how Deitz's admonition not to kill anybody squared with the forcible acquisition of an arsenal big enough to start an insurrection.

He thought, in this odd moment of calm before the shit storm that was sure to come, that now might be a good time to put one into Deitz's skull, but his hands failed him and the moment passed.

Deitz was heading for the doors when one of the standing bears went sailing backwards, and a moment later there was a booming crack that echoed around the upper level of the mall. Deitz kept moving, but Chu looked back and saw two large men in black fatigues running full tilt at them, both carrying stubby black guns that would still have looked lethal if they'd been lavender.

As Chu watched, the guy on the left lifted his weapon—aimed it at Chu's head. Chu saw a blue sparkly crackle flare up at the muzzle—whizzy things plucked at his shirt collar. Then the chattering sound. A machine gun.

To his immense and lasting surprise, motivated by a vestigial gene that may have come down from Tamerlaine, Chu pulled out his gun, pointed it in the general direction of the cops, and pulled the trigger.

The gun kicked back ferociously—God only knew where the round went—the muzzle flew up and the top of the barrel smacked him in the forehead, splitting his skin open—the gun flew out of his tingling fingers and landed six yards away, bounced twice, and went off again, this time spinning itself around on the tiles like a steel top.

Chu stood there half stunned, with blood running into his eyes, and blinked at the pistol while more rounds from the cops skittered off the tiles around him and one slug tugged at his right sleeve.

He heard Deitz shouting at him.

"Chu, for fuck's sake, what the fuck are you doing? Get in here!"

Chu turned around.

Deitz was standing just inside the Pro Shop gates. He had the two glass doors almost shut. There was more chatter from behind him and a series of white splotches stitched across the glass, a line leading right at Deitz's head. Deitz flinched away from the impact and bellowed at Chu.

"Come on, you fucking asshole."

He was through the doors and Deitz slammed them shut just as another line of white blotches chattered along the glass. It dawned on Chu that the glass was bulletproof. Deitz did something to a keypad beside the door, arming the system, grinning at Chu as he did so.

"What the fuck were you doing back there? You shot at those cops? And you've lost the gun. And your forehead is bleeding. They hit you?"

"They were *shooting* at me," said Chu, wiping the blood out of his eyes with the sleeve of his shirt. "I mean, I'm a totally innocent hostage and they were trying to kill me."

"What happened to your forehead?"

"The gun smacked me in the face when I pulled the trigger. I guess I wasn't holding it right."

Deitz laughed.

"I guess you weren't. Well, you're not a totally innocent hostage now, my friend. Now you're a fucking desperado."

Cops in black fatigues were pouring out of alleys and scrambling up the escalators. More rounds were being fired at the doors.

Deitz ignored them, turned away, took a breath.

"There's a first-aid box over there on the wall. Go get some gauze and wrap your head. You're getting blood all over yourself. Then we gotta make sure about the staff. And see if there's any customers fucking around. Orders are for staff to throw out the customers and lock the store down—this place is like a fortress—it was built to withstand full-on armed assault—because of all the weapons—"

"Won't they take their own guns out of the display cases and shoot at us?"

"Nope. Bass Pro management doesn't want any of their staff shooting a customer by accident. It's policy—or they can't get insurance. If they can't get out of the store, they all go into lockdown—they got a panic room behind the gun lockers—and they hole up until the cavalry gets here—"

"How do you *know* all this?" asked Chu, trotting along behind Deitz, dabbing at his bloody forehead with his sleeve, his heart slamming around in his chest. Deitz looked back at him.

"Because we designed their whole security protocol. All the gear. The systems. The hardware and the software. The passwords. How to harden the walls and the floors. We put it all in. I mean our company. Securicom. I know this system better than the cops do. Better than the store guys do. We can hold out here for weeks. They even got dried food. Lots of bagged water. They'll cut the power, but we got auxiliary. They're fucked."

"We put the systems in? Securicom did?"

"Yes," said Deitz. "And now we're gonna secure the position and bunker down in here and figure out how to talk our way out of this situation. You and me. You're gonna tell them all about that Mondex thing, how to trace it. How to find the guys who did the bank. That's your part. You're the IT hero. The rest we can deal with. I can say when the prison van went over I hit my head and wandered off. I can threaten to sue the U.S. Marshals for endangering a prisoner. We'll fuck with their heads.

Maybe even get you off for shooting at those cops, you crazy dink bastard."

"What about the round you put in that guard's knee?"

"Fuck Jermichael Foley. I can say it was self-defense. He wasn't supposed to be shooting at anybody, the dumb fuck. He'll be lucky I don't fire his ass when all this is over. In the meantime, we got work to do. You follow?"

Chu was painfully aware that when it came to chutzpah and moxie and an Olympian capacity for self-delusion, Deitz was in a league of his own, but in the end, Chu got a bandage out of the first-aid box and followed Deitz, wrapping the gauze around his head as he trotted along.

What the hell, Chu thought. *He might even pull it off.*

Endicott pulled over as the black SUVs and choppers and squad cars began to swarm around the Galleria Mall. He was getting no red dot on his GPS screen because he was too far away and the Lexus was probably parked under a lot of concrete and rebar. It looked as if Deitz was either going to die in this mall or go back to prison, and in either case this was, in Endicott's view, far from excellent. Very damn far.

He was not pleased.

He sat there for a while, working through the possibilities, the various courses of action.

Then he called Warren Smoles.

A hundred feet back, slouching down behind the wheel of his mud brown Chrysler Windstar van, Edgar Luckinbaugh drank strong black coffee out of a thermos and set it down on the console beside him. On the passenger seat he had a box of Krispy Kreme donuts, a police scanner, a cell phone plugged into a charger, and a widemouthed one-gallon milk jug, empty, for now, but given enough coffee he'd be making a contribution to it fairly soon.

It had been difficult for him to get sick time cleared, and when he did get it he had to borrow the most nondescript and forgettable vehicle he could locate, which was this piece-of-shit Windstar that belonged to his Aunt Vi, who was too frail and incontinent to drive anything other than her relatives crazy.

Fortunately Vi doted on Edgar because he brought her macaroons and whiskey and Kools, which, according to her doctor, were going to kill her but so far hadn't, so screw him, and she was happy to let Edgar rent the van from her for twenty bucks a day, paid a week in advance, the grasping old bat.

Edgar had no idea that the grasping old bat was wildly rich, in a small way, and that his twice-weekly deliveries of Kools and Jameson's Irish and Pepperidge Farm Macaroons had secured for him a favored position in her last will and testament, which, had he lived, would have run to over fifty thousand dollars.

At any rate, after considerable exertions, Edgar was now parked a few yards behind Endicott's black Caddy in the vicinity of the Galleria Mall and listening to the cross talk on the police scanner. As was Mr. Endicott, Edgar had no doubt.

He had been present when Endicott had set up his own two-car surveillance post near a neat wood-frame rancher at 237 Bougainville Terrace in the Saddle Hill neighborhood of southwestern Niceville.

A quick check of the Reverse Lookup White Directory had confirmed the rancher as belonging to a Securicom employee named Andrew Chu, known as Andy. He had relayed this information to Sergeant Coker's text message center as soon as he had determined that Harvill Endicott had settled in for a long night of watching Andy Chu's house.

He had left the message on a voice mail server that could not be traced to anyone on this planet and had gotten back, a short time later, a brief *heard and understood charlie mike* text message from the same number, *charlie mike* meaning *Continue the mission*. Edgar had no idea what was going on, and he intended to keep it that way.

He was professionally satisfied that his identification of Harvill Endicott as a Person of Interest to Staff Sergeant Coker had panned out. Clearly Mr. Endicott had a strong interest in the whereabouts of Byron Deitz, since he had followed Deitz and Chu all the way from Chu's house to this mall, where events seemed to be overtaking the best-laid plans of practically everyone.

Edgar Luckinbaugh had no interest in any of these events, since too much knowledge was a dangerous thing and frequently led to being indicted, or worse.

So he plucked another Krispy Kreme from the box—honey-glazed, his favorite—and set about it, quite content to be a simple man doing a simple thing and doing it well.

Trail of Tears

Eufaula was there when Kate called from the SUV.

"No, Miss Kate. The boys aren't here. I've been here since two and they haven't called or anything."

Eufaula looked at the kitchen clock, frowning.

"But they should be, shouldn't they? Do you want me to go see if they're walking along North Gwinnett, rambling around like they always do?"

"Eufaula, would you mind?"

"Not at all. I'll take my cell and call you if I find them. Shall I go all the way up to Regiopolis?"

"No, honey, thanks. We just called and they're not there either. The staff went out looking, but neither of them is on the grounds. Nobody knows where they are."

Eufaula had already observed that Rainey had very circuitous ways about him, and that he was having a bad influence on Axel, and that baby Hannah didn't like him at all, no sir, but she felt it wasn't her place to say so. She herself found Rainey to be an unsettling child. Furtive and sly, with a mean streak when cornered.

Sort of like a possum.

Kate thanked Eufaula and shut the cell down. She looked over at Lemon.

"Not at home?" he said, and she shook her head, her chest closing up. They were parked outside Sylvia's house—Rainey's former home—a large stone mansion at 47 Cemetery Hill, tucked up into a stand of trees that ran down a long slope to a tributary of the Tulip.

This part of Garrison Hills was Serious Old Money and looked it. The Teagues had been a wealthy family, but then the Teagues' line, throughout its long and checkered history, had shown a talent for acquiring wealth, if not affection. Sylvia's husband, Miles, was a man Kate had never been able to warm to, and his suicide a few days after Rainey was found alive had struck her at the time as an act of utter narcissistic selfishness.

"Will we go in and see?" said Lemon.

"Yes. And if they're in there . . ."

"Take it easy, Kate. Rainey's not a bad kid, and Axel has a lot of sense for a kid his age."

Kate said nothing and Lemon followed her up the stone steps to the large oak door. Set into the carved frame was a shielded keypad. Kate punched in the code and the latch popped open. They went through the door and into the wide entry hall, a cavernous space that rose up three floors to the vaulted ceiling. The interior of the house gleamed with brass and polished oak and antique carpets in blue and ochre and amber. The hall lights were on but the rest of the huge old house was dark and silent. It smelled of wood polish and still air. Kate walked to the foot of the center-hall staircase and called out.

"Axel? Rainey? Guys, are you here?"

Nothing. Just an echo and the sound of the house ticking as the day cooled down.

They walked through the main-floor rooms—a large formal dining room, and on the other side of the central hall a formal living room done in pale beiges and dark woods, with splashes of bright color here and there. An oil painting of Miles and Sylvia in their early years hung above the stone mantel of the massive fireplace. The house breathed of absence and emptiness.

Beyond the living room there was a wood-lined library full of comfortably threadbare furniture in worn plaids and brown leather. The glass-windowed shelves were heavy with books and framed snapshots.

Sylvia's desk—an antique dresser with a gleaming French polish—was set into the wall opposite the large flat-screen television that rested on a rosewood sideboard.

Lemon put his hand on top of Sylvia's Dell.

"It's still warm," he said.

"See when it was last opened," said Kate. "I don't think they're here, but I'll check the rest of the house."

Kate walked into the kitchen area and looked out the wall of glass to the gazebo where they had found what was left of Miles. Lemon had done the yard recently and the bluegrass was smooth all the way down to the willows and oaks at the bottom of the lawn. No footprints. No Axel. No Rainey.

No one in any of the upstairs rooms either, although it looked as if someone had been lying down on the bed in the master bedroom. The coverlet, a plush and silky duvet, showed a depression about the size of a small kid.

Kate got an image of Rainey lying here and staring up at the carved oak ceiling and thinking . . . what?

Kate had no idea.

After all these weeks, after what she had found out about him today, Rainey was more of a mystery than ever. And what sort of effect was he having on Axel? Or Hannah, for that matter? Axel had never been devious, at least not at this level. Rainey was a different story.

But then he's a Teague, isn't he?

When she got back to Sylvia's office, Lemon was shutting down the computer.

"Whoever's been here—"

"Let's assume it was the boys."

"Okay. First of all, I think they've been using Sylvia's Internet connection to send out phony e-mails. Clever stuff too. One of them has the makings of a great hacker. I can't tell which. They've also been going over all of Sylvia's Ancestry files. From what I can see, they've been looking for . . ."

Lemon hesitated, so Kate helped him out.

"Rainey's story?"

"Yes. That's what it looks like. Rainey was adopted from Sallytown, if I'm right?"

"Yes. From a foster home up in Sallytown. At least, that's the story."

Lemon heard the slightly sarcastic tone in her voice. He sat back and looked at her.

"Well, whatever the truth is, Kate, he's been searching for it. With Axel's help, I guess. And for Rainey's parents who died in that barn fire. The Gwinnetts."

"And they've had no luck?"

Lemon shook his head.

"Not so far."

"I'm not surprised. Neither have I."

Kate sighed, leaned against the wall, closed her eyes.

"Look, Lemon . . . keep this to yourself, okay? Before Dad disappeared . . . I mean, right before . . . he wrote a memo expressing concerns about Rainey's date of birth, about his adoption in general.

After . . . the mirror thing, with Glynis . . . I looked into it. Dad was right. Rainey's adoption papers were—they made no sense. After I was made guardian, I felt I had an obligation to clear up the confusion, make sure everything was in order. What I found just made it worse."

Lemon sat quietly and listened. He knew a bit about this, but Kate had never opened up on the topic. He let her run.

"For starters, there was no record of Rainey's birth as a Gwinnett in any of the databases, local, county, statewide, adjoining states. Canada, Mexico, Jupiter. Nothing. The foster home, no record of it ever existing. The Palgraves, his foster parents, the only Palgraves I ever found were Zorah and Martin Palgrave. Would you like to know when they were married?"

"Yes, I would."

"Zorah and Martin Palgrave were married at the Methodist Church in Sallytown on March 15. In 1893. Dad found an old photograph of a family reunion—*The Niceville Families Jubilee, John Mullryne's Plantation, Savannah, Georgia, 1910*. All four of the Founding Families were there—the Haggards, the Cottons, the Walkers—"

"And the Teagues."

"Yes. The name of the company that printed the photo was on the card. Zorah and Martin Palgrave."

"Maybe a coincidence?"

Kate gave him a wry look.

"You don't believe that yourself. Not after everything that's happened. I don't know what to make of it. Or of this. On April 12, 1913, the Palgraves banked a letter of credit drawn on the Memphis Trust Bank. The letter stated that the funds were to cover costs related to 'the care and confinement of Clara Mercer and the delivery of a healthy male child on March 2, 1913.' The credit letter was issued on the account of Glynis Ruelle. We have every reason to believe that the man who got her pregnant—and started the whole feud—was Abel Teague. He's in the shot, and so is Clara. Beside his name somebody wrote the word *shame*."

"Miles had to know about all this. He was the one who arranged the adoption for Sylvia."

"Yes. He hired a lawyer named Leah Searle to handle it. I found a letter from her to Miles, at least it had her signature on it, dated May 9, 2002, prior to Rainey's adoption, and in the letter she provided a copy of Rainey's birth certificate, which stated that he was born in Sallytown on March 2, 2002. It listed his parents as Lorimar and Prudence Gwinnett.

They were supposed to have died in a barn fire so Rainey went into foster care with the Palgraves. Except none of this was true. Or if it is, there is no way to verify it. To be honest, I think Miles paid Leah Searle to fake the documents."

"Did Sylvia know anything about this?"

"I think she was looking into it when Rainey was kidnapped."

"Have you talked to the lawyer, Leah Searle?"

Kate said nothing for a while.

"No. I couldn't. She died after the adoption."

"How?"

"She drowned, according to her obituary."

"So what you're saying is, nobody knows who Rainey really is?"

Kate shook her head.

"No, I'm not saying that. I sure as hell don't think that Rainey was born on March 2, 1913, and that he is, in reality, the illegitimate son of Abel Teague and Clara Mercer. On the other hand, there's no way that Rainey is eleven either. He's already well into puberty. His voice is changing. He's filling out. Getting muscle. He's almost my height now, and probably just as strong. If he's under fifteen I'll be . . . I don't know. I just don't know. I mean, if his birth certificate is a fake, then how old is he, really?"

"Kids are doing that earlier and earlier, Kate. Growing up too fast. Every generation does it."

"It's more than that. Sometimes, when I'm talking to him, it's like there's something inside there, looking out at me through his eyes. And whatever *that* is, it's not a kid."

She teared up, fought it down.

"Kate, this is all . . . it's just a screwup with the records. Happens everywhere."

She smiled, her eyes bright and moist.

"Yes. It does."

"Boonie said something at the Pavilion—maybe he had a point. Maybe one of us—you and me, or Reed—he's a cop and would have more weight to throw—should drive up to Sallytown and look around the place one more time."

She nodded but could not say anything. Her fears were all on the table, and looking at them was making them worse.

After a tense silence, he changed the subject with an audible clank.

"Okay. We'll think about Sallytown later. I checked the television. It was still warm as well. But I think they always are. The channel mode was set to DVD. I found this in the machine. I guess Rainey was watching home movies."

He held up a homemade DVD with a colorful label on it, a family photograph, Miles and Sylvia and a younger Rainey, taken in front of a brightly decorated Christmas tree.

Kate took it and stared down at it, and the image blurred, and she realized she was crying again. She handed it back to him, and he laid it down on Sylvia's desk. Kate saw a shelf with Sylvia's notepaper on it. She took a blank sheet, sat down at Sylvia's desk, and wrote out a note, but she didn't use Sylvia's pen.

Dear Guys . . . if you're reading this you know we have been at the house. We're not angry at all and we hope you'll both come home and talk about this. Rainey, I think Nick and I haven't been paying enough attention to how much you miss your mom and dad. And Axel, you have to be feeling pretty confused about where your dad is and what he's doing. So don't worry about anything. We love you both and we'll make things better as soon as you get home.

Love and hugs
Kate

She set the pen down, placed a small carved netsuke rabbit on top of the note, and got up.

"Okay. They're not here. Where to now?"

Lemon glanced out the window, saw the light fading as the evening came on, slowly but surely.

"No call from Eufaula?"

"Nope."

"Then we have to go to Patton's Hard."

"I know," said Kate. "I just don't want to."

When It Absolutely Positively Has to Be Dead by Midnight

By the time Boonie and Nick got to the Galleria, the situation had, as the saying goes, hardened. The mall was locked down and all the staff and civilians had been herded to the outer edges of the mall parking lot, where they were clustering around a harried cop like a squadron of Canada geese, squawking that somebody had better *go get their cars and stuff because well because and because* . . .

The cop was close to losing his temper and they heard it finally go with a loud bang just as Boonie pulled through the cordon of Niceville cruisers—their light racks slowly flashing.

A large female staff sergeant in blue and gold with the name CROSS-FIRE engraved on a silver plate on her tunic loomed up out of the crowd of cops and brass and leaned down to look in the driver's window. Mavis beamed down at Boonie, and then noticed Nick in the passenger seat.

"Nick, what in the name of blue devils are you doing here? You're supposed to be in the hospital. Does Kate know you're here?"

"Tig Sutter sent me. Is he here?"

"No. Tig's too smart for that. We got enough chiefs already, now that Boonie's here. How are you, Boonie?"

"I'm fine, Mavis. What's the sitrep?"

"*Sitrep*, Boonie?"

"You know what I mean, Mavis. Gimme a break."

She smiled, blew out her breath.

"Well, it is a cluster—it's a circus for sure. Deitz and a guy named Andy Chu are holed up inside the Bass Pro Shop—"

"How'd they manage that?" Boonie wanted to know.

"Well, I'm afraid we Niceville cops are going to take the heat for that. We got an anonymous call from this party saying that a Securicom employee named Andy Chu hadn't gone in to work and that maybe he was sheltering Byron Deitz at his house. Since Deitz is a multi-jurisdictional problem, well, Chief Keebles decided—"

"Oh jeez," said Boonie, putting his head down on the steering wheel. Mavis patted him on the shoulder.

"There, there, Boonie. It'll be all right. Anyway, Chief Keebles decided to hand the job to our own Emergency Response Team—sorta break them in, they being brand new and all—and by the time they got their pull-ups and onesies on and hit the road on their Big Wheels, it seems that this Chu guy and Deitz were already rolling in Chu's Lexus. So the chief figured, better not try to take him down until they had an idea of where he was going. Chief Keebles felt that maybe he was going to dig up the money he stole from the bank—"

"And he'd share in the glory of its recovery?"

"That's our boy."

"Was there air?" asked Nick.

"Yep. Ours was in the shop, so Chief Keebles asked for help from the Air National Guard, and they sent a Huey over—"

Boonie started bumping his head on the steering wheel. It was distracting. Nick reached over and stopped him. Mavis, paying this no mind, went on in a detached and amused tone.

"Well, of course Hueys tend to attract attention—no mistaking that *thrumpety-thrumpety* sound—one thing led to another and now Deitz has locked himself inside the Bass Pro Shop—"

"Any hostages?" Nick asked.

"Well, maybe. We're not quite sure of the status of this Andy Chu guy who's in there with him. Chu is head of IT at Deitz's company. Chu fired a round at our ERT guys outside the entrance to the Bass store, so maybe he's more of an accomplice. Or he just panicked. They were shooting at him, after all. And he threw his gun away a second later. Could have gone off by accident. Looked like he had a wound. They found blood all over the gun he was using. Deitz went through the store—even knew how to get the clerks out of their hidey-hole behind the gun racks—and he herded everybody he could find up onto the roof and went back down the stairs and bolted the steel fire door shut. They used the Huey to extract those folks."

"Praise the Lord," said Boonie.

"Amen. But it grieves me to tell you that there's a lady out there in the parking lot, name of Delores Maranzano, says her husband, Frankie, and his grandson, Ritchie, were using the bathroom in the Pro Shop and now they're missing and nobody knows where they are."

"So they might still be in there with Deitz?"

"Possibility, Nick. Definite possibility."

"Did they have cells?"

"She says they're shut off."

"How old's the grandkid?"

"Fourteen."

"Has this Frankie guy called out yet?"

"Not a peep. Probably laying low. There's a wrinkle, however."

Boonie lifted his eyes to heaven and said, "Of course there is."

"What is it?" Nick asked.

"Seems Frankie has a concealed carry permit."

Nick sighed.

"And of course he has his piece with him?"

Mavis nodded.

"Delores says he's never without it. He worries about being kidnapped, she says. Apparently he's filthy rich. He sleeps with it under his pillow."

"What's he got?"

"Oh, you'll love this part. Checked the registry. He has a Dan Wesson .44 Magnum—"

Boonie moaned.

"Don't tell me," said Nick. "With the eight-inch barrel."

Mavis nodded.

"She says he has a custom-made shoulder rig with a couple of slots for auto-loaders."

"So he's a shooter?"

"The wife says he goes to those combat simulation ranges. Takes Little Ritchie along with him. Ritchie's a shooter too. A keener, like his granddad."

"How old is this guy?"

"Forty-eight. From his driver's license shot, he looks a bit like a thug. Got a mean mouth and little eyes. He's six one, runs one-ninety. Wife says he's a lifter. He looks it."

"What does he do for a living?"

Mavis shrugged.

"Nobody knows. But Delores fits the trophy wife pattern. They're driving a Bentley. She says Frankie has commercial real estate down in Destin, Florida, but he made his big money in contracting out in Nevada."

"Nevada? Anything against him?"

Mavis shook her head.

"Negative on NCIC and MAGLOCEN and the rest of the databases. Boonie, he ring any bells?"

Boonie wiped his face with both hands.

"There's a Frankie Maranzano lives right across Fountain Square from my office. Top floor of the Memphis. We check out anybody has a clear line of fire into our space, so we looked at him. But his lawyer, fucking Julian Porter, started squealing about how Italian Americans were being targeted by the Feds. There was really nothing solid against him. Like J. Edgar said, 'Not every dago is a don.' "

Boonie pulled himself together.

"Anyway, what counts here is we got an aggressive guy and he has a hand cannon and a grandson he's gonna want to impress and he's prancing around inside that store somewhere."

"That's about the size of it."

"Anybody killed yet?"

"Not yet. Securicom guard named Jermichael Foley got himself shot in the right knee—"

"*Securicom?*"

Mavis nodded, knowing where this was going to go. "That's right. Securicom as in BD Securicom. We checked the records and guess who personally oversaw the design and installation of the security systems for the entire Galleria Mall? Including the Bass Pro Shop?"

Boonie lifted his head from the wheel. There was a bright red bar, slightly curved, marking the pale pink skin of his forehead.

"That place is a fortress," said Boonie.

"That it is," said Mavis. "And Deitz knows it better than any of us."

"We can't leave him in there," said Boonie. "He's got enough supplies to last a month. And there are two civilians in the line of fire. Has anybody tried to reach Deitz?"

"Yep. Our platoon boss got him on his cell phone."

"Deitz want anything?"

"Yep. He wants the Live Eye crew, and his lawyer—"

Boonie put his head back down on the wheel.

"Warren Smoles," he said.

"That's the man," said Mavis. "He's here now. Pulled up in that big white Benz over there. He's been on the Live Eye feed twice already, saying we were about to assassinate an innocent man, demanding immediate access to his client."

"Boonie," said Nick, "you let Warren Smoles in on this—with the Live Eye people along—and he'll turn it into a six-week reality show starring Warren Smoles. He'll deal out the film rights for a half mil. Deitz will have a book deal by Friday. And in the meantime Deitz will have that whole store trip-wired and booby-trapped so tight that it would take a platoon to pry him out of there. The longer you wait, the better prepared his defensive position will be. And Frankie will eventually make a dipshit move and get himself killed. Little Ritchie too. I've seen this all before. You have to take this on the fly, before Deitz gets dug in."

Boonie looked at him.

"You got any suggestions?"

"Yes. First of all, don't let Deitz call out anywhere. To Smoles or the media. Jam his phones."

"Already done," said Mavis.

"We'll need the engineering drawings for the store. The latest. We need to know if anything has changed since Deitz and his crew were there."

"Already got 'em," said Mavis.

"Good. For thirds, I'll need a couple of guys."

A general pause here.

"*You?*" said Mavis, one eyebrow raised.

"Yes. I'm going in and rip him out of there."

Boonie shook his head.

"No goddam way. You just got out of the hospital. That's nuts. I can't let you—"

"Mavis said Deitz was a multi-jurisdictional problem. Tig Sutter sent me down here, so the CID automatically takes precedence over the Niceville folks—sorry, Mavis. Boonie, you take precedence over the State guys—so if *you*—the FBI—the Special Agent in Charge—step back and let me do this, it will all be over by midnight."

"But what about this Frankie guy?"

"That's why we have to move now. So far he's kept his head down. If we can neutralize Deitz, everything else can be handled. It's all we have."

Boonie was thinking it over.

After all, the guy *was* Special Forces. And getting an FBI team down here would take hours. And draw the national media like bats to bugs.

"I have to ask you. Is this personal?"

"Yes. But it's also what needs to be done."

"Not often those two go together."

"Hardly ever."

"You said two guys. Who?"

"My partner. Beau Norlett."

"He's just a kid."

"He's steady and gutsy and I can count on him. I know how he'll react. That's important."

"Okay. And who else?"

"I'll need a base of fire, a sharpshooter to keep Deitz pinned down while we move in on him. I need suppressing fire that actually suppresses. So it has to be somebody good."

"A *rifle* shooter? Not a guy with a SAW?"

"No. A squad automatic weapon's a bludgeon. And if Deitz is bunkered up in the gun section, which is where I'd be, that means there's black powder in there too. Pounds of it, all tight packed in steel cans. Lot of muzzle-loaders shop at Bass Pro. Stray rounds hit black powder, that all goes up, maybe a secondary starts in the ammo crates, and thousands of serious hunting rounds start cooking off. People on the perimeter could die. I want a surgical shooter. Somebody with a cool head."

"How about Coker? He's the best we have."

"Is he available?"

"He's already here. Charlie Danziger too, because it was his Wells Fargo shipment that got boosted. Coker brought his gear with him."

Nick smiled.

"Coker works for me."

Willow Weep for Me

It was twilight by the time Kate and Lemon got to the southern end of the footpath that ran down the middle of Patton's Hard. In the half-light the forest of ancient willows loomed in front of the windshield like a high-walled green basilica roofed in tangled webs of overhanging vines. Beth called them as they shut the truck down.

"Kate, where are you?"

"We're at Patton's Hard. Where are you?"

"Out of my mind. I called the school and talked to a woman named Gert—"

"Oh dear."

"Yes. She says that Axel and Rainey have been getting Early Leave almost since the start of the term? How can that be? Why didn't Alice let us know? How did they get permission for Early Leave? What in hell is going on, Kate? I'm half crazy—"

"Are you driving?"

"Yes. I was on my way home to see if the boys are there yet. I have Hannah with me."

"Pull over and stop," said Kate. "Stop as soon as you can."

"Why—"

"I have stuff to explain, but you need to be stopped. Are you stopped yet?"

"Just a minute . . . just a minute . . ."

Kate could hear crying in the background, Hannah, picking up on her mother's fear.

"Okay. I'm stopped. What's going on, Kate?"

Kate told her the whole story. Beth had Kate's talent for listening and hearing.

"Dear God. Faking notes and e-mails?"

"Looks like, honey."

"And Alice is missing?"

"No. Not missing. There's a note on her door."

"Signed by her?"

A good question. Kate figured being around the FBI was rubbing off on Beth.

"Not that I was told."

A silence.

Then Beth spoke.

"This Gert creature told me that Alice would go out and find the truants and bring them back in her car. She'd even go to Patton's Hard. Is that true?"

"Gert said so, for what *that's* worth."

"And now you're at Patton's Hard too. Are they there? Axel and Rainey?"

"We're still looking. But I'm thinking no."

"God. Kate, what should I do? Should I come down and be with you?"

"You have Hannah. She sounds upset."

"It's the hearing aids. She's hearing now, and I think it frightens her. Kate, I'm . . . you know Byron's out, don't you?"

"Yes, honey. I heard."

"At first I thought he was coming for me. But now I hear he's in the Galleria. Somebody got shot. The police are there. Is Nick there?"

"Yes. He and Boonie went together."

"God. Kate, what's *happening* to us?"

Niceville, Kate thought, but she didn't say it.

"Honey, I think the best thing you could do is go home with Hannah. Eufaula's there all alone, waiting for the boys to show up. If you go there, she can go home."

"You're not at Patton's Hard alone, are you? I hate that place. And it's getting dark."

"No. Lemon's with me."

"Good. I like him."

"I know, Beth. All the women like Lemon."

She looked over at Lemon and smiled.

"Beth likes you."

"Tell her I like her right back."

"Did you hear that?"

"I did. Will you call me?"

"I will, Beth. And you call me if they show up at home. Okay?"

"Okay . . . Kate . . . is everything going to be okay? Will they come home?"

"It will be fine. Just no more Early Leave for either of them."

"I'm grounding Axel for the next ten years."

"Good idea. I'll ground Rainey and they can live in the basement like a couple of trolls."

"I love you, Kate."

"I love you too. Kiss Hannah for me."

"I will."

She clicked off.

Kate looked over at Lemon.

"Well, shall we?"

"We shall."

The footpath, never intended for cars, was barely wide enough to let them run the Envoy down the middle of it, with the willow branches scraping across the windshield and clutching at the sides of the truck. The surface of the path was muddy and uneven and the going was slow. Lemon was looking at the ruts in the pathway.

"We're not the first vehicle to drive down here. See the tracks there?"

Kate turned the lights on, and the beams picked out two shallow trenches, parallel and much narrower than the Envoy's tire prints. Beyond the lights the darkness was closing in as the sun went down. There was a chill in the air and Kate turned the heat up.

"Honk," said Lemon, as they rolled slowly along the path, the huge willows pressing in around them. "If they're around they'll hear you."

Kate blipped the horn a couple of times. There was no response. Patton's Hard was deserted.

"They're not here," said Kate. "I can't feel either of them."

"Let's go all the way through. If they're not here, maybe it's time to call the . . . Hold on a minute."

Kate slowed the truck.

"See that?" said Lemon. "The car tracks turn off there."

"How do you know it's not the parks people on a golf cart thingie."

"You don't golf, do you, Kate?"

"No, I'm too young to die of boredom. So it's not a golf cart?"

"No, it's a car, a subcompact."

Kate peered through the misty half-light. The narrow tracks they had been riding over came to a sharp turn beside a huge stand of willows.

The tracks went under the cascade of hanging willow branches and disappeared into the greenish gloom under the trees.

"I am not," said Kate, "following those."

"Wait here," said Lemon, popping the door. He stepped out, and then leaned back in.

"Have you got a flashlight?"

"In the glove box. Lemon, I've seen this movie."

He flashed a bright, slightly crazed smile and Kate remembered that before he became an "escort" to the Ladies Who Lunch he was a Marine Corps combat vet with two Bronzes for valor.

"Nothing can happen to us. We're the leads."

"What if you're just the faithful sidekick? They always get it first."

"Depends on whose movie it is," he said, reaching into the glove box. He pulled out a Streamlight and, with a flourish, Kate's compact Glock pistol.

"Would it make you feel better if I took this along?"

Kate sighed, reached for the keys.

"Yes. But I'm coming too."

"Why?"

"Because sometimes it's the chickenhearted wimp who stays in the car who gets it first."

Lemon laughed, closed his door, and Kate got out and hit the remote lock. He turned on the Streamlight—a powerful halogen beam—and they followed it down a few yards, reaching the point where the car tracks—if that's what they were—disappeared under the willow branches.

Kate hesitated but Lemon reached out, caught a handful of branches, and pulled them aside, shining the beam in as he did so.

Inside the curtain wall the willows rose up in columns, tall, angular branches arching out like flying buttresses in a green cathedral.

The interior—it *felt* like an interior—retained traces of the glow from the setting sun. It soared over their heads, a hundred feet or more, and spread out around them in a radius of fifty or sixty feet. The soaring space was full of creaking and hissing sounds as the wind off the river stirred the upper branches.

Everybody said that the willows in Patton's Hard would whisper to each other. Kate could understand how an imaginative person could hear voices in those trees.

The air in here smelled of earth and moss and rotting leaves. The ground under their feet was soft and damp. The tracks seemed to fade into the gloom. Something angular and spindly was up against the trunk of the main willow.

Lemon put his light on it.

It was a lawn chair, a battered old ruin that looked as if it had been scavenged from a thrift store or a junk pile. An umbrella was attached to the arm of the chair with a bungee cord. Beside the chair was an upturned wooden crate, and on the crate was a pile of dog-eared paperback books. The space in front of the chair was scuffed and worn. There were candy wrappers and Coke cans scattered about. Another lawn chair, this one folded flat, was propped up against the trunk of the willow. Kate went over and picked up one of the paperbacks.

It was a Harry Potter book—something about a goblet of gloom. Kate opened it and saw what she knew she would see. Rainey had written his name inside the front cover. He always did that.

Lemon was standing close, shining the light down on the page.

"I think we've found their hideout."

"I guess we have. And they're not here."

Lemon turned the light away and shone it deeper into the gloom, following the tracks. Looking at them carefully, he came to the realization that there was only one set of tracks. That is, there was no sign that whoever had driven into this space had ever put the car into reverse and driven back out, smearing and overlaying a second set of tracks on top of the first.

When this thought had worked its way through the levels of his mind, his belly went tight and his breathing got shallow.

"Wait here," he said, walking away towards the far side of the willow curtain. Beyond it he could hear the roaring rush of the Tulip as it raced around the big bend that it had carved into Patton's Hard. As he got closer to the bank he could feel the force of the current through the ground. Kate came up behind him.

"Where do they go?" she asked. "I can't see that anybody tried to turn a car around in this space. You'd see the tracks . . ."

Her voice trailed off as she got to where Lemon already was in one gestalt.

They were now at the edge of the Tulip. Six feet down the muddy banks the dark brown water swirled and hissed and muttered like a living thing. Farther out, twigs and leaves and river junk turned slowly inside the whirlpool generated by the currents as the Tulip powered through the bend.

Years ago Kate had seen a dog slip off the muddy banks and get caught up in that whirlpool. Some kind of hound, it fought desperately for its life. Kate had picked up a tree branch and tried to get the dog to bite it so she could pull him out, and he had tried to do that, but in the end he had just gone under, never taking his huge brown eyes, ringed in white, off her face. She hated Patton's Hard as much as she hated Crater Sink.

On the far side of the river the lights of Long Reach Boulevard were coming on as twilight deepened. In the last of the light they could both clearly see the tracks they had been following.

They ran down the steep bank and disappeared into the Tulip River.

Lemon stepped closer to the bank, shining the light into the water. Through the murk he could see a pale white rectangle. When the light hit it, the reflective paint in the rectangle glowed much brighter. The white rectangle had large blue numbers on it. It was a license plate. He held the light closer to the surface of the water.

Behind him he heard Kate whisper.

"Lemon. You *cannot* fall in there."

He peered down the cone of bright light. The license plate wasn't caught in the willow roots, as he had been hoping. It was attached to something much larger, something round and metallic, and that larger thing was what had gotten tangled up in the willow roots, like a bull caught in a net.

He straightened, turned, and Kate tugged him back up the banks, his boots sliding on the slippery mud. They got back to solid ground.

"Is it there?"

"Yes," said Lemon, "it's there. Some sort of compact car. I think it's light blue. It went down the bank but instead of going all the way to the bottom of the river, it got caught up in the roots of all these willows."

"Did you see what make of car?"

"No. I got the license number. KT987Z. Do you know it?"

Kate went inside herself and came back.

"What you mean to say is, is it Alice Bayer's license plate?"

"Yes, Kate. I think that's what I mean."

"I don't know her license number. I know she drove a small blue car."

She stopped, hoping for the right words to come.

"I guess we'll have to call the police, won't we?"

"Yes," said Lemon, but gently. "I'm afraid we will."

If God Made the Universe Out of Nothing, Did the Universe Make Nothing Out of God?

In many ways Rainey and Axel were just like any other kids who knew they were in major trouble with the parents. Although it was getting dark and they were hungry, neither boy could bring himself to grab an uptown trolley and go back home.

Not just yet anyway.

They were riding the Peachtree Line. They had been riding it for hours, ever since they left Rainey's mother's house on Cemetery Hill.

The Peachtree streetcar was one of the old-fashioned navy blue and gold monsters that Niceville was famous for. Heavy as a tank, it lurched and clattered through the crowded downtown streets, heading east again for the Armory Bridge that crossed the river a couple of blocks south of the Pavilion.

The overheated car was packed with office workers going home at the end of a long day and a few kids from Saint Innocent Orthodox School—Axel and Rainey could pick out their dorky outfits from a mile away.

Axel and Rainey had their Regiopolis blazers folded up and stuffed into their knapsacks. Rainey, in the window seat, was staring across the river at the face of Tallulah's Wall. Axel was tapping away at his iPad, which Rainey thought he probably shouldn't do because maybe there was a way to trace where they were when it was on. That was why he had taken the battery out of his cell phone. Axel had told him that taking the battery out was the only way to shut off a Motorola phone. Axel knew stuff like that because his father used to be an FBI guy. Axel was feeling pretty freaked out about his father being out on the loose. He didn't want to run into him, but he didn't want the police to shoot him either.

Life was complicated for both of them and there didn't seem to be much they could do about it, so Axel was playing Grand Theft Auto and Rainey was staring out the window.

At this time of year the last of the setting sun always lit up the oaks and willows that lined the top of Tallulah's Wall. They glowed now, a bright green, but the vine-covered face of the wall was in a deep purple shadow. There was still a big brown spot in the wall, where six months ago a guy had flown his plane right into it on purpose. Another suicide, just like Rainey's dad.

Rainey looked over at Axel, who was sitting slumped down in his seat, looking sad and worried and tired. They had run out of talk a while back, their sense of a shared adventure had slowly died away, and now they were both just hungry and worried and sleepy.

Axel was a brave little guy and Rainey liked him—he had taken on Coleman Mauldar—but Axel really wanted to go home, and soon they'd both have to decide how to do that. Looking at his reflection in the window glass of the streetcar, Rainey wasn't sure what kind of a state *he* was in.

He felt detached from the grown-ups around him, and from the bright lights of the shops and houses that were passing by on the other side of the glass, detached from the life of the city itself, as if it were a boring movie that he had to sit through because one of the Jesuits thought it would make better men out of them.

He mainly felt detached from Kate and Nick and from everybody else in the current version of his life. Axel was the only person he felt connected to, and even then he knew that Axel and he were very different.

For instance, Axel cared what other people thought and felt. Rainey knew that Axel was feeling guilty and sad and awful. Rainey understood in an intellectual way that this was partly because they had been caught out in a long string of lies and deceptions and getting caught at something sneaky usually made the person who got caught angry and sad and awful. Blowing off school would have to be paid for. Rainey and Axel both understood that.

But it had been fun while it lasted.

Gert the Lesbo had asked for notes and permissions and all that stuff. Axel had figured out how to work the computer—Axel was dead smart at that sort of thing—scary smart—and the notepaper was right there in his mom's desk.

So he and Rainey had been free to do whatever they wanted during school hours. All that was over now. They spent a lot of time in their fort down on Patton's Hard, but Axel said the place creeped him out.

After that, for the most part, they had just gone back to his real home almost every day—except when Lemon was there working on the gardens. They watched television and searched the Internet on his mom's computer and googled for dirty pictures and posted stupid stuff on Facebook and Twitter and ate whatever canned stuff they could eat without having to cook it.

But they had stopped going on Google News after Axel found all that stuff about what was supposed to have happened to Rainey when he was kidnapped.

It had sort of freaked them both out, but Rainey most of all. Rainey had no clear memory of that time, other than there was a mirror with a gold frame in Moochie's window and when you looked into it sometimes you could see a farm inside a pine forest and there was a big horse named Jupiter.

Axel found an article on Google that said Rainey's mother had committed suicide by jumping into Crater Sink. But they had never found her body, and Rainey knew in his heart that his mother wasn't dead and that if he could only listen harder to the voices in the willows then he'd understand what the willows were trying to explain to him. If he listened carefully enough maybe the willows could help him understand why his father had committed suicide after Rainey had been found inside that grave. Even Rainey thought that his father shouldn't have killed himself right when Rainey needed him the most. So it was very important for him to figure out how all these things happened, and why, and then he'd know what to do about all these people in his life.

Including Axel.

The streetcar clattered across Armory Bridge and began to climb up the long, winding streets that ended up at the roundabout on Upper Chase Run, where the streetcar would turn around and head back down and do it all over again.

They had been on the car now for three hours—two dollars got you an all-day ride if you wanted it—and the driver, a young woman with hazel eyes and a big friendly hello for all the passengers—was beginning to pay too much attention to the two kids who never got off and who were always sitting in the last bench on the left at the back of the car.

Axel told Rainey that he could tell she was getting ready to do something adult about them.

They had about a half mile to go before they got to the roundabout again, which was set into the side of Tallulah's Wall, right at the top of Upper Chase Run.

There was a flight of rickety wooden stairs that started at the end of Upper Chase, just past the roundabout. It zigzagged up the easy side of Tallulah's Wall and ended up in a path that wandered around along the crest through all the old trees that lived up there.

The path ended at Crater Sink, but nobody ever took it that far, since Crater Sink had a reputation for being a place where bad things lived.

Although Axel, like every Niceville kid, knew all about Crater Sink, he had never actually gone there. For one thing, it was just plain creepy.

Rainey had visited Crater Sink only once, with his mother, on a kind of picnic. They had driven up there and laid out a brunch but his mother had gotten all twitchy about the way the trees were hanging down over Crater Sink and why there were so many crows all around and why even though it was a bright sunny day the water never showed any blue sky in it. The surface was always black.

So they hadn't stayed, although Rainey often felt drawn to the place, especially now that he had found out that Crater Sink was where his mother was supposed to have jumped in.

They were rumbling slowly past the big mansions of The Chase, all of them sitting on top of their private hills behind their big stone fences. They went by 682 Upper Chase Road, a big wooden house with all sorts of turrets and stained glass and complicated woodwork hanging off it—Rainey thought it looked like it should be haunted. The house was dark and boarded up.

There was a black iron gate, chained shut, and a brass plate on the gate.

TEMPLE HILL

Rainey had looked it up after he'd heard a few of the guys at school talking about it. It turned out that Temple Hill was all about him. He nudged Axel out of his daze and pointed at the house.

"This house is all about what happened to me," he said. Axel sat up, suddenly involved.

"That house? Whoa, it's like a castle! Like a haunted castle. Totally cool!"

Rainey explained how it was the home of this rich old hag named Delia Cotton. According to the story in the *Niceville Register,* she had disappeared like *months* ago, and her handyman too, a guy named Gray Haggard, who had served in World War Two with Dillon Walker, Axel's papa, who was a Big Deal up at VMI and he had *also* disappeared around the same time and guess what, Alice Bayer had been her housekeeper, and it all fit together, and there was even more, because Nick was the guy who had the Cotton case, which never got solved, and Nick was also the guy who got Alice Bayer the job running Attendance and Records at Regiopolis Prep.

Axel had followed this narrative with only half his mind—he was trying to get to the part in Grand Theft Auto where you got to see a naked girl—but the mention of Alice Bayer got his attention, because he had a terrible thought going around inside his head that Rainey knew something bad about her. He was looking up at Rainey while he talked and his suspicions were right there in his face but Rainey missed it.

He rolled on, enjoying the way the story was giving them both the heebie-jeebies.

Rainey had also found out—by sneaking a look at Nick's casebook, which Nick always left on the desk in his office when he was off duty—that the mirror in Uncle Moochie's window had once belonged to Delia Cotton for like a thousand years and that Delia Cotton had decided she didn't want the mirror and she had given it to Alice Bayer, who had sold it to Moochie, and that was why the mirror was in the window of Moochie's store for Rainey to see and get all hypnotized by it and disappear.

He stopped there, because the idea came to him that what had happened to Alice Bayer was just payback, and thinking about it like that was helping to make his guilty feelings go away. But he wasn't going to admit anything like that to Axel.

They clattered past Temple Hill and rumbled around a bend that led up to the roundabout. Axel went back to his Grand Theft Auto game, and Rainey wondered where the mirror was now.

When he'd mentioned the mirror to Nick, he and Kate had exchanged a look that made him think that they knew where it was. Maybe he'd snoop around Kate's house a bit, when that Eufaula girl wasn't around. Eufaula was always following him around like she expected him to steal the silverware or something.

But Rainey had learned a few interesting things pretty fast, these last weeks.

For instance, Rainey had figured out that the more you worked out ways to stop other people from making you feel guilty, the easier it got.

It was like Ninja mind control, and it made him feel tough and confident, not like a kid at all, and the more time he spent listening to the voices in the willow trees, the older and tougher he got.

They were finally at the roundabout.

"We gotta get off," he whispered to Axel.

Axel looked up from his iPad and stared around at the station stop. It was dark now, and the streetcar was the only light.

"Maybe we should just stay on and go home."

"We're gonna, but we should take the next car, 'cause Nosy Pants is looking at us."

Axel sighed and stuffed his iPad into his knapsack. He had finally managed to get to the naked girl part and he hoped he'd remember later how he had done that.

The driver had turned around in her seat to watch as they walked up to the front to get off.

When they got there she asked them if everything was all right but Rainey just said they had skipped school and now they were going to go home and face the music.

"Well, you're such beautiful boys, I'm sure your folks will go easy on you," she said, closing the door after they got down the stairs.

She waved as she worked the car around the turn. They stood and watched it rumbling and creaking off down the street until it was gone and they were standing in a pool of blue light from the lamppost overhead and beyond the light there was only the dark. Axel didn't like this at all.

"Know what we should do, Rain? We should just turn on your phone and call for a taxi."

"They'll know where we are."

"I don't care," he said. "This place looks different at night. I think I just want to go home. They're not gonna like kill us or anything."

"We'll get grounded for a month."

"I don't care if they ground me for a year. Call a taxi or something. Mom'll pay when we get home. I mean it, Rain."

Rainey was staring up at the staircase. It had yellow lights set into the stairs so you could see your way if you wanted to go up to the top at night.

"Come on, Rain. Phone, will you?"

Rainey pulled out his cell phone, put the battery back in, and flicked it on. There were lots of calls, from Regiopolis, from Kate, from Kate, from Kate—there was even one from Lemon, and a text message.

He tabbed it and read it.

BOYS PLEASE COME HOME WE'RE WORRIED SICK
LOVE KATE AND BETH

It had been sent about ten minutes ago. Axel read it over his shoulder.

"See. They're not pissed off. Just worried. Text them back."

Rainey decided to reply.

DEAR K&B WERE OK JST RIDING THE STRTCAR BE BACK HOME IN HOUR
SORRY ABOUT DITCHING CLASSES LV U R&AX

"Send it," said Axel. "Tell them we're getting a cab. Or maybe they could pick us up?"

Rainey thought about it, hit SEND, and then shut his phone off. The air was chillier up here on the side of the wall. He got his blazer out of his knapsack and put it on. Axel pulled his out, slipped it on, and they both stood there, looking at each other.

Axel, who was quick, got it in a few seconds.

"No friggin' way, Rain. We are not going up there. Up there is haunted. Like, are you whack? No way."

Axel plucked the cell phone out of Rainey's hand, stepped back a few feet, and hit the CALL button.

"Yeah, we need a cab at the top of Upper Chase Run. Yeah. The streetcar stop here. Where they turn around. Two of us. My name is Axel Deitz."

Rainey made no move to stop him.

But he felt himself . . . receding . . . going away.

"Yeah, okay," said Axel. "We'll be here."

He shut the phone off, and handed it back to Rainey. "There. They said five minutes, maybe less. Okay. No weird shit. Rain, you look funny. You gonna be sick or something?"

"No. Ax, I gotta do something."

"No you don't. The cab's on the way, man. Just don't go all zombie attack on me. Rain?"

"I gotta see something, Ax. I'll just be a minute, okay. Don't freak out on me."

"Rain, please."

Rainey shook his head, turned, and looked at the stairs, following them as they rose up, a dwindling chain of tiny yellow bars that disappeared into the dark at the distant top. The words *come and be recognized* played in his head.

He had no idea why.

But he began to climb.

"Rain, please," said Axel, coming up a step or two after him. Rainey turned and looked down at him.

"I gotta. I'll catch the next trolley, Ax. Be cool, okay. Tell them I'll be right along. Tell them I had to do something."

Axel's eyes were welling up.

"Rain, there's something wrong with you. I mean it, you look all white and stuff. Your eyes look funny. Don't do this."

Down the road a car turned the corner and came up towards them. The light bar on the roof had a sign—CHASE TAXI. The driver flicked his brights and pulled up alongside the station, beeped the horn, and rolled down his window.

"You guys call a cab?"

"Yes, we did," said Axel. "Rain, come on."

Rainey shook his head.

"Can't, Ax. Gotta do this. You go now. I'll be right along."

The cabdriver blipped his horn again.

"Guys? Let's move it, hah?"

Axel blinked at Rainey, tears in his eyes, his cheeks shining.

"Why are you doing this, Rain?"

Rainey had no answer.

Axel picked up his knapsack and turned away without another word. Rainey watched him get into the cab. The driver asked him something and he heard Axel say, "No, just me."

The driver glanced up at Rainey, standing on the steps, shrugged, and pulled away. Axel watched Rainey as they turned and headed back down Upper Chase Run, his young face a white blur, his big eyes wide. The cab turned the corner and was gone and Rainey was alone in the yellow pool of station light, the black immensity of Tallulah's Wall rising up behind him, a thousand-foot wall of nothing, blocking out the stars.

It took a long time, or seemed to, but he finally reached the landing at the top, out of breath, his knapsack dragging behind him. He set his knapsack down on the landing and leaned on the railing. Niceville was spread out before him, from the lights of Mauldar Field far off to the northwest to the clustered glitter of the Galleria Mall, where something big must be going on, since there were police lights flashing all over it, and the Live Eye news chopper was buzzing back and forth above it.

Closer in he could see the golden glow of downtown Niceville, stitched all over with power lines that, from up here, looked like black netting. Farther down the river the lights of the Pavilion were all lit up like a necklace, and here and there he could see the softer glow of the neighborhoods of Garrison Hills and The Glades and Saddle Hill, buried under all those oaks and willows.

He could even see the dark triangle of the Confederate Cemetery. That was where they had found him, buried alive in a grave with a dead guy inside it. There were boats on the river, blobs of colored light. Rainey imagined people on the boats, a party, pretty girls, rich guys like Coleman and his homies.

Why was he up here?

Come and be recognized?

What did that mean?

Rainey turned away from the view of the pretty little town with a stray line from a poem they had studied in English Lit playing in his head—*anyone lived in a pretty how town . . . he sang his didn't he danced his did*—and walked out onto the path that led through the old forest to Crater Sink.

There were tiny solar lights marking the path. All around him the pines and oaks and willows rose up, getting older and taller and more tangled as he got farther into the forest.

The path was stony and he slipped a couple of times, but as the bony ridge crested, it flattened out and the going got easier. There were no noises at all, just the flip-flop and skitter of his running shoes and the sound of his own breathing. If there were crows around they had all packed it in for the night.

He pulled out his cell phone, put the battery in again, flipped it on, just to see the time, because he felt he had been walking along this path for hours, but it was only a few minutes after nine.

Of course there was a text message from Kate:

DEAR RAINEY THANK GOD WE'VE BEEN CRAZY DO YOU WANT US TO
COME AND GET YOU OR YOU COULD TAKE A CAB AND WE'LL PAY AS
SOON AS YOU GET HERE PLEASE CALL ME PLEASE CALL ME RIGHT NOW
IS AXEL OKAY HIS MOM IS WORRIED BUT EVERYTHING IS OKAY HERE
NOBODY IS ANGRY BUT WE WANT YOU BOTH HOME—

Rainey texted her back.

AX IS GOOD HE IS IN A CAB NOW HOME SOON.

Kate's reply was instant.

WHY NOT YOU WHERE ARE YOU PLEASE CALL US

Rainey shut the phone off, took the battery out.

He stared down at it for a while, feeling suddenly bone-tired. When he looked up there was a girl standing in the pathway, lit up by one of the solar lights.

His chest got all cold and it was impossible to breathe. He stood and looked at her and she stared back at him with a disapproving frown on her face. As he looked at her he saw that she wasn't really a girl at all.

She was a woman, a young and pretty woman. She was barefoot and she was wearing an old-timey dress made out of cotton or something. It was just a simple thing that covered her body from the shoulders down to her knees. She had a scarf or maybe a big necklace around her neck.

Even in the dim light from the solar lamps Rainey could see that she wasn't wearing a bra or anything because her breasts were like right there and her nipples were sticking out like buttons. She had her hands at her side and the necklace looked more like a snake than a scarf, a pretty big snake, with yellow and red and green and black rings all along its body.

As he was looking at it, the necklace lifted up its head where it had been resting on the woman's left breast and it stared right at him with its tongue going all fluttery in the air.

Its eyes were green and shiny and when he looked back to the woman's face he saw that her eyes were green and shiny just like the snake necklace, which, Rainey understood with a shock of recognition, was not a snake necklace at all but a real live snake.

He found that he could not move and when he tried to talk his mouth was so dry that all that came out was a bunch of dry clicking sounds.

The woman opened her mouth and words started to come out of it, but it wasn't like it was a voice.

It was more like the words were coming from someplace else, someplace that had an echo, and she was out of sync with her own voice, the way it happens when the sound track and the film are out of whack.

"You afrighted," the voice said. "That's why you cain't speak. You aright to be afraid."

She had a deep southern accent, and her voice was silky, but there was nothing silky about her.

Rainey worked up some saliva and managed to get his voice going.

"Who are you?"

"My name is Talitha. I knows who you are. I knows why you walking in to Crater Sink."

"My *mother* is in Crater Sink," he said, in a hoarse, defensive croak, while one of his knees quivered like a plucked string. "I have a right to go see my mother."

Talitha shook her head.

"Your momma ain't in Crater Sink. She has gone beyond Crater Sink."

"How do you know?"

Talitha seemed to be listening to someone else. Her attention came back to him. He felt her look settle on him. It had weight and force and it frightened him. She shook her head and her expression was full of warning.

"I knows what is in Crater Sink, boy."

"What's in Crater Sink?"

Talitha paused again, as if listening for something. After a moment, she spoke.

"Nothing is in Crater Sink. Nothing is what lives there."

The way she was saying "nothing" made it come out like a name.

"I don't understand."

"I knows that. That's why Glynis sent me, Rainey. To help you understand."

"How do you know who I am?"

Talitha studied him for a while.

"I believe that deep down you're another one of them Teagues. But not yet. You ain't all the way a Teague just yet. You still got some of your real momma in you. But they trying to get you. They trying real hard."

"Who's trying to get me?"

"They is. Abel Teague, he wants to be alive again. Nothing is helping him."

His chest was tighter now, and tears came.

"How do you know my mother is dead?"

"Your real momma or your step-momma?"

This was too much for Rainey, but not for Talitha. She was without mercy.

"Your real momma was a poor lost child kilt by Abel Teague soon as she had you. Sylvia, she was your step-momma, but she love you like her own."

Now he was fully in tears.

"How do you know?"

"I knows because I am the one who took Anora to the mirror and Anora knows about who your mother really was. Anora and your step-momma, they is blood kin. So is Glynis. Glynis sent me to warn you because part of you isn't a Teague yet. Your mother was a lost girl, but she had good in her."

"Who was she?"

Talitha stopped to listen to the forest again, and then she shook her head.

"Ain't no time for that. Did you ever meet a man named Second Samuel while you was in the mirror?"

This was said with such a note of sadness and grief and longing that Rainey felt like lying to her and saying that he had.

But she did not wait for his answer.

"I can't ever live on that side of the mirror with my daddy, because of what I done. But it ain't too late for you. You ain't a Teague yet. You got good people in your life, Mercer kin, and if you go back now you can be like them and not like a Teague. But you got to leave this place now."

Rainey felt heat in the center of his cold. He knew he'd been adopted, but he had always felt like they were his real parents. His anger rose up.

"My *father* was a Teague."

Talitha's expression grew infinitely colder.

"Your father was a Teague, yes. But his name ain't Miles. You knows that. You knows you was a chosen child. Boy this is cruel hard to hear, but

I will tell you that it was Miles Teague brought your step-momma up here to Crater Sink and pushed her in. That's what Teague men do. It was a Teague man who kilt me."

Rainey's knees went wobbly and his face turned icy cold. He fought for the words.

"My dad *killed* my mother? My . . . stepmother?"

Talitha nodded.

"Why would he do that?"

"Because she was nosy and asking questions about you. Where you come from. Who your momma was. Who your daddy was. What you really are."

"But now my dad is dead too."

"He is. By his own hand, yet he lies in consecrated ground with all his people."

She spoke with such conviction in that disembodied voice that it was impossible not to believe her.

"Why did my dad kill himself?"

Talitha was silent for a time, giving every appearance of listening to something he couldn't hear but she could.

"He killed himself because nothing was coming."

Now Rainey heard the sound of crows.

A long way off, but clear enough.

Talitha heard it too. Perhaps that was what she had been listening for all along.

She looked up into the darkness of the forest roof and then back at him.

"Nothing is coming. Turn away now and run back down them stairs just as fast as you can."

"What is it? What is coming?"

Talitha only stared at him with a look of sorrow and disappointment.

"If you stay you will see. I done what I could do for you. Now I have to go."

"Why do you have to go?"

"Because nothing can kill the dead."

And she was gone.

There was no woman on the dimly lit path. Maybe there never was. The path wound away into the darkness beyond, a dwindling sequence of small yellow lights. Above him the forest canopy shut out the night sky. Black things were fluttering through the branches high up there, and the air was full of chittering and scraping sounds, the clacking of sharp beaks. The black flying things were coming down from the branches and settling onto the ground around him. By the light of the lamps he could see that they were crows. Their glittering eyes watched him, and when he watched them back, they puffed up their backs and shook out their wings, and then settled into stillness. Horror came into him.

Horror and dread.

He turned to run back to the stair-head. His ears suddenly began to ring, a high-pitched drilling whine that seemed to slice through his skull. At first it was a steady shriek, but after a while the tone began to rise and fall. There was a pattern in it. He stood there on the pathway and found that the rising and falling of the ringing had words inside it and that he could understand what was being said. He stood there inside the milling flock of crows and listened to the words for a long time. As he listened he was aware of a *rising up* from the forest floor all around him.

It wasn't a visible rising at all. Nor was it invisible. It was neither visible nor invisible. It was nothing. He could see nothing. Nothing was *here*.

He had come and been recognized.

Deitz Sees the Light

Chu was standing on the upper balcony of the Bass Pro Shop, racks and rows of guns and shelves of boxed ammo lining the wall behind him. He was watching a Live Eye news chopper buzzing past the windows. All the exterior windows of the store were tall, narrow rectangles with bulletproof glass in them—Deitz had called them "security slits"—so the chopper was passing from one slit window to the other in a sequence that reminded Chu of frames in a filmstrip.

The chopper had a searchlight on and the beam was lancing through the windows, the operator trying to probe the darkness inside the store to see if there was anything worth filming. The store was dark because Deitz had shut off all the lights except for a few dim ceiling spots that lit up their own sockets and nothing else.

Chu had his hands on the railing and he was watching the bulky shadow of Byron Deitz as he moved silently down the aisles on the main floor, from Chu's point of view a gigantic box maze packed to the rafters with every kind of testosterone-loaded manly crap the shooting hunting fishing trapping and generally buggering about in the woods dingbats could dream up.

Deitz was a portrait in stealth, a shotgun in his hands, doing what he had described as one last "perimeter check" before they settled in to start the negotiations with whoever was out there.

Some of the display counters had fishing rods by the hundreds standing up in holders like a forest of spindly saplings all in a row. Other counters had paddles and oars and all things boat-like. There were duck decoys and plaid hats and hip-waders and fly-tying equipment and portable toilets and cooking tents and camo-painted bows and deadly looking arrows and bowie knives the size of machetes and all of it bored Chu into a trance.

But the creepiest part of the store, made even more creepy now that the entire cavernous interior was in near-total darkness, was the presence of hundreds of different stuffed animals—foxes, cougars, deer, wolverines, raccoons, possums, lynxes, mountain goats, beavers, owls, hawks, crows, and of course entire families of black bears and brown bears and even a gigantic Kodiak bear.

This golden-furred monster dominated a huge central tower right in the middle of the store. It stood there, reared up and baring a set of teeth that could have been found in the jaws of a Tyrannosaurus rex, a twelve-foot-high two-thousand-pound shape ascending into the shadows near the roof, barely visible, and therefore radiating a kind of supernatural power that seemed to spread out over the entire store and settle into all the darkest places. In short, Chu wished with all his heart that Deitz would turn the goddam lights on.

But that wasn't going to happen.

What made it all even more macabre was what was going on outside. A space had been cleared in the middle of the parking lot and a large blue police van was parked there. At least fifteen other police cars and SUVs were parked any which way around the space, their flashers on, their blue and white and red lights flickering everywhere, and everywhere they flickered they lit up armed cops milling around or standing in tight groups.

Now and then a huge searchlight from the top of the big blue van would snap on and spear a blinding beam in through the slit windows of the store and the beam would break up into these rectangular glowing shafts that would swing through the darkness of the store like Jedi laser swords.

When it touched on one of the stuffed animals, the glass eyes of the animal would flare up and glitter and the bared fangs in its snarling jaws would glow and the animal would look thoroughly alive and terribly pissed off by the light and its shadow would seem to move as the light passed over it. What happened when the beam hit the Kodiak bear in the middle of the store was going to keep Chu out of the woods for the rest of his life.

Eighty feet below him, Nick, Coker, and Beau Norlett were standing at the entrance to a concrete shaft lined with disconnected cables and ventilation ducts that vented to nothing. The shaft was a square, roughly eight feet by eight feet, and it had a narrow ladder made of steel loops embedded in the concrete. The loops, really just sections of rebar twisted into curves, were ridged and looked solid enough, although they were slick with oily rust. The sides of the shaft were streaked with water trails and lime growth. Every ten feet or so, a small red bulb glimmered faintly. The rusted steel rungs and the dim red lights ascended into total darkness far above their heads.

The floor of the shaft was littered with broken pipes, huge gears, twisted cables, and one massive heap of machinery that at one point in its career might have been an electric winch.

"I am not," said Beau, with an air of finality, "climbing up into that thing. It's as dark as a dragon's colon."

"And it smells worse," agreed Coker, "but we have to do it anyway."

"Why?" said Beau, not really hoping to dodge the job, but ready to try *anything else* first.

Since his rhetorical question got the usual answer—blank stares from Nick and Coker—he leaned in to look up the shaft again, his expression a mix of horror and disgust.

He was in plain clothes, like all CID detectives, a pair of black slacks and a charcoal-colored shirt. His tie was canary yellow silk.

Beau liked his ties to pop.

"Nick," he said, pulling his head back out of the shaft, "one slip and we're all gonna die on that metal shit piled up on the bottom there."

"No, we're not," said Coker, who was wearing the duty uniform of the Belfair County Sheriff's Department—crisp black and tan with a six-pointed gold star. "We'll make it all the way to the top and die up there. Like dogs."

Coker felt that nothing eased the pre-fight jitters like a bit of graveyard humor. In this case he was wrong. Nick, who knew that Beau didn't like heights, shook his head.

"Sorry. This is it. This shaft was supposed to be a private elevator for a part of the mall that was going to be a suite of offices for the mall management. It dates back to when the Bass Pro Shop was a Dillard's. When the Dillard's got bought out by Bass Pro, the office part never got built."

"You sure Deitz doesn't know about it?"

"There's a good chance he doesn't, Beau. You saw the plans he laid out. He doesn't even have a notation for this shaft."

"So basically we're hoping he missed it," said Coker, who was clipping his rifle to a tactical sling.

"That's the assumption."

"And if we're wrong?"

Nick smiled back at him. He liked Coker. Coker had a crocodile smile and blood to match.

"We get the posthumous thanks of the regiment."

Coker grinned at that, sliding his rifle around to his back. The weapon was an SSG 550 sniper rifle, Swiss made and Coker's own piece, not out of stores. He liked to say it was a privilege for a bad guy to get shot by a rifle as fine as this.

"Well, that's good enough for me. Beau, no offense, but you need to lose that tie."

Beau had forgotten to take it off. He did so with a sheepish grin, stuffed it into his pocket. All three men looked at each other for a moment, getting ready while they were slipping on their tactical gloves and strapping on their Kevlar.

Nick unhitched his belt radio and gave the TRANSMIT button three clicks.

He got two back from Mavis, in the control van.

Affirmative. Good luck.

"Okay then?"

Beau nodded, looking as pale as his blue-black skin would allow.

Coker said nothing. He just smiled at Nick. This was Coker's favorite thing to do. Possibly getting to shoot Deitz was just a bonus.

Nick did a final press check on a Beretta he had borrowed from Mavis Crossfire. His Colt was a fine piece, but for this work he needed a pistol with lots of capacity. He patted his belt for his spare mags, smiled crazily at the other two men, turned and dipped under the lintel, grabbed the first rung of the ladder, and started to climb. His shoes were grating on the rebar and they made an echoing sound that shimmered up the shaft and came back as a kind of rolling hiss. In a moment he was twenty feet up.

Coker turned and did the *After you, Alphonse* bow. Beau ducked and swung into the shaft, grunting with the effort.

Coker waited a bit to let Beau get his distance, and then he too began to climb.

The phrase *Is this the hill you want to die on?* came to him from a time-less combat memory, and then he was gone into the darkness, moving like a gecko going up a wall. If he'd known that taking down the First Third Bank in Gracie was going to make life this interesting, he'd have done it sooner.

Chu heard the stairs rumbling as Deitz came back up to the second-floor landing.

"Chu," he said, in a low whisper full of intensity, "I think there's somebody in here."

Chu, whose capacity for dread was expanding rapidly, twitched visibly.

"Like guards or something?"

"No. Not guards. Civilians."

"How do you know?"

Deitz shook his head and actually sniffed the air. In the shifting bars of the searchlight he looked inhuman and predatory.

"Cigar. Somebody in this place stinks of cigar. It's in their clothes. I can smell it. It's strongest down there."

"Maybe somebody was smoking and—"

"Can't smoke in this store. There are smoke alarms all over. This is in somebody's clothes, like his jacket or something. Wait here."

Chu huddled by the railing and stared down into the pit-like main floor, plunged back into total darkness now that somebody outside had killed all the searchlights. Which meant something, but he couldn't fig-ure out what.

What it meant was that Nick and Beau and Coker were climbing up a shaft and about to make a combat entry, but Chu wasn't trained to make that sort of tactical leap, and Deitz was too busy worrying about the source of that cigar smell.

Deitz was back in a moment. He handed a complicated black headset to Chu. It looked like binoculars.

"Put these on."

"What are they?"

"Thermal and night vision imaging gear. They can read body heat as well as amplify light. Put them on. The strap's elastic."

Chu put them on and Deitz adjusted the strap. Chu was now quite blind. He felt Deitz adjusting something on the headset, and then the shop floor burst into a pale green field.

"Shouldn't *you* have them on?"

Deitz shook his head.

"No. If somebody puts a light on you, like a flashlight, or those searchlights kick back on, the flare can stun your retinas for thirty or forty seconds. Blind you. Long enough to get yourself shot. You're no shooter, so you just be the eyes. What do you see?"

Chu swept his gaze back and forth around the floor. Inside the green field there were a few hot spots that showed up as red blobs. They were small, no bigger than a dinner plate.

Chu described them.

"No. Those are electrical signatures from the cash registers and alarm sensor nodes. Do you see anything man-sized?"

All of this was said in a whisper, with the two of them crouching by the railing. Chu did a sweep again, this time much more slowly.

"Yes," he said, his heartbeat rising. "On the far wall, where the tents are."

"Inside one of the tents?"

"Yes," he said, studying the red blotch. It was showing through the nylon walls of a large blue tent that looked as if it was a kitchen shelter.

"It's big. Or it's two people."

"Shit," said Deitz. "That's where the cigar smell was strongest."

"Not guards?"

"No. Must be a couple of fucking civilians. Maybe they were in the washrooms or something. I missed them. Now they've got into that fucking tent. Fucking cockroaches."

"What do you want to do?"

Deitz shifted, the shotgun making a metallic *clink* as it rubbed against his belt buckle.

"Keep an eye on them. If they move out of that tent, click me on this."

He handed Chu a small Motorola radio, showed him where to press the TALK bar.

"Just click me. Don't talk. Wait here."

And he was gone again, back into the darkness behind the gun counter. In a moment Chu heard the *beep-beep* of Deitz dialing a number on his cell. Chu kept his headset trained on the tent. *Please*, he was thinking, *don't move. Don't get yourself killed, because then I'm a dead man too.*

Back behind him he heard Deitz start talking.

"Who's this?"

"Hello there, Byron. It's Mavis Crossfire. How's it going?"

"Where's Warren?"

"Mr. Smoles is currently being interviewed by the media. He is telling them that we are about to execute two innocent people because we are night-crawling eaters of the dead who lick the blades of their knives after slitting the throats of kittens because we enjoy that sort of thing."

"I want to talk to him."

"Regretfully, you may not. You must try to be content with my humble self."

"You're the negotiator?"

"Depends. Are we negotiating?"

"I want to see Smoles."

"Then turn on a television. He's having the time of his life out there. Four interviews with local and now he's got the Fox crew up from Cap City. He has them mesmerized, Byron. I believe he arrived with TV makeup on."

"He keeps it in his glove box. You have my phone jammed?"

"We have all cell phones in the vicinity jammed. And all the landlines too. You know the drill. If you want to talk, you have to talk to me. Now are you going to go on with all this crazy juvenile horseshit or are you going to come on out of there like a grown-up and be reasonable?"

"You know what I want, Mavis."

"Please indulge me one more time."

"You all know I didn't do that bank. I want those secrets-to-the-enemy charges dropped. In return, I'll give you the guys who took down all those cops."

"You know I can't make a deal like that. Not under these circumstances. You're a fleeing felon who shot a security guard—"

"Wasn't me drove that van into a deer. I was back in the cage, in fucking shackles. When I came to, I thought everybody was dead. I got out of the van and I was in like a daze. I didn't *escape*. I wandered off. It was like an amnesia thing. Even now I have headaches. God knows what kind of trauma I'm suffering, or how it's affecting my perceptions. I have no clear recollection of how I got here. I'm probably gonna sue the U.S. Marshals for reckless endangerment of a person in custodial care."

Mavis, who, in spite of the seriousness of the standoff, got a major kick out of hearing a guy who was in chains and getting his ass transported by two enormous guards describing himself as being in "custodial care."

She took a moment to regroup.

"Wandered off with two borrowed guns and bought a Hugo Boss suit and sort of sleepwalked into the Bass Pro Shop after shooting Jermichael Foley, one of your own employees, in the knee? That kind of amnesia thing?"

"Yes, exactly that. And negotiators aren't supposed to be smart-asses."

"Byron, this is Mavis. We know each other. I'm just trying to talk sense to you."

"Then get me that deal."

"I can't do that."

"Then get me someone who can."

"Byron," Mavis said, with exasperation creeping into her voice, "this isn't *CSI*. That line was old when Jesus got His first tricycle. What's the story on Andy Chu? Is he a hostage or were you just lonely?"

"Chu's my IT guy. He's not a hostage. He can find the guys who did the bank—"

"Then send him out—"

"Or else?"

"Byron, we can't let you sit around inside the Bass Pro Shop until Christmas Eve. Hunting season is three days off. People need their Day-Glo ball caps and camouflage toilet paper. You're just pissing them off."

Deitz decided to play his ace.

"Then how about this? I think there are a couple of civilians in here."

A pause.

A significant pause.

"I thought you cleared the place out?"

"I thought so too. But now I think I may have missed a couple."

Another significant pause, which told Deitz that Mavis had reason to believe he was right.

"What makes you think so?"

"Come on, Mavis. You got a family member out there, missing anyone?"

Another silence.

"Not that I'm aware."

"No? Ask whoever it is does the guy smoke cigars."

Boonie, who was standing behind Mavis in the blue communications van, turned to one of the uniforms and whispered something in his ear. The cop was gone and back in fifteen seconds, nodding his head vigorously.

Mavis took note.

"Byron, if you have reason to believe that there's an innocent bystander—"

"Or two."

"Or two—inside that store, then you know how important it is for your case that nothing bad should happen to them."

"Yeah. I know that. I didn't ask them to hide out in a fucking tent, did I?"

"So . . . how do you want to do this?"

"Mavis, level with me. Are there a coupla stray civilians in this fucking store?"

"We think there may be—"

"Names?"

"A Mr. Frankie Maranzano and his grandson have so far been unaccounted for."

"Mavis, now you're talking like a fucking lawyer."

"Yeah. You're right. I am. I guess it's the strain. What do you want to do?"

"What do *you* want me to do? I don't want them in here any more than you do—"

Click. Click.

"Shit. Mavis, I gotta go."

"Byron, listen, you need to know—"

Click. Click. Click.

Deitz was gone. Mavis tried calling him back, but the phone went to message.

You've reached the personal line of Byron Deitz. I'm not available to—

She clicked off.

Mavis was going to tell him about the Dan Wesson artillery piece that Frankie Maranzano was carrying, but Deitz was gone. She picked up the radio to warn Nick and Coker but realized that they might be so close that Deitz would hear the transmission. Not being a religious person, she settled for resting her forehead briefly on the desk in front of her.

Boonie watched her do this, wondering if she'd start banging her head on the table, something he often found calming, but she didn't. Perhaps she should have. It might have helped.

Probably not.

Little Ritchie had to go. There was no getting around it. Two more minutes and he was going to pee his pants, and then what would Poppa think? He was sitting in a tight ball of boy tucked into a triangle-shaped corner of the tent. It was black as night all around, so dark that when he held his hands up in front of his face he couldn't see them.

For a while there had been flashing lights all over the place, and whenever they'd landed on the tent it would glow all blue and he'd see the big bulky shape of Poppa sitting cross-legged on the floor in front of the tent zipper, with that Dan Wesson cradled in his lap and his face tight as a fist.

Poppa was in that state of barely controlled murderous rage that Aunt Delores, who was totally whack, liked to call "the crankie-wankies."

Poppa was in that state because he was never really out of it and also because these bad guys who had taken over the Bass Pro Shop were making him miss a soccer game between El Tricolor, Mexico's national team, and their hated rivals, Los Llaneros from Venezuela, a game in which he had a strong financial interest.

As Poppa usually did when he was angry, he had gone as still as the Buddha he had taken Little Ritchie to see on a trip to Thailand. He'd also taken Little Ritchie to a whorehouse on something called the Soy Cowboy in Bangkok to get laid so that, according to Poppa, he wouldn't grow up to be a pervert like Uncle Manolo, who had once tried to do "funny stuff" with Little Ritchie when they were in Uncle Manolo's hot tub.

The evening with the Thai girl had been an eye-opening experience for Little Ritchie, but not in the way Poppa would have thought it was.

Her name was Rose and although Little Ritchie had not quite managed to "do it" with Rose, he had come away madly in love and was sending her half of his allowance money every month by PayPal and soon he was going to buy her the plane fare to come and stay in his bedroom with him until he graduated from high school and got a job in Poppa's business so they could have a family. But right now he had to pee, and it was way past time he told Poppa about it.

"Poppa . . . ?"

He sensed the rustle of Poppa turning in the dark. When Poppa shushed him he got a blast of Poppa's cigar breath right in the face.

"But I got to pee, Poppa," he said in an urgent whisper.

"You can't," said Poppa in a low, growling hiss. "You got to hold it. Sooner or later, one of these mooks is coming around again, and when he does, I'm taking him out. After that, you can piss."

Little Ritchie thought that "taking him out" might be trickier than it looked. When the guy had slipped on tippy-toes past the front of the tent, his shadow on the walls had looked as big as that Kodiak bear in the middle of the store. A Kodiak bear holding a shotgun in its paws.

More cigar breath in his face.

Poppa was real close.

"Here," he said, putting something into Ritchie's hand. It felt like a water bottle. "Piss into that."

"I can't see—"

"Find your *piccolo pezzo* and stick it in. Nature'll do the rest. You have to shut up, Ritchie. When the time is right, I'm gonna take the big one—he's the *capo*—and then the Chink *maricone*."

Little Ritchie was trying and failing to do the thing with the water bottle. He thought it might be better to try to do it standing up. He steeled his bladder against the urge, got to his feet, got everything into position again, and started to let it all go when Poppa shifted his position backwards and Little Ritchie, in an effort not to pee down Poppa's neck, stepped backwards himself, and when he did that the backs of his knees hit a small tin table loaded with stainless-steel cooking gear that was right behind him and over he went with a loud crash and a tiny tinkle taking a section of the tent down with him and that was it for Poppa, who grabbed him by the shirt and jerked him onto his feet and said, "Fuck this, we're gonna go take these assholes out right now!"

And out the door he went, in a low crouch, his gun up, his war face on, dragging Little Ritchie along behind him like a kid who had fallen off a horse and had his shoe stuck in the stirrup-thingie.

It didn't go well.

They had successfully detached the boarded-over vent at the back of the second-floor mechanical room and slipped out into the main hall. They let Coker glide on ahead to get in position.

Coker took a post in the left-hand corner of the upper level—the gun deck, he was calling it—and with the night vision scope he was in a position to cover a wide swath of the store.

Coker did a quick scan with the night vision scope. From a tactical point of view, the upper floor was relatively easy to cover, being largely an open space with few counters other than the gun racks and ammunition displays. It took a careful minute for Coker to establish that Deitz was not on this floor. Chu wasn't visible either.

He clicked his mike button twice.

Immediately he felt Nick and Beau slipping past him, and he tapped Nick once on the shoulder to say that he was set up and ready.

Then he put his eye back to the scope and started scanning the main floor, which was a whole lot more complicated, a wide-open space jammed with merchandise and display cases and stuffed animals and glass counters loaded with stock.

He moved the scope slowly around the terrain, hoping that Deitz would walk into the lens. If he could find any plausible excuse for it, he was going to put a 5.56-caliber round smack in the middle of the rest of Byron Deitz's irritating life.

In his scope Coker could see that gigantic Kodiak bear playing King of the World on that stand in the middle of the store.

He took his eyes off the rubber ring and watched as the darker shadow of Nick Kavanaugh literally flowed over the ground just in front of him. The guy moved well. Beau Norlett was now stationary by a water cooler, covering Nick's advance with his Beretta.

Coker decided that he approved of Beau.

He was young and he worried too much.

Maybe that was because he had a sweet young wife named May and two baby kids. But once he got into action, he did just fine.

Then he heard the clattering sound of something metallic falling, and a sort of hoarse cry, almost a growl. Coker put his eye back on the scope and began to scan the lower room again. The scope picked up movement—a big man was spilling out of a tent—a smaller figure behind him. He jerked his eye away from the scope as the lower floor suddenly lit up in a series of blue-white flashes—heavy-caliber gunshots—two shotgun blasts in return—the booming smack of the muzzle blasts slammed around the enclosed space—big cracking booms—a .44—two deeper explosions—the shotgun again—Nick was now at the top of the stairs—Coker came up fast to cover his descent to the main floor—if he was nuts enough to go down there—and, yes, he was.

Beau looked like he was about to follow Nick, but Coker waved him back—too many targets. Too much random shit was going on. Coker could feel things starting to come apart and he was trying to slow it all down.

Coker could see the large man who had come out of the tent—it wasn't Deitz. The man was holding a very big revolver and pointing it at something Coker couldn't identify—Beau was holding his post ten feet to Coker's right, leaning on the railing, his Beretta trained on the main floor—Nick was going down the stairs—he almost stepped into Coker's field of fire, so Coker jerked the muzzle up—and now more shots flared up on the main floor—Coker lost the large man with the revolver—had to be Frankie Maranzano—he could see a smaller figure lying prone a few feet from the tent door—this figure was moving—crawling—and he heard a sound like somebody screaming—high and thin—another huge slamming burst and then a sharp metallic *clang* and Coker felt a big round buzz by his head, a ricochet. He heard it smack into the ceiling behind him.

Coker moved down two steps, trying to bring more of the main store under his field of fire. He got a scope picture of Frankie Maranzano—he was reloading his Dan Wesson—Nick was down on the main floor—in a crouch—using the counters as cover—snaking through the maze—Coker moved again and reacquired Maranzano, who was now crouched in a position that Nick couldn't see—Coker reached down, thumbed the TRANSMIT button—

"Nick, I have Frankie Maranzano on your right at the end of that aisle—maybe ten feet from your position."

Nick stopped, got down on a knee, his Beretta up—Maranzano jerked into motion—he popped up from behind the counter and now he was coming around the corner with his revolver at the ready—Maranzano, without thinking about who he was shooting at, fired a huge round at Nick—he missed—Nick looked as if he was hesitating—he didn't want to shoot a civilian—Maranzano was shouting at Nick in Italian and Nick was answering—*sono polizia*—but Maranzano still had that bloody hand cannon up, although he had been warned and that was not good, so Coker put a round into the center of his mass and Frankie Maranzano went down.

From another aisle came the concussive boom of a shotgun, and then a smaller brittle crack beside Coker. Beau was firing at the source of that shotgun blast, the muzzle flare from his Beretta blooming white in Coker's peripheral vision.

Another shotgun blast, this time flaring big and blue-white, which meant it was aimed right at their position. Coker heard a solid *thwack* sound and a breathy grunt from Beau. Coker sensed rather than saw him falling backwards.

Nick was on his feet now, stopping briefly to look down at Maranzano as he kicked the .44 away down the aisle. Then he turned the corner, moving fast and low, to take on that damned shotgun.

Coker was moving to help Beau but still trying to keep the rifle on the main floor as he stepped sideways. He heard three quick cracks from Nick's Beretta—one shotgun blast in return followed by a second—the sound of falling glass—then silence.

Coker scanned the main floor—nobody in clear view—this was terrible ground for a firefight—Nick was somewhere down in that maze but Coker couldn't find him—he was about to call him on the radio when he heard someone damn big coming up the staircase, shaking the entire frame as he pounded up the risers.

Too heavy to be Nick.

He was hitting the steps like a sledgehammer. Coker could hear his gasping breath. He lifted the rifle and put the scope on the figure climbing up the stairwell.

It was Byron Deitz.

Coker waited.

Deitz got to the second landing and froze as he saw Coker's outline against the dim light from the corner lamps. He had a shotgun in his hands, held at port arms. A moment later, Nick stepped softly up to the bottom of the stairs, holding his pistol and pointing it at Deitz's back.

Deitz was trapped on the second-floor landing, Coker above and Nick below.

"Coker," said Deitz, breathing fast.

"Hello there, Byron. How are you doin'?"

"Well, I'm just fucking jim-dandy, aren't I? How the fuck are you?"

"Byron," said Nick, a soft voice out of the darkness at the bottom of the stairs. "It's over. You don't have to die here. Drop the shotgun."

Deitz was still staring up at Coker.

"Byron," said Nick, putting real steel in his tone. "Put the shotgun down."

"Nick," said Deitz, not taking his eyes off Coker's shadowy figure, "do you know what this asshole up here did? Do you have any *fucking* idea what he did?"

"One last time," said Nick. "Put the gun down."

"Hey," said Coker, in a teasing tone, "you couldn't even sell out your own country without stepping on your dick. And now here you are, like a hog on a spit, getting it from both ends. Man. I gotta tell you, watching you operate, it's fucking *embarrassing.*"

The words hung in the air like sparks from a fire. Deitz's mind filled up with red light and he stopped thinking about anything.

Coker, who was closer, saw Deitz's sudden twist, the muzzle of his shotgun coming up. He and Nick fired at almost the same time, two distinct muzzle cracks, one slightly deeper, the two bright flashes lighting up Deitz for less than a second.

Coker's round took Deitz in the throat, blowing out the top of his spine and nearly ripping his head off, while Nick's nine-mill slug smacked into Deitz's right armpit, drilling right through his lungs and shredding his heart.

Deitz, effectively crucified by two intersecting bullet paths, dead on his feet, pitched backwards, his tailbone striking the railing. He went over the rail, the shotgun in his right hand triggering one last time, the blast hitting the Kodiak bear in the dead center of the body. Deitz landed with a crash of breaking glass on a counter ten feet below.

With a creaking groan the Kodiak began a slow and ponderous fall that seemed to go on forever, but didn't. It tumbled over onto a display of bows and arrows, rocked once, in that stand-up teeth-baring scary-as-shit Kodiak pose the taxidermist had given him. The actual living Kodiak who used to own this skin had been sitting on his ass in the middle of a mountain meadow in the Grand Tetons, up to his hips in wild wheat and buttercups, quietly downing some overripe chuckleberries, when a Wyoming hunter with a Magnum Express punched a fist-sized hole in his chitlins from a hundred yards out. The stuffed version rocked a couple of times, and then stopped, and everything went quiet.

Coker was kneeling down beside Beau.

"Nick?"

"I'm here, Coker," said Nick, from the bottom of the staircase, his voice steady but tight. "How's Beau?"

Coker was already talking urgently into the radio. Beau was looking straight up at one of the dim ceiling spots right above him. His mouth was moving and his cheeks were coated in sweat. Coker put the radio down and called out to Nick.

"Entry wound in the belly, just below his vest. No exit. I've already called the medics."

"Compress it. Tell him I'll be right there. I got to go see to the civilians. Can you find the damned lights? I can't see what I'm doing."

"What about Deitz?"

Nick moved away.

In a moment he called up.

"Deitz is dead."

"Where's Andy Chu? He's not up here."

Coker was pressing a cloth into the hole in Beau's belly. Beau grunted from the pressure, tried to sit up, put a bloody hand on Coker's forearm and squeezed it hard.

He said "May" in a hoarse croak, and passed out. Coker put a finger on Beau's carotid.

His pulse was rapid but strong.

Coker knew that a gut shot took longer to kill than other wounds, unless it had clipped an artery. But from the sound of it when it hit and the concentrated shape of the entry wound, Coker figured that Deitz had loaded up his shotgun with what hunters called deer slugs, a single solid lead shot instead of the cylinder of lead pellets that made up a normal shotgun load. They were lousy at long range but if you were close enough you could kill a real Kodiak bear with a slug that size.

If Coker was right, there was no way of telling what that slug had done to Norlett's insides. If he lived, Beau Norlett was never again going to be everything he was.

The store lights snapped on, blinding him for a second. He heard voices down the hall and the sound of pounding feet. Cops and medics were pouring into the upper gun deck. Coker stepped back and let them go to work on Beau. Nick had moved off into the store. In a moment he was on the radio.

"I have Chu. He's down by the fishing gear with a big hole in his chest. He's awake and talking. He might make it."

Coker tapped a medic on the back, told him what Nick had said, got back on the radio as a pair of EMT guys ran down the stairs.

"What about Maranzano?"

A pause.

"Maranzano's here. Fixed and dilated. Looks like one of your rounds. Center mass. Straight through the heart."

Coker knew it was a righteous shot, but Maranzano was a civilian and protecting civilians was why they had gone into the store in the first place. There'd be an after-action PISTOL inquiry.

Coker would have to make damn sure their forensics team found that .44 round that Maranzano had fired at Nick. Nick would back him up on the shooting, but Coker's career could depend on that round.

"The kid?"

A moment.

Nick was back, his voice slow and heavy.

"He's here. Got one in the upper thigh."

"Jesus. One of mine?"

A moment.

"No. Looks like a shotgun round."

"Any vitals?"

Another moment.

"No. Blew out his femoral. He's gone."

Endicott sat back in the comfy leather seat of the Cadillac and watched the video streaming on his iPhone. He was looking at Warren Smoles talking straight into the Fox News camera, going on in his usual style about what he was calling *The Galleria Mall Incident*. He had pointed out several times that he was calling it that because what had happened here was a lynching just like *The Ox-Bow Incident*.

Since most of the reporters crowding around him were barely into their thirties and the products of various elite Ivy League universities, with all the monumental cultural ignorance that entails, they didn't have a freaking clue what the hell he was talking about. But they kept the cameras on him because he gave great video.

He was wearing a light gray suit over a shell-pink oxford shirt with a wide-spread English collar and a watered-silk tie in pale lavender. When he spoke, it was in the rounded and assured tones of a practiced orator, a device that, given the caliber of his audience, effectively obscured the fact that he was utterly and totally full of shit.

Endicott, who had personal experience of the man, watched with grim amusement as Smoles, who had absolutely zero actual knowledge of what had gone on inside the Bass Pro Shop, laid out the sequence of events that had resulted in the deaths of three innocent civilians and the grievous wounding of another at the hands of what he was calling "cowboy killer cops." He listened to the narrative for a while and then turned the video off.

What he had gleaned from *The Smoles Report* was directly at odds with what he had been able to intercept on his police scanner, which was good enough to decipher the encrypted chatter between the Niceville PD and the EMT people working the site.

Basically, Deitz had holed up in the Bass Pro Shop because he had to, and Chu went with him because he had to, and the cops went in to get him out because they had to, and it all might have gone differently if there hadn't been an armed civilian lurking in the woodwork.

This civilian popped out with his hand cannon just in time to totally fuck up what could have been a reasonably efficient takedown by two CID detectives—Beau Norlett and Nick Kavanaugh, backed up by a mysterious all-purpose police sniper who was being identified only by the name Coker.

Now Byron Deitz was DATS—Dead at the Scene. His hostage/coconspirator/innocent victim/inscrutable Chinese mastermind/feckless nimrod take-your-pick Andy Chu had been medevacked to Lady Grace Hospital, his condition listed as critical. His companion on the journey was the CID guy, Beau Norlett. His condition was described as grave. And there were two civilians also tagged as DATS, a forty-eight-year-old real estate developer named Frankie Maranzano and his fourteen-year-old grandson, Ricardo Gianetti-Maranzano.

The exact circumstances of their demise were about to become a matter for PISTOL—the Post-Incident Shooting Team Operational Liaison unit—a shooting review board composed largely of feckless civilians and disgruntled ex-cops that was being described by a couple of the troopers on the cross-talk circuit as the Pissed-Off Pogues.

Endicott sat there in the Cadillac watching the flashing lights and the hive of law enforcement activity that was still buzzing around the huge slab-sided fortress of the Bass Pro Shop and wondered where the hell he was supposed to take it from here.

He had given Warren Smoles the heads-up and sent him into the scene in the hope that he'd emerge with something useful to relay, but so far all Smoles had done was to leave four messages on Endicott's shielded message center, each one delivered in the breathless *I'm in the middle of it and ain't I keen* tone that makes Geraldo Rivera so irritating to watch and all of them conveying bugger-all. So now what?

There being nothing for it but to suck it up, Endicott picked up his cell and dialed 913–682–8700. His call was expected and after a long go-round with various stiff-necked guards and assorted turnkeys the line came alive again and Endicott was talking to Mario La Motta, the Man Himself.

La Motta was as charming as ever.

"What the fuck's going on down there?"

Endicott started to lay down the basics but La Motta cut him off.

"I gotta fucking TV up here, Harvill. I can see what the fuck went down. They're saying Deitz is dead. Izzat true?"

"Yes. I haven't seen the body, but they only choppered out two wounded. Three including a security guard who got it in the knee. Everybody else is DATS."

"What the fuck is DATS—never mind. So the Fuckhead bought it?"

"Cops are saying a 5.56 through the throat and a nine-mill through both lungs. The back of his neck is splattered all over a family of stuffed bobcats."

"That oughta do it. If you get a chance, go to the funeral and piss down his throat for us, if he still has one, willya?"

Endicott promised to oblige.

"Okay. Did you get the cash yet?"

Endicott took a breath and went to his Happy Place for a moment, and then came back.

"No. From what I'm hearing, Deitz never had it."

"What? You mean the other guys kept it?"

"No. I mean, from what I'm getting down here, I'm pretty convinced that Byron Deitz had nothing to do with the robbery."

"What? It really was Some Other Dudes?"

"That's what it looks like."

A silence, while La Motta breathed in and out. Endicott found himself thinking of sump pumps. La Motta was back.

"Then why's he fucking dead?"

Endicott laid it out for him. La Motta wasn't a good listener. When Endicott had repeated a few of the salient details often enough to pound them into La Motta's skull, La Motta did more heavy breathing. This time Endicott thought of clogged drains. Apparently when La Motta had to think carefully about something it made his emphysema worse. What he came up with was a surprise to Endicott.

"This Maranzano guy. What's his first name again?"

"Frankie."

"Fuck me," said La Motta. "Frankie Maranzano? How old is he?"

"Forty-eight."

"Julie and Desi had a go-round with a guy by that name, worked outta Vegas. Was a made guy, so we had to be polite. His people got heated up over a jurisdictional thing. What's this guy look like?"

Endicott had to go by the description he'd heard on the police radio.

"Over six feet. A weightlifter. Has money in real estate down in Destin."

"Always drives a Bentley? Keeps a hot young *cumare* with bodacious tits? Name of Delores?"

There was an immense scarlet Bentley alone in an isolated section of the lot, lit up dramatically by a streetlight. A pretty woman was being comforted by the large female patrol cop that Endicott had come to know—and admire—as Mavis Crossfire, although they had never met. He just liked her style on the cop radio.

Delores, the *goo-may*, was all wrapped up inside a Mavis Crossfire bear hug. So, if he set aside the bodacious-tits detail, since they were not currently visible, being pressed up against Mavis Crossfire's gun belt, the markers seemed to be all there.

"I think I'm looking right at the *goo-may* and the Bentley as we speak."

"Fuck. That's him. You come across any of his goombahs, Harvill, you should get outta the fucking road, you follow? With Maranzano dead, there'll be a lotta nasty people coming outta the plumbing looking to take over his interests. First to get it will be Delores. She has any brains, she'll clean out his accounts and fuck off to Brazil."

Endicott expressed his readiness to get outta the fucking road if he ran across any goombahs.

La Motta was quiet.

Except for his breathing.

"Okay. Fuck it. Deitz is dead. Find those Some Other Dudes who did it. Find out who's got our money."

This came as no surprise to Endicott.

To people like Mario La Motta there was no such thing as somebody else's money. They sent Endicott down there to locate and retrieve a couple of million dollars that had somehow become "theirs" and Endicott had better do exactly that.

"I have several leads."

"Good," said La Motta. "Keep me inna loop."

Then he was gone.

Endicott watched as the civilians were slowly being allowed back into the lot to collect their vehicles. Most of the cruisers were pulling out of the mall and they were packing up the large blue control van. The Live Eye chopper had gone off to unnecessarily complicate other police emergencies and the satellite vans were shutting down. Under the streetlamp Delores had been released from Mavis Crossfire's bear hug and Harvill was able to confirm the third identifying element La Motta had mentioned. Endicott realized that he was extremely tired. The suite back at the Marriott beckoned.

He fired up the Cadillac and did a slow U-turn back onto North Gwinnett. In the morning he'd have to go collect the Toyota, which was still parked on Bougainville Terrace, a block up from Andy Chu's house. Chu's house would have Feds all over it by now and it wouldn't do for a curious cop checking for wanted plates to notice the tiny laser sensor strapped to the side mirror.

He rolled back the moon roof, opened all the windows, and lit himself a Camel. He cruised northwest towards Mauldar Field at the speed limit, just as everyone else was doing. The lights of Niceville slowly receded behind him. Ahead of him was a lot of farmland, off to his right the sky-glow of Quantum Park, and away in the north, the blinking light of the control tower at Mauldar Field. A full day.

He put on a Caro Emerald CD and thought about what he had said to La Motta.

I have several leads.

This wasn't exactly true.

Since it was highly unlikely that he'd be able to get anywhere near Andy Chu long enough to have a useful chat with him, he was left with three tenuous threads to pull on.

Thad Llewellyn, Deitz's banker at the First Third and obviously involved with the Raytheon caper one way or another, and perhaps a party to even more.

Warren Smoles, since Byron Deitz may have told his lawyer who he suspected in the First Third robbery, although Smoles, an accomplished blowhard greatly given to celebrating his own insider knowledge, had never led Endicott to believe that he knew anything more than what Deitz had already told the Feds. If he did, he'd have hinted at it.

And Lyle Preston Crowder, the Steiger Freightways driver whose wonderfully convenient rollover on Interstate 50 forty-four minutes before the Gracie bank robbery drew almost all of the state and county police from the scene, allowing the robbers to get clean away. Endicott had a strong suspicion that Crowder was an accomplice in the robbery, and that meant that he had been paid, and how he had been paid might lead an inquiring mind to the person doing the paying. That of course depended upon how one put the question to Mr. Crowder. Interesting? Very.

Endicott was moving, therefore so was Edgar Luckinbaugh. He had listened to the events at the Galleria with professional interest and was gratified to see that Staff Sergeant Coker had been able to make another significant contribution to the cause of law and order, and in a small way Edgar felt that he too had been a part of something greater than himself.

And, since he was out of Krispy Kremes and coffee, he was happy to be on the move again, and on the lookout for a handy 7-Eleven.

After a while it became clear to him that Mr. Endicott was heading back to the Marriott, hopefully to turn in for the night. That was fine with him. There was an old Army cot in the back of the Windstar, and a small portable radio that could be tuned to Niceville's classical music station.

Once he had seen Mr. Endicott safely to bed, he would put a Radio Shack motion sensor alarm under the bumper fairing of Mr. Endicott's Cadillac, tune his scanner to the sensor's frequency, and retire to his bunk. With any luck, he could catch his favorite evening broadcast, *Nocturne*, where surely there would be a soothing Mozart or Debussy to sing him to his sleep.

Stairway to Hell

Kate was at home, in the book-lined study on the second floor, curled up on the sofa in a defensive position, wrapped in a cashmere blanket that had been knit by her mother. She had changed out of her street clothes and was wearing a pair of emerald green velour pajamas.

She had the television on, with the sound off. The images were starting to repeat themselves as the TV stations ran out of what they liked to call "Breaking News."

But the images were self-explanatory and Tig Sutter's call from Lady Grace had come a few seconds before she would have decided to go into a Screaming Hysterical Full-On Panic Attack.

At zero hours minus a couple of seconds, the phone had finally rung.

"Nick's okay. Not a scratch," was the first thing Tig said.

"And Beau? How is he? I wish I could be there, but Rainey hasn't come home—"

"Beau's in surgery. The good news is the slug broke up a lot when it went in and he's a big solid guy so his spine's okay. The bad news is the slug broke up a lot and ripped him up pretty bad. The docs are working on him. They have him listed as grave, but I think they'll bump that down in a bit. I was in to see him before he went under and he was asking how Nick was. He's a fine kid."

"I should be there. Is somebody with May?"

"Yes. Her mom and her sister are here. We sent a female officer to be with the kids. How's Beth taking it—you know, about Deitz?"

"Tig, I think it's fair to say that she's just been through the worst day of her life."

Kate filled him in, briefly, on the situation with Rainey and Axel, with Hannah's hearing aids, and now the televised execution—almost—of her husband and the father of her kids. Tig listened quietly, asking only one or two clarifying questions. When she was finished, he asked where Beth was right now.

"She's in the carriage house, with Axel and Hannah. Axel came home in a cab an hour and a half ago. He was a wreck. He couldn't even talk. Something about Rainey and Crater Sink. He was nearly hysterical, sobbing and . . . out of it. I would be too if it weren't for several G and T's. What an awful thing, at the Galleria, those poor people."

Tig's tone lost some of its warmth.

"I know where your heart is, Kate, but if you mean the Maranzano guy, none of this would have happened—and that Maranzano kid would still be alive—if his idiot grandfather hadn't decided to kick off a firefight inside the Bass Pro Shop."

"I know, Tig. I'm sorry. When will Nick be home?" she asked, glancing at the time marker at the bottom of the television feed.

It was eleven thirty, and although Axel had come home an hour and a half ago—they were all asleep in Beth's bed, Axel in a nearly catatonic state, tightly wrapped in his mother's arms, Hannah wonderfully oblivious on Beth's left side—so far there had been no sign of Rainey, and he still wasn't answering his phone. All she knew was that Axel had left him at the bottom of the staircase at Upper Chase Run.

"I'll pry Nick out of the PISTOL thing in fifteen minutes. He'll be home in forty-five. I'll drive him myself. Don't you worry about any of this, you hear, Kate? Nick's fine and Beau's getting the best care we have and Coker's backing up everything Nick is saying."

"You'll bring Nick home?"

"I will."

A moment here.

"So Rainey's not home yet?"

"No. He isn't. Lemon's gone to Crater Sink to look for him. I know he'll call as soon as he has something to tell me. I'm *this close* to asking the Niceville guys to start an informal search."

Tig had something on his mind, and he was trying to find a way to say it.

"Lemon called in about what you and he found up at Patton's Hard. He came in to the CID office a while ago to make a formal statement about it. It's too dark to do anything tonight, and the current there is too dangerous for a night dive, so we have a Niceville cruiser securing the scene. From what we could tell, without getting the divers down, the car in the river looks to be a 2005 Toyota. The plates are registered to an Alice Bayer."

Kate realized she was holding her breath.

"Were you able to . . . see if anything was inside?"

Tig was slow in replying.

"Well, the auto unit guys lowered a camera on a cable, but it's pretty murky there, with the mud and all, and the windows are all silted up."

"So she might not be in there?" said Kate, not believing that for a second. Neither did Tig, but he was kind enough not to say so.

"We're out looking for her. We asked State to send a unit in to Sally-town to see if she's with her relatives up there. She's not, and they said they weren't expecting her and that they hadn't heard from her in two weeks."

"There was a note. I was told there was a note, on her door, I mean her house on Virtue Place. Did you get that?"

"Yes. We did. Kate, this part is no fun . . . You and Lemon said you found a few of Rainey's things under that willow."

"Yes. Axel's too. We left them there."

As if we didn't want to tamper with a crime scene, she was thinking.

"Well . . . they were still there when we secured the scene. I just wanted to tell you that was the right thing to do. I admire you for it. Not that anybody thinks Rainey or Axel had anything . . . that they might have seen the car there or something. No reason they would have, is there?"

"No. No reason at all," said Kate, realizing that now she was thinking less like Axel's aunt and Rainey's guardian and more like a defense counsel.

"Rainey or Axel ever say anything about going down to Patton's Hard?"

Now the defense counsel was front and center and although she hated herself for it, she had to handle Tig's question carefully, and she was pretty certain that Tig would pick up on that.

"They've talked about Patton's Hard, about why they go there."

"Nothing jumps out at you?"

Voices in the willows.

Forged notes from a dead mother.

Alice Bayer was the school attendance secretary.

"No. Not a thing."

Tig was quiet for a moment.

"Okay. Well, I'll be over in a while, with Nick. You give me a heads-up if Lemon calls in, will you? I want to know the boy is safe."

"Thanks, Tig. As I said, they played hooky today, and Rainey knows we know. I think he's just putting off the confrontation. You know boys."

"I do," said Tig, with a low rumbling chuckle. "I have an office full of them. And they're armed."

"You have people with Beau?"

"Only half the CID and most of the Niceville PD and Marty Coors from State and Jimmy Candles and Mavis Crossfire and your brother, Reed, and Boonie Hackendorff. Other than that the place is deserted."

"Can you ask Reed to call me as soon as we know something about Beau?"

"I will. You stay cool, Kate. Everything will turn out okay."

He was gone.

Kate sat there staring at but not seeing the television, her mind going down various twisted roads. She was still doing that forty minutes later when her phone rang. It was Lemon Featherlight. He was calling from his truck. She could hear sirens in the background. He had found Rainey.

Lemon Featherlight had reached the top of Upper Chase Run ten minutes before midnight. The last Peachtree trolley of the night was in the roundabout station, a female driver sitting at the controls, writing on a clipboard. She glanced up as his lights swept across her trolley, gave him a once-over—dangerous? probably not—and went back to her clipboard.

The lights of the station cast a yellow glow over the bottom of the staircase and on the tree-shaded facades of the last two houses on the street, both of which were shut down and dark.

Behind the glow of the roundabout, Tallulah's Wall loomed up into darkness, except for a small diadem of lights that marked the landing far above.

Lemon parked his pickup beside the trolley car and tapped on the driver's window. She looked him over more closely—a pretty young woman with great bones—hesitated, and then powered her window down a crack, because not all handsome young guys with sea green eyes and a piratical air were nice people.

"Yes sir. How can I help you?"

"I'm here looking for a young kid, looks about twelve, long blond hair, big brown eyes—"

"Like a cartoon chipmunk. Regiopolis kid. He was with another kid from that school, younger, brown hair, also has eyes like one of those Disney chipmunks?"

"Yes. That's right. Rainey Teague and Axel Deitz."

"Deitz? Any relation to the guy just got popped over at the Galleria?"

"I'm afraid so."

"Oh dear. I should have done something about them. They never got home?"

"Axel got home two hours ago. Called a cab from here and got picked up, but Rainey didn't get in the cab. And he's not home yet."

"They spent almost my entire shift riding back and forth between here and the Greyhound Bus Station downtown. I was thinking about calling them in to the local patrol, you know, they had that runaway look, but they both got off here at around nine. I asked them if everything was okay, and they said they had been skipping school but now they were going home. I figured they lived up here on The Chase. God, I wish I hadn't done that."

"My name's Lemon Featherlight. Can I ask you—"

"Doris Godwin."

"Miss Godwin—"

"Doris—"

"Doris. I'm Lemon—"

"You an Indian?"

"Mayaimi. They named Miami after us."

"I'm part Cherokee."

She rolled the window down, offered her hand, and Lemon shook it. It was dry and strong, and she smelled of eucalyptus oil.

"I think I know where he might be," she said. "Last I saw of him, he was staring up at the top of Tallulah's Wall. Like he was thinking—"

"His friend said he went up those stairs."

She paused, looked at him.

"I guess you're thinking about going up there to look for him, aren't you?"

"I have to."

She shook her head.

"Crater Sink is up there. That's been a bad place for as long as my people can remember. We named this wall, long way back, after the thing that lived up there. She's still there, Lemon."

"I know. I've heard about her too. But I still have to go."

"I know."

"Well, thanks, Doris."

She looked at him for a while, and then she picked up her radio.

"Central, this is car thirty. I'm going to be ten-seven for a bit. I got a civilian here, lost his kid. Gonna go look for him."

"Doris, you got a missing kid, call the cops."

A female voice, older.

"Not gone long enough for the cops, June. I'll be right back—"

"You got your cell with you?"

"Yes."

"Take a picture of this parent and e-mail it to me. Before you leave the unit."

Doris glanced at Lemon.

"You mind?"

"No. Please do."

Doris lifted her iPhone, snapped three shots, pressed CONTACTS, and hit SEND.

"I got them . . . Okay, I see what you mean. But you be careful now. What's this guy's name?"

"Lemon Featherlight. He's a Mayaimi Indian."

"He's a hunka-hunka, if you ask me. Take your radio. Be careful. I'm gonna run his name. I don't hear from you in ten, I'm calling this in."

Doris got out of the trolley, used a remote to lock it up, leaving the interior lights on.

"Okay, Lemon. Let's do this."

And they climbed that staircase. They were both breathing raggedly when they reached the top. Niceville glittered far below, and the solar lights marked a winding path off into the old forest. A moon was rising over the southwest horizon. They turned to face the pathway. The trees were motionless and towering. They blocked out the stars.

Neither of them said anything.

"Call him," said Doris.

"Rainey. It's Lemon. Rainey?"

His voice got swallowed up by the silence. It was as if he'd spoken into a ball of cotton. Lemon sighed, put his foot on the path, and took a step, and then another. Doris followed close behind. About fifty yards in, they found Rainey.

Lemon took one look at him, and got on his cell. There was no signal.

Doris, seeing this, pulled out her radio, kneeling beside Rainey's body, touching a finger to his throat.

"June, this is Doris."

"Doris—you okay?"

"We're at the top of the wall. We found the kid. It looks like he's in shock. We're going to need the EMT guys."

"I'll call 911. Stay there."

Lemon was kneeling beside Rainey. Doris tried her iPhone. No signal either. And now there was a kind of vibration in the air all around, rising and falling, as if something immense was out there in the dark, breathing. It chilled her blood.

Doris stood up, took out her iPhone, and snapped off a series of pictures, her flash strobing in the dark, turning in a full circle, shooting as she turned.

"Why'd you do that?"

"There's something out there."

"Yes. There is. We're getting him out of here."

Lemon picked the boy up in his arms and strode quickly along the path toward the staircase landing. Doris followed, stopping every few feet to take another series of flash pictures. They were at the stairs now and going down as fast as they could, Lemon cradling the kid in his arms. There were flashing lights at the bottom of the stairs, blue and red and white. Halfway down they met the firemen and the medics, coming up fast.

A Trick of the Dark

That night, Thursday night, after Rainey had been released by the medics and brought home by Lemon Featherlight, Nick and Kate made Rainey a late-night bowl of soup. Beth and Axel and Hannah were in bed, but Rainey wasn't.

Not yet.

And it was long after midnight.

Rainey understood that this had something to do with the trouble he and Axel had gotten into. He had heard Nick and Kate talking in the living room, about Patton's Hard and Lieutenant Sutter, Nick's boss, and about Judge Theodore Monroe, the guy who had given Rainey to Kate in the first place.

None of it sounded good to him.

From the way they were sitting, not really looking at each other, and saying things in that way that grown-ups had when they wanted to talk about stuff that involved you without giving you a part in the conversation, Rainey knew something big was headed his way, and it wasn't anything good.

By the end of the snack, in spite of their best efforts, Rainey had begun to suspect that the cops had found Alice Bayer's body in the Tulip and that tomorrow morning he wasn't going to school because Kate was taking him to see Dr. Lakshmi, the brain doctor who had looked after him when he was in the coma.

From what Nick and Kate were saying, and not saying, Rainey understood that going to Dr. Lakshmi was supposed to help him with the cops. Rainey was pretty sure that meant something like what they called an "insanity plea" on all those cop shows he watched.

As far as he could figure it, an insanity plea meant that Kate and Nick were planning on sending him to a crazy farm.

Ordinarily Rainey, being just a kid, would have handled this by screaming his guts out and crying and weeping and begging.

But now he had this new thing going on inside him, this squeaky scratchy buzzy insect voice that had come to live in his head.

Rainey had tried to ask this new thing if it had a name—it felt like it was *in* him but not part of him—but all he was getting was ***nothing*** and then a sort of quick sharp pin-stick in his skull as if he had been stung by a bee.

Rainey didn't think this buzzy stingy thing in his head was a . . . a *kind* thing. He didn't think it was a very *nice* thing at all.

To Rainey it seemed like what he had in his brain was like an earwig or a snake, and that thought scared him.

Like what if it had earwig babies inside his brain and then those earwig babies had earwig babies and they all started to eat his brain from the inside out and what if one day while he was having breakfast or playing with Axel and one of the earwig babies crawled out of his ear or out of his mouth and everybody could see it—

These were scary thoughts and part of him felt he ought to tell Nick and Kate about it . . .

But . . .

But whatever it was inside his brain it had words all mixed up inside the buzzing and the clicking and the words were kind of helpful when it came to thinking about what to do in this . . . situation . . . he was in.

Right now it was saying **say nothing say nothing these people are not your friends say nothing wait,** which Rainey took to mean not to do anything right now, to keep still and quiet and wait and see.

So he was eating his dinner—even the peas—and keeping his head down while Nick and Kate talked over it.

From the tone and not the words Rainey figured that while Kate was more or less on his side, Nick was not. For one thing, Nick was usually a smiley kind of guy, especially when Rainey and Axel and Hannah were around, but tonight he wasn't even looking at Rainey, other than those times when Rainey wasn't looking at him and he'd look up and Nick would be watching him—studying him—with those pale cop eyes.

So the thing in his head—he had to call it something—**we are no thing**—was telling him **lay low but keep your head because tonight is a big night.**

Need to *name* this thing, Rainey was thinking and after a lot of buzzing the name came to him—**we are Cain call us Cain** so that was how it got its name and after that Rainey felt less like it was an earwig or a snake and more like it was just a kind of ghost in his head.

So that was a little better.

Not okay, but better than earwigs.

After the snack he got handed around for hugs and kisses—as fake as Harry Potter's glasses—and sent upstairs to have a shower and get ready for bed because "tomorrow was going to be a big day."

So that's what he did, and it was almost two in the morning, and now he was standing in the shower and letting the warmth pour down on him.

The part of him that was still a kid was glad that Axel was safe and that although he was in pretty big trouble about Alice Bayer, he was still just a kid and what could they do to a kid anyway, no matter what had happened to some old lady?

This was the part of him that wasn't **Cain** because **Cain** was talking to Rainey about the mirror.

Cain *really* wanted to see the mirror.

The idea that **Cain** wanted to see that mirror again and the belief—amazingly strong—that the mirror was **not far away from where you are now**—became impossible to put aside.

He reached up and shut the shower off and stepped out into the fog of his own bathroom. The mirror in here was coated with mist so all he could see of himself was a slender pink cloud.

He took a large soft towel off the rack—the rack was heated, so the towel was warm, a pleasant thing to wrap around your body after such a cold night. He dried himself off and put on his big white terry-cloth robe—it was actually one of Kate's, who was about his size—and he stepped out into the upstairs hallway.

He went, barefoot, to the top of the stairs and listened. He could hear Kate working in the kitchen and there was music coming from the downstairs study where Nick had his home office. Nick was in there doing his detective thing, and Kate was cleaning up after dinner. Rainey didn't know much about the kind of music Kate liked and this was a tune he didn't recognize at—

it's in the linen closet at the back it's—

all but it had a lot of strings and sounded like home used to sound when his mother was still—

wrapped in a blue blanket go look at it—

alive. Part of him felt ashamed that he had lied to Kate because all she was really trying to do was take care of him—

now—

and here he was playing mean tricks on her and lying to her and staying out all hours—

now go now go now—

Cain was getting screechier and when she did that she could really make Rainey's head hurt, like his skull was full of needles, so Rainey turned around and walked back up the hall past the door to his own bedroom and past the door that led into Kate and Nick's room.

There was a long side hall that led back to the guest room and Kate's office, which she had set up in a kind of sunroom that opened out onto a wide gallery with a roof made of lacy black wrought iron and railings that looked like vines.

The linen closet, actually more of a walk-in supply closet and storage room, was at the far end of the side hall, which had a soft Oriental carpet runner in green and white flowers and the walls were painted a warm yellow like sunlight and had oil paintings of Savannah and Marietta and Sallytown and old Niceville all along both walls.

The hall was dimly lit with a series of ceiling spots that cast pools of warm light onto the carpet. The door to the linen closet had a special light shining on it because it was really sort of a painting all by itself.

It wasn't very big and looked really old, kind of homemade. It was made of thin slats of cedar held together in a big wood frame. The entire door was painted a soft, warm yellow that matched the yellow of the walls, but on top of the yellow paint were all these white star-shaped flowers hanging from these curling green vines.

The vines and the flowers covered the entire door right to the edges and looked as if they had at one time been part of something much larger, maybe a whole room that was painted like that.

The paint had faded a bit and the cedar boards were all warped and cracked, but you could still make out the tiny white flowers and the green vines.

Kate had told him that the flowers were jasmine and that the door had been painted a long time ago, by an artist from Baton Rouge, Louisiana, for a relative of hers whose name was Anora Mercer, and it had originally been part of an entire room called the Jasmine Room.

According to Kate, the Jasmine Room had been one of the rooms in a big plantation home called Hy Brasail, a huge estate in southern Louisiana that had been built right on the banks of the Mississippi River, and was owned by a distant relative of Rainey's named London Teague.

Rainey noticed that when Kate started talking about London Teague her voice went sort of funny and she moved past him pretty fast. He didn't know—couldn't have known—that, prior to a powerful dream she'd had six months ago, the story about the Jasmine Room had just been some old fairy tale that her mother used to tell. After the dream Kate knew that the Jasmine Room had also been the scene of a murder. But she kept the boards anyway.

Rainey had asked Kate if the plantation was still around but she had shaken her head sadly and said no that it hadn't been a happy place and it had been bombarded by Union gunboats as they came down the Mississippi in the final year of the Civil War. The door was one of the few things that the people were able to salvage out of the wreckage and it had been brought to Niceville by a freed slave who had come to spend his last years in Savannah with the Gwinnett family.

Rainey had asked why the plantation was called Hy Brasail—which was a funny name—and Kate had said it was from an old Irish poem and she closed her eyes and recited the poem, which had stayed with him for a while, but now he only remembered the last line, which was . . .

and he died on the waters, away, far away

Rainey thought it was weird to name a plantation after something as sad as that last line and as he gathered his courage together and reached out for the doorknob he wondered what had happened to London Teague that had made his name so difficult for Kate to speak out loud and was there a warning in it for him too.

But he opened the door anyway.

Everything was cleaned up and Kate was sitting at the kitchen table with a glass of wine and a mind full of white noise, listening to Nick talk on the phone in his office—it sounded like he was talking to Lemon—when she realized that Rainey had not come down after his shower.

She walked to the foot of the stairs and listened, but the rushing sound that the shower in Rainey's bathroom always made was absent.

Thinking that he might have fallen asleep on his bed, she came up the stairs quietly, barefoot on the soft cream-colored carpeting, making no sound.

She reached the second floor and looked down the main hall. The door to Rainey's room was open and although his clothes lay scattered on the floor the bed was untouched. His bathroom was still foggy from the shower but Rainey wasn't there either.

Some faint ripple of concern kept her from calling out his name as she passed by their own bedroom, glancing in to see if Rainey had gone in there. But she could feel the emptiness of the bedroom and the bathroom door was open, the lights off, the suite of rooms dim and silent and empty, their big four-poster a shadow in the light from the street-lamp.

The mirror.

Kate came down to the turn into the second hall and saw Rainey at once, a bent figure hunched over on the floor of the linen closet, his back to the hall, his head lowered, as if he had something in his lap and was staring down at it.

Kate saw the glint of gold frame at his sides and knew at once what Rainey had done.

She came softly down the hall, not wishing to frighten him, her chest cold and her throat tight, hardly breathing. Rainey was motionless on the floor of the closet, although the whisper of Kate's bare feet must have been loud enough for him to hear. If Rainey could still hear.

She reached him, hesitated, knelt down behind him, and touched his shoulder. His head came up and he began to turn around, bringing the mirror with him. Kate pulled back when she saw his face, because the expression in it was nothing she had ever seen there before—shock, fear—anger?

"I found it," he said, a hoarse croak.

"Yes. You did," said Kate gently, glancing down at the surface of the mirror, seeing only the dull glimmer of the ornate gilt frame and the stained silvery reflection in the ancient glass. The ceiling light over their heads. The shelves of linen. Part of Rainey's body where he was leaning over it. And, by his shoulder, her own pale, tight face staring back at her.

Her chest relaxed slightly.

It was only a mirror, at least for now.

"I looked into it," Rainey said.

Kate reached out and lifted it out of his hands, turning it to the wall and leaning it there. The card was still attached to the ancient wooden backing—

With Long Regard—Glynis R.

"And what was there, Rainey?"

His angry look shifted into something else.

Loss?

Confusion?

"Nothing. It's black."

Kate looked at him.

"Black?"

"Yes," he said, in an abrupt accusatory tone, packed with indignation and resentment. "You've painted it over, haven't you? So I couldn't look into it again. You painted it black, didn't you?"

"Rainey, sweetheart, we haven't touched the mirror."

"No?" he said, reaching out and jerking it backwards, holding it out to her.

"What do you see?"

Kate saw her own face, pale and drawn and her anger rising up, two small round pink spots on her cheekbones.

"I see my face."

Rainey jerked it back, turned it to face him, staring into it. Kate leaned forward and saw his reflection in it, his hair hanging down over his eyes, his face bright red, his mouth slack.

"I see you, Rainey. What do you see?"

Rainey looked up at her, his skin going from red to pale white.

"It's black. Why is it black?"

She leaned back against the wall and spoke as softly as she could, although all she could think was *neurological damage visual hallucinations brain damage dear God please no.*

"Is that what you see when you look into it, honey? Do you see black?"

He looked back into it, and yes, that's what he really did see, but now that he really studied it, it wasn't a black like it had been painted, but a black like a cloud or a scarf—a clingy black scarf—had been pulled over it.

This frightened him and made him angry and he wanted to yell at her but **Cain** spoke up and said **these people want to put you in the crazy farm for the rest of your life you can't act crazy you can't let them know that you know what they are planning** and her buzzy electrical voice calmed him down.

He put the mirror down, and leaned back, and closed his eyes, and Kate's heart went out to him, he looked so sad and confused.

She took the mirror away, gently, and wrapped it up in the blue blanket, and put it away. Then she helped Rainey to his feet and walked him back down the hallway to his room.

He was so tired he was staggering by the time she got him into his bed.

"Why couldn't I see into it?" he said, as she sat by him and looked down at him.

"Well, sometimes when a person is very tired, they don't see things properly. But after a good night's sleep, everything is better. You're just exhausted, and you've had a terrible time recently. Too much is going on. Everything will look better in the morning."

make nice now make nice

"Should I say good night to Nick?"

"If you want. Or I can say good night for you."

"Maybe that would be okay."

ask about the others

"Axel . . . is he okay? I didn't get a chance to ask him."

"He's fine. He's trying to cope with a lot."

"Yes. They killed his daddy too, didn't they?"

not good not good get off that

Kate's skin changed and her eyes grew darker.

"Well, he lost his daddy too, but Rainey, honey, nobody killed your dad."

he had it coming

"That lawyer guy, Warren Smoles, I watched him on the television and he said that Nick and Sergeant Coker executed Axel's dad, that they didn't even give him a chance."

shut up go to sleep shut up

Kate was shaking her head.

"Mr. Warren Smoles is a bad lawyer who takes money to tell big fat lies and make up things so bad people don't have to pay for what they did. That's what he does. It's how he makes his living."

smolessmoleswarrenwarrensmoleswarren

"Now Axel is an orphan too, isn't he?"

don't talk get rid of her

"You're not an orphan, Rainey. You have us now. We're your family."

get rid of her get rid of her or we will

He closed his eyes and said he was sleepy.

Kate flicked off his light, walked softly away, and closed his bedroom door.

Cain had a lot more to say and she was still saying it when Rainey finally drifted away.

But when he woke up on Friday morning, he knew what he had to do and exactly how to do it.

Friday

The Roots of Evil

The divers from the U.S. Coast Guard Air Sea Rescue base at Sandhaven Shoals came in to Patton's Hard on an MH-60 Jayhawk just after dawn on Friday, rattling windows all over Niceville and sending the willows along the riverbank into a swirling riot of whipping branches as it settled down onto a cleared section of hardpan lit up by the headlights of four squad cars.

Tig Sutter and Nick, and Lemon Featherlight, were waiting for it, had been waiting for an hour, nursing their coffees.

No one was talking about Rainey or Axel or Beau Norlett because they'd already talked it out—Beau was in the ICU and many more operations were ahead of him, and the Rainey and Axel thing was a subject they couldn't discuss at all right now.

Lemon wasn't asking questions, mainly because he didn't want to attract too much attention. He was here at Nick's invitation because Lemon and Kate had found the car in the first place. It was a compliment and Lemon valued it, and right now was honoring it by being silent.

So they were all quietly watching the light change as the sun came up behind Tallulah's Wall and the city slowly emerged from its long shadow. The rising sun first lit up a ruffle of lacy branches as it touched the tops of the taller oaks and pines. Against the pink sky they could see the tiny black swirling flecks of the crows as they flew up into the morning light.

They swarmed into flocks that looked like smoke clouds and the sunlight bounced off their shiny wing feathers so that shimmers of gold rippled through the flocks like flames. They were too far away to hear and anyway the thrumming beat of the approaching chopper as it thundered in was too loud for anything else, even for clear thought.

The Jayhawk set itself massively down onto its struts, sinking into the hardpan. The gate popped and several fit-looking men and women in

Coast Guard flight suits emerged, bending low to deal with the prop rush even though the rotors were several feet over their heads.

Lemon held back while Tig and Nick came forward to meet them, as their obvious leader, a wiry young woman with the blue and silver bars of a CWO-4 on her shoulders and a tag on her chest with the name FARRIER engraved in black on a gold plate came up to them.

She had a broad smile and careful eyes and the muscles in her neck stood out like wires.

Tig, looming over her, wearing a tan suit and a blue shirt, held out his huge hand and she bravely put hers into it, still showing that smile.

"Lieutenant Tyree Sutter?"

"I am. Call me Tig. This is Detective Nick Kavanaugh."

"I'm Chief Warrant Officer Farrier."

She turned around and introduced the uniforms gathered behind her, six people, all petty officers in different grades, four men and two women. They were all lean and mean-looking and, as far as Tig was concerned, much too young to be flying around in a Jayhawk without notes from their mothers.

In the way of all military people, they were cool and friendly and politely distant and had nothing much to say after they had all said "Good morning, sir."

Chief Warrant Officer Farrier gave a few soft-voiced orders and the crew walked back to the chopper to off-load their gear. She turned around to face Tig and Nick again.

"So we're thinking a Toyota?"

Nick answered that.

"Yes, Chief—"

Farrier held up her hand.

"Please. I'm Karen. You're the Special Forces captain, am I right? Fifth SOG out of Fort Campbell. You're the one who—"

Nick deflected this as gently as he could, with a wry smile.

"These days I'm just plain Nick, Karen. If that's okay?"

She seemed to pick up at once that Nick didn't do war stories and she let it go, although her whole crew had talked about him all the way in from Sandhaven. She sized him up in a friendly way and nodded.

"Nick? Okay. Works fine for me. Have we got a crane or a tow truck, if we can get a cable onto this car?"

"Yes," said Nick. "Niceville PD has a heavy lifter on the way. It's a stabilized crane with extendable pads and has a good reach. It was strong enough to pull a Humvee out of the Tulip down by the Cap City Bridge."

"That'll do it," said Farrier. "Can we go look at the site?"

"We can," said Tig, motioning for Lemon to come up. He introduced him as the person who had located the car in the first place. She gave him a once-over and said, "Marines?"

Lemon smiled, a rarity with him lately. Nick watched with a flicker of amusement as Farrier reacted to that pirate's smile.

"Ex. Is it that obvious?"

"We get kidded a lot about being the Knee-Deep Navy. Usually by Squids. The Navy left its mark on you, but you didn't give me any attitude. So, you're probably a marine. A lot of Seminoles in the Corps. So I made a leap."

"Mayaimi, not Seminole," said Lemon, taking her in and liking it. "Other than that, a perfect score."

Farrier smiled back at him, held it for a moment longer than she needed to, and then broke off, all business now.

They walked down the wet grass to the head of the narrow path that led under the arch of willows. It was colder inside the tunnel of trees and the mud squelched under their shoes. The air smelled of mold and wet leaves. The trails that Lemon and Kate had followed in were still partially visible, although they had been heavily overlaid by the larger wheelbases of Crown Vic squad cars.

The ground was pretty chewed up along the track, but once they got to the bower entrance the narrow ruts the Toyota had carved out were pretty clear.

Two uniformed Niceville cops, a man and a woman, were waiting for them by the edge of the willow fall. They were both new to Nick, but Tig seemed to know them. He spoke with them briefly, introducing Chief Warrant Officer Farrier, Lemon, and Nick.

They had been on duty at the site since midnight and they both looked happy to be handing the place over.

The female officer, a Middle Eastern–looking woman with almond-shaped brown eyes and round cheeks, held up the curtain of willow branches for them to step under, saying, as she did so, "It's pretty weird inside there, ma'am. Like a big green tent and the trees are talking all the time."

Farrier stopped and looked at her.

"*Talking*?"

The officer nodded, her expression quite serious. She glanced at her partner, a slender kid with restless eyes and a tense way of holding himself. "Am I right, Kenny?"

"They whisper," he said, backing her up without hesitation or any sign of embarrassment. "Not like in words, but after a while, you're here all night, it starts to make sense. I know it's just the wind in the branches and the sound of the river, but it's . . ."

"Freaky," said the woman. "Just plain freaky. We're off duty now. Ma'am," she said, addressing the Coast Guard officer, "you be careful if you have to go into that river here. There's a big whirlpool about fifty feet offshore, because of the way the river bends through here. And the current is really strong. You lose your grip on the bank and you're gone, ma'am, you're gone."

"I will," said Farrier, smiling at her, and then she stepped through the curtain and found herself in what looked like a large green vault made out of willow branches and supported, like a circus tent, with three huge willow trunks, intertwined sixty or seventy feet overhead into a tangled green web. Farrier looked up at it, craning to take it in.

"Man," she said, "reminds me of a church. How old are these trees, anybody know?"

"They were old when Niceville got started," said Tig, "and Niceville got started in 1764. There are engravings of the town, over at City Hall, made around 1820, and you can see them there along the Tulip. An arborist from Cap City told the mayor that these may be the oldest willows in America."

"That's difficult to believe. We had willows when I was growing up in Maryland and most of them didn't last longer than a hundred years. These sure look old, don't they?"

"They smell old, anyway," said Nick, who shared Kate's dislike of Patton's Hard. "You can see the tracks run right through here."

Although the sun was rising fast it was still shadowy under the willows and he used his Streamlight to pick out the twin ruts that had carved a path through the mud and dead leaves. The tracks ran through the curtain fall on the river side. The inference was pretty obvious, and Farrier was all business from there on in.

As she and Tig went on to look at the site, Lemon and Nick stopped to look at the battered old lawn chairs that were all that remained of Rainey and Axel's hideout collection.

Everything had been photographed and tagged and bagged and taken back to the forensics lab at the CID HQ on Powder River Road. For what purposes, neither man was ready to speculate.

Especially not Lemon Featherlight, who, after what he and Doris had seen on top of Tallulah's Wall, was beginning to think that dark things were swirling around Rainey, and the fact that he was the only person who had been able to see Merle Zane meant that he was tangled up in it somehow, whether he liked it or not. Brandy Gule, the half-feral young woman with whom he had been living, had fought with him over what she called his obsession with "that creepy crypt kid" and now she was gone.

They heard a rustle of leaves. Tig and Farrier came back under the canopy, Farrier's expression verging on grim.

"That's a hell of a river you guys have there. Diving it's going to be like catching a ride on a moving freight. We'll need that hook set up before I put one of my divers into that current."

And that's what they did.

The operation took over six hours, from the time the mobile crane managed to power its way into the willow line—cutting a huge swath through the trees, but there was no help for that.

The operator had no faith in the load-bearing quality of the river-bank, so he set the apparatus up on solid ground at least thirty feet back from the bank and extended the crane at a forty-five-degree angle until the hook was over the place where the car had gone in. Once the rig was set and fixed, the divers came down to the site, four of them in dry suits and carrying full-face masks with closed-circuit cameras attached.

Only two of them were wearing single-tank backpacks. The other two were dressed to go in if they had to, but their job here was to pay out the running lines attached to the divers and monitor their safety while they were in the water.

The divers, both petty officers, one a rangy kid named Evan Call and the other a short bulky fireplug of a guy named Mike Tuamotu, hooked their safety lines onto the strongest tree trunks they could locate, did a final check-down, and eased into the murky water about twenty feet upriver from the point where the car had gone in, paying out their safety lines and riding the current down along the riverbank.

Farrier had turned up the loudspeaker on the CCTV system, so Tig and Nick, standing back from the console, could see what the divers were seeing, and hear their cross talk.

Lemon was standing at a distance, less caught up in the process than he was by what was at stake.

On the screen the image was coming from the camera of the lead diver, in this case Mike Tuamotu. The Tulip was a muddy river, and running fast. On the diver's left as he eased down the riverbank they could see an immense wall of matted and tangled tree roots, an unbroken thicket of twisting vines and branches that disappeared into the dark water below the divers' flippers.

"Stay out of that stuff," they heard Tuamotu say as he brushed past a section of willow roots that seemed to reach out for him.

"Heard that," said Call. "Looks like a mangrove swamp, doesn't it?"

"He's right," said Farrier. "Those roots must go down to the bottom of the river. Like that all along here, you think, LT?"

"These willows here are the largest in Patton's Hard," said Tig. "But, yeah, I'd say so."

"How long's this park, anyway?"

"A mile. Little less."

Farrier shook her head.

"Man, look at that root system. It's like a dragnet. Or a sieve. Look at all the stuff that's caught up in there."

They could see every kind of debris that a river could carry embedded in the wall of roots, shreds of old clothing, a rubber boot, beer cans and plastic bottles, bits of matted fur that looked like roadkill. A lot of what looked like baskets made of bone, hundreds and hundreds of those, large, small, varying in color from gray to brown, trapped deep inside the root mass all the way along the bank. The current swirled and tugged around the divers and their lines were wire-tight.

"Mind that whirlpool, guys," said Farrier, as the divers got closer to the eddying pool of spinning water that lay just a few yards offshore.

"Roger that," said Tuamotu. "I can feel it right here. Real strong clockwise spin on it. What you figure those basket things are?"

"Lots of animals go into the river," said Nick, thinking about the dog that Kate had tried to save right about here almost twenty years ago. "I guess the roots catch them up and there they stay."

Apparently the divers could hear him.

"Bones don't last in water," they heard Tuamotu say over his microphone. "At least not in warm water like this."

"I guess he'd know," said Farrier with a smile. "Mike's plucked a lot of bones out of deep water."

"Yeah," said Tuamotu. "Not all of them stripped clean like these things either. If they're bone, something's picked all the meat off them."

"Got pike in this river," said Tig.

"That'd work," said Tuamotu. "Okay, there's the car, boss."

On the screen they saw a small pale blue blot begin to materialize out of the murky water. As Tuamotu moved closer it took on shape and form and clarity. It was Alice Bayer's blue Toyota, almost vertical, nose down. Nick, watching the image sharpen, realized that he wasn't breathing.

Lemon moved farther away and stood looking across the river towards Crater Sink, where the crows were soaring high in a blue sky.

Let it be empty, he was thinking, and although he knew he was praying, he wasn't sure to whom.

Or what.

Nick and Tig watched as Tuamotu reached the side of the car. It was tangled up in a massive snare of tree roots, coated in river silt, with only a tint of blue showing.

Tuamotu reached out and wiped a gloved hand across the driver's-side window. The interior was dark. Call came up and put a light on the window.

Through the speaker they heard heavy breathing and the rushing scatter of bubbles rising up.

"It's empty," said Tuamotu.

"What about the trunk?" asked Call.

"It's a freaking Toyota, Evan," said Tuamotu. "It doesn't have a trunk. It has a back pocket. You can't even get a set of golf clubs back there."

A ripple of relief ran through everyone on the surface.

Lemon felt his shoulders loosen.

Farrier waved to the crane driver. He hit a lever and the hook began to drop down on the end of a corded steel cable. Evan Call came to the surface, caught the hook, and guided it back down.

"Weeds," they heard him say. "Like trying to run through a thicket of thorns. Catches at you."

Through Tuamotu's camera they watched as Call came back down the root wall, struggling with the weight of the hook, which tended to force him back into the matted growth that lined the bank. He was breathing rapidly. They could hear it through the speakers.

"Evan," said Farrier. "Slow down. You're starting to hyperventilate."

"Hate these roots," he said, mostly to himself.

A few seconds later he was at the tail of the car. Tuamotu moved up to brace him as he reached under the chassis to find a solid place to set the hook. They heard him muttering to himself, and his raspy breathing as he struggled with the cable. Tuamotu was holding Call's belt and keeping the roots clear of Call's tank frame. It took a while before they heard a solid muffled clank.

"That's got it," said Call. "Mike, get me out of here."

Tuamotu pulled at Call's equipment belt until the diver was able to untangle himself from the roots that were wrapped around the rear of the car.

"Take us back ten feet," said Tuamotu.

The topside attendants went back to the safety lines and began to reel the lines in.

"Good enough," said Tuamotu. "We're clear. You can take it up."

Farrier waved to the crane driver, who shoved the lift lever forward. The diesel began to grind and the steel cable pulled taut with an audible twang, droplets of water flying off as it took the weight. The engine seemed to be struggling.

"Liable to pull the car apart," said the crane man. Farrier made a circling motion with her hand.

Wind it up.

The operator shrugged, increased the power.

The crane boom dipped and a groaning creak came from the stabilizer pads. Everybody moved back from that shivering cable. Another groan, and the diesel engine grinding low.

Then a burst of muddy water as the roots let go, and the crane settled back as the cable began to come back in.

"It's going up," said Tuamotu.

In a moment the tail of the Toyota broke the surface and then it was hanging clear, a muddy blue ball with water pouring out from every crevice.

The crane man lifted it up about fifty feet and slowly swung the crane around until he could lower the car down onto a patch of cleared ground. He worked it so that when the front wheels came down, he pulled the crane arm back to allow the car to settle down on all four wheels.

As soon as the slack came back on the cable line, Nick leaned down and jerked the hook clear. Then he came around to the driver's side, gave Tig a look. Tig nodded, saying nothing.

Nick popped the driver's-side door, stepping back as dirty water cascaded out from the interior, carrying with it the detritus of a life, a purse, sodden, open, spilling its contents on the ground, what had been a box of tissues, a wad of paper that might have been a three-ring binder, a Starbucks coffee cup, a pulpy mass that had once been a pack of Kools. Nick waited until the torrent became a trickle and then he leaned into the car, looked around, extracted himself, being careful not to touch anything.

"She's not in here," he said, thinking that although this was a relief, it didn't solve anything. Alice Bayer was still missing. He looked at the shift lever. It was in DRIVE. His heart got stony as he considered what that meant. Farrier came up to Tig and Nick.

"Tuamotu's on the horn," she said quietly, with an edge. Everyone caught her tone and they looked at her, waiting for it.

"She wasn't in the car. She was under it."

They listened while Tuamotu and Call worked it out. The body was female, that much was clear, and partially clothed. Probably an elderly woman, for reasons neither diver wanted to make plain.

She was bound up, literally, in a cocoon of twisted willow roots. From the body's position—they were all looking at it on the screen now—the subject had been trying to climb back up out of the river—they guessed she had fallen in—and gotten herself tangled up in the roots.

She drowned there, and stayed there even when the car came down on top of her. Or maybe she was going to get out okay and then the car came down on her. If that was the way it happened, nobody had to say the word *murder* but it was hanging in the air anyway. If she wasn't at the wheel of that car, then somebody else was.

The divers—and the people watching, Nick and Tig and Farrier and Lemon—all agreed that the weight of the car coming down was what had pressed her body deeper into the root mass.

"Can you get her out of there?" Farrier wanted to know. There was a silence.

It went on.

Farrier was about to ask again when Tuamotu came back on the radio.

"Boss, these roots . . . they're moving."

Farrier frowned.

"Sure they are. Current's running at seven knots and there's a whirlpool at your back."

Call came on.

"Not the current, boss. Mike's right. They move. It's like they're curling around that woman's body. You can see them tightening."

Farrier gave Tig and Nick a look, went back to the radio.

"Evan, get a grip. Put your light on it."

Call did. The cone of white light burned through the murk and into the root mass. Nick found himself looking into Alice Bayer's distended face, her swollen eyes open, two opaque green marbles. Her mouth was stretched in what looked like agony and her dentures had come loose, a comical obscenity. Roots were wound around her and her arms were stretched out and up, her hands ending in fingers that were raw and torn at the tips, the palms shredded as if she had been fighting out of a trap. It was easy to imagine what her final moments had been like.

Nick studied that image, letting it burn into him, because he'd need it to keep him centered on what was important here.

It was likely that someone had done this to her, and whoever it was, Nick was going to find him and put him in a cell.

Whoever it was.

"What's that behind her?" Tig asked.

Call moved the light in closer. A small rounded object was a few feet deeper into the root mass. It looked like a cage made of twigs. Or bone. There was something round inside it.

An egg, Nick thought. *An egg in a basket.*

"One of those bone basket things."

Farrier was losing patience.

"Evan, you and Mike go in there and get that poor lady out of there or I'll suit up and do it myself. And there will be consequences. Am I clear?"

A silence.

"Yes, ma'am."

"Then do it."

They did.

It took another half hour, but Call and Tuamotu managed to untangle Alice Bayer's body from the root mass and bring her up to the surface, where she lay in the current, her long gray hair streaming, her flesh waxy and soft. She had swollen up so severely that a silver necklace was buried in her neck and the watch she had been wearing, something quirky by Fossil, had cut a trench into her wrist. It was a day/date watch, stopped of course, but maybe useful for setting a time of death. Nick made a note of it and bagged her hands.

By that time Tig had called the medical examiner's van in and the morgue attendants had managed to get all of her into a body bag and close the double doors.

"There any eels in this river?" one of them asked Tig, in a low voice meant only for him.

"Yeah. Why?"

The man shrugged, lifted his palms.

"She'll have live ones inside her."

The other attendant, an older man with a sallow, waxy face and bloodhound eyes, simply nodded, looking apologetic and pained.

"Happens. If a body's in the water long enough. They go down the throat. Or up the—"

"Thanks," said Tig, cutting him short. "That really made my day."

"Hey. Weird things happen, Lieutenant," said the younger man. "Yesterday, somebody stole two cadavers out of a refrigerated truck. What the heck are you gonna do with two frozen stiffs?"

Tig was about to turn away.

He stopped.

So did Nick.

"A refrigerated truck?" he asked. "Where?"

The man grinned at his partner.

"Out of the State Police lock yard near Gracie."

The bloodhound man spoke up.

"It was those two guys, got killed in that police pursuit the other day. The brothers. Shugrue? Shogun? Wanted by the Feds. Got killed in the crash where all those bystanders got hurt? At the Super Gee?"

"You mean the Shagreen brothers?" said Tig, glancing at Nick.

"That's it. Knew it was something like that. Everybody was talking about it at the ME's office. Nobody knows how long they been gone, but they're gone, that's for sure. They figure the guys were in this White Power cult and the cult came and took them, maybe gonna have a weird cult ceremony over them."

"And they're *gone*?" said Nick. "Both bodies?"

"Gone as gone can be, Detective. Staties are all in a tizzy. They seek them here. They seek them there. Those Staties seek them everywhere. Anyway, there you go. Weirdness lives."

Tig looked at Nick.

"I'll call Marty Coors," he said. "Ask him why he didn't give us a heads-up. Maybe you better let Reed know. Could be biker guys in town thinking about payback."

"I will. What do you make of it? You really thinking bikers?"

Tig looked out across the river. The sun was glittering on its surface. How could something so pretty hide so much that was so ugly?

"Nah. Even the Nightriders wanted these guys out of the gang. I'm with these guys," said Tig after a moment. "Weirdness lives."

"That's my take on it," said the bloodhound man. His partner laughed, they shrugged again, and were about to get in the van and pull away when Nick asked them to hold on.

"Tig, wait one. I gotta do something."

Tig nodded, and Nick went back to the river, where Mike Tuamotu and Evan Call were just getting ready to come out of the water. Lemon was kneeling by the bank, talking to the divers as Nick came up.

He stood up and looked at Nick.

"I know. I've already asked them," he said.

"Yeah. And we sure as hell don't want to," said Tuamotu, with a sullen edge.

"But we will," said Evan Call.

Forty-five minutes later they had seven of the "bone baskets" lined up on the riverbank. They had washed off as much of the river silt as was possible. Up here in the light of day the objects looked even stranger than they had down in the root mass.

Nick and Lemon were squatting and studying them, but not touching them. Tig was standing over them, looking like a man who would like to be in another kind of story. One with palm trees and naked dancing girls and drinks with tiny umbrellas.

Farrier and the divers were squaring away their gear and talking quietly among themselves. The morgue attendants were smoking cigarettes and telling each other horror stories about various floaters they had known and loved. The crane guy was gone and Alice Bayer's car was sitting on a flatbed trailer, leaking muddy water and smelling like a dead skunk.

"What the hell are they?" Tig asked, for the ninth time.

"What do they *look* like?" asked Lemon, for the eighth time.

Tig shook his head, considering the larger one at the left end of the row. It was about a yard long and a foot wide, and it looked like an oblong cage made of calcified stone that had been colored a deep amber by the river mud.

The bars of the cage looked like stone ribs, in that they tapered as they rose up, and where they touched at the top, they looked like steepled hands, with the spiky fingertips making the roof of the church. Inside the cage there was a floor of cylinder-shaped stones, linked in a row that ran the length of the cage. And resting on the chain of linked cylinders was a small round object, about the size of a five-pin bowling ball, uneven, muddy brown, with markings on the surface that looked like the canals of Mars.

Tig grunted, said nothing.

"Come on, Lieutenant. What does it look like?" Lemon asked again.

"Okay. I'll say it," said Tig, in a raspy tone, clearly unwilling to have this conversation. "It looks like a skeleton. With the skull down inside the rib cage. Happy?"

Lemon reached out and touched the side of the basket, pushed it gently.

"Maybe these ribs are hollow. To come down the river and get caught up in these roots, these things would have to be light enough to get carried by the current. But it feels like stone. Like it's not organic."

"What's that?" asked Nick, pointing to something embedded in the base of one of the cage bars—*face it*—*the ribs*—of the basket.

He touched his fingertip to a vaguely greenish bump. He rubbed his fingertip across the bump and there was a sudden flash of dark green.

Lemon leaned in to look at it, and then he pulled out a long, slender knife, black, with a ribbed steel handle, a small oval hilt, and a tapering double-edged blade that came to a needle tip. The blade was black except along both edges, where the sharpened steel glittered in the sunlight. Tig jumped a bit, but Nick, who had seen where it had come from, was less surprised.

"A Fairbairn-Sykes?" he said.

Lemon grinned at that.

"Yes. Won it from an SAS guy in Iraq."

"How?"

"He was sure I was an Apache."

"You're not?" said Nick, but Lemon ignored him. He leaned in and used the tip of the knife to pry the green object from the stone. It came free with a dry pop and tumbled into Lemon's palm. It was shaped like a beetle, oval, and it had crude markings scratched into its surface. Lemon rubbed it and the shine came up stronger.

He handed it to Nick, who hefted it in his hand. It was heavier than it looked. He handed it up to Tig, who turned it in the light.

"Looks like a piece of jewelry."

"It is, in a way," said Lemon. "It's a trade stone. Made of malachite. You see hundreds of them up and down this coast. Mostly in museums. They were in use long before you guys came and screwed everything up. They were like a coin. All the tribes agreed on their value, based on the weight and the color. Mayaimi used them. Cherokee. Choctaw. Seminole. You'll find them in collections and museums as far west as Santa Fe, north as far as the Dakotas."

"So it's part of somebody's *collection*?" said Tig. Lemon looked down at the bone cage.

"Or maybe he's a lot older than we think and it was something he carried in his medicine bag."

"*His*," said Tig, his voice going higher. "You think this thing here is . . . *human remains*?"

"I'm beginning to think I do," said Lemon.

"But you said it yourself. It's made of *stone*."

"It is now," said Lemon. "I don't think it started out that way. It's like it went through fire or something. It got . . . changed."

Tig literally snorted.

"Hello? Lemon Featherlight? Come back. Earth needs you."

Lemon stood up.

"You ever see a mouse after an owl has eaten it? That tiny ball of bone and fur the owl sicks up?"

"Yeah. Sure. All over the place. Little egg-shaped packets of skin and bone. So what?"

Tig stopped, did a take.

"No, wait—that's what you two think these things are? *Bodies* that have been . . . eaten? By what? No. Never mind. They're *stone*, Lemon. Not bone."

Nick stood up, brushing the dirt off his hands.

"Tig, we might have to find a way to get all the bone baskets we can find the hell out of that root mass."

"For why?" asked Tig. "There must be hundreds of them."

"I'd say thousands," said Lemon. "Maybe more."

"Okay. Thousands of whatever the hell they are. Why do we have to dam up the Tulip to get them?"

"Because this might be a crime scene," said Nick. Lemon nodded.

"Or at least a graveyard," he said.

Tig went silent, thinking it through.

"Look, here's what I can do. We'll take these things back to the lab—along with poor Miss Bayer over there—and we'll see if we can figure out what the hell they're made of. And if they're made out of anything human—which I seriously doubt—I'll think about what we're gonna do about that. If they're really old bones, maybe Native Americans, then it's a matter for the Bureau of Indian Affairs. And maybe you, Lemon, seeing as how you're a Mayaimi Indian. If they're newer bones—and I'm saying *if*—then maybe there's foul play involved and then it belongs to Nick here. How's that sound?"

"Fine with me," said Lemon.

"Me too," said Nick.

Tig sighed and put his hands on his hips.

"Okay. But what's most on my mind is this. Nick, this Alice Bayer thing looks like a suspicious death, at the least, and maybe even manslaughter. Or worse."

He paused but both of his listeners knew what was coming. It was inevitable, but after it was said, nothing was going to be the same between Kate and Nick. All three men knew that.

"Okay," he said, in a warning tone, "here it is, Nick. We're gonna have to talk to Rainey and Axel about what happened here. Is that gonna be a problem?"

"Not for me."

"Kate, maybe? Or Beth?"

Nick shook his head.

"No. Kate's an officer of the court. She knows how it works. Beth's been around law enforcement and the courts for years. She knows how it works."

"Kate's also a lawyer. If we're gonna talk to a minor, they're both going to need a lawyer there when we do it. That's state law. Will she act for both of them?"

"I don't know. It's tricky. She's also his legal guardian. And Beth will have a say."

"Who was the judge who sat on the Rainey Teague custodial hearing? It was Teddy Monroe, wasn't it?"

"Yes. He's still the supervising adjudicator."

"Maybe Kate should talk to him, get his advice. Teddy's a reasonable guy. If he thinks Kate will have to recuse, he'll know a good alternate to stand in for her with Rainey. See that he's protected properly."

"I'll talk to her about it."

"And Beth? About Axel."

"I don't know."

"Maybe I should do it."

"Be an idea, I think."

Tig looked at Lemon.

"We're gonna need what you've got, Lemon. Can you do that? You and Kate found the car. You were first on the scene. Sooner or later you're going to have to make a formal statement. If there's . . . a hearing, say, you'll be called. I know you were—you are—tight with the kid?"

"I haven't seen anything that makes me think Rainey or Axel had anything to do with what happened here. What *may* have happened."

"Neither have I," said Nick.

Tig looked at him, and then came back to Lemon.

"I'm hearing a *but*. But what?"

Lemon paused, thought about it.

"But yes. I'm ready to do . . . whatever."

Tig nodded, as if his expectations had been confirmed.

"Okay. I figured you'd see it that way. Both of you. I'm gonna go get the morgue guys to bag these . . . *things* . . . up. While I'm gone you two guys may want to take a minute to come on back to our home planet, okay?"

Tig stalked off towards the morgue van, anxiety and frustration in his wake.

Lemon and Nick watched him go.

Nick turned to Lemon, speaking low and urgently.

"We have a problem with Alice being down here looking for truants."

"I know it," said Lemon, who was thinking exactly the same thing, and had been since dawn.

"So . . . I got a question."

"I'm here."

"Rainey. You knew the kid before this all happened. Before he got disappeared, the coma, the whole thing. Do you think he put Alice Bayer in the Tulip and sent her car in after her?"

Lemon said nothing for a time.

Nick waited him out.

"I'll say this. The Rainey Teague I knew would never have involved another little kid in playing hooky. He would never have been sneaky enough to get the entry code to his old house out of Kate's notebook. And he wouldn't have been cold enough to fake a note from his dead mother."

Nick studied his face.

"That's what I think too."

Both men worked that through in silence, and then Nick said something that surprised Lemon.

"So where does this take us?"

"*Us?*"

Nick looked over at Tig, and then back at Lemon.

"There's no getting around this one. You're as wrapped up in this thing as anyone is. You knew the Teagues, you knew that Sylvia was worried about Rainey a long while back. You're the one who saw Merle Zane walking around Lady Grace twenty hours after he died. None of these people here—Tig, Boonie, the rest of the cops—none of them know deep in their guts that what's going on in this town is real."

"Boonie said he believed us about the mirror. He's the one who asked you to look at Merle Zane's body and try to explain it."

"When Boonie has time to think about it, he'll decide that I'm a Section Eight Discharge suffering from post-traumatic stress and you're this crazy Indian mystic and Merle Zane needs to go in the ground and have a big rock put on the grave to keep him there. What else can he do? No. There's nobody else but us. Whether you like it or not, you're stuck in this thing."

Lemon looked away, indecision in his expression. Nick picked up on it, figured he knew why.

"What the hell happened with the Corps anyway? I've never asked you that."

"I met three MPs who didn't like me."

"You or your skin?"

"Started with my skin. I made it about me. They got put in the hospital and I got put in the brig."

"Good for you."

He paused, thought it over.

"Wanna know why I'm not still in Special Ops?"

"I know you miss it like crazy. I know you tried to get back in."

"They turned me down. Why? I killed three disabled girls in a place called the Wadi Doan. Shot them down in an alley."

Lemon shook his head.

"That's not the whole story."

"Never is. I need your help in this. It's all connected somehow. These freaking bone baskets. What happened to Rainey last night. The way he's changing. There's a way it all fits together. I need you to help me figure out how."

"You should have had Beau Norlett. He's a good cop. You could ask him for anything."

"Yeah. He is and I could. But I don't have him. Even if everything goes right, he's looking at a lot more surgery and six months of rehab."

"What about Reed? He's a cop. And he's family."

Nick waved that off.

"Reed's too fucking *sane* for this. I need somebody totally whacked, somebody who can see dead men walking. I need a crazy Indian mystic and you're the only one I've got. Besides, Reed's on his way to Sallytown. He left this morning."

"What's he going to do in Sallytown?"

"You know damn well. You and Kate have already talked about it. His bogus birth certificate."

"He's going to try to find out who Rainey is?"

"Yes. So that leaves you and me."

"And Kate and Beth."

"Yes. But we're going to have to keep them out of the line of fire. We're going to have to keep a lot of this from Kate."

"She won't like that."

"I know. But we're going to try anyway."

Tig was headed back, looking grim, trailed by the two morgue guys.

Lemon had one last thing.

"Back at the Bar Belle, when we were trying to explain all this to Boonie, at the end, when he said he believed us but he had no idea what the hell to do about it, do you remember what you said?"

"Yeah. I said FIDO. Fuck It Drive On."

"And you told Boonie to put Merle Zane in the ground and walk away."

"I remember."

"So what's changed?"

Nick gave it a moment.

"What's changed is this stuff isn't going away. It's coming closer and closer to me and my family. It's not just a bunch of people I don't know. It's already been in my house, and now, with Rainey, and maybe even with Axel, I think it's back again. So I can't just say FIDO. I have to try to do something about it."

"Nick . . . what we're talking about . . . what's wrong with Rainey and Axel . . . these bone baskets . . . with Niceville, there may be no *solution* to *any* of it. It might be something we just . . . can't handle. At all. Any of us. You have Kate. You have Beth and Axel and Hannah to think about too. You have a good life here. What we're talking about . . . maybe it's not something you can *solve*, like a murder or a bank robbery. I don't believe it is. I think it's something from . . ."

"From *outside*?"

Lemon smiled.

"Yes. I said that. In Lacy Steinert's office at the Probe. Just before Rainey woke up."

"Well, I think the *outside* is already in."

Nick dropped Lemon off at his apartment in Tin Town, drove a block up, and took out his cell phone.

"Nick?"

"Kate. Where are you?"

"I'm at Lady Grace. But I've got a hearing—"

"How's Rainey?"

"They gave him an EKG. No sign of anything. They're releasing him right now. Shock, is what they're saying. And stress. I'm taking him home and putting him to bed. Beth and Eufaula will take care of him. I can't miss this hearing. How did it go at Patton's Hard?"

"Alice was there, honey."

He heard Kate's breathing stop, and then start again. "Was it . . . bad?"

Nick told her almost the whole story, editing out the grisly details, but including what Tig had said, about talking to Rainey and Axel, about getting them legal representation. Kate heard him out and was silent for a time after he stopped.

"Tig doesn't really think that Rainey and Axel pushed Alice Bayer into the river and then shoved her car in on top of her, does he? I mean, he can't think that. They're just little kids."

"I don't know what Tig is thinking. I don't think he does either. But

Rainey and Axel left stuff of theirs at the scene, and Alice Bayer was the attendance secretary at Regiopolis. And she was known to go looking for truants. So Tig has to look at that. That means Rainey and Axel will need legal representation."

"I think I can represent Rainey. Maybe both, if Beth will agree. I'll talk to Judge Monroe. And to Beth. But I think it would be okay."

"Kate, you know how this looks."

"Yes. I do."

"I've done a couple of things—"

"I know. Reed called me. He says he's on the way to Sallytown. I'm okay with that. Maybe he can come up with better details than I could. It has to be done. Especially now."

"This thing looks . . . it's going to be rough on everyone. I was thinking, about Rainey, this seizure thing, on top of the wall. And everything that went on over the last year and a half. Have you thought about getting him in for tests? I mean, more than just an EKG. We talked about this last night."

"I've got a call in to Dr. Lakshmi. She was the chief neurologist on Rainey's case. I haven't heard back yet."

"I think it would be a good idea to call her back right now, Kate. Get something started. Get Rainey in as soon as you can. Let him get some rest, and, if you can, get him in to see Dr. Lakshmi right now. And don't let him out of your sight until you get him in there. He needs to be under medical care by this afternoon. At the latest. Do you understand what I'm saying? Tig's not going to move all that fast, but he will move."

Kate didn't need any of that explained to her, and saying it out loud would have come close to being a breach of ethics for both of them.

What neither of them was saying was that if Rainey or Axel had been in any way responsible for what had happened to Alice Bayer—and both of them were very afraid that might be true—then the only possible explanation—and the only viable defense—would be a neurological finding that would diminish—or erase—Rainey's culpability.

And Axel's defense—if he needed one at all—was that he was just a kid and had no way of forming any kind of culpable intent that the law would consider. It was highly unlikely that Axel would even be considered for charges.

On a fundamental level, Kate understood the conflict going on in Nick's heart. She knew him well enough to know that he hadn't told her a tenth of what he had seen at Patton's Hard, and she knew that as a cop he had a reflexive contempt for concepts such as *diminished capacity* and *fugue states* and *mens rea* and all the rest of the lexicon of exculpatory medicolegal jargon.

But she also knew that sometimes those arguments were true, and fair.

There wasn't much else to say, except one thing.

"Nick, I know how you feel about all of this."

"It won't be my case, Kate. After he has time to think it over, Tig will have to put somebody else on it. I'll try to see it's somebody smart. Maybe Stephanie Zeller. She's a single mom, got two kids. Maybe it'll give her a little empathy."

"I know, honey. But I also know how you feel, and I think what you're doing for the boys is wonderful. I admire you for it. I love you for it."

"Kate, thank you . . . but I have to be straight. I may be doing it for Axel and Beth and Hannah. But I'm not doing it for Rainey. I have a lot of doubts about that kid. Something's not right there. I'm doing this for you and Beth and the family."

"Nick, Rainey's family too."

Nick was quiet.

She left it there.

"Bye, babe," she said, and clicked off.

Harvill Endicott Confers with Lyle Preston Crowder

The taking of Lyle Preston Crowder came as a huge surprise to Lyle Preston Crowder. At around two on the Friday, the last day of a six-day week, he unhooked a flatbed loaded with Sheetrock at the dock of a Home Depot ten blocks away from the Galleria Mall in northwestern Niceville.

The drop took about a half hour since the flatbed was ancient and the jacks were rusted and cranking the damn thing off the hook on his Kenworth was a real bitch.

But he got it done and pulled his rig away from the lot, thinking about getting to the nearest 7-Eleven to pick up a twelve-pack of Dos Equis beer, a DVD of Tres Equis porno, and a humongous pepperoni pizza, and going back to his semi-regular room at the Motel 6 on North Gwinnett for a rest, which, after six days on the road, he felt he had well and truly earned.

He was giving his employers an honest day's work every time he logged on because he was glad to still have a job after that "accident" he'd been involved in last spring.

It was the only truly rotten stunt he'd ever pulled in his life—things had gone horribly wrong—people had died—and he had spent the next few weeks sick with fear of every phone ring and every knock on the door.

But the time had passed and no one had come to arrest him and even the guilt was fading. He had his life back, praise the Lord, along with a cool ten thousand dollars, and he'd never risk it again. This was a kind of internal prayer that he recited to himself every day at quitting time, and he was saying it again as he pulled the Kenworth into the lot at the Motel 6 and climbed down from the cab with his beer and his pizza and his porn, a pale-skinned kid with a compact build and a threadbare goatee, wearing jeans and a T-shirt with a faded MARGARITAVILLE logo on it.

He was twenty-seven, separated from his high school sweetheart, a recovering cocaine addict, hence the separation, an avid supporter of the Green Bay Packers, and not really a bad guy, in spite of what he had done last spring, but payback seems to be woven into the warp and woof of the universe. His was waiting patiently for him inside room 229 of the Motel 6 on North Gwinnett.

He had chosen the room—a monthly rental—because it had a view of the courtyard pool and of the parking lot out back, so he could watch over his truck and admire the girls getting tanned around the poolside.

He juggled the sack and keyed his lock open and stepped into the dimly lit room, immediately aware of the smell of cigarette smoke.

A man was sitting in the battered vinyl recliner in the middle of the room, facing the door, and he was holding a large gray steel pistol.

The pistol, fitted with a long steel tube that registered with Lyle as a silencer, was being held in a steady hand and at the other end of the arm attached to that hand was a cold face staring back at him. The man was in a nice-looking gray suit and a white shirt and a black tie. It struck Lyle that maybe he was a cop, although he looked more like a funeral director.

"Who the fuck are you and what's your fucking problem?"

"I have no problem, Mr. Crowder," said the man, in a cool, soft voice with an accent but nothing Lyle could name. "Please come in, put your groceries down, and sit over there by the desk."

Lyle looked at the gun. He wasn't afraid yet. Young people in America have witnessed this sort of confrontation many times, although only on television or in the movies, but nothing ever happened to the hero, and all young people are heroes in their own movies.

So Lyle got lippy.

"If you're a cop, show me your tin. Otherwise, how about you just fuck off, old man—"

The old man did not show tin. Nor did he fuck off. The old man shot Lyle in the meaty part of his left thigh.

The muffled crack of the shot bounced around the room but hardly registered in the outer world, where the chuffing whisper of the round being fired got lost in the general roar and bustle of the traffic out on North Gwinnett, in the howl of a plane taking off from Mauldar Field, which was close, and in the bass-heavy music coming from a group of teenagers, boys and girls, hanging around down by the courtyard pool.

Pretty much the same thing happened to Lyle's scream, which at any rate only lasted until he hit the carpet, at which point Mr. Endicott was kneeling down beside him and sticking a needle into the side of his neck, and after that the thinking and feeling and screaming part of Lyle Preston Crowder left the building.

Nor did the sound of the shot reach Edgar Luckinbaugh where he was sitting in Aunt Vi's moth-eaten Windstar across the street in the parking lot of a Wendy's restaurant. He had watched an hour ago as Mr. Endicott had parked his Cadillac in the Wendy's lot and extracted a small leather case from the truck, locked the car with the remote, and walked across North Gwinnett to the Motel 6, where he climbed a set of outside stairs to the second-floor walkway and made his way to room 229, where he used—or showed every sign of using—a key to let himself in.

Nothing had happened for quite a while, and Edgar, happy for the break since single-man surveillance was damn trying, had gone into the Wendy's to use the facilities, buy himself a burger and fries, and come back out to the Windstar in time to watch as a huge red Kenworth truck pulled massively into the Motel 6 parking lot, sliding neatly into a slot at the side of the motel.

A young man wearing a MARGARITAVILLE tee climbed down from the cab carrying a large paper sack. He closed the truck up, locked it, patted the grille the way a cowboy would pat his horse, and then he took the outside stairs and walked along the exposed upper gallery to room 229, where he used a key, or seemed to, and went inside.

The door closed, and that appeared to be that.

Edgar was at a loss what to do.

He decided to text Staff Sergeant Coker.

REPORTING
    ENDICOTT MEETING UNIDENTIFIED SUBJECT AT AIRPORT DRIVING
MOTEL 6 ON NORTH GWINNETT.
    ADVISE?

A few minutes went by while not much happened anywhere around him, and certainly not over at the Motel 6. Then the text came back.

DESCRIBE UNIDENTIFIED SUBJECT

Edgar thought it over.

YOUNG WHITE MALE APPROX 25 YRS FIVE TEN 180 GOATEE DRIVING
KENWORTH RIG WITH STEIGER FREIGHTWAYS MARKINGS NO TRAILER
ATTACHED

This text zipped into the ether.

Moments later the reply came back.

CAN YOU ESTABLISH ID UNSUB ASAP RPT ASAP

Edgar stared down at the text message, sighed theatrically, and texted back.

WILL ESTABLISH WAIT FIVE

Edgar got out of the van, slowly, since he had been in it a long time. He went back into the Wendy's and ordered a double cheeseburger and

a Frosty, took the sack and the receipt and jaywalked across North Gwinnett, dodging traffic.

He walked into the office of the Motel 6 and set the sack down on the
desk in front of a young redheaded man who was listening to something
screechy on his iPhone headset.

The man pulled out one of the two earpieces. Apparently Edgar
Luckinbaugh looked like a guy you should pay only half a mind to.

"Help yuh?"

"Guy here ordered this from us. I got the room number but I can't
read the name here."

"What's the room number?"

Edgar pretended to consult the receipt in his hand.

"Two two nine."

"That's Lyle. Does it say 'Lyle'?"

Edgar kept the receipt close.

The music coming from the kid's one open earpiece sounded like a
pig being fed backwards through a bark chipper. Edgar figured the kid
would be deaf in a year but in time would probably come to appreciate
the silence.

"Whole name?"

"Lyle Crowder. Drives for Steiger. That's his rig out in the lot. He
calls it the Big Red One."

Edgar looked at the receipt, shook his head.

"I think I got the wrong hotel. I'll go back and check it again."

"Whatever," said the kid, plugging in "Pig Fed Backwards" again.

Edgar stepped outside and texted Coker.

ROOM 229 REGISTERED TO A LYLE CROWDER DRIVES FOR STEIGER
FREIGHTWAYS

There was only a short pause.

YOU CARRYING?

Edgar was, his old service Colt .45.

He hadn't fired it in anger in six years. Hadn't fired it at all in six years,
if you wanted to be picky about it.

YES BUT NOT HAPPY WHY NOT COPS?

The answer took a couple of seconds.

NO COPS FIVE G BONUS IF U GET IN THERE NOW WE ARE ON THE WAY
HOLD SUBJECTS AND WAIT

Edgar stared down at the text message.

It was plain enough. It was shouting inside his head: FIVE G BONUS IF U
GET IN THERE NOW

Five thousand dollars to do what he had done as a cop many times.
Except he wasn't a cop anymore, he couldn't call for backup, and he was
a rusty old man who had gotten into something way over his head. On
the other hand, there was Coker, and the certain consequences of disap-
pointing him.

He was in a pickle, all right. What wasn't clear was what he was going
to do about it.

Endicott straightened up from the naked and bound figure lying on the
bed and set the bloody Dremel tool down on a towel on the night table,
stripped off his latex gloves, took off his painter's filter mask and his safety
goggles—he was aware that workplace injuries cost the nation billions
every year—and untied the barbecue apron he was wearing.

He'd bought it at a Stein Mart. It was navy blue and had a saying on
it in white letters.

Everyone has to believe
in something.
I believe
I'll have another beer.

The letters were no longer quite so white.

The cords of the kid's neck were standing out like the ribs of an
umbrella and his face was scarlet, coated in sweat. The gag in his mouth
was soaked in blood and tears and his chest was going up and down like
a bellows.

There was a lot of blood spattered around, and other unpleasant
events had taken place down below but Endicott had dabbed Vicks
VapoRub on his upper lip, so that wasn't too much of a problem for him.

He studied the kid's body, and the kid stared back up at him, his blue eyes as wide as Kansas. Endicott stared back at him and thought.

Five thousand dollars up front and five thousand after to create a major shunt on Interstate 50 at mile marker 107, shunt to occur at 14:49 hours. Shunt to create maximum blockage of interstate.

How did the money arrive?

Federal Express. Fifties with mixed numbers.

Do you still have the package?

No. Threw it away. I swear it.

Where was it sent from?

New Orleans. The airport I think.

Any secondary contact?

Yes. Another five thousand by FedEx.

For doing the job?

Yes.

Keep that package?

No. I swear no. It was evidence.

Sent from the same place?

Yes. New Orleans.

Are you lying to me?

No. I swear it, please no more.

Of course Endicott hadn't stopped there—due diligence and all that—but he was beginning to think the kid was telling him the truth.

It was standard procedure to poke around at the person being interviewed a bit longer, if only for the practice, and of course the amusement it provided—but time was an issue—there were still Warren Smoles and Thad Llewellyn to be "interviewed," and if they disappointed him, he would have to find a way to get at Andy Chu—word was he was awake and talking—and if time was the issue as previously noted, then this Lyle Crowder kid was looking like a complete waste of—

The front door of the motel room slammed backwards and there was a tall black figure filling up the doorway, silhouetted in the golden light of the fall afternoon, a black figure holding a large blue steel pistol. Endicott noted a minor muzzle shake but the man was already advancing into the room far enough to kick the door shut behind him. And now Endicott could see him clearly.

"Why, Edgar, it's you. What a lovely surprise."

Edgar kept the pistol on him, glanced briefly at the naked kid on the bed, and came back to Endicott, taking in the bloody apron and the painter's mask slung around his neck.

His sallow face flushed bright red.

"You sick fuck," he said, in a low hoarse snarl that was entirely convincing. "Back up! Back away. Get your fucking fairy ass up against the wall."

Edgar didn't sound like a bellhop to Endicott. He sounded like a cop. An angry cop. A dangerously angry cop who was pointing a very serious pistol right at him. Endicott regretted not taking closer notice of a bellman who did not want to leave his room even after he'd been tipped twice. In the future he'd be more attentive to such things.

Endicott did as he was told, backed away, raising his hands as he did so. Edgar was keeping his distance like a smart street cop, but the noises coming from Lyle Preston Crowder were pretty distracting and he kept cutting his eyes back and forth from Endicott to what was left of Lyle.

Endicott kept his hands up, but he was watching Edgar's index finger where it rested inside the trigger guard of the pistol. The skin over the knuckle was pink, not white, which it would be if Edgar was putting pressure on the trigger blade. If what Edgar was holding was what it looked like from this angle, a standard 1911 Government Model Colt .45, almost an antique now, the hammer might not be at full cock. Too risky to carry it that way. Most people rack the slide to put a round in the chamber, and then ease the hammer down and flick the safety switch upwards.

Endicott had no doubt that Edgar had thumbed the safety off and cocked the hammer, but firing might be strong trigger pull. On an old Colt like this one, even a well-maintained piece, the trigger pull could be as much as two pounds.

But Edgar's Colt looked worn and dirty. So the trigger pull might be more than two pounds. Perhaps he didn't use it much.

And perhaps he kept the magazine inserted and loaded all the time, even when the gun was in a drawer, which tended to damage the magazine spring that pushed the round upwards so the slide could scoop the next round out of the magazine.

This didn't help Endicott much if there already was a round in the chamber, although it might mean that if Edgar's first round missed him—which wasn't likely—the second round might not come up far enough to be engaged by the slide.

Which meant the gun would jam.

These were serious questions, and he went through them all in a few seconds. The main issue here was how committed Edgar was to shooting Mr. Endicott. From where Mr. Endicott stood, Edgar looked like a man with a serious commitment indeed. Endicott had to admit that he was in a tricky situation that could go either way.

Edgar was poking around inside his jacket with his off hand, still keeping that muzzle steady on Endicott's middle mass. He came up with a set of black steel handcuffs. He threw them at Endicott.

Endicott fielded them neatly.

He hefted the cuffs.

They were old and heavy. The chain connecting them was about five inches long. They looked like antiques, more like shackles than regular police handcuffs.

And they weighed a ton.

The fact that the handcuffs were leaden was an important detail and deserves to be repeated in light of what happened a few seconds later.

Danziger was at the wheel and Coker was riding shotgun. They were in Danziger's Ford F-150 pickup and fighting traffic on their way down from Danziger's ranch, racing down Arrow Creek and across to Rural Route 40, which would take them to the top end of North Gwinnett. They were maybe ten minutes away from the Motel 6 and covering the distance as fast as possible without attracting any police attention. Neither man was saying much.

Both of them were armed, Danziger with a Colt Anaconda and Coker with his service Beretta.

Coker was not in uniform.

Edgar's text had come in as he was driving in to the deputy sheriff substation on North Ring Road. His shift was eight to eight this evening, a twelve-hour ride as shift supervisor.

Coker had pulled over to take the text and then called in to the station to tell Jimmy Candles, the other duty officer, that something had come up and he was going to be late. Jimmy Candles didn't mind. It was a slow night anyway. He told Coker he'd take the full shift and Coker could cover him off tomorrow. Coker thanked him—he was owed a lot of sick time anyway since he never ever got sick.

He clicked off and called Danziger.

Danziger met him at the crossroads where Ring Road connected with Arrow Creek. Danziger wasn't too worried, but he had brought his favorite sidearm, which said something.

The fact that this Endicott mutt had tagged Lyle Crowder was a matter of concern to both men. Not because they cared for Lyle Crowder all that much, but because there was a chance—slight but real—that Crowder could give this Endicott guy a thread that might take him on to Danziger, who had sent five thousand to the kid along with detailed instructions, and followed it up after the job was done with another five thousand.

Danziger had sent the packages from a FedEx drop box, but airports had security cameras, and if Crowder gave Endicott a time frame and a starting point, a determined investigator would, sooner or later, find a bit of security video that would open up a whole world of trouble for both of them.

Coker had the Radio Shack cell phone in his hand, the anonymous one he only used to communicate with Edgar. He also had his police scanner on, tuned to the Niceville PD frequency. There was some cross talk about changing the patrol units that were guarding a crime scene at Patton's Hard.

Coker picked up on that.

"Patton's Hard. You know who they're looking at for that? Rainey Teague."

"No shit. Why him?"

"Jimmy Candles said Tig Sutter's looking at him and some other brat for that floater they pulled out of the Tulip yesterday morning."

"Who was the floater?"

"Nobody's saying. But the kid's stuff was at the scene."

"What's he, twelve or something?"

"Not the point. Youngest killer I ever put in cuffs was ten. Up in Gracie. Name was Joey La Monica. Slit his mother's throat for her welfare check. Same with his baby sister because she saw him do it. Week later the neighbors smelled something bad. First Responders found the kid on the couch, playing Nintendo. His mother and sister were in the tub upstairs. He told me later he wasn't strong enough to get his mother's body up the stairs in one piece so he had to cut her up. Wanted to finish his Nintendo game before I took him away. Stony little fuck. Shanked in Angola."

"Now that's a real heartwarming story, Coker. Thanks for sharing."

Coker had his cell out again.

"You're welcome. Some of them, they're just born that way. Where the hell is Edgar?"

"Don't you go pulling on Edgar's sleeve right now, Coker. He's just done a solo kick-in. He's got his hands full. He was a good street cop. He knows how to do things like that. We'll hear—"

Coker's cell phone beeped.

GOT BOTH NEUTRALIZED ADVISE PLS

Coker showed Danziger the screen, took it back.

"Could be Edgar. Could be Endicott," said Danziger.

"Yeah."

"Did you have a tell set up?"

"No. I never thought Edgar would have to go in hot. Got a suggestion?"

"Ask him how's the wife."

"His wife's dead."

"Yeah. I know."

Coker keyed the board.

HOW IS FRANCIS?

A pause.

STILL DEAD REPEAT GOT BOTH ADVISE PLS

"Still don't like it?" asked Danziger.

"No."

"You could voice him?"

"Not on this. I don't want my voice track anywhere near this stunt."

"Maybe you're being a bit fastidious."

"*Fastidious?* What the fuck is—"

His cell beeped again.

HAVE THEM NEUTRALIZED. DO NOT APPROACH HOTEL. ID RISK. MEET IN WENDY'S ACROSS GWINNETT IN FIVE. BROWN 1985 WINDSTAR VAN.

Coker paused a moment, and then texted back

OK. CLEAN SCENE AND MEET IN FIVE

A pause.
The reply beeped back.

ROGER THAT IN FIVE OUT

"Man," said Danziger, as the exchange ended. "What did we offer him?"

"Five large."

"Cheap at twice the price."

"Fuckin' right."

"Guess there was still a lot of cop in Edgar."

They were about a minute away from the motel now, and Danziger slowed down a bit to ease into the time frame. Coker was still worried about Edgar.

"Maybe there's too much cop in Edgar."

Danziger looked at Coker.

"Coker, we are not gonna whack Edgar."

"He's gotta be wondering, Charlie. Lotta money in it for him, he starts putting things together."

"Never happen. Edgar's more afraid of you than he ever was of Francis, and she was fucking scary."

"We're there. Come in from the back way."

Danziger found a left-hand turn a block away from the Wendy's lot. It was almost four and the traffic on North Gwinnett was dense and chaotic. The Wendy's lot was jammed full, but as they came around the right side of the building they could see a mud brown Windstar parked in a slot facing the main street, nose in.

Across the way was the Motel 6, a squat rat-brown breeze-block structure covered in siding and as purely butt-ugly as, well, as a Motel 6.

The motel lot was half empty but they could see the big red hood of Crowder's Kenworth parked in a side lot. Danziger slowed the pickup to a crawl as they approached the Windstar.

There was no other parking spot open so Danziger came to a stop behind it. Immediately someone in a car behind them hit his horn.

Danziger waved him around and the guy shot them a finger as he squeezed past. Coker's cell phone beeped and he plucked it off the dash.

"Bingo," said Endicott, standing at a slit in the motel window curtains, looking through a pair of Zeiss binoculars. He watched as the man in the passenger seat of a large white Ford F-150 picked up his cell and looked at the screen. *Rough trade*, Endicott thought, looking at the guy.

Endicott couldn't see the driver, just a pair of large-veined brown hands on the steering wheel, big strong hands, cowboy hands. Faded jeans. Another big guy, and no fat on him either. A tooled-leather belt with a big cowboy buckle. A white shirt. Some kind of thick gold ring on his right hand, looked like a Marine Corps crest.

The butt of a large steel revolver was sticking out of a hideaway holster tucked into the driver's waist. *Okay. There you go.*

These are the guys running Edgar.

The leathery cowboy with the silver hair was still looking at the cell screen. Endicott knew what it said because he'd had the message ready to go as soon as he saw anyone showing the slightest interest in Edgar's Windstar.

86 MEET. MAIDS DOING ROUNDS. WILL CLEAN SCENE AND RESET MEET.

The man with the silver hair put the cell away and looked up at the second-floor gallery of the Motel 6. In the double lens the guy's face was like something chipped out of a gravestone and his eyes were as yellow as a wolf's. They seemed to be boring straight up through Endicott's Zeiss glasses and drilling into his brain.

He knows I'm here, came the irrational thought, unbidden but piercing. *He knows.* Endicott's groin got tight and he stepped back away from the window.

The Ford suddenly accelerated away from Edgar's van, turned the corner, and was gone. But Endicott had the plate number memorized. He was good at that sort of thing, even when he was scared brainless.

Endicott watched through the slit for a while, expecting the Ford to pull into the Motel 6 parking lot any moment. But it didn't.

After a long, tense time, Endicott drew the slit closed, feeling deeply rattled, which was highly unusual for Endicott.

He pulled himself together and started to work on the room, and the unholy mess it contained. Drill enough holes in people and all sorts of stuff comes running out. As he went at the job, which was unpleasant, and likely to get more so as he worked his way through the scenario he was going to create, most of his mind was on the work in front of him.

But a small screen at the back of his skull was running a text loop over and over:

GOING TO NEED SOME HELP WITH THOSE GUYS
GOING TO NEED SOME HELP WITH THOSE GUYS

"You know what the fuck happened back there?" said Coker, as they worked their way north.

"I do. Edgar's dead and we just got burned."

"He'll have your license plate."

"Yep."

"I figure Crowder's dead too."

"I certainly hope so."

"Edgar must have talked, Charlie."

"Not necessarily. Maybe he was alive when you asked him how his wife was. Maybe not. Maybe Endicott already knew Francis was dead. I have no idea how, but did he tell the guy everything? I don't think so."

"Why not?"

"Because Endicott still had to go to the trouble of reeling us in for a visual. If Edgar had talked, told him who he was working for, Endicott wouldn't have run that risk. He would have known about us already. Why take a chance on us coming right at him, once we figured out we'd been burned? Edgar had to know he was a dead man either way. Edgar had a lot of *fuck you* in him. He wouldn't want to go out crawling."

A pause.

"Good point," said Coker. "Neither would I."

"Did Edgar have people?"

"He had an Aunt Vi. Loved whiskey and macaroons. You think we should send her a bit of money?"

"Yes. I'll take care of it."

Another pause, while both men worked it out.

"We're gonna have to kill this pesky fucker," said Coker, with an edge. "We should have gone in and taken him out right there."

Danziger shook his head.

"Edgar said Endicott had a big Sig Sauer and lots of ammunition.

Holed up in there, only one way in. It would have been a gunfight. Hard to explain why we were there when Niceville PD showed up. We're gonna have to lay back in the tall grass and work this out."

"We know anything about this guy?"

"Only what Edgar sent us. Resident of Miami. Single. Calls himself a collector. Probably working for those guys in Leavenworth. Or at least he was."

"You think he's gone freelance?"

"Two million buys a lot of loyalty, Coker."

They were out of the suburbs now and pulling onto North Ring Road.

"You gonna go to work?"

"No. I called in before I called you. Jimmy's okay with it. I can't be buggering around in a black-and-tan with this Endicott guy running loose. He has your plate. I figure he'll come for you tonight. We'll be ready."

Danziger pulled up beside Coker's car, a green Crown Vic, shut the engine, put out a hand to stop Coker before he got out.

"He's not coming for anybody tonight, Coker. He's gonna want to bring in help."

Coker considered this.

"Got a point."

Danziger gave him a sideways grin.

"He's read the file. You smoked four cops with a Barrett. He's gotten a look at you already. Even I think you're a scary-looking guy. From the way he's handled himself, he's no fool. He'll check out of the Marriott, hole up somewhere secure, and call for backup. Give him a day for his shooters to get here, get ready. Then he'll come."

Coker grinned at Danziger.

"You'd love that, wouldn't you, Charlie? Be just like the big fight at the end of *The Wild Bunch*."

"Except in my version they die and we don't."

A Beryl Is a Jewel

It was after three o'clock Friday afternoon when Reed pulled into the main square of Sallytown, parked his shiny black Mustang under a spreading willow, and climbed out of the car, stretching his back muscles. He was still sore in all kinds of places—he'd been bounced around pretty good in that crash at the Super Gee and his safety harness had left welts across his chest and shoulders. It felt good just to stand in the sunlight and take in Sallytown.

He knew the town pretty well, since he'd spent a year patrolling it for State before he got reassigned to pursuit. It was a sleepy Main Street kind of town, population around three thousand, just like thousands of others scattered across the South, and the main square had what most main squares in the South had, a redbrick town hall with a Confederate flag flying on the pole outside, a flowered central garden with a statue of a Rebel cavalryman in the middle, and live oaks all over the place, every one trailing wisps of Spanish moss.

On the far side of the square was the Episcopalian Church of Christ the Redeemer, built in 1856, rebuilt in 1923 after the lightning strike and the fire. It was a white wooden structure with a needle-sharp spire painted silver. The spire could be seen for miles around, sticking up out of the trees and glittering like a spear tip.

A historical plaque beside the town hall said that it had been built in 1836 and during the war it had been the headquarters for Robert E. Lee and his staff for three months in 1864. A soft fall light lay over the square and the buildings and the people walking up and down the main street, going in and out of the shops.

The vehicles were mainly pickups and older Detroit steel. The pickups had bumper stickers with sayings on them like THIS TRUCK INSURED BY SMITH AND WESSON or OUT OF WORK? HUNGRY? EAT YOUR

IMPORT! Reed, a man of the South himself, had no problem with that Confederate flag either.

Although a bunch of pig-eyed redneck dimwits had defiled it back in the sixties—and were still doing it—to him the flag of the Confederacy would forever stand for Chickamauga and Shiloh and Manassas and Vicksburg and the thousands of wildwood boys who had died at those places.

Not that he'd try explaining that to anyone north of the Ohio River.

He stretched again, worked out a kink in his neck, and headed across the square to the town hall, which was where the Archives and Records Office was located, on the second floor facing the parking lot out back. He was in plain clothes, jeans and cowboy boots, a white tee and a navy blue blazer, but he had his service Beretta in a holster at his waist and his badge was in his coat pocket. He wasn't on official business, but nobody had to know that.

As he climbed the stairs to the old carved doors he remembered the call he had taken from Nick earlier in the day, telling him about the theft of the Shagreen brothers' corpses from the State HQ lock yard. He had no thoughts on it other than to be thoroughly amazed that the Shagreen brothers had friends who cared enough about them to steal their corpses. Nick had suggested that those friends might be out looking for Reed Walker.

Reed had no position on that other than to hope it was true because he would truly enjoy shooting them.

Archives was open until five on a Friday. When he stepped into the dim, shadowy space with the slowly turning ceiling fan and the tall sash windows, he was greeted by the slender shape of Miss Beryl Eaton, who had been expecting him for over an hour now.

Miss Beryl was in her seventies at least, but still a beauty, with soft pale skin and vivid blue eyes. Her long white hair was swept up in a spiral arc and pinned by a silver bar. She had been the archivist for Sallytown since the fifties, a widow now, and kind of a living monument herself.

"Reed, how lovely. You look well."

"I am, thank you, Miss Beryl. You are, as always, stunning."

"And you are, as always, a charming liar."

She asked after the family and she required details, not just a few vague pieties. She said how sorry she was about Dillon's disappearance and asked him if any progress had been made in finding out the circumstances of his "passing."

Reed was forced into a series of evasions that he hoped Miss Beryl did not notice while she walked him back into the records area, where there was a long trestle table, shiny with age, on which she had laid out a silver pot that smelled of strong black coffee, a tall china cup, and several ancient green ledgers. Each one was as thick as the King James Bible. She pulled out a chair for him and watched while he got himself squared away.

"I took the liberty of bringing the parish records over from Christ the Redeemer for the time frames you mentioned. That would be the newer-looking book on the left. These others are property records and tax rolls and of course the various census books we have for the period you requested. Do you wish any help at all?"

While Reed had told her that he was here to look into a birth certificate matter dating from around 2000, he hadn't been more specific than that, and Miss Beryl was too tactful to pry, apparently feeling that his visit was an official one, and therefore something not to be poked at by a clerk.

"I think I'm good, thank you, Miss Beryl."

She nodded and slipped silently from the room, leaving a faint scent of mimosa. He pulled the parish ledger over, flipped it open, and went to work. And the work was grim. Page after page of chicken-scratch handwriting or faded type, and the smell of must rising up from every open book. None of the relevant documents had been scanned into a searchable database, although there was talk of doing it when the economy got better. Kate had told him that Sylvia had done all her searching through Ancestry and had come up with zip, so maybe a database wouldn't have helped anyway.

Reed drank his coffee and dug in and went at it and he was still at it an hour later, when Miss Beryl ghosted back into the room and stood looking down at him. He was slumped over a pile of ledgers and records books, looking rumpled and frustrated.

"Dear boy. You look quite terrible."

Reed, who had never liked clerical work, looked up at her and smiled.

"I'm getting bogged down here, Miss Beryl."

"Perhaps I can be of some help?"

Reed looked down at the heap of open books. He was getting nowhere. And time was running. Miss Beryl sat down on the far side of the table, folded her long-fingered hands, and smiled at him.

"This isn't an official investigation, is it?"

Reed gave her a wry smile.

"Yes. No. And it might become one. How's that for an answer?"

"Perfectly sensible. Let me help you. I infer from the specific pages you have open that you're trying to determine a birth. Am I correct?"

"You are."

She sat back and considered him.

"I've always liked you, Reed. Many of the young policemen with whom I come into contact are dismissive of the doddering old bat who runs Archives. You have never been that sort. I think you're worried and unhappy. The tenor of your unhappiness leads me to conclude that this is a family matter."

"In a way."

"And that would be . . . ?"

"The Teague family."

Miss Beryl's expression altered slightly. It became both cooler and more guarded.

"I know the Teague clan quite well. Which branch?"

"Miles Teague. And his wife, Sylvia."

Miss Beryl paused. When she spoke her tone was reserved and careful.

"Miles Teague. He's dead now, is he not?"

"Yes. He is."

"By his own hand."

"Yes. And Sylvia's gone too."

"Yes. I know. May I venture a guess?"

"Please."

"You're looking into an adoption that Miles arranged. A young boy named Rainey. Rainey is now in your sister Kate's care, and she has questions?"

"Yes. Several. Many."

"Rainey was the boy who was at the center of that tragedy last year, was he not? His abduction and his odd return, found in a sealed grave. Sylvia's disappearance, Miles' suicide?"

Reed nodded, waiting.

Miss Beryl was silent for a long time. She was obviously torn between tact and truth.

"I am going to make a leap of faith here, Reed. I hope I won't be sorry that I have done so."

"Whatever you have to say stays between us."

"That may not be possible. Do you recall a Leah Searle, Reed?"

"I know the name. She was the lawyer Miles hired to do the adoption paperwork for Rainey."

"I knew her. We met during the early days of her work for Miles. I was impressed by her. She was an able young woman. Initially, our relationship was purely professional. I helped her with the Archives, and the parish books. The issues were complex and the records utterly chaotic. We persisted. And we failed. Over time it became clear to both of us that there was no reliable record of Rainey's birth in any available archive or database."

She made a sweeping gesture over all the books on the table.

"You can ruin your young eyes going over these materials, Reed, and you will go away as puzzled as you were when you arrived. You're aware that Leah Searle is dead?"

"I understand she drowned."

Miss Beryl raised an eyebrow and smiled.

"In her bathtub. An *accident*, we are told."

Reed looked at her.

She held his look.

"We come to the heart of the matter. She was in Gracie at the time of her death, following her researches. I believe by this point she was no longer working for Miles. I believe she was following her own line of inquiry."

"Into Rainey?"

Miss Beryl shrugged.

"Not only him. It had become a more wide-ranging investigation. You know the Teagues have a reputation, here in Sallytown, and elsewhere?"

"I know about London Teague. I know that he probably had his third wife killed, back in Louisiana, before the Civil War, and that her godfather called him out over it."

"That was Anora."

"Yes. She was—"

"A Mercer, as are you, on your mother's side. Anora's godfather was John Gwinnett Mercer. After her death, he and London Teague came to a stand at John Mullryne's home in Savannah. The fight was inconclusive."

Reed was wondering why Miss Beryl had taken such an interest in the history of his family. She knew it better than he did. But he said nothing, and she went on.

"London Teague had two wives before Anora. The first one, whose name is not known, died of malaria in the West Indies, where London ran a slave market catering to ships bound for the Carolinas. The second wife, Cathleen, had two sons, Jubal and Tyree. She died by her own hand after discovering that London Teague was a philanderer and a brute. Tyree was killed at Front Royal, during the War of Secession. Jubal, a cavalryman, survived the war and, very late in his life, had a son named Abel Teague. Anora had two girls, Cora and Eleanor. After her death, London sent them to live with John Gwinnett Mercer in Savannah. Cora died of influenza in the last years of the war. Eleanor went on to establish the Mercer line from which you derive, Reed. But Abel was born too, of Jubal, and in him the sins of London Teague came back into the living world. Abel Teague was a scoundrel, a rake, and a coward. Many men wished him dead, men of your line, or men married to women of your line. In the year before the First World War, Abel defiled a young woman named Clara Mercer. And then he refused to marry her. Clara had an older sister named Glynis. She was married to a fine man named John Ruelle. They owned a large plantation on the eastern slope of the Belfair Range. They took Clara in. She had suffered a nervous collapse. She may have been pregnant. John, and later his brother, Ethan, called Abel out for his offenses, but Abel would not come to a stand. That is to say, he refused to fight a duel. Refused many times. He was immune to shame, and cared nothing for anyone's honor. Not even his own. I doubt he had any honor to protect."

Reed reached into the inside pocket of his blazer and pulled out a sheet of paper folded in three. He held it out to Beryl, who took it.

"What is this, Reed?"

"It's a memo I found in my father's printer the day he disappeared. It was one of the last things he wrote. I gave it to Kate and Nick. This memo is why I'm here. To see for myself if it's accurate."

Miss Beryl unfolded the sheet.

Rainey Teague DOB questions:
memo for Kate.

    Searched Cullen County census for period surrounding R's DOB with Gwinnetts found no entry. No entry in surrounding parishes no entry in Belfair, no State or County Records show any certificate of R's birth or baptism. No record in adjoining states, counties, or parishes. No sign R was born or baptized anywhere in US, Canada, or Mexico in any date range corresponding to his stated age. Foster parents Zorah and Martin Palgrave: found entry Cullen County Registry of Birth Martin Palgrave born Sallytown November 7th 1873 married Zorah Palgrave Sallytown Methodist March 15 1893. Palgraves received credit letter signed G. Ruelle April 12 1913 "for care and confinement Clara Mercer and delivery of healthy male child March 2nd 1913."

Martin and Zorah Palgrave operated printing shop that created tintype print Niceville Families Jubilee 1910.

Indications Leah Searle made same findings re Rainey adoption and communicated same to Miles Teague at his office in Cap City on May 9 2002 prior to adoption from alleged "Palgrave foster home," no actual trace of which can be found in any taxpayer list or census other than in Cullen County census of 1914.

Conclusion: further study required to verify place of birth, true identity and origins of person now known as Rainey Teague.

Query Miles Teague suicide possible result of his realization that Rainey Teague's recovery from Ethan Ruelle crypt was related to R's uncertain origins. Otherwise it is inexplicable.

Must place all this before Kate now, since she, as his legal guardian, will be the obvious choice to provide him home until he comes of legal age. These issues need to be resolved ASAP.

She finished reading it and set it down on the table. "So Leah and your father were following the same lines. I'm not surprised. Do you suspect that the child Clara delivered was Abel Teague's?"

"I'm convinced of it."

"So am I. What a terrible man he was. For his sins, Abel Teague deserved death many times over. Yet he lived a long time. An abnormally long time. Do you know how long, Reed?"

"No. I don't."

"Abel Teague died at the age of one hundred and twenty-two years, give or take a year or so. He spent most of his later years right here in Sallytown."

"Here?"

"Yes. He was a resident in a palliative care facility not far from here, called the Gates of Gilead. Do you know it?"

"I've had calls there, when I was on patrol. But no, I'd have to say I don't know it well. I know I never ran into an Abel Teague."

"You would not have had the opportunity. He maintained a private room in a remote wing of the facility, at great expense, a room without windows or mirrors. He was particular about that. It amounted to a mania. He had several strange men, creatures really, who saw to his needs. The staff abhorred them. The creatures allowed no one else near his suite. Other than Abel's private doctors, of whom he had many. Abel Teague moved into that suite in the 1950s. He never left it until the morning he died. Would you care to know *when* he died?"

"Please."

"He died last spring. He was found lying on his back in a small forested park adjacent to the facility. He was wearing pajamas and a bathrobe. The cause of his death was a large-caliber bullet that had been fired into his left cheek, just below the eye. According to the rather cursory report compiled by the coroner and by your State Police, the wound was self-inflicted, although the weapon, a .45-caliber pistol, was never found. It was assumed that someone happening on Abel's corpse had stolen the gun. If you wish, you may visit the Gates of Gilead yourself, to confirm my narrative."

"I don't need to confirm it, Miss Beryl."

She sighed, and seemed to grow sad.

"I wish someone would try. Perhaps a rational explanation would arise."

She was silent for a time.

"I know you're wondering why I know so much about this matter. I told you I liked Leah Searle. This is not accurate. I loved her. She was young and bright and smart and sweet. I was attracted to her, and she to me. Not an appropriate match, I know. I am old and she was not, but it was a strong attraction nonetheless."

Miss Beryl, Reed thought, *has hidden depths.*

"I watched her disintegrate during her employment with Miles Teague. She grew secretive. Where we had once shared the work, and the time, she drew away, and spoke less and less about Rainey and his adoptive parents. Her attention moved to Gracie, where I gathered she was following a line of inquiry. She admitted as much, but would say no more about it. Then she died. Drowned. In her tub. In a cheap hotel in Gracie. It was ruled a misadventure. She had been drinking, and had also taken several tablets of Ativan. The Gracie police maintained that she passed out and slipped under the water. I believe she was murdered."

Reed had seen this coming.

"By Miles Teague."

"Yes."

"In order to stop her from finding whatever she was looking for?"

"Yes. Either here in Sallytown, or in Gracie."

"And what she was looking for was where Rainey had come from and who his parents really were."

She shook her head.

"That is where it began. The search for Rainey's true origins was what led her to Gracie. I believe that she brought what she found there to Miles Teague. And he killed her for it."

"Miles committed suicide."

"With a shotgun and I was delighted to hear it. Why did he do it? I am persuaded that he had something to do with Sylvia's death as well. She was in touch with me, shortly before Rainey disappeared, following the same lines that Leah had been following. I tried to help, but as you have seen, as your father reports, there really is no trail here at all, and Leah refused to tell me what she had found in Gracie. She felt that it was the kind of truth that is dangerous to know. As it turns out, she was right."

Her blue eyes were shining and wet. Reed looked around, found a box of tissues. She took one, touched her eyes, and folded it into her hands.

"Miss Beryl, Kate has papers supposedly provided by Leah Searle, birth certificates and other records, that show a date of birth for Rainey as the year 2000, right here in Sallytown. They're *signed* by her, at least. And by a notary."

Miss Beryl's lips tightened and her cheeks flushed pink. She answered with real heat.

"Forgeries. Complete *forgeries*. Miles had them created by a counterfeiter. There are no such records in existence and Leah would never have tried to fake them. *Never*."

Her certainty was pretty convincing.

She went on.

"I know that Sylvia began to investigate these things herself. And then she disappeared. Threw herself into Crater Sink, we are expected to believe. She may have gone into Crater Sink, Reed, but not willingly. I think Miles put her there, for the same reason he killed Leah."

"A man who was cold enough to do those things isn't likely to take his own head off with a shotgun, Miss Beryl."

"That would depend on what he was afraid of. Perhaps he saw something coming that he did not care to face."

"Justice?"

She shook her head.

"Not ours, certainly. Perhaps it was something darker. And older. How do you imagine Abel Teague managed to stay alive and healthy for one hundred and twenty-two years?"

"Money? Luck? Fiber?"

"Don't be pert, young man. I believe he had . . . allies. I believe he had found a way to prolong his life. An unnatural way. I have no idea what shape it may have taken, but Abel was tapping into a darker power."

"The devil?"

"Abel Teague was a devil, yes, but I don't believe that Satan as we understand him has anything to do with this. Or God, whom I am completely persuaded has as much interest in His Creation as a careless child has in the ant farm he has long ago abandoned at the bottom of his yard. I have tried to discern the shape of this force, at least from the effects it seems to produce, in people such as Abel Teague, in places such as Crater Sink. It's like trying to detect a new planet simply by observing the alterations in stars and planets nearby. Some *gravitational* force *twists* reality in this part of the world. I am convinced of it. Abel used this force to survive far beyond man's natural span of years, and I have no doubt that it—whatever it is—used Abel in return. I know that Abel Teague was a lecher and a degenerate and addicted to opiates. I wonder if whatever the *power* is, it uses people such as Abel Teague to allow it to *experience*, to savor, the sensual elements of the living world. A fancy, but I believe there is something to it."

She smiled, and shook her head.

"I'm old, Reed, and Leah Searle was the last love I will ever have. I imagine I am shocking you, and you must try to bear up. But I lived a false life for all my years with Walter, and when he died I decided never to be false again. Leah's gone and I'm fading. I'm glad you came. I think the answer to your question is not here in Sallytown."

"Where, then?"

She stood up. So did he.

He was being dismissed, but with style.

"There's a place in Gracie. It's called Candleford House. Have you ever heard of it?"

"Yes. It was an asylum, wasn't it? Back in the twenties. Didn't have a very good reputation."

Miss Beryl shook her head.

"It had the reputation it fully deserved. Candleford House was a barbaric prison run by sadistic guards and quack medics and assorted charlatans, and the inmates were routinely tormented, raped, and ultimately poisoned for what money they possessed. Candleford House was a portal into hell, Reed, and it was the last place Leah went to before she died. She wouldn't tell me what she found there, but as we have already discussed, Leah confirmed that Clara Mercer was forcibly removed from Glynis Ruelle's care in 1924 and locked up in Candleford House. And there she stayed until 1931, when she was taken from Candleford House to Lady Grace Hospital in Niceville. We are agreed that she was there for an abortion, probably the result of a rape. Clara escaped from Lady Grace Hospital and threw herself into Crater Sink. Leah found something in Candleford House and Miles Teague killed her to suppress it. I was going to go there myself, but I'm too damn old. Gracie isn't far. I want you to go for me, Reed. Today. Right now."

"But it's empty. A ruin, isn't it?"

She came around the table and took his hand. Her fingers were bony but her skin was dry and cool. The scent of mimosa floated around her.

"It's a ruin. But it's not empty."

The Remains of the Day

Nick was on his way to a crime scene at a Motel 6 on North Gwinnett, lights and sirens, when Kate got him on the cell.

"I've been calling and calling, Nick."

Her voice was completely wired. Nick shut off the siren, kept the roof rack going.

"Don't tell me. Rainey?"

"Who else? WellPoint Neurological lost him."

"Lost him? Lost him how?"

"Dr. Lakshmi said she'd see Rainey right away, so I took him straight to WellPoint. He said he needed to go to the bathroom. I told them he was a flight risk, I told them that, so they assigned a male nurse to stay with him. But the nurse wouldn't go into the bathroom with him because there were rules about it—sexual abuse liabilities—so he went down the hall to talk to the other nurses, and poof!"

"When was this?"

"Just now. Maybe fifteen minutes ago."

"You weren't there?"

"No," she said, with a hysterical edge to her voice. "They wouldn't let me, because of Hannah!"

"I don't—"

"I had Hannah, that's why! Look, Beth took Axel to school, and then she had to meet with the lawyer about Byron's estate. So I kept Hannah with me and we drove Rainey to WellPoint. But Hannah was having a fit in the truck. She said Rainey was giving her a headache. I mean, what now, but okay, so I asked her how, and she said Rainey was making her hearing aid buzz—"

"Rainey was where?"

"In the front seat, beside me. Hannah was in the back. Nick, Rainey wasn't even talking. He was staring out the window, stony silent. He didn't have his phone on or anything. He wasn't paying any attention to her at all. But Hannah's screaming—"

"What's she saying?"

"Saying? Nothing sensible. She's a kid, Nick. Something about buzzy talking in her head. Screechy talk, she says. But she's obviously in pain, I mean, severe pain. I couldn't leave her in the truck, so I had to take her in with me, with Rainey and me, and we got Rainey signed in, and they told me I couldn't bring Hannah into the clinic—no kids as visitors—and she's hysterical by now—so I let them walk Rainey away—Nick, he never even looked back—but as soon as the big steel doors closed, she shuts up, stops crying. Now her hearing aids are fine, she says. So I leave her in the front office for a second, and I go ask Reception where Rainey is, and they say he's been taken to the prep room for X-rays, fluoroscopy, an angiogram, something called a computed tomography, and later they were going to do a lumbar puncture. It was all in-house. They said it would take several hours and no I couldn't be there if I had Hannah with me. I went back out to look after Hannah. She was hungry. We went to McDonald's. Drove around. Met Beth for lunch. Called in to see how he was doing—he's gone! I've been calling and calling, Nick!"

"I'm sorry, babe, really. I was in a meeting with Tig, talking about Rainey. Then I went to see Beau. I had to turn my cell off to get into the hospital. I'm sorry, babe. Where are you now?"

"I'm in the car, looking for him. Beth is with me. Eufaula is taking care of Axel and Hannah. I called the Niceville police but they don't seem to be doing much. So we are."

"Where are you looking?"

"We've checked out Patton's Hard. The place is covered with crime scene tape and there are two cop cars keeping everybody away. Now we're heading over to Sylvia's house to see if he's there."

"Have you called Lemon?"

"Yes. He's meeting us there. Can you come?"

"Kate, I can't. I'm on my way to a crime scene. Two dead. I can't break away."

"But what about Rainey?"

"I spoke with Tig. Like I said, he's moving slow on this, I think to give us time to prepare. So far Tig hasn't made any announcement about Alice Bayer. She's just a Jane Doe we took out of the Tulip. But if Rainey's gone again, Tig will put out a notice that the Niceville guys will take seriously. They'll pick him up in an hour."

"But they'll question him, won't they?"

"Not without a lawyer. It's illegal to ask a minor any questions about a case unless he has a parent or a lawyer present. If they find him, they'll bring him to wherever you are. Tig will see to that. We can trust him. Rainey will turn up."

"We're still going over to Sylvia's house. Aren't you going to meet us there?"

"I can't, babe. I just can't."

"Fine. I guess it's Lemon and Beth and me again. Maybe you should put him on a retainer. Like Miles did for Sylvia. Our own private escort. That's what Lemon used to do, wasn't it? Entertain lonely wives whose husbands are too damn busy at work."

That stung him, but he controlled it.

"You're angry and upset, Kate. I get that. But that's a cheap shot and we don't play it that way. Don't call Lemon if that's the way you feel. And since you ask, I do have him on a retainer."

That stopped her.

"Why?"

Nick laid it out for her. He'd hired Lemon to help him figure out what was going on with Rainey and, for that matter, with Niceville itself.

"But why Lemon? Why not one of your people in the CID?"

"Because no one but Lemon would buy any of it. And he buys it because he's *seen* it. But if that's not okay with you, then he's gone. I'll call him as soon as you get off the line."

She was quiet.

He could hear her breathing, and Beth in the background, on her own cell, talking to the cops again, and the sound of music playing, the hum of tires on the road. Kate was still moving, on the cell, and he was distracting the hell out of her.

"Honey, you should pull over—"

"No. I'm sorry. You're right. It's just—we're trying to help Rainey, but he's making it pretty tough. Do you know what else he did?"

"I'm afraid to ask."

"I just went to an ATM to get some driving-around cash. My ATM card wasn't in my purse. It was there last night, but it's gone. I called the bank and they said someone just used my card to withdraw a thousand dollars. I think it was Rainey. This is no coincidence!"

"How did he get your PIN?"

"Same place he got the entry code to Sylvia's house. My daybook. I can never remember pin numbers and codes. Rainey knew that. This kid's out of control, Nick. But he's not stupid. He's actually making *moves*, Nick. Like an experienced criminal would. Making *plans* and getting access to cash. He's *operating*. It's like some adult is *helping* him."

"Are you still driving?"

"Yes. We're going to Sylvia's house."

"Okay. Hang up. Keep your phone on. I'll call Tig. He'll get the Niceville PD moving. They'll have him in an hour. Okay? This will all work out. Really, babe."

"Even after this?"

"You and I have seen wild kids before. Their parents pay your salary. They all worked out, sooner or later, didn't they?"

Some moments went by.

Nick could feel her thinking about it.

"That's true. They all did. Mostly."

"There you go."

More quiet breathing.

"Thank you. I feel better."

"Good. That's what I live for."

She even laughed. Weak and full of worry, but still a laugh. So he laughed too.

"No, really, babe. You complete me."

"Dear God. What horseshit. Go to work, Nick."

"Be safe, babe. Keep me in the loop."

"You be safe too, Nick. Bye."

When he got to the Motel 6 the Niceville patrol guys had the scene isolated. There were two cruisers down in the parking lot, their roof racks spinning, sending that crazy flickering light flying around the walls and windows like fireflies from hell. The sun was going down in pink and golden glory, all the streetlights were on, and assorted gawkers were crowding the perimeter.

A patrol cop held up the crime tape and he rolled his Crown Vic under it, coming to a stop at the foot of the stairs that led up to the second floor. Mavis Crossfire was standing at the top of the landing, looking down at him, her hands on her hips, smiling a crazy smile.

"Jesus Mary and Joseph, it's Himself," she said. "Didn't I see you at the Galleria Mall? Don't you have a life?"

"No. I don't. Neither do you, I see."

"I got promoted. I'm section supervisor for six precincts now. You look a little freaky, Nick."

Nick told her that Rainey was in the wind again.

"Jesus. Slippery little bugger. That kid will end up teaching escape and evasion to Navy Seals."

"I really don't want to talk about him, Mavis."

"Okay. We won't. How's Andy Chu doing?"

"He's out of danger. Boonie has two gigantic FBI guys sitting in his room and frowning at him. He's on IV and he'll wear a cast on that shattered shoulder for a long time. So far Boonie hasn't figured out whether he was a hostage or an accomplice. He's leaning towards accomplice."

"Has Chu lawyered up?"

"Not yet. But he's pretty sedated. Boonie hasn't tried to question him. Anyway, I dropped in to see Beau this afternoon."

"I was gonna ask."

"He's drugged out of his gourd, but they re-sectioned his bowel and did what they could for his liver and spleen, and there's no internal bleeding now. His spine's okay, but he's going to be on glucose and saline for a while. Only solid he can take is Jell-O. They're talking about a temporary colostomy, which he's not gonna like."

"Nor would I. How's his morale?"

"He's a tough kid, but I'd say he's . . . shocked. Young kids never imagine anything bad can happen to them. I saw a lot of it when I was regular Army. Round comes in out of nowhere, and the main thing is the kid just *cannot* believe it. Some of them died and the main thing they were when they died was *surprised*. Beau's got a lot of that going on. May's there right now."

Mavis shook her head.

"How'd the PISTOL thing go?"

"They cleared us. What else could they do, with a cop down? Coker had no choice but to take out Maranzano. The grandkid they laid on Deitz. And then Coker and I did Deitz. Eventually."

Mavis gave him a look.

"What does that mean?"

Nick thought about his answer.

"This is just us, okay?"

"Always is, Nick. You know that."

"We had Deitz on the staircase. It was dark, but there was enough to aim by. I was below him, and Coker was at the top. Deitz was in the bag. Only sensible thing for him to do was drop the shotgun and take his chances with a jury."

"But he didn't. He tried for a shot at Coker."

"Yeah. But only after Coker goaded him into it. Coker said it was embarrassing to watch Deitz operate. Deitz lost his temper."

"Deitz always had a bad temper. And Coker's as cold as they come. He likes to kill bad guys."

"Yeah. But it . . . bugs me. Sticks in my throat."

"Byron Deitz was a racist misogynist sadistic son of a bitch, Nick. And greedy. And a bully to his wife and kids. Did I mention butt-ugly? And now he's dead. The world's a better place. Maybe Coker shouldn't have goaded him, but Coker saved my life back there at Saint Innocent Orthodox. And he also saved the janitor, remember? He's a stone-cold snake, Nick, but he's *our* stone-cold snake. Keep tugging on hanging threads and one day your pants will fall off."

Nick did a take, grinning in spite of his miserable mood.

"How, exactly, would that work?"

Mavis shrugged, grinned right back at him.

"I have no idea."

"Okay. What have we got here?"

Mavis lost her smile, glanced over in the direction of a laundry cart, where an elderly black maid, her eyes red from crying, was sitting down on a wash bucket and talking to a policewoman Nick didn't know.

"Two white males. Dead at the scene. I'll let you figure out how. Lady over there found them when she came to do the room. We've already taken her prints and mapped out how far she got into the room before she saw the bodies, which was about a foot. You ready to take a look?"

This was a rhetorical question, so he just let Mavis lead the way. There was a patrol cop holding the door, and he nodded at Mavis as they came up.

"Tommy, this is Detective Kavanaugh, with the CID. Nick, this is Tommy Molto. He's been guarding the scene. He was first officer here."

Nick looked him over, a strong-featured Italian kid. He seemed to be having the time of his life.

"Crime scene secure, Officer Molto?"

"Sir yes sir! It's as clean as my . . . it's clean as a whistle, sir. I personally guarantee it."

Nick thanked him, and Mavis gave him a scorching look as they went by him and stood on the threshold, Mavis a bit behind Nick, letting him see it for himself.

There were two bodies in the room, one a muscular young man with a goatee, naked, covered in blood, mutilated, bound at the wrists, ankles, and neck by a white cord. He had a gag in his mouth, a large bullet hole in his forehead, and a slightly smaller bullet hole in his left thigh. He was lying in his own mess. His blue eyes were open and the expression fixed on his face was a mixture of shock and terror.

The other body was lying in a tumbled heap on the floor in the middle of the room, a sallow-skinned big-boned older man in a black suit, a white shirt, a narrow black tie. He was lying on his back, splayed out, and had a star-shaped exit wound in the top of his skull.

As Nick came around to look down at him, he saw where the round had gone in, under the man's chin, a bulging hole where the muzzle blast had billowed out and torn open the soft skin on the underside of his jaw. There was a spatter of black spots around the entrance wound. Powder stipple. Which meant the weapon was close to, if not in contact with, the man's throat when the round was fired.

The guy also had a vivid three-inch gash on his forehead, done while he was still alive, because it had bled like crazy until the bullet took out his brains. Nick looked up and saw the droplet spatter and brain bits stuck to the ceiling, in the middle of which was a large black hole where the round had gone into the plaster.

So the man was standing in the center of the room when he took the round.

Nick looked down and saw the Colt .45 pistol lying on the orange shag carpet a few feet away. The man's right hand was stretched out in that direction, as if the Colt had flown loose after the round smacked home.

Nick knelt down and sniffed at the man's hand. Mavis stood back and watched him work, saying nothing, although she had her own view of what had happened here.

After a while, Nick stepped away from the bodies and walked around the perimeter of the room once again, not touching anything, as he slipped on a pair of latex gloves.

Even with the door open and the breeze running, the smell of blood and bodily fluids was rank and choking. If Nick wasn't going to complain, neither was Mavis. But she was breathing through her mouth and wishing for Vicks VapoRub all the same.

Nick came back and stood beside her.

"Okay. This is what we're supposed to see here. Some kind of twisted sex thing. We have the vic on the bed, bound and gagged. Been shot in the upper thigh with what looks like a nine-mill. Another, much larger round in his forehead. Typical star-shaped entry wound there, with lots of powder stipple, so another close-contact shot. Somebody went at him with a small power drill. Knees and ankles and elbows and hips and jaw. Into the bone wherever it could reach. Would have hurt like holy hell. BTK is what we're supposed to see here. Bind. Torture. Kill. Motive? Sadistic sexual thrills."

Mavis said nothing, but she smiled.

Nick went on.

"We're given the older guy in the suit as the perpetrator, and the handsome young kid as the vic. The old guy gets his . . . has enough. He puts a round into the kid's forehead, and then, in a sudden fit of remorse, he puts that big Colt over there under his chin and stuccos the ceiling. Flops to the ground, the pistol flies loose, and there we are."

"A tableau of bitter remorse?"

Nick gave her a sideways smile.

"Exactly. There is the smell of cordite on his gun hand, so it's possible that the gun was in his hand when the round went off. How'm I doing, Mavis?"

"Work of art," she said, waiting for it.

"Yeah. Except the dead kid is Lyle Preston Crowder, who came to fame last spring when he rolled a flatbed loaded with rebar on Interstate 50, killing a bunch of church ladies and tying up every available patrol unit for miles around."

"And forty-four minutes later, the First Third Bank in Gracie gets hit," said Mavis.

Mavis had gotten the kid's ID from the hotel clerk, but Nick had simply remembered the kid's face. She was impressed.

"I don't know about you, but I was convinced at the time that the kid had something to do with it."

"So was I," said Mavis. "But Boonie never bought that, and it was a federal case."

"Well, *somebody* agreed with us, I think. Looks to me like he was asking Lyle about that robbery, and emphasizing the importance of the question with a power drill. So far the money's never been recovered, not even partially, has it?"

"I don't have it, I know that, and I checked my undie drawer and my laundry bin and everything."

"So it's still out there," said Nick, "and somebody figured Lyle might know where. And of course we both know this other guy."

"Edgar Luckinbaugh," said Mavis, happy to contribute.

"I guess we have to toss this place, don't we?"

"What you mean *we*, white man? I'm just a humble patrol person."

"Can you do chain of evidence anyway?"

"How about I just take pictures?"

Which she did, starting at the edges of the room and working her way in, finally getting several detailed close-ups of the bodies and the wounds. Then she stepped back and bowed to him, waving him forward.

"The duty ME been called?" Nick asked, as he bent down to go through Edgar Luckinbaugh's pockets.

"She has," said Mavis. "She's finishing up something called a fractured supraorbital process."

"Cracked eye socket."

"My goodness. Those are real big words for a young fellow like you."

Nick tapped the bruise on his forehead.

"I got one when the marshals' van rolled over."

"Jeez," said Mavis, "I'd forgotten about that. Been a full week, hasn't it? Remember when nothing at all ever happened in Niceville?"

"No," said Nick, extracting the man's wallet from his breast pocket while trying to avoid the bloody bits on his shirtfront.

"Neither do I," said Mavis.

Nick stood up and flipped through the wallet. Driver's license, Social Security card, a memorial Mass card for a Francis Louise Luckinbaugh, born Gillis, died in 2006. A Capital One credit card, a prepaid cell phone card, a magnetic employee card for the Marriott Hotel, receipts for Krispy Kreme donuts—several of these—a receipt for Wendy's dated today, from the Wendy's just across the street, as a matter of fact.

Nick went to the window, looked out across North Gwinnett.

"Anybody ID a ride for Mr. Luckinbaugh yet?"

"No. All the cars in the lot are accounted for. Nothing in the name of Luckinbaugh."

"Work with me here, Mavis. He has a cuff key in a slot on the big fat cuff case on his belt, but I see no cuffs anywhere in this room. He has a huge premortem gash on his forehead, quite fresh, that must have smarted a bit. Unlike most of the Western world, he does not seem to have a cell phone. Yet he has a prepaid cell phone calling card in his wallet. He has a shoulder rig fitted for that big old Colt, which I'll bet was his duty gun when he was on the job. He's been stuffing his face with Krispy Kreme donuts, which, according to the receipts, he's been buying all over town, and all in the last forty-eight hours. And he's saved all of his gas and food receipts too, like he was going to hand in an accounting of expenses to somebody else. Does it feel to you like it feels to me, that Edgar was still on the job this afternoon?"

"You mean, was he doing a private detective thing? Yes, it does. Else why the cuff case and the Colt?"

"Cuff case, but no cuffs. So where'd they go?"

"Excellent question, Nick. He forgot them?"

"Or he was in the process of cuffing someone when things went terribly wrong. He got overpowered—maybe he was trying to cuff the guy and the guy used the cuffs to rake him across the forehead there—hence the laceration premortem. Guy comes in close, grabs the weapon by the muzzle, turns it upwards, which is what you do when you're fighting for control of a gun. Pistol goes off under Edgar's chin and Edgar's brain bits stucco the ceiling."

"He wasn't shot by Lyle over there."

"Nope. By a Third Party, is my bet, a Third Party with a nine-mill that he used on Lyle's upper thigh. My guess is he shot Lyle with Edgar's .45. He then takes Edgar's cuffs with him. And his cell phone. But not the cuff key, and not his Colt."

"You know what this scene really plays like, Nick? It plays like Edgar followed Mr. Third Party to this location, that he was being paid to follow Mr. Third Party around by Mr. Unknown Client, and that he decided to do a solo kick-in, and got himself killed for it."

"Like he thought a crime was in progress? And the cop in him decides to do something about it?"

"Along those lines, yes."

"Does this hotel have a security system that covers the staircase?"

"Yes, it does. I've got the hard drive for you downstairs. I looked at the video. You see people coming and going. Clerk says they were all regular tenants or service workers. One guy the clerk didn't know, tall thin guy, he kept his face away from the camera. He was well dressed, elegant, even. Gray suit and really nice shoes—the clerk's a shoe guy. He went up the staircase to the second floor at 14:56 hours by the time clock. He was carrying a leather bag. Camera doesn't pan, so there was no telling where he went, or where he came from, but the clerk's sure the guy wasn't a tenant."

"Can we get a still?"

"Being done right now. More people come and go, and then, at 15:29 hours we see Lyle coming up the stairs with a pizza and a sack with groceries in it."

"That's the beer and junk dumped into the bathtub?"

"Yes. Next there's a long period where nothing much happens—a couple of maids pass by—and then, at 15:52 hours we see Edgar going past the camera lickety-split, with his war face on. Thirty minutes later, Mr. Third Party comes down the stairs with his leather case. He keeps his face averted from the camera and steps out of the frame."

"I'll want stills of that too."

"You'll have them."

Nick was studying the cars in the Wendy's lot.

"Does Wendy's have security cameras?"

"I haven't asked, but I'd be surprised if they didn't. Cameras are everywhere now."

"Makes our lives easier, anyway. So we've confirmed our various players, at least in a general way. We need to ID Mr. Third Party and we need to figure who the Unknown Client was. One more thing. We figure he took Edgar's cell with him. Why do that? If he's caught with it, it's evidence that links him to a murder."

"He took it because he doesn't want anyone else—say the cops—finding out who Edgar was calling on it because he was probably calling the Unknown Client, and Mr. Third Party doesn't want us to know who that person is."

"Yes. Very nice, Mavis. Tell me, what do private dicks usually do?"

"They get hired by worried spouses to follow people to cheap motels just like this one and take pictures of sexual degenerates doing naughty stuff to each other's nobbly bits with whips and feather dusters and goldfish and such like."

"So a typical Saturday night at your house?"

"In your dreams, Nick."

"See that piece of shit Windstar over there?"

"I do."

"Do you notice, Mavis, that it's so blinking dull and boring and awful that it's actually impossible to keep looking at it without falling asleep?"

"Therefore a perfect vehicle for surveillance."

"And in a perfect position to watch this very room. I propose we go over there and toss it. What do you say?"

"Whither thou goest."

Mr. Teague Is Not Receiving

Lemon parked his ancient pickup a few houses away from the Teague mansion on Cemetery Hill and shut the engine down. From where he sat the house looked closed up and empty, but that didn't mean that Rainey wasn't in there. He figured Kate and Beth were ten minutes away, and he wanted Kate to be the first face Rainey saw, if Rainey was there at all. But the kid was really troubling Lemon.

Back when Sylvia and Miles were still alive his relationship with Rainey had been, all things considered, a pretty good one. Lemon had never had a son, or even a brother, and they were both Gators fans—Rainey used to kid him about the Seminoles—and when they had time they'd throw the football around in the Teague backyard.

Throwing footballs around hadn't been something Miles enjoyed. Neither was parenthood. Or being a husband, for that matter. Lemon wouldn't have been around at all if he hadn't been more or less in love with Sylvia, and Rainey meant the world to her. But this new Rainey?

In his heart, Lemon believed that Rainey was, one way or another, involved in the death of Alice Bayer. And now that he was dodging it all again—on the run, acting like a spoiled shit—acting like a *guilty* spoiled shit—it was impossible to reconcile the two kids.

It was like something very bad had come to live inside the kid, and was sitting there like a spider, tugging at Rainey's strings and cables. Lemon checked his watch, looked in his rearview.

No Kate.

Thinking it over, Lemon thought maybe he'd just do a walk around the yard, see if there was any sign that Rainey had been there. If doing that gave him a chance to have a moment alone with Rainey, a kind of brotherly heart-to-heart that might involve a loving smack to the side of the head, maybe that wouldn't be such a bad thing. Nick was his guardian, but he had to stay away from anything physical, any kind of rough discipline. Nick's feelings about Rainey were too flammable.

So Lemon climbed down out of the Suburban and walked up the block in the direction of the Teague house. He reached the bottom of the drive.

And then he stopped.

The house looked perfectly ordinary, a large stone mansion resting on a rolling lawn, surrounded by oaks and willows, a dappled afternoon light lying on it. *The warm glow of old money* was the expression that came to Lemon's mind as he stood there looking up at it. But there was something on the big stone verandah that had never been there before. It was like a shadow, or at least a darker kind of light, and it was resting on the porch. Looking at it Lemon knew it wasn't a shadow.

It was a *darkness*.

And it was aware of him.

Lemon's gut did a slow roll and the muscles all over his back and belly started to crawl. The shadow got larger, lengthening and spreading. It separated into two distinct shapes, and then into the figures of two large men.

They were standing on the landing, staring down at him, not yet clearly defined figures, but men nevertheless, blurred and shimmering as if his eyes were watering, but solid enough. He shook his head and they came into focus.

They both wore blue jeans and heavy black boots. Their big bellies pushed the white cotton of their shirts out like spinnakers and sagged down over their belt buckles. Although one had a shaved head and a black biker goatee and the other one was clean shaven, with shaggy blond hair, they had a family resemblance.

Lemon had seen their pictures, a couple of mug shots, above the headline in the *Niceville Register*, the morning after the crash and the carnage at the Super Gee. Dwayne Bobby Shagreen and Douglas Loyal Shagreen, ex-Nightriders, wanted by the FBI, and until two days ago, lying dead and frozen in the back of a meat wagon at the State Police HQ lock yard outside Gracie.

Lemon knew they weren't really there, no more than Merle Zane had really been standing at the elevator in the hallway at Gracie when the door opened and they stood face-to-face and spoke to each other. Whatever these things were, they were fully present now, looking as solid as the stones they were standing on, arms limp at their sides, dull cow-like faces devoid of expression or feeling, staring back at him, waiting for him to come closer. He got his heart rate under control and stood his ground.

"Why are you here?"

The one with the long blond hair looked confused, and then he said, as if he had just recalled this, "We are here for Mr. Teague."

There was no edge or venom in his voice. No emotion at all. It was low and flat and soft. A faint Virginia accent.

"Why?"

"We take care of his needs."

"Where are you from?"

The blond one looked puzzled again.

"We see to Mr. Teague's needs. There is no place to be from. There is no other place to be. We are here for Mr. Teague."

His lips were numb and his mouth was dry. There was a high-pitched buzz in Lemon's ears. An artery in his neck was pulsing so intensely he could actually hear it.

"Is Mr. Teague home?"

"Yes."

"I want to talk to him."

"No."

There was a voice behind him, a woman's voice.

"Lemon? Are you okay?"

He looked back and saw Kate. She was on the far side of the street, standing beside her Envoy. Beth was in the passenger seat, staring out at him.

Lemon looked back to the landing. It was, of course, empty. Kate and Beth came up to him. Kate looked as if she had been crying, and Beth just looked shell-shocked.

"Are you all right, Lemon?"

"Yes. Sure, Kate. Of course. Why?"

"You were talking to someone on the landing. At least you looked like you were. We called your name twice but you didn't hear us. What were you doing?"

Lemon looked back up at the landing, saw the Shagreens standing there. Obviously Kate wasn't seeing them. He looked at Beth, who was simply looking back at him with the same puzzled expression. He shook his head.

"I guess I was talking to myself."

"Is Rainey there?" Beth asked.

"In the house?"

Beth smiled at him.

"No, Lemon. On the roof."

Lemon shook his head.

"No. He's not."

"You've already looked?" asked Kate.

"Yes."

"You looked *inside*?"

"Yes. He's not there."

Please believe me, both of you.

"Fine," said Beth. "Now what do we do?"

We get you both away from here, was his thought. What he said was "Are you hungry?"

Kate looked surprised at the suggestion, as if being hungry had never occurred to her. She suddenly felt that she was starving.

"I'm famished," said Beth. "But what about Rainey?"

"The Niceville cops have more cars than we do. They'll find him. I'm hungry too. You two pick a place. I'll follow you."

Beth and Kate walked back to the truck. All Lemon could think about was getting them into that Envoy and as far away from Cemetery Hill as possible.

"How about Placido's?" said Beth. "It's just around the corner on Bluebottle Way. Can you do Italian?"

"I know Placido's. I'll be right behind you."

"Okay," she said. "See you in five."

Kate got into the Envoy, started it up, rolled down the window. She was looking past him at the Teague house.

"When you were standing there, we thought it was like you were talking to somebody. Not yourself."

"Did you see anybody there?"

Kate focused on him, a sharp, searching look.

"Not that I could see."

"Beth, did you?"

She looked uneasy.

"Maybe something. Like a shadow, sort of."

"Look, let's get out of here. I'll see you at Placido's."

Beth hesitated, glanced back up at the house, and then smiled.

"We'll talk about this over carpaccio. Okay?"

"Sounds great."

They pulled away.

He waited until they turned the corner onto Bluebottle, and then he walked back up to the bottom of the stone staircase.

The dark light was still there, a pool of nothing that somehow made the sunlight weaker. Lemon put a foot on the first step and the dark light got more solid.

"I'll see you again," he said, and walked back to his truck.

Candleford House

Gracie was only about forty miles away from Sallytown. Reed pulled into town as the sun was going down behind the Belfair Range. Gracie was a bigger place than Sallytown, but not by much. Since it was set in a kind of hollow between the eastern and western elevations of the Belfair Range, twilight came early and all the streetlights were on along Division Street, Gracie's main drag.

At the intersection of Division Street and Widows Lament, the center point of the town since all the streets radiated out in spokes the way they did in Washington and Paris, Reed saw the local branch of the First Third Bank, the scene of that spectacular robbery six months back.

It was an old stone structure built to look like an Egyptian temple, which made the huge illuminated plastic bank signs stuck on the elegant old facade look as out of place as Ray-Ban sunglasses on a marble bust of Cicero.

This Friday night Gracie was jumping as high as an old broad named Gracie can jump, which meant the crowd at T.G.I. Friday's was bulging the windows out and the line at the Ruby Tuesday had spilled out onto the sidewalk. Something involving penguins in 3-D was playing at the Chantilly Pantages, and Jubilation Park, Gracie's village square, had a traveling carnival set up.

The Tilt-A-Whirl was a spinning octagon of neon filled with shrieking teens, and the merry-go-round was putting out a calliope version of "The Skaters' Waltz." *Got to love small-town America*, Reed was thinking, as he rolled through the center of Gracie and out along Division Street. *God bless the USA.*

Reed had driven by Candleford House many times while he was working patrol for State, but he had never paid too much attention to it.

Now, as he brought the car to a stop in front of it, he gave it a closer look. It seemed just as he remembered it, a tall, forbidding gray stone building with two projecting tower-like bays on either side. Four stories high, with Norman turrets topping the towers. Money had been spent in the building of it. It had leaded casement windows, a central gallery with a couple of ornate pillars and a smaller upper balcony framed by carved stone arches. There was a huge wooden door on the street level, set in under a ponderous stone portico.

Candleford House was stained by rain and wind and time and it looked as grim as death. Since it was a memory that Gracie devoutly wished to forget, it carried no historical plaque. It had been left to rot in a large weedy park behind a barrier of chain-link fencing. The local kids had done for all the leaded glass in the windows, except for the upper floors. The windows there were still reasonably intact. The last of the setting sun was reflected in the highest windows, which glittered gold like wolf eyes at night.

There was a NO STOPPING sign right in front of the place, so Reed went farther along Division and found a 7-Eleven lot where he could leave the car. He got out with his Maglite, took his mid-sized bolt cutters and a pair of gloves out of the tailgate lockdown, keyed the car remote, and strolled back to Candleford House.

It was getting colder these fall days and with the sun down there was a bite in the air. There were no houses or stores on this block, other than the 7-Eleven down the street. Live oaks crowded the street, looming and dense, shutting out the sky. Streetlamps burned a sickly yellow inside the branches. It was a lonely, gloomy, and unpleasant stretch. Why the city felt it had to put up a NO STOPPING sign was a mystery. The entire block was empty and there were no cars around.

It was pretty obvious that Gracie people didn't want to come anywhere near this place.

He stood on the sidewalk in front of the sinister old pile, wondering what in the hell he was supposed to find inside this dead-eyed zombie of a building. Especially in the fading light, and that was assuming that he could even get inside the damn thing in the first place.

Looking up at the facade, having it loom over him like a gigantic tombstone, Reed was finding it difficult to feel kindly towards Miss Beryl.

But he'd said he would do it and he was a man who kept his word. He would get in there somehow, poke around, likely find sweet bugger all, get the hell out. Then he'd go back to T.G.I. Friday's on the square for a couple of beers and a rib-eye steak, find himself a motel, call Kate and Nick, fill them in on what he had, including Miss Beryl's conviction that Miles Teague was a cold-blooded murderer.

Reed suspected she was right. He had never warmed to Miles, and his suicide when Rainey had been found alive had struck Reed as impossible to explain in any sane way.

Miss Beryl's theory answered a lot of questions and Nick and Kate would want to hear about it.

Then he'd get himself a good night's sleep, and maybe drive back up to Sallytown, check out the Gates of Gilead, and then stop by Miss Beryl's place to fill her in on . . . whatever he had found.

He did a slow walkabout along the perimeter of the fence. It was ten feet high and topped by razor wire that tilted inwards, as if it was there to stop whatever was inside from getting out.

So climbing *that* was off the table.

He went around to the back of the lot. There was a hinged gate here, chained and padlocked. He looked for alarms. There weren't any. Nor did he see any power or phone lines running into the building. It stood there, dark and dead-eyed and silent.

There was a glow in the evening sky that promised a moon later. He had no intention of being around long enough to need moonlight.

He checked behind him, looked right and left, put his gloves on, and snapped the chain with his bolt cutters. The chain rattled to the ground and he pulled on the sagging gate. He had to lift it to move it, and it groaned as it came, but all he needed was a couple of feet.

He slipped through the opening, walked across the big yard, which was mostly weeds and stones and broken glass. The back of the building had what looked like a cookshack attached to the main structure. The roof had fallen in, but it looked like a soft spot to probe.

There was a slatted door hanging off a hinge. He jerked it away and the black hole of what had once been a summer kitchen lay before him. He flicked on the Maglite. It had a powerful halogen beam. He laid it on the interior and saw a stone floor littered with what was left of the roof beams. There was a door—open—at the back of the summer kitchen, and a flight of stone stairs that led upwards into the gloom. The place smelled of mold and seepage and rot.

Great way to spend a Friday night, he thought, but he went in anyway. It was his intention to see if anything remained of an office or a registry, or a reception area, and his best bet was the main floor hallway. The stairs were marble, worn smooth by time, and he was surprised that no one had bothered to strip the place for its fixtures.

He reached the main floor landing. It was like walking onto the deck of the *Titanic* after a hundred years at the bottom of the ocean. There was a huge central hallway with a checkered tile floor. The ceiling was lined with decorative tin tiles and a large chandelier, rusted and ruined, dominated the air space. Reed put his light up into the darkness and saw a kind of central atrium that went all the way up to a stained-glass roof.

The atrium was lined with tall galleries on all four sides, supported by carved wooden pillars. There were four levels of galleries. They receded into the gloomy dark far above.

The comparison with the *Titanic*—or at least pictures he had seen of its ballroom—was sharper than ever.

There was a brown ruin to his right—what was left of a large oak counter, behind which stood a wall of pigeonholes for either keys or mail. Clearly the reception desk, as if Candleford House was a place where you checked in for a spa weekend. He walked over to it, his boots crunching on broken glass and years of plaster dust.

The desk was barren, just a rotted-out pile of dead wood. The wall of pigeonholes was empty. There were no ruined ledgers lying around, no paper of any kind at all. There was a door to the right of the reception desk, with faded gold letters on it. PRIVATE. Reed honored that sign by booting the door open.

The heavy wooden door boomed backwards and he put a light into the room. There was nothing in it, just an overhead dome light hanging from a chain, and rotted floorboards peeling up. Not finished flooring either. Just the rough planks of a subfloor. There was a row of windows along the back wall, and through their shattered glass he could see the lot, the chain-link fence, and down the street the blue glow of the 7-Eleven.

If there had ever been anything in this room, it was taken out long ago. The same was probably true of every other room in the place.

What the hell had Leah Searle seen here that got her killed? There was *nothing* here.

The place was an empty shell.

It held nothing but the smell of rot and plaster dust and mold. He wasn't even getting the stink of rats or mice, and he had seen no roaches. No pigeon shit on the floors, no bats fluttering around the upper floors. "No rats no cats no wolverines," as the song went.

Which was, come to think of it, damned odd.

Patrol cops spend a lot of time in ruined buildings, rousting homeless people, chasing felons, looking for lost pets. Reed had been in hundreds of them, and every last one of them was teeming with vermin of every stripe. They usually reeked of ammonia from bat droppings and there was always the murmuring ruffle of pigeons in the rafters.

Candleford House was empty.

And *silent*.

Reed couldn't hear traffic noises from outside, and that carnival a few blocks back was putting out enough bad music to drive dogs crazy for miles around. But inside here? Not a sound. It was like the place was holding its breath. When he moved across the floor even the crunching sound of his boots on the debris was muffled and dull.

It struck Reed then that Candleford House wasn't empty at all. It was packed full of *silence*, a thick fog of deafening silence.

For the first time since he'd stepped inside this place, Reed felt his chest and neck get tight, and the skin on his back grew hot in some places and cold in others. He knew this feeling. This was fear.

Of what? he thought.

Of *nothing*, came the answer, out of an ancient place deep down in his limbic system.

Nothing is in Candleford House.

Nothing is in this hallway with you.

Nothing is standing behind you.

Reed pivoted, bringing his Beretta out, running the light around the main floor, and then shining it up into the dark shadows of the upper galleries.

He saw . . . nothing.

He shook himself, forced his body to relax.

This was crazy. If *nothing* was what spooked Leah Searle, then this whole exercise was absurd.

He decided he'd give the place a quick look, all four floors, room by room, do it right, and then he'd get out.

He found the first staircase, tested it with his weight, and then went up it carefully, keeping his weight on the sides of each riser, not trusting the centers at all.

He reached the first gallery. Each side had four large bedrooms, with gaping windows, and all sixteen rooms were empty. It took another hour to search all four floors, and his expectations were completely fulfilled. Nothing was in every room.

Nothing filled the central atrium. Nothing was in the dining room, nothing was in the long-deserted spaces that might have been hospital wards. Nothing was in the tiny windowless rooms on the top floor, the ones with the heavy doors with the small iron-barred windows in them. Reed checked each and every one of them. At the end of the fourth-floor gallery, past a row of what could only be called cells, he saw an open door.

He followed the cone of his flashlight through the door and found himself in what must have been, at one time, a very nice room.

It still had its oak flooring. Four tall windows, each with its glass intact, let in a pale glow that had to be coming from the rising moon.

Reed went to the window, looked out, and saw Division Street far below, through the screen of live oak branches. It was still deserted, as was the entire block, but the forceful silence that seemed to choke off all the sound in the rest of the house wasn't as strong here.

Faintly, across the tops of the forest that Gracie lived in, he heard the shouts of laughing kids, and the wheezy music from the merry-go-round. Even the air in here was sweeter and fresher.

He turned around and looked at the room. It wasn't large, but the shreds of an Oriental carpet in the middle of the room carried an appealing pattern of white flowers and green vines that reminded him of the painted doorway at the end of the upper hallway in Dad's—no, Kate's—house.

There were marks on the carpet, deep indentations that could have been made by furniture. They were spaced in a way that suggested a bed rather than a couch. A large lamp, green tin, in a cone shape, the kind of lamp you saw in old factories and brand-new loft condos, hung from a chain in a way that would have lit up the middle of the bed. The room had an arched roof and the walls were capped with ornate crown molding.

Except for that ugly damn lamp, the effect of the room, even now, was sort of appealing, and it stood in stark contrast to the Victorian-prison feel of the rest of Candleford House.

What really troubled Reed about the lamp was its positioning. It was directly over the middle of the carpet and if he was right about those marks having been made by a bed, then it would have put all its harsh factory light down on the bed in a way that would have been pretty useless for anyone who wanted to use it to read by. Instead, it would have lit up the middle of the bed like a spotlight.

Or the person lying in the middle of the bed.

Which struck Reed as not only odd, but damn creepy, as if the idea of the room was for a person to be able to stand at the end of the bed and watch someone lying on the bed, under the harsh glare of the hanging light.

He looked up from the carpet and put the light of the flash around the walls. They were covered in flowered wallpaper, faded and peeling, but pretty, in a fussy, old-fashioned way. There was a lighter spot, a square shape, where a picture must have been hanging, and placed pretty low, for a picture, only about halfway up the wall.

Rather than step on the carpet, which he was unwilling to do, though he had no idea why, Reed came around the edges of it and stood looking at the lighter square in the wallpaper.

There was no nail or hook in the space. Now that he was close, he could see that the wallpaper inside the square didn't match the pattern around the edges. It was the same paper, but the piece in the square had been cut from a different part of the wallpaper and patched in.

Why?

Reed tapped the center of the square.

It gave off a hollow-sounding thump and the square shifted a bit. Reed looked around the edges and saw seams. This board had been cut to size and put in this square to cover . . . what?

A window?

He tapped around the edges of the board.

It rattled and the bottom left corner popped out a bit.

Reed got the blade of the bolt cutter and pried at the corner. The entire square popped free, and he was looking into a dark space.

He put the light into the square and saw a small closet-like space, windowless, about five by three. In the middle of the space was a large padded chair covered in moth-eaten velvet cloth, at one time purple. There was a table beside the chair, with an ashtray and something that looked like it might have been a tobacco box. The chair was placed so that anyone sitting in the chair could see directly through the opening. There was no getting around this one. The meaning of it was unmistakable.

A rape room, that's what this pretty sitting room was set up for.

And a rape room with a closet and a window where someone else could watch the rape take place.

He looked back into the closet space and saw the vague outline of a wooden panel door that had been cut into the back of the closet. So the person watching the rape, or the torture, or whatever it was, could come and go without being seen.

Reed stepped back, and then kicked out at the wall under the open square. It cracked and bent.

He booted it again, and again.

The wall cracked wide open. He kicked the opening into shards and splinters, stepped into the closet, shoved the chair aside, and slammed his boot heel against the door in the paneling.

The door was just a piece of shaved spruce. It flew back on rusty hinges, and he was looking at a large high-ceilinged room with a wall of leaded-glass windows running along one side.

The light of the moon was pouring into the room. There was a massive four-poster bed in the middle of the room, bare wood now, the mattress and bedsprings long gone. It was covered with dust but it was still intact. It was set in the middle of a Persian carpet, the rug white with dust and slowly rotting into pieces from the damp.

There was nothing else in the room except a tallboy dresser on the wall opposite the windows, all its drawers pulled open, as if it had been ransacked by a thief in a hurry.

Reed walked over to it and put a light into the top drawer. It had been lined with newspaper, now yellow and cracked and peeling. He pulled at one sheet and it came up.

It was a page of ads for farm tools, straight razors, curling irons, suspenders, hair oil, dentures, all of them in faded sepia. There was a dateline in the upper left corner.

September 23, 1930

He pulled the drawer out, turned it over. Nothing. The next. Nothing. And more nothing.

But on the underside of the bottom drawer a maker's mark was branded into the wood:

J. X. HUNTERVASSER & SONS
OGILVY SQUARE SAVANNAH
FINE CABINETRY TO THE GENTRY

There was a small square of yellowed paper glued to the drawer bottom, just below the maker's brand. It was a typed form, the letters faded but legible:

KINGSFIELD STANDING DRESSER
GENTLEMEN'S DELUXE MODEL B-2915
CUSTOM MADE FOR
MASTER ABEL TEAGUE
GIFT OF HIS FATHER COLONEL JUBAL TEAGUE
DELIVERY CHRISTMAS DAY

Reed held the light on the drawer for a while, and then he set the drawer on the floor.

Was this what Leah Searle had found? If she had, there was obviously an easier way to get into this room than kicking down two walls. But it was proof that Abel Teague had been . . . what?

Living in Candleford House, or at least staying in this room whenever he was in Gracie, until at least 1930? Clara Mercer had been forcibly remanded to Candleford House on June 14, 1924.

Because of the fire in the Niceville archives in 1935, no one knew who had signed that order. The documents had been destroyed. Was Leah Searle closing in on a copy? If so, what would it prove?

Well, for one thing it might prove that Abel Teague arranged to have Clara Mercer taken away from the Ruelles and brought here to Candleford House as a captive toy for his amusement. Which, after everything he had done to her already, was a refinement of sadistic cruelty almost too bloody awful to contemplate. It meant that Clara Mercer had spent seven years locked away in Candleford House, enduring unspeakable abuse at the hands of the same man who ruined her young life all those years before. The paper lining might mean that Teague was still living here, or at least coming here on a regular basis, when Clara got pregnant. Clara went into Crater Sink in 1931.

Was it possible that Abel Teague left here shortly afterwards, and in such a hurry that he forgot to take a family heirloom, a Christmas gift from his father, and left it to rot in this room?

It certainly would explain why Glynis Ruelle would have carried a hatred for Abel Teague that would have seared her soul black for the rest of her years. But Glynis Ruelle died in 1939.

And all of this was ancient history now.

Why would Miles care enough about any of it to murder Leah Searle and his own wife? And then take his head off with an antique Purdy? The fact that Miles Teague had an evil relative wasn't news to anyone in

Niceville. The bitter memory of London Teague's crimes was the reason the golf and country club in Niceville was named after Anora Mercer.

Whose signature was on that order of committal? And why was Abel Teague occupying the nicest room in Candleford House? Was Candleford House being run for Abel's personal amusement?

An entire hospital full of victims, and an elaborate facility set up on the top floor to cater to his corrupted tastes. Why would the people who ran Candleford House take that risk?

Unless it was Abel Teague's money that created Candleford House in the first place. And kept it going. Did he pay for the staff and the guards and the quacks? Was it Teague money that got the archives burned? If Teague family money created and supported the most notorious private hell house in the Deep South, would Miles Teague kill Leah Searle and his own wife to keep *that* a secret?

Hell yes.

Reed turned to leave.

A young woman was standing in the middle of the room, glowing in the moonlight shining through the windows. She was barefoot, and wearing a dress made of very thin fabric. It looked gray in the moonlight but might have been green. She was pale but pretty, with wide eyes and long auburn hair. She was naked under the dress, her lovely body outlined by the moon's glow. She cast no shadow on the floor in front of her. Her hands were folded together and resting on her rounded belly. She was looking at him with an odd expression that Reed realized was curiosity.

My first ghost, was the thought in Reed's mind. He felt no fear, only that he wanted to be very still and silent and not to do anything that would make this image flicker and disappear. The woman looked around the room, and then back at him.

"Who are you?" she asked.

Her accent was pure Savannah, her voice low and soft and clear.

"My name is Reed Walker."

She seemed to take this in.

"Your mother is Lenore, isn't she?"

"Yes."

"She's with Glynis now. She's happy."

"Is my father there?"

"No. I'm sorry. Nothing took him. Nothing keeps him. Nothing keeps everything it takes. Nothing is in this place right now. Can you not feel it? You need to go."

"Are you Clara Mercer?"

"Yes. I used to live in this place. Now I live with Glynis. Why did you come here?"

"To find out what happened here."

She looked around the room.

"Terrible things happened here. This was Abel's place. For a long time I lived here with him. And with nothing. They fed on me. They were one thing and no thing at the same time. They still are."

"Why did you come here?"

She looked around the room.

"I come to remember that I am not here anymore. Sometimes I find that I cannot remember that. Glynis says that coming here helps me to remember. But I don't stay. You should leave too."

"You said Abel Teague is still alive?"

She shook her head.

"No. Not in the way you mean it. Not in the way you and I are alive. Glynis has him digging in her fields. He suffers there. And does no harm in the world. Sometimes I go down to the fields to watch him. But nothing is trying to get him back. Through the boy. You must see that this does not happen."

"How will I do that?"

"Nothing is using the boy to bring Abel back. He's already changing. You must stop that."

"How?"

"He still has the power to turn away from that path. If he does not, you must kill him."

She turned her head, stood very still.

"Nothing is here. I have to go. So must you."

"Why?"

"Because nothing is thinking about you."

And she was gone.

But the room wasn't empty. It was as if a compressor was pumping air into the room. Reed felt the pressure building on his skin, in his lungs, in his throat. His ears ached, as if he were sinking down into deep water. The pressure was coming up from the floor and closing in from the walls.

Reed backed up to the windows and faced the room. There wasn't a sound. The silence was crushing. Reed couldn't hear his own heart beating but he could feel it hammering in his chest. He had the sensation that the silence and the pressure were part of the same thing. And it was *close* now, almost touching his skin. Hovering there, an inch away from his face. And there was a *mind* in it. Cold and alien and profoundly different from Reed Walker and all of his kind.

He felt himself being *studied*.

Considered.

Appraised.

He knew that if he opened his mouth the silent thing would pour itself into him and stay there forever, feeding on him. He pulled out the bolt cutters, smashed the glass, and rolled backwards out the window. He fell for a long time before he crashed into the branches of a live oak, tumbled again, struck another limb, clutched at it, managed to stop, and then felt it give way, and he was dropping again, the branches lashing at him, and then the branches were gone—a moment of silent falling—he hit the grass hard, bounced once, and he was out cold.

Endicott Calls upon the Black Widow

Frankie Maranzano's newly minted widow was now the only occupant—other than Frankie Il Secondo, the flatulent Chihuahua—of Frankie Maranzano's 3,200-square-foot two-story penthouse suite in a sixty-four-story green glass obelisk called The Memphis. Although Frankie had retainers—mercenary muscle and gun hands—living in the building, Delores wasn't ready to be alone with them until she had sorted out where their loyalties were likely to fall. So she was keeping them busy with the funeral arrangements for Frankie and Little Ritchie while she played the Inconsolable Widow up in the penthouse.

It wasn't that she didn't mourn Frankie and Ritchie. Frankie and Delores had been very happy for many years. And then they met.

Delores thought it might have been Coco Chanel who said, "If you marry for money you earn every penny." And Frankie was doing a fine job of turning Little Ritchie into his Mini-Me, and the world did not need two Frankie Maranzanos.

Now that they were gone, her world, especially this suite, felt a lot more like home.

The Memphis was part of a cluster of towering condo complexes that had sprung up around Fountain Square, the center of the Cap City business and shopping district. It was directly across the Square from the Bucky Cullen Federal Complex, where Boonie Hackendorff, of the Cap City FBI, enjoyed a corner office with a view of Fountain Square, dominated, of course, by The Memphis. Conversely, Frankie Maranzano had a reciprocal view of the back of Boonie Hackendorff's bald head as he sat at his desk in that corner office.

Frankie Maranzano, not an admirer of the FBI or of law enforcement in general, had often entertained his guests by aiming one of his high-powered Remington rifles at the back of Boonie's head—the range across Fountain Square was about a thousand yards, and although a down-angle shot plagued by the tricky crosswinds that swirled around the towers, it was still quite makeable.

Although not by Frankie.

But he didn't know that. Of course all of Frankie Maranzano's guests would laugh wildly when Frankie would say "POW!" and pretend that the rifle had recoiled into his shoulder. They would laugh like that no matter how often he repeated it.

And he repeated it often.

Frankie Maranzano's sense of humor was not complicated, but his business affairs had achieved a complexity that approached byzantine, and Delores, his ex-*goo-may*—actually she had ceased being his *goo-may* when he married her—was extremely awake to the precarious nature of her position.

She was sitting at Frankie's desk—a single slab of black granite held up by two carved stone Saint Mark lions taken from a piazza in Venice. Evening had come and on the other side of the wall of glass behind her chair Cap City glowed like a constellation of diamonds and emeralds and rubies, but the glittering condos and office towers and hotels filling the skyline behind her blazed in vain upon the back of her neck, since Delores was diving deep into the problems presented by her not-quite-so-dearly-beloved Frankie's untimely passing.

The chief problem presented by his *sudden-onset mortality experience*—this was how she had described it in an e-mail to her mother back in Guayaquil—was that Frankie's various business associates in Denver and Vancouver and Singapore were having some difficulty accepting that a trashy, gold-digging South American whore should, simply by the accident of being Frankie's third wife, presume to sit in Frankie Maranzano's chair and busy herself with matters that no mere *putana* was capable of understanding, let alone managing.

One of Frankie's associates, phoning to express his condolences and inquire into the funeral arrangements, had ended his call by advising her to consider who among Frankie's business partners she was going to call on to take over the Cap City end.

When Delores hinted that she might take it on herself, Tony had laughed and said, "Fuck, Delores, you're a very fine piece of ass and I've always liked you, and you kept Frankie in line, fucked if I know how, but you're not a *Guinea* piece of ass. That's the problem. Nobody's gonna work with a Spic whore. A *Wop* whore, sure, no problem. But a *Spic* whore? It just ain't *dignified*. No offense, hah?"

So Delores was feeling under the gun, literally. And when a person signing himself Mr. Harvill Endicott, Private Collector and Facilitator, sent her a personal note, hand-delivered by a private courier, on expensive stationery, accompanied by a Mass card stating that Mr. Endicott had taken the liberty of paying for a novena for her late husband at Holy Name Cathedral to be said on the Sunday next, she was intrigued. The note was simple and direct:

I apologize for intruding upon your grief at this unhappy time. I am in possession of details relating to your husband's death which may be of advantage to you. If you wish to inquire into my credentials contact Warren Smoles of the law firm Smoles Cotton Heimroth and Haggard at the number below.

I offer my counsel in this matter as a courtesy and will not accept any sort of payment for my advice, now or at any time afterwards.

Our conversation will of course remain completely confidential. I ask only an hour of your time as soon as you may be able to receive me. I ask you to consider that time is an issue.

With sympathy and respect,
Mr. Harvill Endicott
Private Collector and Facilitator

The note had been accompanied by a return envelope and a blank reply card. Mr. Endicott had provided no hotel suite or business address or cell number. Not even an e-mail address.

Delores had read the note a couple of times, considered calling Frankie's personal legal adviser, and then realized that Julian Porter was not now, and had never been, a friend to her, nor had he ever shown any interest in her other than the forty-seven times he had tried to get her into bed.

So she called Warren Smoles, who had been front and center at the whole Galleria Mall fiasco. Smoles seemed to be distracted—he was in a public place and he was being shouted at—nevertheless, he found time to express, in a rich baritone, his boundless regard for Mr. Endicott and all his good works.

Delores put the phone down and googled "Harvill Endicott." The search returned nothing.

She called Warren Smoles back and advised him of this, to which he replied that of course there would be no online traces of Mr. Endicott since his services were of a confidential nature and that his nonexistence in the Google-verse was an indication of his discretion and exclusivity.

This was also why Mr. Endicott did not reveal his location or details other than in person and then only after mutual trust had been established.

Delores consulted a martini or three on the matter and decided to take a leap and see this Harvill Endicott person.

The narrative of her husband's death, and that of Little Ritchie, was, in her opinion, crafted by the police to put Frankie in a bad light and portray him as the victim of his own volatile temper.

However, Delores, no fool, found this narrative totally persuasive—Frankie's *crankie-wankies* were legendary in his business circles. But if there was information floating around that might undercut this interpretation, and perhaps lay the groundwork for a massive lawsuit, which she was already contemplating, then she was happy to hear it.

By return courier, she invited Mr. Endicott to call upon her in her rooms on the Pinnacle Floor of The Memphis at seven o'clock Friday evening.

In the note, she informed him that, due to the nature of her late husband's business concerns, he would be subjected to a rigorous body search by the security personnel in the lobby, for which she apologized in advance. She had sent the note off two hours ago, and had received a reply within the hour, in which Mr. Endicott expressed his extreme pleasure at her acceptance and confirmed that he would call upon her at the appointed hour.

Which was about a minute from now.

And the phone on Frankie's desk commenced to ring. The security detail down in the lobby had just admitted a Mr. Harvill Endicott to the elevator floor and did Miz Maranzano wish them to send this person up.

"Have you searched him?"

"Quite thoroughly, ma'am. Do you want one of us to come up and stay with you during his visit?"

The guards downstairs were neutral—they worked for whoever was paying the condo fees—but they lived for gossip to retail to the local media, and Maranzano gossip was the finest around.

"No thank you, Michael. Send him up."

She reached over to Frankie's iMac and turned on the video feed from the lobby. It showed a tall, well-dressed older man in a navy blue pin-stripe and a white shirt. He was looking into the camera as if he were aware that he was being watched and wished to convey how harmless he was. He had a long, pale face and deep-set eyes and a general air of book-ishness. He entered the elevator and, after a swift ascent, arrived on her private floor a minute later, where Delores watched as he walked across the complex tiles of her foyer and rang the bell.

Frankie had been lying on the huge white leather sectional that dom-inated the living room. At the sound of the bell, he erupted into a fit of hysterical yapping that reminded Delores that she was sending him to the vet in the morning to have his vocal cords clipped.

She crossed the immense white carpet that helped to quiet the echoes of this minimalist suite, booted Frankie briskly in the slats, and opened the door. Mr. Endicott stood in the warm pool of light from the fixture above the door and smiled back at her, his expression one of amiable interest.

"Mrs. Maranzano, a pleasure," he said, a slight bow without offering his hand. "I am Harvill Endicott. Thank you for seeing me."

"Not at all," she said, stepping aside and watching as he took in the suite.

"Magnificent," was all he said, thinking *classic goombah baronial* as he waited for her to direct him to a destination.

"Let's talk in Frankie's office, shall we?"

Endicott followed her delightful ass and her swinging hips with real enjoyment. She was wearing a tight black leather skirt and a scarlet leather jacket and the soles of her black stilettos were also a vivid scarlet.

She got him seated in one of Frankie's Eames chairs and took her place behind the desk. She pressed a button and a silver tray laden with ice, decanters of various liquors, and mixes arose through the top of a credenza behind her.

"Would you like something to drink, Mr. Endicott?"

Endicott, who was sitting with his legs crossed and his long-fingered hands resting in his lap, shook his head.

"Sadly, my constitution does not tolerate alcohol. I metabolize poorly."

"Some Pellegrino, then?"

"That would be lovely."

Frankie Il Secondo appeared at Mr. Endicott's feet and glared up at him. He twitched, growled, showed his needle teeth, farted with intent, and sat his bony ass down, radiating bug-eyed hostility. Mr. Endicott returned the look with interest, and then focused again on Delores, who was upright in the chair and watching him over the crystal brim of a glass full of gin and tonic.

"So," he said, "to business."

"Yes. I'll go first. Was my husband's death the result of police incompetence?"

"You're contemplating a suit, I take it?"

"I'm undecided."

"Then I'd recommend against it. I have listened to the radio conversation between the officers on the scene and, to be direct, your husband was firing on a police detective when he was shot. He was warned twice to cease and desist, but he continued, and was duly shot dead by a police sniper. This is an inconvenient element that seems to be, in this case, incontrovertible. Issues such as this have been tried in civil litigation many times. The result is usually a massive expenditure of time and treasure on the part of the plaintiff which accomplishes nothing but the further enrichment of a battalion of lawyers. I am not here to counsel such a course. Indeed, given your current vulnerable circumstances, I would strongly advise against it."

"Then why *are* you here?"

"Your husband's business affairs are in a transitional phase, I would expect."

"What do you know about my husband's business affairs?"

"A great deal, since I am routinely employed by men who are in the same business. And I have done researches of my own, of course."

"Yeah? And even if I knew what you were talking about, so what?"

"I know your position is precarious. Wives are often faced with uncertainty in transitions such as this one. No doubt you are worried about it right now. You need not be. In fact, I believe you stand on the threshold of a great opportunity. But decisive action is required."

"And what would that be?"

"As I've said, I've looked into your husband's affairs and it's clear that his various partners across the country have doubts about your ability to run Mr. Maranzano's portion of the conglomerate with the same vigor and decisiveness that he was able to command."

"If you're saying they think I'm a greedy Spic whore who needs to be kicked to the curb, or worse, you're right on the money."

"Just so. And you've been wondering what to do about it?"

"Of course. I'd be crazy not to. And I'm still waiting to hear something useful from you."

Endicott sipped at his Pellegrino, glanced down at Frankie Il Secondo, who, although tiring rapidly, was trying to maintain his malevolent glare while puffing out a steady stream of lethal emissions. Endicott briefly considered dropping the heavy crystal tumbler on Frankie's bony skull. He looked up and smiled at Delores, who may have been reading his mind.

"Here's my advice to you, ma'am. *Avenge* him."

"Avenge Frankie? You mean, go after the guys who killed him? The guys who killed him were cops."

"I do mean precisely that."

"Okay. You *are* fucking bats."

"Not in the slightest. The specific officer who shot your husband is a rogue cop responsible for the deaths of four police officers several months ago. Do you remember the First Third Bank in Gracie? It was robbed of over two million dollars?"

"Frankie said he wished he'd done it himself."

"The man who engineered that robbery and executed four police officers who were pursuing him is the man who shot your husband."

"The *sniper*?"

"Yes. Staff Sergeant Coker of the Belfair County Sheriff's Department. He is an accomplished marksman and a decorated law enforcement hero. He is also, in my opinion, a dangerous psychopath."

Not that there's anything wrong with that, Endicott was thinking. *Noth-*

ing more steady and reliable than your true psychopath. Endicott had realized long ago that he was one himself.

"You *know* all this?"

"I am utterly convinced of it."

"Can you prove it?"

Endicott smiled, took a sip of Pellegrino, and used his foot to gently edge Frankie Il Secondo a few inches farther away. Although the dog was apparently asleep, his emissions were proceeding apace, leading Endicott to reexamine his views on cap and trade.

"I don't wish to *prove* it in a court of law. I wish to confront Staff Sergeant Coker and his accomplice and extract the two million from them, a process I do not intend for them to survive. In return for your assistance in the area of men and materials, I am prepared to share the proceeds of this project with you."

"I see. And what's my end?"

"For one evening's work you receive one hundred thousand dollars, a mere bagatelle, I acknowledge. What is most vital here is that you are seen to swiftly and decisively avenge the death of your husband and his grandson. This will also bring home to your husband's retainers the realization that you are every bit as ruthless as he was. Frankie's business associates will duly note the implications and I believe they will accept that the transition of power here from Frankie to his widow will be in their interests, if they do not wish to provoke a shooting war, which is in no one's interest. You will come into secure control of a business which my research leads me to estimate to be in excess of thirty million a year. And all this in exchange for one evening's work performed by people already in your employ. It would be what the French call a *coup de main*. It would be bold and audacious."

"My husband's friends might just think I'm as fucking nuts as you are."

"Perhaps. But they will also fear you, and the most important component of respect is fear."

She liked that argument, he could see.

But she was still wavering.

"And if I tell you to get lost?"

"Then I will promptly get lost. I will pursue other means to achieve my goal. But you will remain in a precarious position here, one that might prove fatal. As I said, decisive action is required."

"You're *totally* fucking nuts, aren't you?"

"Not at all. And I'm in deadly earnest."

"How do I know you're not an FBI asshole?"

"Your point is well taken. If we can reach an understanding, I can provide persuasive credentials. I assure you I am merely a private facilitator."

She laughed.

"Yeah. And you want to facilitate yourself into a cool million five. If you know made guys, why not go ask them for help? Why come to me?"

"The gentlemen who sent me here have no intention of sharing the two million with me. They are of the view that the stolen money belongs to them. I am merely an employee. A manservant."

"They're not going to be happy if they think you fucked them."

Endicott was amused to see the true gutter girl emerging here. It pleased him to see that Delores Maranzano was as much a thug as her husband. He knew how to do business with thugs.

"They're in Leavenworth and likely to stay there. Leave them to me."

Delores was quiet for a while.

"When do you want to do this?"

"Tomorrow afternoon. I have studied the property in question. It will require forceful people to accomplish this. Your husband has people who are capable of being hardhanded?"

"Four of them are ex-Army contractors who worked for Blackwater. The other two are related to Frankie by blood. They're all pretty skilled."

"Can you command them?"

"I never tried. They're Frankie's people."

"Are they nearby?"

"They all live in the building."

"How many are available now?"

"Six guys usually. Five right now. Manolo's in Ibiza on a holiday. He's flying back tonight."

"What would it take to have them shift their loyalties from Frankie to you?"

She shrugged.

"The contractors are freelance. They'd have to believe that I can run Frankie's end of the business. That they'll still get paid. Manolo and Jimmy are relatives. Don't know which way they'd jump. Mainly, they'd all want to see that I've got the balls to keep the business going."

"Then we need to persuade them of that."
"How do we do that?"
"Invite them up for drinks."
"Right now? Right this minute?"
"Yes."
"What have you got in mind?"
"A demonstration."

Good News Never Arrives Wrapped in a Baby Blue Folder with a Gold Seal

Nick called it a day around nine and left Mavis and her people working the forensics angle at the Motel 6. He got the Crown Vic rolling and called Kate to see if there had been any sign of Rainey yet. She answered on one.

"Where are you?"
"Southbound on Gwinnett—"
"Are you heading home?"
"Yes. Anything on Rainey?"
Kate laughed, but not a funny kind of laugh. It was more of a snarl.
"Oh my yes."
"Is he there?"
"Nope."
"Where is he?"
"Frankly, my dear, I don't give a damn."
That stopped him.
"What is it?"
"Oh no. I'm not going to tell you over the phone. I want to see the look on your face."

Nick came in the door and found Beth and Kate and Lemon Featherlight sitting around the dining room table and staring at a sheaf of papers folded in three and wrapped in a pale blue binder with a gold seal on it.

There was also an open bottle of champagne on the table. It was empty, but a second one was chilling in an ice bucket on the sideboard. From the state of their glasses, they were well along the way to Blessed Oblivion. From the looks on their faces, they were doing the right thing.

Nick sat down at the far end and looked at the three of them, and they looked back at him.

"Okay. What's in the blue wrapper?"

Beth shook her head.

"No. First, have a drink. Lemon, pour the man a stiff one."

Lemon got a fourth flute from the sideboard, popped the cork on the second bottle of Veuve Clicquot, and filled Nick's glass.

"Mine too," said Kate, and the way she said it let Nick know she was a little bit tipsy.

"Me too," said Beth. "And don't forget your own."

Lemon shook his head.

"Can't. Got to get some sleep. I have a meeting early tomorrow, down at Lady Grace."

"With who?" Nick asked.

"*Whom*," said Kate.

"It's about the bone baskets," said Lemon. "The expert from UV is coming down."

"What are *bone baskets*?" asked Beth, speaking as carefully as Kate was.

"Long story, Beth," said Lemon. "Maybe we better fill Nick in on this thing here," he said, tapping the blue packet. Nick picked it up.

"It's a subpoena, looks like."

"More or less," said Kate. "You're gonna love it. We've all read it with great interest. Go on. Open. Enjoy."

Nick unfolded it and laid it out.

NOTICE OF HEARING:
EXIGENT CIRCUMSTANCE APPEAL
IN RE RAINEY TEAGUE ET AL

An informal hearing will be held on Monday at 10:00 A.M. before Judge T. Monroe to hear arguments and rebuttals regarding the continuation of custodial care under respondents listed:

KATHERINE ROSEMARY KAVANAUGH
NICHOLAS MICHAEL KAVANAUGH

WHEREAS a Writ of Exigent Circumstances Child Endangerment concerning the custody and guardianship of Rainey Teague alleging physical and mental abuse and exploitation of fiscal assets by the above listed respondents and associated parties (see addendum) including but not limited to the Niceville Police Department, the Belfair and Cullen County Criminal Investigation Service, and the Law Practice of KAVANAUGH LLB ET AL.

YOU ARE HEREBY DIRECTED AND REQUIRED:
To attend at the Belfair and Cullen County District Court Offices—Judge T. Monroe presiding—on Monday next at 10:00 A.M. to hear and respond to allegations of Child Endangerment and Abuse of Office relating to events and circumstances contained in WRIT 65271 filed by W. Smoles of Smoles Cotton Heimroth & Haggard contained in an INFORMATION attested to and signed by COM-PLAINANT/PETITIONER said RAINEY TEAGUE and duly notarized and witnessed.

WHEREAS:
This subpoena has been issued under the SAFE HAVEN LAW of this jurisdiction, no contact will be permitted prior to the hearing between the COMPLAINANT/PETITIONER and any or all of the RESPON-DENTS and PARTIES listed above under Penalty of Law. Although this is an informal hearing for the purposes of preliminary discovery only, legal representation is strongly advised.

ISSUED THIS DAY UNDER MY SEAL
THEODORE MONROE, JUSTICE
BELFAIR AND CULLEN COUNTY COURTS

Clifton Fowler,
Clerk of the Court

Nick laid the paper down and stared at it for a while as if he expected it to burst into flames.
"Rainey went to *Warren Smoles?*"
Kate didn't answer.
Beth did.

"I spoke to Cliff Fowler about this. As far as we can tell, as soon as he got out of WellPoint, Rainey called Smoles—"

"What the hell would give him an idea like that?"

"I may have," said Kate. "I was putting him to bed last night. He asked me about Warren Smoles because he'd seen a news tape of Smoles at the Galleria shooting. Some kind of wrap-up report the next day. Rainey was upset about the things Smoles said about you and Coker 'executing' Axel's father. I said that Warren Smoles was the kind of lawyer who made his money by telling lies and making sure bad people never had to pay for what they did. I think that's what put the idea in his head."

Nick sat back, drank some wine.

"Son of a bitch. I don't *believe* this."

"Believe it," said Kate, looking straight at him. "You were right all along, Nick, about that kid. There's something wrong with him."

"Anyway," said Beth, "Cliff says that Smoles sent a car and took Rainey to what Cliff described as 'an undisclosed third-party location' that had a registered nurse to take care of him. Smoles interviewed Rainey over the course of a couple of hours. Cliff doesn't know exactly what the kid told Smoles, but it was obviously serious enough for Smoles to file this writ. Cliff says that Smoles has a sworn statement from Rainey, signed and notarized, appointing Smoles as his attorney and alleging fear of his life. Not just from us, but from law enforcement officers as well—"

"I know," said Nick. "That's the Safe Haven law. In cases where the complainant alleges that local law enforcement is either corrupt or biased, his attorney can provide shelter and protection until the matter can be heard by a judge."

Kate leaned back and closed her eyes.

"What do you want to do, babe?"

She opened them again.

"I'm not dumb enough to say it in front of a cop and two witnesses. Beth, how are the kids?"

"They're watching *The Kid* again."

"Then that's what I'm going to do too."

She got up, kissed Beth on the cheek, walked around Lemon and gave him a pat on the shoulder, leaned down and gave Nick a kiss. Then she filled her glass again and walked with a slight weave and wobble out of the dining room. Beth got up, swayed a bit, and did pretty much the same thing, except both Lemon and Nick got a kiss.

Lemon and Nick sat at the table in silence, both of them looking at the subpoena.

"Where in hell," said Lemon, "would a little kid get an idea like going to Warren Smoles?"

"Maybe right where you said. In hell."

Lemon got up, patting Nick on the shoulder.

"I gotta get some sleep."

"Let me know how it goes with the bones?"

"You going to be okay?"

"Yeah. I'm waiting for a call from Mavis."

"That thing at the Motel 6?"

"Yeah. She's pulling surveillance video. She said if she found anything tonight she'd give me a call."

She didn't.

So, after a while, dead beat, he went to bed.

A long time later, Kate slipped in beside him.

"You asleep?" she asked.

"No."

"Good."

The morning came up like thunder, or at least it sounded like that in Kate's head. It wasn't thunder. It was Nick's cell phone.

She snatched it off the night table, looked at the screen, dropped it on Nick's chest, and got up to go to the bathroom. Nick watched her cross the room, thinking *oh my lord buy me somma that* and then he answered the cell. It was Mavis.

Saturday

Say It Isn't So

Mavis Crossfire was waiting for Nick in the parking lot of the Wendy's across from the Motel 6. She was in her private ride, a black Lincoln Navigator. She was in plain clothes—cowboy boots and jeans and a plaid rodeo shirt with mother-of-pearl buttons—but she was wearing her side-arm and she had her badge clipped to her belt.

She honked at Nick as he turned his Crown Vic into the lot. There was an open slot beside her and he slipped into that. Mavis rolled down her tinted window. Her usual happy smile was nowhere around.

"Hey, Nick. Come on around and get in."

He climbed up and got comfortable. It's not really possible to be uncomfortable in a Lincoln Navigator, but Nick was in a pretty bad mood, which Mavis picked up on right away. Mavis had the motor running and the air conditioner on. She rolled up the window and turned the radio to something cool and jazzy. Nick interpreted this to mean that she had something to say that she didn't want anybody else to hear.

"Thanks for coming. Any word about Rainey yet?"

Nick shook his head.

"Oh yeah."

"He come home?"

"Not if he wants to stay alive."

"Pardon?"

Nick filled her in on the subpoena.

"You've got to be kidding me."

"Would that I were."

"Poor kid. I mean, he's gotta be scared shi—"

Nick shot her a cold look.

"With respect, Mavis, fuck the poor kid. How about Alice Bayer?"

"I know. I know. I just mean, he's gotta have a malfunction, right?"

"Excuse me while I jot that down in my Big Blue Book of Who Gives a Shit?"

Mavis looked at him sideways.

"This isn't you. You were there when we pulled that kid out of that grave. I know how you took it when he went into a coma."

"Something's not right with him, Mavis."

"You cutting him loose?"

"I think so. Yeah. Yes. I am."

"Kate won't."

"Don't bet on it. This thing with Smoles broke her heart."

"You really think Rainey did Alice?"

"More to the point, I think *Rainey* thinks Rainey did Alice. The little shit has lawyered up."

"Does Kate?"

"In her heart, yes."

"He's just a kid, Nick."

"Coker once took down a kid named Joey La Monica. Ten years old. Up in Gracie—"

"I know that story. Rainey's not that kid."

"Mavis, how about we just agree to disagree, okay? You wanted to see me, about a video?"

Mavis could see that this part of their conversation had come to an end.

"Okay. I have it on my laptop. Hold on a minute."

She reached into the backseat, lifted out a bright red Mac laptop.

"Jeez," said Nick, looking at it. "What's that red called?"

"Ashes of Men," said Mavis, putting the machine down on her lap and opening it up. She tapped a few keys and brought up an mpeg file.

"Okay. What I'm going to show you, I only found after going through a lot of pointless crap. It's just a short mpeg. It was taken from a camera inside the Wendy's, covers the front door and the customer spaces. Here, take a look."

She hit a button and a color video began to play. The quality was surprisingly good. It showed the customer area of the Wendy's, people sitting at tables, moving around the room, in and out the doors. The view included part of the parking lot outside the big front window, where cars and trucks were parked. The sun was bright on them and the inside of the Wendy's was shadowy as a result.

Mavis tapped a button and the video halted.

"That's Edgar's Windstar. You can see from the marker that we're right in the middle of the time where this all happened. Let me do this frame by frame, okay?"

"Sure."

She tapped another button and the video turned into a series of freeze-frames, herky-jerky people walking like Charlie Chaplin. People getting into and out of cars. Cars pulling in and backing out. Halfway through the video a big white Ford F-150 came around into the frame, moving from right to left. It slowed down behind Edgar's Windstar, came to a stop. Sat there for five or six frames. Then it accelerated out of the picture.

"Okay," said Nick. "What'd I miss?"

"I missed it too, at first. I had to look at it a whole lot of times before I noticed it. Let me back it up."

She did, and everybody did the same thing they had done before, only backwards. The white Ford backed into the frame, stopped. The camera angle was direct and a couple of degrees high. It showed a hand hanging out the driver's window, and a section of his shirt, his other hand resting on the steering wheel. The driver was wearing a white shirt and a belt with a big cowboy buckle. He was big, but lean. He gave the impression of being a rough man. There was someone in the passenger seat but he was in shadow. Just an outline.

"Can you magnify this?"

She ran a fingertip across the touch pad. The still frame filled the screen.

"I took this single frame and sharpened it. It's the best we're going to get. Look at his right hand, on the steering wheel. What do you see?"

"A big gold ring with an insignia on it."

Nick peered at it, narrowed his eyes.

"It's a crest. The Marine Corps."

"Yeah. Now look at what's in the guy's belt."

The image was starting to pixelate, but it was clear enough to show the butt of a large revolver and part of the frame.

"Gun. Looks like a Colt Anaconda."

Mavis sat back and looked at Nick.

"Yeah. So what do you think?"

Nick was quiet for a while.

On the radio a sinuous trumpet solo was playing the theme to *China-town*.

"Damn," he said finally.

"Me too," said Mavis.

"Lot of people in Niceville drive a big white Ford One-fifty with the premium package. And a lot of Niceville folks go around heeled. And a lot of Niceville folks go to Wendy's. And a lot of people have Marine Corps rings."

"Yeah. But put this together with the fact that a kid we think had something to do with the Gracie job is getting killed right across the road, and where does that take us?"

"Where I don't want to go."

"Let's say it, Nick. Get it over with. Charlie Danziger."

"Yeah. That's where we are, I guess."

"Danziger always carries a Colt Anaconda. He wears a Marine Corps ring and drives a big white Ford pickup. His armored car delivered the payroll cash. He's the Wells Fargo route manager. He pulls up behind Edgar's Windstar and stops. There's another guy in the passenger seat, from the shadow another lean, rangy cowpoke type. I'm thinking maybe it's Coker. Coker's a sniper. The passenger leans forward and looks across Gwinnett in the direction of the Motel 6. Then the Ford accelerates out of the lot. What do you think happened there?"

Nick was trying to cope with this, but he had no doubt about what was going on.

"Edgar Luckinbaugh was working for them. Edgar called to tell them that the guy he was following had just made contact with Lyle Crowder, which, if they knew he had guilty knowledge about the Gracie robbery, which we have to assume he did, totally freaked them out. They sent Edgar in to stabilize the situation until they got there. Things went to shit before they pulled up. Maybe they tried to raise Edgar on his cell, and when he didn't respond, they got the hell out of Dodge."

Mavis nodded and they both fell silent.

The *Chinatown* theme ended and Harry James came on with "Cherry Pink and Apple Blossom White." They both felt sick and empty and angry, but there wasn't a thing they could do about that.

"Sometimes this job sucks deeply," said Mavis.

"Yes. It truly does."

"Four dead cops. For what? For money they won't get to spend? Money they didn't even *need*? Danziger's well off, and so's Coker. I just don't get it."

"I guess we never will."

Another silence, while they stared across at the Motel 6. A yellow crime scene tape had been strung across the door to room 229. A Niceville PD cruiser was parked in the lot.

"We need to know who Mr. Third Party is before we make any other moves, Mavis. Do we have anything on him at all?"

"We got zip out of Edgar's Windstar other than a jug of pee and a pile of empty Krispy Kreme boxes. And a receiver for a Radio Shack motion detector, but no motion detector."

"Edgar was doing single-man surveillance. Night and day. If his subject was down for the night, Edgar would want to get some sleep himself, but not lose the guy. He had a cot in the back for that. He buys a cheap motion detector and plants the transponder in the subject's car. Car moves, Edgar hears the buzzer and wakes up."

"Still no help to us unless you want to drive all over Niceville with Edgar's receiver, hoping for a signal."

"Gotta be something," said Nick. "Gotta be."

They sat there together for a time.

"Mr. Third Party," said Mavis. "His moves were pretty professional, right? I mean, most of the murders we get around here, the body is on the floor in the bathroom and the guy who did it is sitting in the front room with a beer in his hand and blood all over his shirt and he's crying that the bitch had it coming. This guy is a pro."

"Which means he's from out of town. Flew in for the job, whatever it is."

"The job was probably to find the Gracie bank robbers and take the money away from them."

"Yes. Maybe he's working for himself, or maybe he's on a commission. Maybe somebody from out of town feels they've got a claim on the money. But one way or another, our pro's from out of town. And where did Edgar work?"

"The Marriott," said Mavis, her smile coming back a bit. "You think Edgar picked up on something weird about the guy?"

"And told Coker about him? Maybe. It makes sense. If Coker was worried about people coming into town to take the money away, who better to put on a retainer than the ex-cop who worked at the best hotel near the airport? Can we get a record of everybody who checked in at the Marriott in, say, the last three days?"

"Sure. But why only three?"

"The receipts tell us Edgar began his surveillance Thursday afternoon. My bet is he gave Charlie a heads-up and Charlie put Edgar on the surveillance right away. You know what, Mavis, forget three days. Can you find out who checked in on Thursday?"

"I can. You hungry?"

"I am, come to think of it."

"Go get us burgers and coffee. I'll get on the horn to Mark Hopewell. I'll ask him for a list."

"Cheese or plain?"

"I'm on a diet."

"Plain then. And no fries?"

"I said I'm on a diet, not a death march."

Nick was gone for ten minutes. While he was standing in the line, he called Kate. She said she was okay, just a little woozy. She was still in bed.

He told her he loved her.

"I don't blame you," she said. "I'm irrezissible. G'night."

He clicked off.

His cell rang immediately.

REED WALKER.

"Hey, Reed. Where are you?"

"I'm on my way down from Gracie. Where are you?"

Nick stepped out of the line and found a quiet corner in the hall outside the bathrooms.

"You sound like hell, Reed. You okay?"

"No. I jumped out of a building."

"What?"

"Yeah. Candleford House. The fourth floor. I bounced through a bunch of tree branches and hit the dirt. Out cold. Lay there for a couple hours, until two State guys found me. They took me to the clinic there. I just got out a while ago."

"You *jumped*?"

"Fucking well told you I did. You would have too."

"You lived?"

"Here's your sign."

"I mean, are you hurt?"

"I think maybe my left thumb is okay. Everything else hurts like crazy. We have to meet. I'll be in town in maybe an hour. Where are you?"

"I'm on a case."

"Whatever it is, I need to see you right now. I found out a lot of crazy shit up in Sallytown. And I saw *seriously* crazy shit in Gracie. You ever need a thrill, Nick, you go for a walk inside Candleford House on a moonlit night. I gotta talk to you."

"What about?"

Reed gave him the A version, short, sharp, and memorable, ending with Clara Mercer's warning about what was happening to Rainey and what needed to be done about it.

"Kill him," Nick said, and watched heads turn. "A ghost told you to kill him?"

"I know. Nuts. But we gotta figure this out. Weird shit is going on. Where are you?"

"I'm at the Wendy's on North Gwinnett. Mavis and I are on a double homicide."

"Where'll you be in forty-five minutes?"

"I don't know."

"Call me when you do. You call me as soon as you know where you're gonna be later. Okay?"

"I will."

Reed clicked off.

When he got back to the big Lincoln with the burgers, Mavis was still on the phone. He climbed in and set the bag down on the console. Mavis looked at him, held up a finger—wait one. Fine with him. He had a lot on his mind. *Kill Rainey?* And that was where it was going to stay, for now.

"Okay. Okay . . . thanks, Mark. Thanks a lot. You did great. Yeah, I know. Poor Edgar. Well, we're on it. I'll call you."

She closed the call.

"Guy named Harvill Endicott checked into the Marriott on Thursday afternoon. Asked for a smoking room. Edgar was on duty. Mark thought the guy was an undertaker or a minister. This Endicott guy said he was a "facilitator and a collector." He ordered up two cars, one a black Caddy and the other a beige Corolla. Two cars for one guy—"

"Corolla for surveillance and the Caddy for his ride."

"Would you like to hear his description?"

"Absolutely."

"Tall. Skinny. Pale skin. Seemed pretty fit. Well dressed. Gray suit, two bags. Mark said he thought Edgar was taking a real interest in him too."

"Sounds like he could be Mr. Third Party in the motel video. Is he still there?"

"No. He checked out last night. Left the Caddy and the Corolla in the lot out front. Took a cab to Mauldar Field. I asked Mark to go out and poke around the cars. Guess what he found under the Caddy's rear bumper?"

"Edgar's motion sensor thingie."

"That's it. You want to go over there? Mark's pulling the video from behind his desk when this guy was checking out. Full front, face and all. He says he'll have it waiting."

Nick thought about that.

"No. Endicott's in the wind. Send a cruiser to get the video from Mark and run it down to Cap City. Siren and lights all the way. We'll get Boonie to run a full background on him, put out a still shot and a description. Get State and County on it too."

"What do you want to do right now?"

"You know what we have to do."

Mavis nodded.

"Go see Charlie."

What Is Written in Stone

Mid-morning on the Saturday: Lemon and the prof from UV were in the morgue at Lady Grace, standing around a stainless-steel gurney. In the middle of the gurney was one of the bone baskets that the Coast Guard divers had pulled out of the willow roots under the banks along Patton's Hard. The bone basket was lit up by a harsh overhead halogen. It looked alien and strange and yet still somehow human. This one was colored a steel gray.

Like all the others, it had what looked like human ribs tapering up from a central spine, the rib tips touching each other lightly. Inside the bone cage, sitting on a row of narrow cylindrical objects that looked like a spinal cord, was a large gray shape, roughly spherical, with creases on its surface that looked like the canals that Mars was once thought to have.

Lemon Featherlight was standing on one side of the gurney, and across from him was a stunning Nordic woman almost as tall as he was, a full-figured Valkyrie with long blond hair so pale it glowed. Her eyes were cornflower blue and large and far apart, her nose long and narrow and hawkish. Her name was Helga Sigrid and she was originally from Reykjavik but now she worked as a forensic anthropologist for the University of Virginia at Charlottesville.

She was telling him, in layman's terms now, since her previous explanation had been so technical that his brain felt like burning steel wool, what they were looking at here.

"Fossils," she said, in a clear bell-like voice with a distinct Icelandic accent, or so Lemon assumed, since he'd never heard an Icelandic accent before. "Fossils happen when organic material is slowly replaced by mineral material. Each molecule of the mineral material replaces and duplicates the molecule of organic material that it has consumed. In a sense, the mineral uses the *shape* of the organic object as a mold, which is why at the end of the process, we have what looks like the body of something that was once alive but has somehow been magically turned to stone. Because, in a way, it has. That is what we have here."

"So this thing was once alive?"

She shook her head.

"No. To be precise, what was once living material that looked *exactly* like this was once alive. But this object here is not organic and never has been. It is stone. At least, a kind of stone."

"What kind?"

She frowned.

"Well . . . this is why I wanted to talk to you. Are you the owner of this . . . fossil?"

Lemon had to think that through.

"Well, not the owner—"

"Are you in a position to grant the university the privilege of taking these objects back to Charlottesville for further study?"

If not him, then who?

"Yes. I probably am."

She smiled upon him.

"That is wonderful. We have never seen objects such as these. No one has. They are absolutely and profoundly unique. This is an unprecedented find, Mr. Featherlight. It is historical. Scientists will study these objects for years. Papers will be written. It is . . . simply thrilling!"

"But what were they? Originally?"

She frowned again.

"That is the puzzle, yes? I have examined the interior of one of these ribs and there can be no doubt that the molecular structure the minerals replaced was that of a human bone. In this case, lying before us, we have a fossil record of a male Caucasian in excellent health who died at the approximate age of forty. Perhaps forty-five. This spherical object inside the rib cage shows the outward characteristics of a human skull, but it has been misshapen by geological forces I do not understand. It will be necessary to do MRIs and CAT scans to get an idea of what is inside. Further, the process of fossilization takes thousands of years, and yet this seems to be the fossilized remains of a very modern human. That is, a human exactly like the kind of human who emerged from the Olduvai Gorge three hundred thousand years ago and spread out across the planet. A modern man. Homo sapiens. A man exactly like you. It is a puzzle. Some force we do not yet understand has worked upon it. As I said, this is all so very exciting."

"It looks as if it's been . . . consumed."

"Yes," she said, looking down at it. "It does create that impression. As if it has passed through a process that transformed it into this shape. We do not generally see bodies this intact. As if the bones had been fused together by some kind of heat or energy. Animals scatter bones. Winds and tides have their way. Erosion. Sand. Yet here we have so many fossilized human remains, and all are intact. You say there are more? Many more?"

"Yes. The divers saw them all along that riverbank. Hundreds in plain view. More buried deeper in the root mass."

She looked as if she might faint from ecstasy. Lemon was perfectly willing to help her with that if she asked him.

"So many? How magnificent! They will have to be excavated. A formal dig must be initiated. Mr. Featherlight, this find will put your town in the forefront of anthropological research. I can see these remains being named after you."

"But they are *human* remains, right?"

"Oh yes. There can be no doubt. If you mean fossilized human remains, of course. There is no organic material here. Otherwise we would have the complication of finding out what sort of culture this person may have come from, and then determining their specific burial practices, and then, once our studies were complete, we would have to return this relic to the earth in a manner that suited those spiritual beliefs and rituals. In this case, we do not have that complication. These are replicas of something that was once human, rather like those poor sad figures that have been found in the ruins of Pompeii. From what I have observed, I suspect that these *objects* may have been accumulating along the banks of your lovely river here for hundreds, perhaps thousands of years. By what process they have been consumed—one could almost be dramatic and say *devoured*—will be a fascinating line of inquiry."

She finished her breathless recitation and looked as if she was thinking about hugging him.

"Yes, Mr. Featherlight, it is an extremely exciting find. The most important and exciting find of my career. Are you not thrilled?"

Lemon was thrilled, for a while, and then he worked out what this Valkyrie was telling him.

Something was *eating* people and spitting out their remains into the Tulip River. And whatever it was, it had been doing it for a very long time. Hundreds if not thousands of years, according to the Valkyrie. The Cherokee had a name for what it was. *Tal'ulu*, the Eater of Souls.

And she lived in Crater Sink.

He was sitting in his truck thinking about the implications of all this when his cell beeped.

DORIS GODWIN

Doris Godwin. He got the name in a moment. Doris Godwin was the streetcar driver who had helped him get Rainey down off Tallulah's Wall.

He pressed ANSWER.

"Doris—"

"Mr. Featherlight—Lemon—I'm a bit shook up here. Maybe you can help me? By the way, how's the little boy?"

Lemon's answer was careful.

"It was a kind of a seizure. He's going to be tested for some neurological issues—"

"Yeah? Me too. I'm having a very bad day here. Can I send you some jpegs?"

"Sure. Yes. Of course. Right now?"

"Yeah. I've got them all loaded up."

"I'm ready."

"Okay. They're on the way. What I want is for you to take a good look at them and then call me back tonight. I'm not going to stay on the line because I'm working right now. I'm at that turnabout at the top of Upper

Chase Run, but I got to get on the tracks again and I can't take personal calls. I'm off at five."

As she was talking, the jpegs came in. Lemon remembered that while he was tending to Rainey up at Crater Sink, she had gotten to her feet and taken a series of shots of the woods all around them. At the time he had his hands full with Rainey. Now he was looking at her shots.

"Jesus," he said.

"Yeah. That's what I said too. You call me!"

"I will."

Behold a Pale Horse

Nick called Reed as Mavis was pushing the Navigator up Arrow Creek. They were about fifteen minutes away from Charlie Danziger's ranch. Reed answered the call on the second ring.

"Nick. Thanks for the call back."

Nick put the cell on speakerphone.

"You still want to meet?"

"Yeah. Say where."

"You know Charlie Danziger's place. Up in the grasslands on the south slope?"

"I do. What's at Charlie's place?"

Nick glanced at Mavis, who nodded.

"You still have your badge and your sidearm?"

Reed was silent for a while.

"This is police business?"

"Serious as it gets. We think Charlie might have had something to do with the Gracie thing."

Silence.

"No *fucking* way. Not possible."

"Reed, I have you on speakerphone. Mavis is driving."

"Damn. Sorry, Mavis!"

"That's fine, Reed. You want in on this?"

"Yes. I do. Does Charlie know you're coming?"

"No. But we had a County car cruise by and his truck's parked outside the ranch house. You have any Kevlar?"

"Yeah. It's all in my trunk. You want to meet on the perimeter and go in together?"

Mavis looked at Nick.

"No," said Nick. "Keep your cell on and hang back. You know that old logging run that used to go down to Belfair Mills?"

"I think so. I'll find it on my GPS."

"It's screened from Charlie's place by the south slope. You can get within a hundred yards on foot. Can your ride take you there?"

"If I have to carry it."

"Okay. When can you be in position?"

A pause.

"Give me fifteen."

"We'll go in. If it looks like it's going south, I'll double-click you."

"Okay. Jesus. Charlie. I can't believe it."

"Neither can we. Maybe we're wrong."

"I hope so."

"What about the meet? You wanted to tell me something?"

"We live through this, we can talk about that."

Danziger was out on his front porch, sitting on a rail-back chair that was tilted up against the boards of his rancher. He had his boots up on the railing and a cup of coffee in his hand. He was smoking a Camel.

He squinted into the sunlight as he watched the big black Lincoln make its way up the long gravel drive to his front door. He had the Winchester leaning on the wall beside him and a small two-way radio clipped to his belt.

He had a pretty good idea who that big black Navigator belonged to and when it got close enough for him to make out who was inside it, he sighed, stubbed out his Camel, picked up the Winchester, and stood up. The Navigator came to a stop about fifty feet away, and Mavis shut the engine down.

The doors popped open. Nick and Mavis stepped out, keeping the doors between them and Charlie. Mavis had her doors lined with Kevlar. On his own advice, Charlie recalled.

So this wasn't a social call.

"Nick. Mavis. Nice to see you."

"Hey, Charlie," said Mavis. "How you doing?"

Nick stepped out into the clear.

He was wearing blue pin-striped slacks and a white shirt. His gold badge was clipped to his belt and his Colt Python was in his holster.

He smiled at Danziger.

"Charlie, can you put that Winchester down?"

"I'm always glad to see you, Nick. You too, Mavis. But right now is a bad time."

"Why is that?"

"Because I'm expecting company and I don't believe they'll be friendly."

Nick and Mavis worked that out.

"Where's Coker?"

"He's around."

Nick knew what that meant.

They were standing in his sights right now.

"Are *we* the company?"

Danziger shook his head.

"No. Me and Coker, we've been having a disagreement with these out-of-town people. We're just sorta waiting for things to develop. Wasn't expecting you folks to step into this. I think it would be best if you two either put this off for another day or you came up and sat down and we talked about things. You standing out in the open like that is making me nervous. Come on, for Pete's sake. You two look like rolling thunder."

Nick looked at Mavis, who shrugged.

"You know why we're here, Charlie."

"Believe I do."

"Can't walk this one back, Charlie. Unless you can convince Mavis and me it just isn't so."

Danziger pushed his hat back, rubbed his forehead. "Probably can't do that."

Mavis seemed to settle into herself. Nick shook his head and fought down his anger.

"Was Coker in on it?"

Danziger shook his head.

"Nope. It was all me."

"The sniper stuff?"

"All me."

Mavis had to smile.

"Charlie, you couldn't hit the backside of a bullock if you were sitting on it sidesaddle."

Danziger looked up at the hills.

"We can argue about this later. Time is running. If you're gonna stay, then stay. If you want to get out from under this, then you two oughta pull out now. Might be that when you come back I'll be dead, which sorta solves the whole thing."

"We're not leaving," said Mavis.

"Then you better come on up the stairs."

They stood staring at each other for a time. The wind hissed in the long grasses. Somewhere out in a field one of Danziger's horses stamped and snorted. Nick took a long breath, let it out.

"Okay," said Nick. "We're coming up there. Mavis, put your piece away."

Mavis slipped her Beretta back into her holster and stepped clear of the door.

Danziger set the Winchester down.

Nick and Mavis came up to the top of the stairs. Danziger smiled down on them.

"Well, might as well sit down and have a drink. I'm sure as hell not going to try shooting my way out of this, especially with my friends. What'll it be?"

"Beer, if you got it," said Mavis, after a long beat. She sat down on a rocker beside the door. It groaned as it took her weight. Nick leaned against the railing, watching Danziger's hands, feeling Coker's gun sights on the back of his head.

It was an uncomfortable sensation.

"Got no beer," said Danziger, with a lopsided grin. "All I got is white wine."

"That's what I figured," she said. "Other than maybe you have a forty-year-old bottle of lime cordial back there. Sure. I'll have a glass."

"Nick?"

"Sure, Charlie. Thanks."

Danziger fiddled around inside a cooler for a time, came up with a large bottle of Santa Margherita and two extra tumblers. He set them down on the table beside his chair and poured out two brimming glasses. He handed one to Mavis and the other to Nick, and then he refilled his own. Going back to his chair, he put his boot up on the railing and tilted himself back up against the wall.

He lifted his glass.

"Here's to perdition."

"Perdition," they said.

A moment passed.

Everyone was aware of Coker, of his presence in the air all around them.

"What's Coker gonna do?" asked Mavis.

"He's gonna stay where he is until our company gets here. Then we'll see what happens."

"Who are you expecting?" asked Nick.

"You ever hear of a Harvill Endicott?"

"We have."

"Thought you might have. When I heard you two were on that double homicide at the Motel 6, I figured, That's all she wrote. Better make your peace."

Mavis and Nick said nothing.

"Poor Edgar. Wouldn't-a sent him in there, we'd known that Endicott was so damn tricky. Anyway, Endicott burned us in the Wendy's lot. Me and Coker figure he'll be along, with a few people."

"Maybe not," said Nick. "Endicott checked out of the Marriott last night. Took a cab to the airport."

"Any record of him flying out?"

"We haven't looked. Boonie's on that."

Danziger winced at the sound of Boonie's name.

"Boonie know about all this?"

"He does now."

Danziger winced again, shook his head.

"Damn. He say anything?"

"No," said Nick, lying through his teeth.

"Anyway, even if Endicott's gone, we'll see his people sooner or later."

The radio in Danziger's hand squawked twice. Danziger picked it up, thumbed SEND.

"Hey there."

Coker's voice came back, full of static but clear enough.

"Looks like you're having a party down there. Give my regards to Nick and Mavis."

"They heard that."

"I got a black Mustang coming along the Belfair Mill logging road."

Nick looked at Mavis.

"Tell him that's Reed."

"Nick says that's Reed Walker."

"He's getting out. Has a piece in his hand. Heading for the ridge off to your left."

Nick broke in.

"Tell Coker not to shoot. I'll bring him in."

"Nick is asking you not to shoot Reed. Says he'll bring him in."

Silence. The same wind in the long grass, eternal and uncaring. The sound of that big old horse whinnying a long way off.

"Okay. That's how it is, hah? Tell Nick okay."

Nick got on the cell.

"Reed?"

"I'm here. I'm not in position—"

"Coker's got you cold, Reed. Stop moving."

More silence.

"Shit. Where is he?"

"Reed, that's Coker out there. Nothing you can do and you know it. Just come on in, okay? Reed. Don't go crazy. Just walk down the slope and have a glass of wine."

Coker's voice crackled and snapped over the radio, a sharp edge in his tone.

"Tell Reed he's got five seconds."

"Reed, you have to come down. Put your piece away and come in slow. Coker's all over you."

A pause.

"Okay. Goddammit. Okay. I'm coming."

Reed came down the grassy slope, his hands raised. His face was marked with bloody streaks and he was limping badly. He came up to the bottom of the steps, lowered his hands, and looked at Charlie Danziger.

"Did you do the Gracie job?"

"All by myself," said Danziger. "Now if you'd slip that pistol out of your holster and set it down on the step, I'll see if I can persuade Coker not to kill you."

Reed put the gun down, straightened up, pain flickering across his face as he did so.

"What happened to you?" Mavis asked.

"He jumped off the roof of Candleford House," said Nick.

"Fourth floor, actually."

"Why'd you do that?" asked Danziger.

"It was better than staying on it."

"Well, come on up and take a pew."

Reed took them all in.

"What are you all waiting for?"

"Company," said Mavis. "Bad company."

Coker's radio crackled into life.

"Okay. We have movement."

Danziger stood up, looked at Nick and Reed and Mavis.

"You all want to sit this out?"

Nick stood up.

"No. Guess I'm in."

"Me too," said Mavis.

Reed stared at his hands, his whole body tight and his mind full of hot wires. He just nodded.

"I'll take that as a yes," said Danziger.

"What happens after?" Nick asked.

Danziger grinned at him.

"My luck keeps running like it has lately, there won't be any after."

"But say you make it? What then?"

Danziger looked around at their faces.

"Well, I'm sure as hell not gonna shoot any of you folks. No, I live, guess I'll take what's coming."

"What about Coker?" asked Mavis.

"Well, Coker's a different story. I doubt he'll come in peaceful. You guys will have to go root him out, is what I figure. Good luck with that."

"Why'd you do it?" asked Reed, in a hoarse snarl. Danziger's smile faded.

"At the time I was angry. Now, I couldn't tell you. Never even spent a dime of it."

Reed glared at him.

"Angry? The way you got treated? By State?"

"Cut deep, I'll admit. I deserved better."

"So did those cops who died on that blacktop."

"No argument from me."

"And Coker? Why'd *he* do it?"

"Coker? He was nowhere around."

"So you execute four cops? Because you're bored?"

Danziger hardened up a bit.

"Yeah. And when all this is over I'd be happy to gun up and toe the scratch with you anywhere and anytime."

Reed was on his feet again.

"Now would be just fine with me."

"Reed," said Nick. "Not now. Back off."

"Nick, this—"

Coker's radio again.

"Cut the chatter and take up a post, people. I got one man coming down the slope behind the house. Don't know how he got so close. He's moving pretty good. Like a recon marine or a ranger. Probably another couple guys flanking in the long grass. They'll have somebody in the tree line, covering their backs. Remember, they're gonna have to close with you. They need Charlie alive."

Reed looked at Nick, tugged out his pistol, and moved into the house, heading for the back door. Charlie handed Mavis his Winchester and pulled out his Colt. He tossed the radio to Nick.

Mavis went inside the house and set up a firing position on Danziger's dining room table. It had a view out three sides of the house. She assumed that Reed was covering the fourth.

Reed had never been in a firefight. She hoped he'd do okay. In a gunfight, being fast and brave wasn't as important as being accurate.

Nick dropped onto the ground and moved into the long grass, slipping into it without a sound. He stopped to turn the volume on the radio speaker down to the lowest level. As he did so, it squawked twice.

"Nick, you have a man in the sweetgrass at your six, maybe fifty feet behind you. He's moving."

Nick stopped, flattened himself into the grass, and listened. He heard the wind, the ticktock of the sweetgrass blades as they moved against each other. A huge brown toad was staring up at him from a thicket. He had golden eyes and a round white belly. He blinked at Nick, opened and closed his mouth, crossed his forelegs, laced his fingers, went on staring. Nick heard something sliding through the grass. Irregular.

The sound stopped, held for thirty seconds, and then began again. Nick put his Colt into his holster and waited. The sound came again, moving slightly away from him. He moved with it.

There was a pale mound inside the sweetgrass, cream and brown. Maybe ten feet away. It was a man in camouflage fatigues. He had an M-4 rifle, light brown in color, slung across his back.

He had been moving, but now he was very still. Nick figured he had sensed something and was now listening as intensely as a soldier can listen.

Nick stayed as still as the other guy was and waited the man out.

There was a gunshot, the short sharp crack of Reed's Beretta, and the chuffing rattle of an M-4 set on three-round burst, and then two more shots from Reed's Beretta.

At the first shot the man in camo began to move. Nick was on him, a knee in the small of the man's back, his left hand on the man's chin, his right on top of his skull. He jerked the man's head back and twisted it sideways. He could feel the spine go, a dull, meaty crack muffled by the corded muscles of the man's thick neck.

Nick slipped by him, moving left toward the tree line. A loud crack off to his right and a round hummed past his eyes. He could almost see the blur as it went by and the air it was pushing was like a puff on his right eye. He heard a meaty *thwack*, a distant *thump*, as a round came in and struck hard just a few yards away from him.

He heard a man grunt.

A second round smacked into the same position, followed by a faint booming sound coming from a long way off—Coker's sniper rifle.

This time there was no grunt.

More rounds now, coming from the house, mixed fire, the heavy bark of Danziger's Winchester, the sound of glass shattering, Mavis shouting something that Nick couldn't make out.

He got up and started to run toward the house. He was on the bottom of the stairs when a man came staggering out of the front door. He was young and brown-eyed, wearing tan slacks and a brown tee. There was a large hole in his chest and he had his hands crossed over it. The expression on his face was surprise and confusion.

He saw Nick and said, *"Mai che cosa?"*

Coker's round came in and hit the kid right in the middle of his face. It collapsed into a bloody red horror and he went backwards into the darkness behind him. That was the last round fired.

Silence came down.

Nick came up the stairs and stopped at the door.

"Mavis?"

"In here, Nick."

"Where's Reed?"

"He's in the back. I could use some help here."

Nick came into the room.

Mavis was bent over a figure lying on the floor. It was Charlie Danziger. He was staring up at the ceiling, his lips working. At first there was no blood visible. Then, in a coughing black eruption, it was everywhere. Charlie was bleeding out.

"Where's he hit?"

Mavis rolled him onto his back. There were two holes in his chest, small and black, but blood was spreading out around the holes. Nick put his hand on Danziger's throat. His pulse was weak and fluttering. Mavis was holding Danziger's head up and trying to clear blood from his airway.

She looked across Danziger's body and shook her head. Danziger started to convulse. Mavis held him as steady as she could. Blood poured from his mouth and nose. He was trying to say something, but all that came out was a strangled cough. He turned his head, looked at Nick. His left eye socket was full of blood but his right eye was blue and clear.

"Some kid in civvies got past Reed, I guess," said Mavis, holding Charlie's head in her hands. "I was looking out the window, didn't see him come in. He had me cold. Charlie moved into the line of fire, but he got hit before he could get his gun up. He went down, but I got the kid with the Winchester. Charlie saved my ass."

Danziger's lips were moving, but all that was coming out was blood. An artery at the side of his neck was distended and the sinews in his neck were all corded up. His one blue eye was full of pain and regret. Nick put a hand on Danziger's chest, looked into his eyes.

"It's all right, Charlie," said Nick. "You paid in full. God loves you. You're good to go."

Charlie's hand went down to his shirt pocket. He patted it, coughed up more blood, and died.

Mavis sat back on her heels, wiped her face with both hands.

"Jeez. What a lousy goddam day."

"Where's Reed?"

"He's out back. Throwing up, I think. He's never been in a gunfight before. You might want to give him a moment. We get everybody?"

"I got one. Coker took out another guy in the sweetgrass."

"He also took out a third guy, up in the tree line. Reed saw that one go down. Then another guy popped out of the weeds, real close. He put a burst by Reed's head and Reed snap-shot him in the throat. It was ugly. Reed got distracted by the gurgling and thrashing the guy was doing and he let the fifth guy get by him. He was the kid in the slacks. He get away?"

"No. He was standing on the front porch looking down at the hole you put in his chest. He spoke to me. Something Italian, I think. Coker punched a round into his face."

His radio crackled.

It was Coker.

"Nick, I have no other targets. No movement anywhere. What's the story down there?"

"All the bad guys are KIA."

"Any of ours?"

"Yeah. Charlie's down."

A pause.

"How bad?"

"He's gone, Coker. He took two meant for Mavis. Saved her life."

A long silence here, maybe a full minute.

"Did he?" said Coker, his voice thick and strained. "Good for him. I've always liked Mavis. You sure he's gone? All the way gone?"

"I'm sure. Maybe for the best, Coker."

"Yeah. I get where you're coming from. Damn. I'm gonna miss him. He was good company. He say anything?"

"No. He was looking up at me. You could see what he was thinking. I told him that he was good to go. That he was paid up in full. What about you, Coker? You gonna come down and pay up in full?"

Coker's radio crackled and popped.

His voice came back.

"No. I don't think so. I got things to do. Check his shirt pocket. You'll see a blue card. Mondex card. Half the Gracie money is in there. Charlie's got the PIN number on a piece of paper stuck on the fridge. Never could do numbers. You take care, Nick. I always enjoyed your company. Will you do right by Charlie? See the word gets around about what he did for Mavis. See he gets a good send-off?"

"I will. You might as well come in, Coker. You have nowhere to go."

"Well, I was thinking on that, Nick. If you don't have me, you can lay it all on my head and leave Charlie's piece out of it. Leave it that he went out like a stand-up and not a cop killer like me. He wasn't the shooter that day. You know that. He thought I was just gonna take out the engines."

"Coker, we *do* have you. Mavis has already called it in. Cars are on the way. Where you gonna run to? Where you gonna hide?"

"You sound like that fucking gospel song, Nick. I fucking hate gospel songs."

A pause, the wind hissing in the long grass.

"You take care of yourself, Nick. Sorry about all of this. You kiss that pretty girl for me."

"Coker, there's no point. They'll shoot you down where you stand."

Silence.

"Coker, you hear me? Come back?"

Silence.

"Coker, you there?"

Silence.

Monday

Res Ipsa Loquitur

The Belfair and Cullen County Courthouse had originally been a Catholic church, and it still had ten wood-frame leaded-glass windows along either side, old whitewashed wooden plank walls, and a row of wooden fans along the cedar-vaulted ceiling.

Where the altar had been there was now a carved wooden judge's bench, built up on a dais so that it dominated the room. On the face of the bench was a wooden panel with an oil painting of a Civil War cavalry battle—Brandy Station on the second day. A faded American flag edged in golden cording hung from a cavalry lance behind the judge's chair.

In the judge's chair this Monday morning was Justice Theodore Monroe, a gnarled old vulture with a hawk-like nose and small black eyes. He was in his black robes and the expression on his face as he peered through his steel-framed half-glasses at Warren Smoles was so fixed and malevolent that even a man seraphically free from any taint of self-doubt could not help but feel a tremor of concern.

The long cedar-and-sandalwood-scented room was virtually empty, since Judge Monroe had declared that the custody hearing was to be conducted in camera.

No members of the public and no press people were allowed inside the building. Kate and Nick and their lawyer, Claudio Duarte, a lean young man with olive skin and an angular face made even more striking by large brown eyes, sat at the desk usually reserved for the prosecution.

Warren Smoles, working alone, had been assigned the defense desk. Rainey was waiting in Judge Monroe's chambers, in the unlikely event that he might be called. One of Smoles' "nurses" was sitting with him. What may have been going on in Rainey's mind was anyone's guess. He *looked* nervous and defiant and sullen.

Lemon, neither a family member nor a lawyer, was excluded from attending, which was fine with him since the temptation to punch War-ren Smoles' lights out would probably have been irresistible.

A solitary clerk sat off to the left, speaking into a funnel-shaped mouthpiece which covered the lower part of her face.

One of the first exchanges she had recorded was an opening skirmish between Smoles and Judge Monroe. Smoles had objected to his place-ment at the defense desk as "prejudicial to his argument," an objection Judge Monroe had handled with a short, sharp reply.

"Duly noted. Poppycock. Now sit down."

Smoles, red-faced, had wisely done so.

Judge Monroe had chosen to conduct the matter seated on his bench, rather than in chambers, mainly because he was profoundly disgusted by the substance of Warren Smoles' petition, and he wished to be able to sit high above him and glare down upon the bald spot at the back of Smoles' head whenever Smoles lowered his head to read from his papers.

Judge Monroe looked around the room at the various people present, illuminated by the colored light streaming in through the stained-glass windows on the courthouse's eastern wall. His gaze rested for a moment on Kate's face and marked the anguish and pain that was in it.

He liked and admired Kate, had known her and her family for years, which was why he'd asked her to be Rainey's legal guardian in the first place.

That his seemingly harmless request had brought her to this outra-geous and insufferable ordeal had created a slow burn in his belly that he was medicating with sips from a tall glass filled with ice and a clear liquid that was not tap water.

He looked at the clock at the back of the courtroom, waited until the minute hand ticked onto the numeral ten, and banged his gavel down.

"All right. Let's get this farce on the road. I don't intend to screw around with a lot of legal jargon here, I'd like you all to know. What I want from Mr. Smoles here is a clear statement of his argument con-cerning the matter of Rainey Teague, any evidence that he wishes to provide in support of that argument, and, if necessary, I shall require the boy himself to come in and say his piece. Once Mr. Smoles has had his say, then it will be the turn of Mr. Duarte here—good morning, Mr. Duarte."

Duarte jumped to his feet.

"Good morning, Your Honor."

"I doubt that. It will be the turn of Mr. Duarte to present his reply to

Mr. Smoles' arguments, to provide counterfactual evidence if he has such, and, if Rainey is brought in—which remains my decision alone, be aware—I won't have the boy dragged into a messy squabble—I intend to question Rainey myself and to—"

Smoles, who could not help it, stood up to object and got promptly gaveled down again.

"Mr. Smoles, I will remind you that this is an *informal* hearing and that I will tolerate none of your usual courthouse theatrics. I run a court of law here, not a goddamned carnival. Are we clear?"

Apparently he was, since Smoles seemed to shrink into himself under Judge Monroe's incandescent glare.

"Fine. We're all on the same page. Ruth, are you ready? All in order?"

"Yes, Your Honor," said the clerk.

"Good. All right, Mr. Smoles. How about you fire up your calliope and play us a tune."

Smoles stood, said nothing for a moment, staring down at the papers on his desk. The court waited in silence. The minute hand at the rear of the court ticked off ten seconds.

"Your Honor, and my esteemed colleagues here assembled—"

"Mr. Smoles. Skip the lapidary crap."

Smoles stiffened at that, made a show out of marking something down on his yellow pad.

"Thank you, Judge. Look, this is as difficult for me to do as it will be for Miss Walker—"

"Mrs. Kavanaugh," said the judge.

"For Mrs. Kavanaugh and her husband to hear. And I wish the record to show that I did suggest that, since they are in a sense being judged here, that they not be subjected to the ordeal directly."

"My clients are staying," said Duarte. "They're not witnesses. They're respondents."

"We've dealt with this, Mr. Smoles."

Smoles smoothed back his hair and patted the lapel of his charcoal gray Brioni.

"Very well. The essentials are these. Friday afternoon I received a call from Rainey. He was in a McDonald's on Kingsbane, and he was in a very agitated state. He wished to hire me—to retain me—to help him deal with a very unhappy home life. We spoke awhile and I made the decision to consult with him in person. I sent my driver to pick him up at two thirty that same afternoon. When the boy arrived at my office a number of details were immediately obvious. He was distraught, sobbing uncontrollably. I decided to videotape our meeting."

"Just move it along, Counselor. Summarize."

"Yes. Of course, Your Honor. To *summarize* the events as Rainey laid them out, it seems that Rainey had been skipping school and of course Kate, as his guardian, was upset at that. A kind of confrontation ensued when he came home on last Thursday night, during which Rainey became very frightened at the anger in her demeanor. He tried to explain that he just wanted some time to think, that he was being bullied at school, and that he was very upset by the loss of his parents. According to Rainey, Kate got very cold then. She informed him that she was worried about his mental state and that she and Nick had decided to get him checked out to see that he was okay. Make sure that there wasn't anything wrong with him. Mentally. Rainey expressed the fear—to me, I mean—that his guardian was planning to have him committed to what Rainey called 'a crazy house.' "

He paused, pretended to consult his notes.

"You will see from the video that I stopped him there, because I felt we might be getting into . . . actionable . . . territory and I didn't want to prejudice any subsequent discovery process—"

"You were anticipating criminal proceedings?"

"Well, Your Honor, I was trying to be—"

"I'm sure you were. Move it along, Mr. Smoles."

"Certainly. I asked him why he thought that his guardian would want to have him sent into a mental facility. He had trouble formulating an answer and I waited while he did so. There was no coaching of any kind. I assure the court of that. Finally he told me that his family was worth a lot of money and that since his parents were dead, maybe Mrs. Kavanaugh wanted to get control of the money herself."

Duarte was on his feet.

"Your Honor, even in an informal hearing, this amounts to slander, to libel if it's written—"

"Mr. Duarte, I suspect we haven't heard the worst of this yet. And I remind you that an assertion is not a fact, and accusations or implications made in an informal hearing are not public statements, spoken or written, and therefore do not fall under the libel and slander laws. I understand your position, but you must rely upon me to run my own hearing, Counselor. Mr. Smoles, I think we can dispense with the blow-by-blow. How about you cut to the chase here. What's on the table?"

Duarte sat down, put his hand out, and rested it on the desktop, lightly touching Kate's. She had gone very still. Her face was bone white. Beside her sat Nick with an expression like a stony mask.

Smoles put his head down, examined the papers on his desk.

"Your Honor, what I am about to say is very . . . volatile . . . and may carry implications that go far beyond the matter of Rainey's custody and the guardianship of his family fortune, which amounts to over ten million dollars."

"Say your say, Mr. Smoles. I'll deal with the fallout."

"Yes, Your Honor. After talking to Rainey for quite a while, and then doing due diligence into past events, I think we must take very seriously the possibility that a conspiracy exists between a known felon named Lemon Featherlight and Mrs. Kavanaugh here to gain control of the Teague estate by having Rainey committed to a mental facility on charges of having murdered a Regiopolis school attendance officer named Alice Bayer—"

Nick was on his feet and moving.

Duarte got to him before he got to Smoles. Smoles, a nimble fellow when properly motivated, was already halfway out of the courtroom.

The walls echoed with Judge Monroe's gavel blows. He restored order at the top of his lungs, and when he had it he went on in a low but vibrating voice.

"Do go on, Mr. Smoles."

Smoles looked uncertain, as if surprised that he was being allowed to continue. He wondered if he might have been overlooking something vital here.

"Well, of course, this is just one interpretation of the facts on the ground. But it seems that a Lieutenant Tyree Sutter of the CID has already contacted Detective Kavanaugh to arrange for Rainey to give testimony concerning the discovery of Alice Bayer's body in the Tulip River. Close to the scene were items belonging to Rainey, and his young friend Axel Deitz. The fact that Rainey was skipping school and that Alice Bayer was the attendance officer became the basis for Lieutenant Sutter's suspicions. I have questioned Rainey in this regard and he maintains that he has no idea how his books and papers got to Patton's Hard. He knows nothing at all about what happened to Alice Bayer. He thinks that Mrs. Kavanaugh and someone else—probably Lemon Featherlight— may have taken his belongings down there and set the scene. Perhaps Miss Bayer was lured to Patton's Hard by information that Rainey was there. Miss Bayer was known for her willingness to go out and retrieve boys who were absent from school. It is possible that the conspirators made that call, overpowered her when she arrived, pushed her into the river, and then planted incriminating evidence that would suggest that Rainey himself was responsible."

Duarte was on his feet again, partly because he was afraid that if he didn't break Smoles' oration Nick, who was armed this morning, would shoot him.

"Your Honor, this is the grossest kind of—"

"Mr. Smoles is entitled to the grossest kind of distortion. The court is required to hear it. The serial exchange of lying distortions and the deceptive cherry-picking of competing facts is the essential nature of our justice system. Go on, Mr. Smoles. Please. Consider me utterly rapt."

"Thank you, Your Honor. To be alleging such things about a colleague for whom I have the greatest esteem is as painful for me as it must be for Mrs. Kavanaugh to hear."

"I'm sure it is. You must endeavor to carry on regardless."

"Well, as unlikely as this scenario may seem, there are corroborative elements that lend it credence. For instance, the people who first reported the presence of Alice Bayer's Toyota to the police were Mrs. Kavanaugh and Mr. Featherlight. One might wonder why a respected official of the court, and a married woman, would be keeping company with a person of such dubious character as Mr. Featherlight, who received a Dishonorable Discharge from the Marine Corps after assaulting two military police officers so severely that they were hospitalized, and whose subsequent income sources came from his work as an "escort" for various wealthy married women who frequent the cafés along the Pavilion."

He's a dead man, Nick was thinking, *as soon as Lemon hears about this. No, wait. He's a dead man anyway.*

"And a further cause for concern is the fact that, according to Rainey, Mr. Featherlight was a frequent visitor to the Teague household when his mother and father were alive. At all hours, Rainey says, and often when Miles, his mother's husband, was not at home. I do not go so far as to suggest a link between Featherlight and the death of Sylvia Teague, not without further investigation, but it's a fact that Sylvia Teague disappeared shortly before Rainey's return from his abduction, that Miles Teague was found dead of a shotgun wound a few days later—*allegedly* a suicide—and that while Rainey was lying in a coma in Lady Grace Hospital, Lemon Featherlight was a frequent visitor. I contend that Lemon Featherlight is the linking factor between all these different events."

He paused here, mainly for effect, and also to take a sip from a bottle of Perrier. He glanced across at the opposition table and made accidental eye contact with Nick Kavanaugh, flinched away from that, and busied himself with a sheaf of papers before taking a breath and starting up again.

"So, to be clear, I contend that there are reasonable grounds to suspect that Lemon Featherlight insinuated himself into the Teague household and once there began to formulate a plan to eliminate Rainey's father and mother and then seek to establish an unnatural relationship with Rainey in order to have access to his wealth. Rainey, a mere child, had already reached this conclusion, as he explained to me over the weekend."

He paused to let all this percolate. Kate was dimly aware of the sound of his voice. She was in a private hell, and Nick was down there with her, but in a different room.

Nick was thinking that no matter how this turned out that kid was never setting foot inside his house or coming within twenty yards of Kate again for the rest of his life.

"Finally, I have obtained information that as recently as last Friday evening, Mrs. Kavanaugh and Lemon Featherlight were seen dining together in a cozy bistro on Bluebottle Way known as Placido's. I do not intend to suggest anything improper about this, only to support the argument that a close relationship exists between the two of them. Perhaps, in the beginning, it was not Mrs. Kavanaugh's intention to conspire with Featherlight to gain control of Rainey's wealth. One might say she has been *seduced* by a practiced manipulator of women. It is with profound regret that I present these disturbing facts to the court—"

"Implications and innuendo do not amount to facts," said Duarte, his face white with shock and anger. "Your Honor, I ask that this offensive display be brought to a halt. Mr. Smoles' allegations—"

"Are total horseshit," said the judge. "And allow me to say that I agree completely—"

"Your Honor—"

"Sit down, Mr. Smoles. I think we have had enough of you for the nonce. Mrs. Kavanaugh, I wish to compliment you on your poise and control throughout this thuggish display on the part of Mr. Smoles. Mr. Smoles, I salute you. You have managed to slither lower in my regard than you ever have before, and believe me, there are creatures lying on their backs at the bottom of ponds that I hold in higher esteem than I do you."

Smoles was on his feet again, but Judge Monroe snarled him down.

"I have heard you out, Mr. Smoles, because I wished to have your verbal statement made a matter of record so that I might forward the transcript to the State Bar Association. I apologize to the Kavanaughs for requiring them to endure it. It was, I will admit, a far more vicious and loathsome display than I expected, even from you. Listening to you today was an education in the depths to which a person such as yourself can sink. If you'll permit me to express myself in a colorful way, I hereby anoint you the Sultan of Slime. You are a hog happily rolling in his own filth—"

"Your Honor, I can verify—"

"It has not been my experience that lies and deliberate distortions of the existing evidence are all that easy to verify. Please sit down and shut up. I have a few things to say and then I will listen to whatever Mr. Duarte has to say and then I will render my judgment in this matter. Ruth, do you wish to take a break?"

"No thank you, Your Honor."

"Anyone else? No? Well, then, I'll begin. As a member of the legal edifice in Niceville I am often apprised of information that would not normally fall across my desk. I heard through the grapevine that Lieutenant Sutter was contemplating an investigation into the suspicious death of Alice Bayer. I was also apprised of the reasons why the name of Rainey Teague had arisen. I anticipated the line Mr. Smoles might take if he were in possession of similar information, so I made a few inquiries on my own, mainly by calling on Lieutenant Sutter personally at his offices on Powder River Road, something you could easily have done, Mr. Smoles. You are—or were—an officer of this court as well as the instigating party in this action. Lieutenant Sutter would have been required to provide information relevant to your petition. You neglected to do so. I did not. We met on Saturday afternoon, and I asked him to walk me through the elements of Miss Bayer's death insofar as he had been able to reconstruct them."

"That's a breach of—"

"Not another word, Mr. Smoles. Not one. This is an informal hearing. I can set fire to a bobcat and stuff it down your pants if it amuses me. How about you just sit down and take this like a man? I'll make it short. The estimated time of death for poor Miss Bayer was inferred from the electric wristwatch she was wearing, a time-and-date affair made by a firm called Fossil. The watch ceased to function at seventeen minutes after two on a Tuesday afternoon more than fourteen days ago. Naturally Lieutenant Sutter looked into the whereabouts of everyone connected to the case, starting, as is usual, with the people who discovered the body, since it often happens that they turn out to be the killers. He established that, at that time and on that day, Mrs. Kavanaugh was standing before Mr. Justice Horn in Part Four Room Three of this very building in a matter related to a plea bargain for a juvenile client of hers. The court records reflect this fact, Mr. Smoles."

"Your Honor, I was not made aware—"

"You might have been if you hadn't rushed into this case without doing any serious background work. As it is, it took me one interview to shatter your basic premise even before I had heard it. And you did not disappoint me. You leapt upon a chance to attach yourself to a wealthy young boy with obvious emotional problems, in order, I suspect, to suck his estate dry. You are now reaping what you sow, Mr. Smoles, and to quote Jackie Gleason, 'How sweet it is.' As I have said, I intend to refer your conduct in this matter to the Bar Association and the Board of Judicial Standards, along with all the supporting documents, including the transcript of our proceedings this morning. I fully expect you to be censured, but so far has your profession sunk in honor that I do not hold out the hope that you will be disbarred."

He paused, took a drink of that clear cold liquid, savored it, and went on.

"Having satisfied myself as to Kate's alibi, I asked Tig—Lieutenant Sutter—if he had managed anything equally conclusive with Mr. Featherlight, who, by the way, is not a convicted felon, having been charged in a DEA-related sting which was later dismissed, so in fact Mr. Featherlight has no criminal record of any kind. And his discharge from the Marine Corps is a General one, not a Dishonorable. Concerning his relations with the women of the Pavilion, I have no opinion other than to admit to a vague sense of envy. Tig was indeed able to establish that on the date in question, Mr. Featherlight was in attendance at the National Guard flight training facility near Gracie, and was actually sitting in a helicopter flight simulator at the time, where he was apparently failing to safely land a virtual Eurocopter AS350. It appears that Mr. Featherlight spends four days a week, twelve hours at a time, working towards achieving his Rotary-Wing Pilot Certification in the Air National Guard, for which I honor him."

He paused here, took another long sip of his drink, sighed, and set it down. The clunk of the glass on the desk was the only sound other than the ticking of the Westinghouse at the far end of the courtroom.

"So, where does this leave us, Mr. Smoles? In the matter of the death of Alice Bayer, I have no opinion. I leave it to Lieutenant Sutter to sort that out. In the matter of the custody of Rainey Teague, I think you all may have anticipated my decision, but if not, I stand ready to hear your counterarguments, Mr. Duarte."

"Your Honor, I'm happy to hear your decision, if I may stipulate a right to respond for the record?"

"You can and you just have. In the matter of Rainey Teague, I reaffirm and reinstate Mrs. Kate Kavanaugh as his legal guardian and return to her full custody of the boy and all his affairs, with a proviso. Kate, I understand that because of Rainey's erratic behavior you and Nick were considering getting the lad medical attention. I think this is an excellent idea. Clearly the boy has run off the rails. God knows he has every reason. He needs to be looked at, and you need to do it as soon as possible. He's in my chambers right now, if you wish to go and see him?"

Kate sat there and stared back at the judge.

Nick said nothing.

She looked at him.

I have to, Nick, was her unspoken thought.

I know you do, was his unspoken answer.

Will you come with me?

No.

Judge Monroe's chambers, as all chambers must be, were lined in leather-bound copies of legal decisions, both in the state and at the Supreme Court level, going all the way back to 1856. The long wicker blades of a huge ceiling fan circled slowly in the humid air. Morning light was pouring in through a tall sash window and illuminating a massive rosewood desk with a marquetry inlay depicting the last stand of the Twentieth Maine under Joshua Chamberlain at Little Round Top on the second day of the Battle of Gettysburg. This unlikely scene was present only because the desk had been liberated from a Yankee officer's tent after his position had been overrun by Confederate forces under the command of Teddy Monroe's great-great-grandfather. In front of this desk were two large green leather wingbacks which had been bought fair and square from an antiques shop in Richmond.

Seated in one, reading a copy of *Vanity Fair*, was a small-boned, sharp-featured young woman in a blue skirt and a crisp white blouse. Sitting across from her and staring down at his cell phone screen was Rainey. He was wearing his school slacks and a rumpled white shirt. When the door to the chambers opened they both looked up, expecting to see Judge Monroe. When the arrival turned out to be Kate Kavanaugh, Rainey got to his feet and headed for the door that led to a private hall and down a flight of stairs to the rear parking lot.

"Rainey," said Kate, "don't go. It's all right. I just want to talk for a minute. Please stay."

The nurse was on her feet and moving to intercept Kate. Kate held up her hand, palm out, not looking at her.

"Stay out of this. We won. If you need that clarified, go find Warren Smoles."

"He was supposed to text me."

"Last I saw of him, he was in that white Benz and headed down Burke Street. Like a hare. Get it? Burke and Hare. Never mind. Good luck trying to catch him."

The nurse glanced back at Rainey, shrugged, and left at a trot. Kate stood by the door and looked at Rainey, who was now standing by the other door, his hand on the knob. He was glaring at her.

Kate tried to keep her expression as soft as she could manage it, but it was difficult for her feelings not to show.

"Rainey. Please. If you don't want to live with me anymore—"

"I don't."

"Then we can work something out."

Rainey's expression tightened.

lying and lying is what she does

"Oh yeah. Working stuff out is what you do best, isn't it? So you won. What now? I get locked away in a crazy house and you get all my money."

Kate stayed by the door and swallowed her anger.

"Rainey, this thing about your money, even if I wanted it, which I don't—I have all the money I could ever need—your family's finances are all protected by layers and layers of legal rules. The only influence I have over it is to see that all the taxes are paid every year, and that any corporate papers that have to be filed get filed on time, and that your family's home on Cemetery Hill is kept in good order and all the property taxes paid. All of the detail work involved is handled by lawyers and bankers who are retained by your estate. I monitor their billings and help make decisions about how to keep the money working for you. As soon as you're twenty-one you gain control of all the yearly interest and dividends your estate pays, which amounts to around six hundred thousand a year. And you get full control of the principal on your thirtieth birthday. I can show you the papers. Your fortune simply *cannot* be taken away from you."

they can do whatever they want

"Yeah? What if I'm dead? Or in jail."

"You're not going to jail, Rainey. And if you die without leaving a will, then your family's money would very likely be divided up among your various relatives."

"Right. Like you."

"I'm a very distant relative, Rainey. A judge would determine the—"

"Like that old judge in there? The guy who's always on your side? The guy who stuck me with you in the first place?"

His venom was so intense that the force of it pushed her into silence. She went back on her heels as it washed over her. It struck her that Rainey hated her. Or that something inside Rainey hated her. There was a loud knock on the door behind Kate's back. Neither Kate nor Rainey reacted to it. They were locked inside this awful thing, and Kate had no idea what to do about it.

The knock came again.

"Who is it?" she said.

"It's Nick. Can I come in?"

that one will kill us stay away from him

Rainey, stepping away, crossed the room, pulled the back door open.

"He comes in, I'm gone."

"Rainey, please—"

Nick opened the door.

Rainey turned to run and slammed into Tig Sutter, who had been waiting in the hallway outside the door. Rainey bounced back and tried to push past him. It was like trying to move a bank vault.

There just wasn't much give in Tig Sutter.

Kate looked at Nick.

"What is it? What's happening?"

"Tig needs to talk to Rainey," said Nick. "This is as good a time as any, I think."

"No it's not. First of all, I have a problem with you being here. You might be intimidating Rainey."

That got to Nick.

"I'm *intimidating* the kid?"

"It's possible. Rainey, are you worried about Nick being here? Is that why you don't want to say anything?"

good say nothing these people want to trick you

Rainey didn't respond.

Kate repeated the question.

"Maybe."

"Because if you'd feel better Nick can go. Am I right, Nick? Tig can handle this, can't he?"

Inside his head Nick was screaming at her, *Take a good look at this little creep*, but what he said was, "If you think it'll help, I'll go."

"Actually, Nick," said Tig, with a wry smile. "Come to think of it, maybe you should step back. This goes any further, a lawyer could argue you had a bias one way or another."

"Kate's his lawyer, Tig."

"For now," said Kate. "If this goes any further, we'll probably bring Claudio Duarte in. Really, Nick. Maybe you should go. Okay?"

Nick stared at her for a long time and Kate realized they were in serious trouble for the first time in their marriage. But there was nothing she could do about that right now. Then he turned and left the room without another word.

"Rainey," she said, once the door had closed, "I'm here to represent your best interests. And I swear to you that your best interests are not being served by swearing at us. If you can control yourself maybe you'll find out that what Tig has to ask you isn't so terrible. And I won't let you answer any questions that I think you shouldn't answer. But if you refuse to say anything at all, he isn't just going to say oh well and walk away. He can't. Can you, Tig?"

"I'm afraid not."

"So Rainey . . . look at me, please?"

the smell good one we like her

He didn't move and seemed to be trying to turn into stone. *Where did he get the iron*, she was wondering.

And *Where the hell was Reed?*

"Well, he's not saying no, Tig. Give it a try."

"Okay. Rainey, you know who Alice Bayer was, don't you?"

Rainey muttered something.

"Sorry, Rainey. I didn't catch that."

go slow be careful

Rainey looked up at him.

"She was the attendance officer at school."

"Okay. That's good. And how did you get along with her?"

"Tig," said Kate, a warning in her tone.

"Okay. Scratch that. You know a place called Patton's Hard?"

"Yes."

"Do you ever go there?"

"Yes."

"A lot?"

"No."

"Just now and then?"

"Yes."

"Do you ever go there when you should be in school?"

"Sometimes."

"Were you down at Patton's Hard two weeks ago Tuesday?"

"I can't remember."

"Were you in school that day?"

"I can't remember."

"Rainey, did Alice Bayer ever come down to Patton's Hard when you were there?"

Rainey was silent.

need to stop now

Tig repeated the question.

More silence.

"Rainey, please—"

need to go away now right now right now

Kate saw Rainey's eyes change color and then they rolled upwards and he passed out. They called for medics. Rainey was awake by the time they got there, on his back on the floor, blinking up at the ceiling, Kate kneeling beside him.

The EMT people—a matched set of bouncy blonds, one male and one undecided, checked him over, sat him up again, and took his vitals, conferred in a whispered exchange packed with medical jargon, and pronounced him fine.

Rainey sat up, and Kate stood to face Tig.

"We can't do this anymore. Not today."

Tig looked uneasy, but he knew she was right.

"Okay. But when?"

"Judge Teddy wanted me to get him some tests. We started that on Friday, before all this happened. That's why he was at WellPoint. Let me take him back there, get some results. Then we can see about talking to him again?"

Tig thought it over.

"Okay. Get him to WellPoint. Call me tomorrow."

Kate and Rainey had nothing to say to each other until they got to Kate's Envoy. They got inside and Kate started it up.

Rainey was staring straight ahead, breathing rapidly through his open mouth.

"Rainey, are you okay?"

He nodded.

"I'm going to take you back to WellPoint."

And this time I'm staying right with you.

"Okay." A faint, defeated whisper.

we can't go there they'll find us with machines

"Will I have to stay overnight?"

"Maybe. But I'll be right there with you."

"Why are you working so hard to help me? After what I did to you?"

Kate considered the kid for a while.

She had the strange impression that the old Rainey was here in the car with her, instead of the other Rainey.

"Because I promised to take care of you. No matter what. And that's what I'm going to do. Now before we go there, is there anything you want to get? Clothes? A video game? Your books?"

Rainey seemed to think about it.

"Will they let me have my portable DVD player?"

"I don't see why not. We'll pick out a few DVDs to take along."

Rainey was watching her now, but inside his head he was listening to **Cain.** When she stopped buzzing and crackling in his brain, he said, "I'd really like to have that Christmas video of my mom and dad and me."

"Okay. Where is it?"

Rainey looked at his hands.

"It's at my house," he said.

"You mean your old house?"

"Yes. Mom and Dad's place. I think it's still in the DVD player."

"You want to go to Cemetery Hill and get it?"

Rainey had his head down again.

"Could we?" he said.

Kate thought it over.

There was time.

"Sure. Buckle up. We'll go there right now."

Rainey smiled then, and pulled in a long, ragged breath, holding it a while.

smells so good so many good smells so many

Tidy as You Go

Warren Smoles had the satellite radio in the Benz playing as he rolled it up the driveway to the garage door of his château-style house in The Glades. It was the largest house on a long, meandering block lined with hard-bitten palm trees and scattered thickets of holly and bougainvillea. The rest of the houses were the original fifties-style Frank Lloyd Wright ranchers and Old Hollywood Art Deco bungalows, so Warren Smoles' house stood out pretty much the way Warren Smoles did. The song he had on was "So You Had a Bad Day" and he was playing it because it matched his mood.

He was not at all used to being handled the way Teddy Monroe had handled him this morning, and he intended to barricade himself in his mini-mansion for the rest of the afternoon and self-medicate with a bucket of Tanqueray and a few hours of *Best of the Bowl Games* DVDs. Perhaps, when he was more himself, he'd think of a way to counter-fuck the old son of a bitch, but for now it was time to fall back and regroup.

Smoles lived alone in this huge house for several reasons, the main one being that no one else wanted to live there with him. He had quite a time keeping staff and his dogs kept running away and he'd tried goldfish but they all ran away too—he could never figure out how, but he'd come home and find the bowls empty and the fish just plain gone.

So he went for cats, who are no less particular than dogs but far more willing to sell themselves out for a soft bed and regular meals.

Smoles had fifteen of them scattered about the house, mostly tabbies, a couple of six-toed grays like Hemingway had, and three Maine Coons as big as Rottweilers. He hadn't named any of them—naming cats was like naming seagulls—and keeping his house smelling as good as it did required the work of a phalanx of visiting maids every third day. On the other hand, he had no rodent problems and no fucking noisy songbirds loitering about either.

He locked the Benz in the garage and came in through the connecting hallway to his side door, where he keyed in a long and complicated password.

He was carrying a sack of cat food tins, a forty-pounder of Tanqueray, and three fresh limes, so when the door clicked loose he just shoved it open with his toe and walked through into his open-plan kitchen and entertainment area and set the sack down on the Corian counter.

There were no cats around.

This was odd.

They usually came slinking in or they were already gathered around the door waiting for him when he came home. Not that they loved or even liked him in any way, but none of them could handle the electric can opener or change the kitty litter.

But no cats today?

He walked around the counter and out into the great room, a large stone-walled space centered around a gigantic flat-screen TV and an entertainment system capable of reaching out into the stars and catching talk shows live from outer space, if outer space had talk shows, which so far it did not.

The walls were covered with pictures of Warren Smoles sharing handshakes and glassy-eyed grins with all sorts of celebrities and sports stars and politicians, none of whom looked as delighted to be in the picture as Warren Smoles did.

No cats here either.

He looked down the hallway that led to the front door.

No cats there.

Odd. Damn odd.

Well, fuck 'em, he thought, turning around to start in on his bucket of Tanqueray. A tall, well-dressed but vaguely funereal gentleman was standing behind his Corian counter and smiling at him.

"I know what you're going to say," he said.

"Who the *fuck* are you?"

"There you go. Now ask me how I got in."

"I don't give a fuck how you got in. What the fuck are you? An insurance salesman?"

"No. I'm a private collector. My name is Harvill Endicott."

"Jeez Louise!" said Smoles, relief in his voice. He had never met Endicott personally. All their business had been conducted over phone lines or through the Internet. Even the way Endicott had retained him had been through PayPal.

"I did not mean to alarm you," said Endicott in a soothing tone.

"Fuck that. I want to know why my *alarm* didn't alarm me, that's what I want to know. And where the hell are my cats?"

"Your alarm system is not very effective. I suggest you invest in a better one. Your cats were gathered around the side door when I came in. When they saw that I was not you they took the better part of valor and skittered away. I'm sure they'll be back when things quiet down."

"Thanks. Setting aside the break-and-enter thing for now, what do you want?"

"I do apologize. I dislike waiting about in the open. So I came in. I wanted to thank you personally for your help in establishing myself with Mrs. Maranzano. We have reached an understanding. For which I am grateful."

Smoles walked over to the fridge and pulled out an ice tray, got a silver bucket down from a cupboard, and started to build himself a drink.

"Glad to be of service, Harvill. What was the understanding?"

"A confidential matter. Forgive me."

"I got paid. No skin off me. You want a drink?"

"Pellegrino, if you have it?"

"Perrier do?"

"Lovely."

Smoles, still a bit rattled but calming down, got the man a Perrier. His gin and tonic came together out of habit and he walked across the slate floor to his big burgundy armchair by the fireplace. He sat down, put his feet up on an ottoman the size of a Cape buffalo, crossed his lizard-skin cowboy boots, and sipped at his drink.

"Well, I don't like you coming in like this, Harvill. I'll let it go for now. But don't do it again, or I'm not gonna be so fucking amiable."

Endicott came over and stood in front of him, holding his Perrier in his left hand. His other was in the pocket of his gray sharkskin pants.

Smoles gave him a once-over.

Guy looks like a cross between an accountant and a mortician. Dresses pretty good. Pants a bit baggy. Wouldn't go for pleats myself. Well, like the Froggies say, shack-oon a son goot.

"Nice pants, Harv. Are they sharkskin?"

"They are."

"Who's the maker?"

"Zegna."

"Yeah? I'm a Brioni guy myself. This suit's a Brioni."

"I can see that it is. Well, your health."

"Yeah. Salut! This you bailing out? Work all done? I trust I gave satisfaction?"

"You were all that I expected. And more."

"Yeah? Good. I got a rep, like to keep it. Tough about Deitz, hah? He was an impossible guy to control. That thing at the mall, that was pretty fucking extreme. I've heard about this Coker guy. Whispering Death, right? He's taken out a whole shitload of perps."

"So I understand."

"Sit down, will ya? I don't like people standing over me. Makes me cranky."

Endicott stepped back a few feet.

"Sorry about that. People say I have a tendency to loom. I have a question, actually. It concerns Byron Deitz."

"Okay. Here's me turning my meter on. *Ching-ka-ching ching.* Now, how may I be of assistance, Harv?"

"Deitz transferred a substantial amount of money to an unknown recipient. I have now established to my own satisfaction who this recipient was—"

"No shit? Who was it?"

"Allow me to keep my own counsel. My inquiry is ongoing—"

"Anything to do with that shoot-out up at Charlie Danziger's ranch on Saturday afternoon?"

"Again, I shall keep my own counsel. What I still need to know is the means by which this exchange was effected."

Smoles narrowed his eyes.

"Hey. You're still *working*, aren't you? You're still chasing that fucking bank money! You cagey old prick. I'd be careful with that. Whoever did that bank, he's a crazy mother—"

"I was asking about the method of transfer?"

"Well, it was an offshore thing."

"Deitz never told you the details?"

Smoles took a long swig of his gin and tonic, drained it, and let the ice drop into his mouth, where he started cracking it, with his mouth open, all the while staring up at Endicott with a sly grin on his leonine face.

"Might have, Harv. Might well have. He dropped hints, for sure. How bad do you want to know?"

"How badly do you want to tell me?"

Smoles hooted at that.

"Not too fucking badly, Harv, 'less I see something in your hand. Show me something makes it worth my while and maybe we can do business."

Endicott smiled down upon his broad grinning face, pulled his Sig out of the pocket of his sharkskin pants, and shot Smoles in the meaty part of his upper left thigh. Harvill Endicott was a creature of habit.

Smoles shrieked and blew out a whole lot of ice chunks and clutched at his leg.

"What the *fuck*?"

"I'll ask you again, Warren. How badly do you want to tell me?"

Mr. Teague Is Now Receiving

Lemon called Nick while Nick was driving down to the CID HQ to file some Monday afternoon paperwork. The shootings at Danziger's house had generated more PISTOL interrogations, and the investigation into Danziger and Coker's involvement in the Gracie robbery, and Coker's subsequent disappearance, had drawn media in from all over the country. They were all descending on the CID HQ on Powder River Road. So Nick was headed down there, thinking about Coker and Charlie and Kate and Rainey and what Reed had said about killing Rainey if it came to a crisis, and he also had the words of a Billy Ray Cyrus song going around in his head—*Where'm I gonna live when I get home*—

In other words his plate was full and what was on it wasn't at all appealing. LEMON FEATHERLIGHT CALLING appeared on his cell screen, so he scooped the phone up and hit RECEIVE.

"Nick, how did it go?"

"Depends on your point of view. We still have custody of Rainey. Kate's pleased. I'm not."

Lemon gave that some thought.

"Kid went pretty far, didn't he?"

"Too far for me, Lemon. I've seen wild kids. This one is something else. You got a minute?"

"I do. I was only calling to see how it went."

"Let me pull over . . . How'd the bone basket thing go?"

"I'll wait until you're stopped."

A pause.

"Okay. I'm on the shoulder."

"Me first?"

"Yeah. I'm interested."

Lemon filled him in, just the basics, but the basics were crazy enough. Lemon ended with the connection to the old Cherokee legend about the soul-eating demon that lived in Crater Sink.

"You buying that?" Nick asked.

"Those things are real, that much I'm buying. How they got there, and what happened before they got there, I have no idea."

"Maybe your pro from UV will sort it out."

"She was a happy lady. Thinks there's a Nobel Prize in it. They're going to name the things after me, she says. One of those Latin names."

"Good for you."

"Look, there's another thing . . ."

"Okay."

"Remember the streetcar lady who helped me get Rainey down those stairs—"

"Doris Godwin. A babe, you said."

"Yeah, that too. When we were up there she took a sort of 360-degree bunch of shots—"

"Why?"

"Why. Because she was scared bootless. She thought there was something out in the woods. She sent me the jpegs the next day. They're pretty hairy, Nick. You'll want to see them."

"What was in them?"

"People. The entire forest was full of people, standing there, staring back at us. There might have been hundreds of them. Far back into the woods. Maybe even more. Maybe thousands. Just standing there, those old trees hanging over them."

"Like what? Ghosts? Zombies?"

"No. Nothing like that. Citizens, that's all. People of Niceville. People you'd see on the streets. But I'm looking at the shots, and they're all dressed different. Style, I mean. Some old-timey, some yesterday. Mostly men, too, but a couple of older women. Some old cowboy types, even. Some soldiers, Confederate and Union. Now I'm looking, I can even see some men, look like they might be Indians. Cherokee or Creek, looking at their clothes, the way they're painted up."

"Fakes?"

"No. Doris was pretty freaked. So am I. It's like they're ghosts from a bunch of old-time photographs. But they're not, are they?"

Nick was quiet for a bit.

"Man. It all fits."

"Fits what?"

"With the general weirdness of Niceville."

Nick told Lemon what had happened to Reed up at Candleford House, and what he had learned from Beryl Eaton at the Archives and Records Office in Sallytown.

"Reed *saw* Clara Mercer?"

"He's pretty convinced he did."

"Man. How'd he take it?"

"Like I said. Out the window and four floors down. He's lucky to be alive."

"Where is he now?"

"Believe it or not, back in an Interceptor. Marty reinstated him after the shoot-out at Charlie's place."

"Still can't believe that. Coker, I could see it, but Charlie?"

"Well, keep the Charlie end to yourself. Charlie got shot taking a bullet for Mavis Crossfire. That oughta be worth something. I talked it over with Mavis and she thinks we may be able to work it that Coker takes the freight."

"Whose idea was that?"

"Coker's."

A silence.

"Man, what a town."

"Niceville?"

"Yeah. A Hell of a town."

"No argument from me. Lemon, I gotta—"

"Yeah. Just one thing. Where's Rainey now? In a clinic, maybe?"

"On his way to WellPoint. Kate's taking him—"

"Kate's *alone* with him?"

"I think so. After the trial, in chambers, she and I had a blowup over the kid. I got told to leave. I left. Tig Sutter was there—"

"She was going straight to WellPoint?"

"That was the plan. Look, Lemon, I really gotta run. There'll be media all over the HQ in a couple of hours. You okay?"

Probably nothing to worry about she won't go to Sylvia's house she'll take him to WellPoint and everything will be fine.

"Yeah, I'm fine. Whole thing has me rattled."

"No shit. Send me those jpegs. Talk later."

Lemon shut his phone down, looked at the screen, picked it up again, speed-dialed Kate's cell.

It rang six times and went to voice mail.

"Kate, this is Lemon. If you get this—"

Forget that!

No time!

Wherever Kate was, there was one place she could not go. Not alone, and sure as hell not with Rainey. He hit the pedal and powered out into traffic. He figured he was fifteen minutes away.

Ten if he broke all the rules.

He decided to break all the rules.

Lemon parked his truck across the road from 47 Cemetery Hill. The big stone pile looked exactly the same as it had last Friday. Dappled sunlight on the slate roof, the wind sighing in the live oaks. Down the way a dog barking. The sound of the traffic on Bluebottle. Kids shouting in a backyard somewhere. Kate's Envoy wasn't there.

He tried her cell again. Three rings and voice mail. Was she in the house already?

He had to go look.

Lemon got out of the truck and walked across the street to the foot of the driveway. The dark light was still there. He moved closer and it solidified into two separate shapes that gradually took on the form of the Shagreen brothers. They stood there, lifeless but living.

"Is Rainey Teague here?"

"Leave this place," said the blond one.

Lemon pulled out a large black Smith & Wesson and pointed it at the blond man. There was no reaction from either of them. He put a foot on the staircase. The blond came closer, becoming quite solid now. The same dappled light that was on the roof was now moving over his face and shoulders.

"You leave now."

Lemon aimed the revolver at the thing's head. He heard an engine behind him, and a woman's voice.

"Lemon?"

He turned and saw Kate sitting at the wheel of the Envoy. Rainey was in the passenger seat, leaning forward so he could see Lemon.

Lemon backed away down the driveway, but he kept the Smith in his hand. He came across to the truck, put his hands on the window frame.

"Kate. Thank God. I was afraid I'd missed you."

"You look awful, Lemon. You're white as a sheet. What's wrong? Why do you have a gun?"

Lemon was looking at Rainey, who was now sitting back and staring straight ahead. Still glaring at Rainey, Lemon asked, "Kate, I've been calling you. So has Reed. Your phone's off."

"No it isn't. It's right here."

She pulled her phone out of a slot on the outside of her purse, pressed the screen.

"It *is* off. I never—"

"Rainey been alone with it?"

Kate turned to look at Rainey, who was still staring straight ahead, breathing through an open mouth, looking pale and hungry.

Cain was drilling through his brain.

this one is worse than the others he can see

"We stopped for lunch. I left him in the . . . Rainey, did you turn my phone off?"

"No. I never touched it."

He was still staring straight ahead.

"Why are you here, Kate?" Lemon asked. "Don't you have to be at WellPoint?"

"He will probably have to stay there overnight, so he wanted a few things. There's a DVD of his parents. He thinks it's still in the player in Sylvia's house. Then we're going to the clinic."

Lemon looked at Rainey.

"Kate, I'm going to have to show you something. You may not be able to see it, but I think Rainey can. So may I?"

"Certainly. What is it?"

"You'll see. Park the car. Come with me."

Lemon took Rainey by the elbow, a firm grip on the bone, and steered him toward the driveway. Kate followed a few feet behind. When Lemon and Rainey reached the bottom of the stairs, the Shagreen-shaped things came into being again. Lemon could feel Rainey's body vibrating under his grip.

this one can see kill him kill him he can see

"Kate, do you see anything on the landing?"

"On the landing?"

"Yes. Do you see anything?"

Kate stepped closer.

One of the Shagreen shapes came down a step.

Lemon put the Smith on it and said, "No."

Rainey was staring at it, fixed and rapt.

yes take them now take them both

"I can see . . . you're talking to something," said Kate. "Is it kind of a shadow?"

"Is that all you see?"

"Maybe there are two. The sunlight looks . . . like it's bending."

"Rainey. Tell Kate what you see."

now do it now

Rainey said nothing.

Lemon put the muzzle of the Smith up against the side of Rainey's head. Kate reached for his hand to pull the gun away.

"Lemon, what are you *doing*?"

"Tell Kate what you see, Rainey, or I'll kill you right where you stand."

An acid smell was coming off Rainey. His breathing altered. He looked at Lemon with different eyes and smiled. When he spoke it wasn't his voice. It was a woman's voice.

"they belong to us."

"What are they?"

"they are guardians they're a gift."

"A gift from whom?"

"from nothing."

"From *nothing?*"

"yes we got them from nothing at crater sink."

Lemon took the revolver away from Rainey's temple.

"What would have happened if Kate had gone up those steps?"

said too much say nothing

Kate came around and looked into Rainey's face. There was nothing human in it. He opened his mouth wide and sucked in a gulp of air, held it.

"Dear God."

Lemon was looking up at the things on the porch. They were staring back down at him, as still as gravestones, faces blank. The same stink was coming off them too. Even Kate could smell it now.

She looked up at the porch. The light bent and wavered, and darkened, and then she saw the figures clearly. The Shagreen brothers, at least their shells. She turned back to Rainey, who was smiling up at her, and then to Lemon.

"Lemon, we have to fix this."

Lemon's expression was remote and cold.

"How do you figure we can fix something like this, Kate? There's no *fixing* this."

Kate was staring into what was in Rainey's eyes. There was *nothing* in there. She was looking at nothing and dead-eyed nothing was staring back at her. It was in him and it would have to be driven out. She didn't know if that was even possible.

But she had to try.

"He has to go back."

"To WellPoint?"

"No. To Glynis Ruelle."

the harvest we can't go there

In Rainey's head the voice abruptly stopped, went down deep, and hid itself. Rainey's eyes rolled up and he dropped like a dead thing.

Lemon caught him.

"Kate, we have to call Nick."

She shook her head.

"No," was all she said.

The Way Is Shut

Delia Cotton's rambling Victorian house on Upper Chase Run was sealed and shuttered, as it had been ever since her disappearance last spring. It spread itself out in gables and porches and galleries and glass-walled garden rooms under the blue shadows cast by ancient live oaks and towering willows. Pools of sunlight shimmered on the rolling lawn that led up to the house. The shutters on all the windows were closed tight and padlocked. The black iron gates at the bottom of the long curved drive were chained shut.

Kate pulled the Envoy to a stop in front of the gate. Lemon got out and walked up to the chain, looked at it. Then he came back to the Envoy and got the tire iron out of the storage space under the rear loading deck. He went back to the gate, set the blade of the iron between the fence and the chain link, jerked it downwards. The chain snapped off and fell to the ground.

Lemon walked the gates back and Kate rolled the Envoy up the drive, Lemon following along on foot. She stopped the truck under the lacy gingerbread roof of the portico and turned the engine off.

Rainey had come around a while ago and was sitting up and looking at the house with a blank expression. It was as if the thing inside him had gone away and all that was left was a boy in a walking trance. Lemon came up just as Kate was stepping out of the Envoy.

"Is he awake?" he asked.

"His eyes are open. I'm not sure he's in there. Can you get us inside?"

"Sure. The trick is to do it without bringing down the security patrol."

Lemon walked up the stairs while Kate stood beside the truck, watching Rainey.

"Rainey. Can you hear me?"

Rainey looked at her.

"You want to send us to the harvest."

A flat declaration without sentiment.

And a pitch-perfect accusation.

Rainey could still feel **Cain** inside his head, but the thing had gone down very deep. Rainey could feel it curled up at the base of his skull, blinking in the dark, waiting, saying nothing.

It came to him that **Cain** was afraid.

Kate ran her fingers through her hair, shook her head to clear it.

"Rainey, did those Guardians come with you?"

"I don't know," he said. "I don't smell them. I think they can't come to this house."

"Why not?"

"You know why."

Again, no pitch or tone.

Just a flat, emotionless statement. It was so devoid of hope or fear that Kate had to look away.

Lemon was back.

"Okay. How about this? The front door's not locked. It's shut, but not locked. I looked in. The place is boarded up, so it's dark. But the power's on. What do you want to do?".

"What we came to do."

Lemon wasn't happy about it. But he opened Rainey's door and helped him down, keeping a strong grip on his left arm. Rainey was slack and silent. He offered no resistance, and that *smell* was gone.

They went up the steps to the main door and walked into the hallway. It was like stepping into a jewel box. The walls and floors were polished oak. Brass sconces lined the entrance hall and a narrow Persian runner led down to the base of a broad flight of stairs. In the dim light they could make out a galleried second floor. An enormous crystal chandelier dominated the central hall.

Halfway down the hall, double-glass doors opened onto a wood-paneled study on one side, and on the other a light and airy music room in an octagonal shape, with stained-glass windows on every wall. The windows were shuttered and the music room was dim and shadowy.

They stood at the bottom of the central staircase and listened to the old house creak and groan as the heat of the day slowly faded.

"Where to now?" asked Lemon, who had never been inside Delia Cotton's mansion before. All he knew of her was that she was one of the famous Cotton clan, that her husband had made a fortune mining sulfur, and that she had been a stunning beauty when she was young.

Before her disappearance, she had lived alone at Temple Hill in the kind of Victorian splendor that old money favored and then one sunny afternoon she had virtually walked off the planet, never to be heard from again.

"I think it's this way," said Kate, leading them down a side hall that opened up onto a large paneled dining room. At the far end of the dining room French doors led back into the music room. Beyond the dining room was a huge kitchen and past that was a glass-walled solarium full of ferns and palms and orchids.

"Someone must be watering those," said Lemon. The smell of rich, damp earth and the scents of jasmine and lavender floated in from the solarium.

"The Cotton estate keeps the house the way it was on the day Delia disappeared. It was in her will. She left a separate fund to pay for the maintenance. That's why the power is on. The door to the basement is over here."

They crossed the checkered tiles of the kitchen and stopped at a large wooden door painted the same buttery yellow color as the kitchen.

Rainey halted a few feet away from the door.

Kate looked back at him.

"Rainey. We have to go down."

"I'm not going down there."

"We have to."

"I know what's down there."

"How do you know?"

"Nick took a video of it, when he was looking for the woman who lived here. I found it. There's a wall down there, and it was like a movie was playing on it. It was a farm and people were working in the fields. It was where I went when I was in the mirror. Where Glynis lived. You want me to go back into that place and not be in this world anymore. I'm not going down there."

Kate opened the door and stood beside it. The stairs led down into darkness, but there was a faint glow in a far corner.

"Rainey, I can't do anything else for you. It's all I can think of to do."

Lemon, quite ready to force the kid, took his arm. Rainey was vibrating and his face was white, but he went down the stairs without a struggle. Inside his head he could feel **Cain** buzzing.

Although it was dark, there was enough light to let them see that the basement was a huge open space with a stone floor. Rough-cut beams ran overhead from one side to the other, supported in mid-course with standing girders that must have been added years after the original construction. A gigantic oil-fired furnace with conduits running everywhere stood in the shadows.

But there was light in the room.

There were slit windows set into the thick stone walls just below the beams. They were boarded up and sealed with tape.

Except for one.

There was a circular hole in it, about the size of a quarter. A beam of sunlight that looked as solid as a laser was shining in through the hole. The beam was playing on a wall of stone opposite the window. There was an image there, blurry and indistinct, but moving. There was a band of dark green running along the top of the wall, and then a line of black spikes, and a field of clear blue along the bottom of the wall.

"It's a pinhole camera," said Kate, looking at the image. "The image is upside down."

"What are we looking at?" asked Lemon.

"You have to work at reading it. The green line along the top is the grass outside the house. The black spikes are the fence that lines the property. And the blue is the sky. Can you see it?"

Lemon got it in a moment.

The indistinct shapes, luminous but faint, gradually emerged as an upside-down picture of what was on the other side of the window. Lawns and trees and fences and beyond the fence Upper Chase Run. The live oaks were moving with the wind and the pale blue sky had clouds gliding across it.

Rainey had backed himself into a corner as far away from the image as he could get. Lemon looked at him, and then back at Kate.

"What happens now?"

"I don't know. Nick said the image changed into a farm, people working in the field, pine trees."

"All I'm seeing is the street outside."

"And that's all you will ever see."

They all turned at the sound of this new voice, and there was a woman standing on the basement stairs. She was tall and slender and very old. Her silver hair was long and it flowed down over her shoulders. She was wearing a Chinese robe in sky blue silk embroidered in gold thread. She was staring at Rainey with a cold eye and her mouth tight.

"Glynis Ruelle will never let that thing come into her world."

"You're Delia Cotton," said Kate.

"I am. You're Kate Walker. I knew your mother very well. Is this child Rainey Teague?"

Rainey jerked when she said his name.

"Yes," said Kate. "Miss Cotton, I thought you had—that nobody knew where you were?"

"Perhaps. But I knew where I was, which is all that mattered. I have chosen to live this way. I have the money to make it possible. I am very weary of Niceville and the problems it presents. Such as the one presented by this creature here."

"Where have you been?"

"Right here," she said, making a gesture that took the entire house in. "In Temple Hill."

"But the place is all boarded up?"

"I have become wary of windows. And basements. I hardly ever come down here."

"Why not?"

"This trick of the light you're looking at. It always happens at this time of the afternoon, at least if the day is sunny. I heard the boy describe it and he is quite right. The room reproduces the effect of a camera obscura, a pinhole camera. I suppose I should board up that hole, but I haven't yet. I have no idea why. But if you're waiting for Glynis Ruelle to open the way, you must think of something else to do instead."

"She let Rainey in once."

"The boy hadn't gone to Crater Sink then. Now he has. Nothing is in him now. I can smell it on him."

"Do you know what's happened to him?"

She looked over at Rainey.

"Yes. Nothing has happened to him. Nothing happens to most of the Teagues. You don't actually know who this child is, do you? I mean, his antecedents are obscure, are they not?"

"Yes. We can't find any trace of his birth."

"This boy was conceived in April of 1999, in Abel Teague's hospital room at the Gates of Gilead Palliative Care Center in Sallytown. It was not a consensual transaction. This boy is the consequence of a sustained and brutal rape. I do not know his mother's name. His father was Abel Teague. She was confined to that room for nine months. When she delivered this boy, she was killed by Abel Teague's Guardians. Abel is a terrible man. Glynis Ruelle managed to bring him to the harvest, where he suffers. He wishes to escape. He is trying to become a living man again. Now that this boy is almost grown, and the heir to great wealth, Abel Teague wishes to come back and have a new life inside this boy's body. The presence inside this boy is helping him."

"But we have to stop that!"

"Yes. You do. That is easily done."

"How?"

"Kill him."

"What?"

"Your friend here has a weapon. Kill this creature and it all ends. The portion of the presence that is in him will dissipate and be gone. The Guardians that the presence has created will fade. Abel Teague will remain where he is, a part of the harvest."

"We can't just *kill* him!"

"You have no choice."

Delia looked at Lemon.

"Young man, you must be strong. For the woman and the boy. Do it. Kill him now!"

Lemon hesitated, and then he walked over to Rainey and put the gun to his head. Deep down in his skull, Rainey heard **Cain** begin to hiss, like a trapped snake. Rainey closed his eyes and waited.

Anything was better than this.

Kate screamed at Lemon to stop.

He didn't.

Lemon cocked the hammer back, pressing the gun muzzle in tight. Kate came across the room at Lemon.

"Lemon, how do you know this woman is real?"

Lemon looked over at Delia.

Delia Cotton nodded at Lemon.

"She may be right. For some time now I have suspected that I might be dead. Time has a way of moving around me and it isn't always where I left it. It doesn't matter. The thing inside the child has to be driven out. There is no other way."

Hannah's hearing aids.

"Lemon, listen. There may be another way."

"There is no other way," said Delia quietly.

Kate's eyes were locked on his.

His heart changed.

Maybe she was right.

Maybe there was another way.

Lemon took the muzzle away from Rainey's temple. Through it all Rainey had neither flinched nor shown any kind of emotion.

Delia waited until Kate looked at her.

"I pity you, Kate. You are making a grave error and you and your family will come to bitterly regret it. But it is done. Now please take that creature from my house."

She looked at Rainey, and he met her look.

"To what lives in this body, hear me, the way is shut. Shut and barred and I guard it. Never come here again, creature, or I will put an end to you."

No, Really, Harvill, You Shouldn't Have!

It was a fine, clear Monday evening and the view across Fountain Square was particularly stellar. Delores Maranzano was standing at the long floor-to-ceiling window in the living room of her suite on the Pinnacle Floor of The Memphis and watching the lights of the city glitter and sparkle in the cool fall air. She was wearing one of Coco Chanel's little black dresses because she had just come from poor Frankie's memorial service at Holy Name, where the novena that Mr. Endicott had kindly paid for had just been performed, against the medieval background of a magnificent Roman Catholic cathedral and a full choir.

Now she was having a bracing gin and tonic and admiring the panorama. But her mind was not at ease. Events had not gone well at that ranch up in the foothills. In fact they had gone quite badly.

Not only had she lost four nice young men in her employ, but she had also lost her nephew Manolo, who had somehow managed to get himself shot in the face during that fiasco, and now he lay on a tin tray in the morgue at Lady Grace, with four other bodies nearby to keep him company.

His condition had been described to her by a Special Agent Boonie Hackendorff of the FBI—whose offices she was looking into right this moment, on the other side of Fountain Square—as "a closed casket deal, ma'am. A closed casket deal."

Apparently his investigation into the entire affair would be clouding her future for quite some time, and he showed every sign of being very persistent. Well, that was a concern for another day. There *was* an upside.

She had heard from Tony that Frankie's associates were impressed by the energy Delores had shown in the abortive attempt to avenge the wrongful death of her husband, and that while things had clearly not gone well, her display of steel had gone a long way to improve her standing with the organization. At that point in her ruminations the doorbell rang.

Frankie Il Secondo was at the vet recovering from having his vocal cords sliced apart, so there was no earsplitting crescendo of falsetto yapping to contend with as she made her way across the carpet to open the door.

Mr. Endicott, as expected, stood there in the glow of the overhead light, holding a bouquet of white roses and wearing a sad, sympathetic smile.

"Thank you for agreeing to see me," he said.

"Not at all. Please come in."

She stood aside and bowed him into the room.

He noted the improvement in the atmosphere at once and looked around for Frankie Il Secondo, who was nowhere to be found. He came to the center of the room, still holding the flowers, waiting, she assumed, for her to do something clever with them.

She smiled, carried them into the kitchen, filled the sink with water, set the stems into it, and came back out with a bottle of Pellegrino and two glasses. She set them down on the coffee table and poured a glass for Mr. Endicott, who seemed ill at ease.

"I am very grateful to you for seeing me, Mrs. Maranzano—"

"Please. After what we've been through? It's Delores to you."

Endicott bowed slightly.

"Delores, then. I am painfully aware that the events of the weekend have created a number of problems for you. And I am very sorry for that. It is unfortunate that when your people arrived, several law enforcement officials happened to be visiting the residence. I understand you have been called upon by Agent Hackendorff of the FBI?"

"Oh yes. This morning. Early."

Endicott sipped at his sparkling water.

"Was he . . . unpleasant?"

"Not really. He was under the impression that my nephew, Manolo, had taken matters into his own hands. I told him that I had no idea what Manolo had been planning and that if I had I would have done everything in my power to stop him."

"Excellent. May I ask . . . ?"

"Did *your* name come up?"

He inclined his head.

"Not at all. Why complicate things, right?"

"Excellent. I thank you for your discretion. I was hoping to hear you say that."

"I'm sure you were," she said, with a sly up-from-under look that was decidedly flirtatious.

Good Lord.

Is the woman making a pass at me?

He had been planning to use one of the kitchen knives on her—the security detail downstairs was too thorough to risk bringing up a weapon—but dear God she did have a lovely figure on her, and it was a poor heart that never rejoiced.

Tidy as you go was his motto, and after he tidied up the Delores problem, he was going to go back to Warren Smoles' house and tidy him up too.

He had taken up a very discreet residence at Warren's lovely home, since hotels and motels were a trifle too hot for him right now. He had even let Warren live for a while longer. He was back at the house right now, lying on top of his king-sized bed, naked and bound and gagged.

He had kept Warren alive largely because, now that Warren had become talkative, Endicott was learning so much about All Things Cap City. Niceville and Cap City had all sorts of possibilities for a talented and enterprising psychopath. Concerning Delores here, he could always slice her up after they made love. He was pretty certain that there was a Jacuzzi somewhere in this flat. They were perfect for that sort of work. He watched her with renewed interest as she went about seducing him.

She was wearing a black dress. She crossed her legs to great effect and leaned over to pour out more Pellegrino, giving him a glimpse of her marvelous breasts. From this vantage he concluded that she wasn't wearing a bra. She handed him his glass, still leaning forward and opening her legs slightly.

Endicott felt his skin beginning to burn.

She sat back in her chair and crossed her legs again, this time more slowly, to even better effect.

"Delores, may I say you look *perfect* this evening. Grief often makes a woman—"

Delores was on her feet.

"I'm going to slip into something more comfortable, Harvill. Give me five minutes."

He gave her three. He had his shorts and socks on but was otherwise naked when he pushed the door of her bedroom open with his left foot. He had two glasses of white wine, one in each hand, so there wasn't much he could do when Desi Munoz clubbed him across the back of his head with the barrel of Frankie Maranzano's Dan Wesson .44.

The glasses went flying and Mr. Endicott went sprawling. He rolled over onto his back and blinked up at Desi's towering bulk. Even a happy Desi Munoz was not an endearing sight, and right now Desi Munoz was very far from happy.

"Desi. You're supposed to be in Leavenworth."

"Yeah, well, I'm not, am I? I'm fucking *here*."

Delores was standing behind him, half-naked.

Unlike Desi, she looked quite happy.

"You said they were in Leavenworth. I asked around and found out that Desi was already out. I felt I had to call, Harvill. I mean, we're all part of the same *family*, aren't we, Desi?"

"Fucking well told we are."

"Desi has agreed to help me run my end of things here. He has expertise in the business. Mr. La Motta and Mr. Spahn are flying down later. Isn't this exciting? And it's all because of you, Harvill. Desi, are you going to shoot him right here? Because, you know, the carpet and all?"

Desi frowned.

"Okay. Where you want him?"

"How about the tub in the guest bathroom? It's a Jacuzzi. You know, for the blood and icky bits and all that stuff?"

"Okay. The bathroom. Get up, Harvill."

On the way into the bathroom Mr. Endicott's mind was racing. He knew he could come up with something. And sure enough, he did, and it was absolutely brilliant, but before he could really get things off the ground Desi shot him in the back of the head. Getting shot in the back of the head at close range with a .44-caliber revolver renders the entire concept of *having* a head retroactively moot.

Being a gentleman, at least where half-naked ex-*goo-mays* worth thirty million dollars were concerned, Desi Munoz dumped what was left of Harvill Endicott into the Jacuzzi to bleed out.

Then he and Delores went back out to the living room and got to know each other better.

(As a footnote to Harvill Endicott's premature decapitation, it's worth mentioning that Warren Smoles' absence from the Niceville social whirl was not remarked upon for almost three weeks. His partners at Smoles Heimroth Cotton and Haggard were aware of the spanking he had gotten from Terrible Teddy—it had been the talk of the legal community for days afterwards—Judge Monroe's phrase "the Sultan of Slime" was on everyone's lips—and they were not surprised that he was lying low.

Smoles had no personal friends and when the cleaning ladies arrived on Wednesday only to find the house closed up and the entrance code changed, they simply marked him down as "Account Suspended." No one else gave much of a damn about him.

Except of course for the cats.

After a while, when the new guy didn't come back and the dry food ran out and the electric can opener continued to defeat their best efforts and all they had to drink was the trickle of water dripping into a bathtub on the third floor, the cats began to take a more active interest in Warren Smoles.

Smoles was laid out on top of the king-sized bed in his master en suite, just as Endicott had left him. He was trussed up like a Christmas ham and he had a bullet hole in his thigh.

But he was still alive.

Whenever the cats would wander into the room, he'd jerk around on the bed and make weird noises at them. Sadly, if the electric can opener was simply impossible for creatures without opposable thumbs, there wasn't much the cats could do about the knots and gags and plastic cord cuffs that were keeping Warren Smoles right where he was.

He was, however, fun to watch.

Being cats, they'd soon lose interest in what he was doing and wander out again to look a bit harder for something good to eat. Eventually it became clear to all of them that there really wasn't *anything* left to eat in the whole damn house.

On the morning of the fifth day they began to gather around Smoles again. He wasn't jerking and twisting and making weird noises by then. He was badly dehydrated and slipping in and out of consciousness. The cats, all fifteen of them, sat around him on the bed and considered him through half-closed eyes.

After a period of indecision, one of them—a tabby, of course—ventured an experimental bite. This seemed to energize Smoles quite a bit and he did a whole lot more of that writhing and twisting stuff and he went back to making those high-pitched noises. But soon it became obvious that other than doing his usual herky-jerky shrieking and squealing thing, Smoles was basically harmless.

The Maine Coon cats were the first to get down to serious business. Soon all the others joined in. Everyone agreed that he tasted like ham.)

Wednesday

I Sing the Body Electric

It took two days to set it up but now they were here—a Wednesday morning—and Kate was using all of her considerable powers of persuasion on the woman behind the desk.

Doctor Lakshmi had very large almond-shaped eyes and full lips, which she colored a deep rose red. In the normal course of her day she radiated a calm, competent, and even loving nature. Today this was not so, and she sat looking at Kate with great resistance, even some anger.

"One does not administer ECT to a child without very good reasons, Kate. WellPoint is not some third-world quack shop. I'm very sorry to—"

Kate looked at Nick, who was sitting across the room, keeping his distance from this. They were back together, if they had ever been apart, but he had very little hope in Kate's idea, no matter what may have happened with Hannah's hearing aids.

"It was *electrical* interference, Doctor. The audiologist confirmed it. He replicated the effect by using an oscilloscope. He even provided the frequency range that—"

She waved that aside.

"An audiologist is not a neurologist. There are professional standards, and I adhere to them. What you are proposing could not even be contemplated without a whole battery of diagnostic tests."

"All of which you've done, CAT scan, an EKG, PET scan, even a lumbar puncture. I've read your own website, and on it you clearly state that in cases where no other anomaly is present Electroconvulsive Therapy is often successful in treating mental health conditions like severe mania, schizophrenia, catatonia—"

"Rainey is not catatonic. He's resting quietly in the ward. There has been no repetition of that interior voice effect that Rainey reported."

Kate sat back.

"Look, Doctor, I'll be blunt. This is Rainey's last hope—"

"Kate I don't for one second believe that Rainey has a demonic presence inside him. WellPoint does not do exorcisms—"

"I'm asking you to treat his mania—his *belief* that there actually is some kind of demonic presence inside him. You yourself said that ECT is very often the answer to that kind of delusional condition, especially when all else has failed."

Dr. Lakshmi was silent for a time.

"There are risks—"

"I'll sign any waiver you put in front of me."

"There may be short-term memory loss. He will experience nausea, headache, jaw pain. During an ECT treatment, heart rate and blood pressure spike. Although his heart is strong, the risk remains. Slight but present. We are inducing what amounts to a seizure. It is performed under a full anesthetic, which carries its own risks . . ."

Her voice trailed away.

Kate held her breath.

"I will need to consult an ethicist . . ."

"But you'll consider it?"

"You are set upon this course?"

"I am committed to it."

Dr. Lakshmi studied her for a while and then looked over at Nick.

"And you, Nick? You are also Rainey's guardian. Do you support this treatment?"

"Doctor, if he doesn't get it, then Kate and I have a problem, because I'm not allowing Rainey to live in our house until his condition is resolved."

He glanced at Kate, gave her a wry smile.

"So far what this has actually meant is that I'm in a hotel and Kate lives in our house with Beth and Hannah and Axel, and Rainey is confined in your ward—"

"That's because he's a flight risk and the center of an investigation into the drowning of a school official. Are charges being considered?"

"No. Because of Rainey's mental . . . issues . . . the prosecutor has declined to lay any kind of responsibility on Rainey, but the fact is he may well have had something to do with it. If this treatment can help him live a normal life . . ."

"Then you fully support it?"

"Yes," said Nick. "I do."
"Very well then."

She was down deep down deep curled tight inside a web of tasty memories savoring them tasting them breathing them eating them. She had been thinking of the pleasures to come when the oldfamiliar came to live here again—the things they had done together—tasted together—that neither could do alone. In the beginning there had been no one that nothing did not simply consume in anger but in this aftertime as the crack between the worlds cooled and changed and she changed with it old habits had changed too and some of the life that came to her she did not consume or did not consume all at once and a few of these lives slipped into her and stayed and she was less alone and the new aftertime had been very rich and tasty—this entity she had entered was unformed—unready—powerless to make things happen—but he was the matrix for the oldfamiliar and soon he would come again—

—she was aware of the entity trying to see her—trying to fight her—it drew her—buzzing and clicking to herself she moved into that part of the entity's mind where vision lived—

Rainey's eyes were closed tightly, and he was strapped down on the gurney as the nurses moved about him in the cold white room, but he *saw* the thing burning against the inside of shuttered eyes—his heart was pounding but he could not move—*nothing* looked back at him—

—her eyes were yellow sparks inside a field of black diamonds—she was spinning like a wheel of fire and smoke but the eyes held him—he could feel the heat of her on the surface of his mind—the electric crackle of her glittery skin—inside her eyes there was a wasteland—a burning yellow plain under an emerald sky swept with blue fire—her eyes grew wider—she *knew* that Rainey was looking at—looking into her—seeing her—she felt his raw terror—it was silky and silvery and living—she opened her mouth and

—there was a hissing crackling flood of fire—blue and white and violet flames slithered and arced along all the wires and walls—they were so hot so burning such pain she had never known—she flitted down caves and leapt across glowing canyons and snaked farther down and farther down tunnels of pulsing flesh with the violet flames pursuing her . . . she went down deep and down deep and down—

Three Weeks Later

A Dappled Day

The weather was changing, but it was still warm enough for the kids to play outside in the backyard. Kate and Beth had set out the lawn chairs, and they were watching Rainey and Axel and Hannah play some kind of game that they had arranged on a blanket at the bottom of the lawn, down where the creek ran through the pines and willows there, at the edge of the little forest. Sunlight filtered through the trees and lay like scattered gold coins all over the grass and flowers and on the heads and shoulders of the children.

All things considered, they were almost happy, and although there was loss—their father was still gone—life had calmed down to a degree and Rainey's *voices* had not returned. He and Axel had stopped skipping school and their marks were improving. The matter of Alice Bayer's death had been filed under Misadventure, and she'd been decently buried in the Methodist Cemetery up in Sallytown.

Deep in Kate's heart she knew that Rainey had been there when Alice had gone in, but she found it impossible to believe that Rainey had in any way made it happen. Rainey was, after all, just a kid.

Kate had managed to talk Nick into coming back home, even though Rainey was still living with them. He was distant and polite to Rainey. The Alice Bayer Question, among many others, weighed heavily on him.

But Kate felt that Nick had a soft heart and a fair mind and would, in time, come to forgive the kid for what he had done with Warren Smoles and to accept that whatever happened to Alice, Rainey hadn't *made* it happen.

About Smoles, who seemed to have dropped off the planet, Kate was trying to forgive Rainey herself, and every calm day made it a little easier.

Hannah had gotten a brand-new set of hearing aids, partly because she simply refused point-blank to allow the old ones anywhere near her.

With the new hearing aids, there had been no reappearance of that *interference* thing, the kind that had occurred before Rainey's ECT treatments.

Kate had begun to hope that, whatever had happened to Rainey, it was over now, and that perhaps they could all just settle down and have as ordinary a life as possible in a town as strange as Niceville.

Things were changing with the grown-ups too.

Lemon Featherlight was seeing a girl named Doris Godwin. It looked like a serious affair. They were spending a lot of time checking out these shots Doris had taken, at the top of Tallulah's Wall. And the thing with the "bone baskets" had grown into a project that took Lemon and Reed up to UV once a week to talk to Dr. Sigrid, the anthropologist. Kate was beginning to suspect that Reed had developed an interest in Dr. Sigrid, who was, by all accounts, a genuine Valkyrie.

So Kate and Beth hadn't seen much of anyone for a couple of weeks, although Lemon had met with Nick a few times to talk about the bone baskets and the pictures. Nick wasn't saying anything about any of this stuff. Kate figured that when he was ready he'd fill her in.

Meanwhile, she was happier not knowing.

Now that Byron was dead, the Chinese had turned their attention to a young Asian man named Andy Chu, a Securicom IT guy who had been with Byron on the night he died. Chu was in the hospital, guarded by the FBI. According to Boonie, the Chinese wanted him very badly, and Chu was talking up a storm with Boonie in an effort to avoid being deported. Boonie said if Chu kept on talking he might be able to keep him away from The *guangbo*. Kate figured Boonie was starting to like the kid, who seemed to be—to a degree—an innocent hostage at the Galleria.

Charlie Danziger's funeral had come and gone—he'd gotten buried with full honors and Mavis Crossfire had given him a lovely eulogy.

Beau Norlett was there, in a wheelchair but on the mend and due to go back to the CID—desk duty at first—in a month.

About the Gracie robbery, the official word was that Charlie Danziger had nothing to do with it—that it was all on Coker—who was still missing, along with his girlfriend, Twyla Littlebasket.

They were both now on the FBI's Most Wanted List, which probably made Coker smile.

Kate wondered whether she was getting the whole story—it was hard to see Coker doing anything that Charlie Danziger wouldn't know about—but Nick and Tig Sutter weren't moving off that line and it had now become The Official Version.

Kate was a smart enough wife to leave it alone. Niceville was a town that had buried a lot of secrets far more strange than that one. Maybe everybody was just relieved to be taking a break from . . . Niceville. That suited Kate and Beth.

"Can I get you a glass of wine, Kate. A nice warm red?"

Kate looked a little odd.

"Well, I think I better not."

Beth stared at her.

"You're pregnant, aren't you?"

Kate smiled, blushing a bit.

Beth jumped up and hugged her sister. "That's wonderful," she said with tears in her eyes. "Have you told Nick?"

Kate's mood dipped and recovered. She had had two miscarriages in the past, both early, and had waited until now to tell anyone.

"I am going to tell him tonight."

"I'll take the kids to dinner. The two of you can be alone."

"Perfect."

They sat for a time in companionable silence, smelling fall in the air. Somewhere in the neighborhood, leaves were being burned and the tangy scent of them drifted on the wind. A burst of laughter came from the children down at the bottom of the yard, and Axel sat back, waving something in his hands, a wand of some sort. Apparently he had won something, a hand or a round or a prize. Hannah was sitting back—blond and happy—and staring up at the boys, her blue eyes wide.

"What are they playing?" asked Kate.

"That new game Rainey and Axel made up. They're teaching it to Hannah."

"What are the rules?"

"No idea. It involves a lot of whispering. I think there's a secret language too. Kids only, anyway. No adults allowed. They all stop and stare at me like owls whenever I go down there."

The sun went into clouds and the dappled gold coins disappeared. It got cool. The children were whispering together. Kate felt a chill. So did Beth.

"Getting colder," she said. "We should go in soon. Can I get you a wrap?"

"No. I'm fine. We'll go in."

They watched the children for a while longer.

"Kids do love their secrets," said Beth.

"They do. Probably harmless."

"Probably," said Beth, suppressing a dark feeling. Kate was doing the same while they listened to the children murmuring at the bottom of the yard.

Beyond the kids, the river bubbled and flashed in the deep shadows under the old pines. The sun stayed behind the clouds. It got colder. Kate looked up at the sky and thought, *Winter is coming.*

Acknowledgments

First and foremost I am profoundly grateful to my wife, Linda Mair, for her wit, her style, her acute sense of business and writing, and above all for her amazing ability to put up with me.

Beyond Linda, I need to thank Barney Karpfinger, my rather steely agent, and Cathy Jaque, who runs the Foreign Office, for their loyalty, patience, and fire. I need to thank Carole Baron, my editor at Knopf, the consummate pro who taught me that *better* is not acceptable when you're capable of *best*, to Ruthie Reisner, Carole's indispensable Two-IC, to Victoria Pearson—who brought it all home—to Jason Booher, who gave the Book the Look, and Cassandra Pappas, who gave the pages their grace, to Emily Stroud, for utterly brilliant graphic design and a killer website, and to all the copyeditors around the world who saved me from myself a hundred times.

And of course, thanks to Sonny Mehta, who took a flier on *weird* and made it all possible.

Carsten Stroud is a *New York Times* best-selling writer of fiction and nonfiction, including the true-crime account *Close Pursuit*. His novels include *Niceville, Sniper's Moon, Lizardskin, Black Water Transit, Cuba Strait,* and *Cobraville*. He lives in Destin, Florida.

A NOTE ON THE TYPE

This book was set in Janson, a typeface long thought to have been made by the Dutchman Anton Janson, who was a practicing type-founder in Leipzig during the years 1668–1687. It has been conclusively demonstrated, however, that these types are actually the work of Nicholas Kis (1650–1702), a Hungarian, who most probably learned his trade from the master Dutch typefounder Dirk Voskens. The type is an excellent example of the influential and sturdy Dutch types that prevailed in England up to the time William Caslon (1692–1766) developed his own incomparable designs from them.

Composed by North Market Street Graphics,
Lancaster, Pennsylvania

Printed and bound by Berryville Graphics,
Berryville, Virginia

AVAILABLE IN ARROW

Niceville

Carsten Stroud

The first book in the Niceville trilogy: a terrifying psychological novel about a small US town where nothing is quite what it seems . . .

When ten-year-old Rainey Teague disappears on his way home from school, Detective Nick Kavanaugh and his team are baffled. CCTV shows Rainey staring into the window of a pawn shop – he's there one minute and simply gone the next.

And that is only the beginning of the nightmare as a chain of terrifying events is triggered in idyllic Niceville.

As Nick struggles to uncover what happened to Rainey, his investigation takes him deep into the history of Niceville, and it soon becomes clear that there's a much higher than average rate of abductions in this town. And there'll be more victims to come . . .

arrow books